ASHES UPON THE SNOW

Carroll C. Martin

ISBN: 1497431867
ISBN: 978-1-49-743186-7
Library of Congress Control Number: 2014912050
CreateSpace Independent Publishing Platform
North Charleston, South Carolina

DEDICATION

Dedicated to Mother and Daddy, Grandma and Granddad Keller, Grandma Martin and the pioneers of Erath County, Texas, who enriched our lives and left this world a much better place.

CONTENTS

ACKNOWLEDGMENTS

Thanks to all those who encouraged me to finish writing and publishing this book. A special thanks to Le Jones and Judith Martin Meador for editing the manuscript. And a very special thanks to my brother, David, for all his help, encouragement and editing.

PREFACE

The telling of the Snow murders was a tale I had heard all my life, particularly in my younger years. My grandparents, parents and many relatives were alive when it all happened and often talked about it, interweaving their fear and that of the entire community into their tales. Growing up in the 1940's and 1950's, even we kids would tell the story over and over — on a moonless night, in the dark corner of a closet, or just sitting in the shade of a tree on a hot summer day.

In my early grown-up life, it came to mind that although I had heard the story of the Snow murders a thousand times or more, the details of the story weren't always the same and I became very curious about what really happened. I decided to discover the real story and thus began an extensive research in the 1960's. I investigated old detective magazines found in the Stephenville and Tarleton University Libraries; newspaper accounts found in the microfilm archives of the *Empire Tribune* and *Fort Worth Star Telegram*. I researched the original trial transcripts found in the Erath County District Clerk's Office, and I talked to the few survivors who had firsthand knowledge. This research continued off and on for several years but with the life changing events of starting a family, I put away my pile of gleaned material.

Then about the turn of the century, I once again found myself with a little free time, and my thoughts once again turned to the gruesome murders. What I had not realized before is that while collecting facts of the Snow murders, I had also amassed a wealth stories about the everyday lives of everyday people. Why not put the two together? Thus began my quest of lacing the murders with the stories of people I knew, stories of people my parents knew and stories of people my grandparents knew. Thus began the birth of *Ashes Upon The Snow,* and when I had finished writing the story, I mentioned it to a few close friends and relatives, and without much ado, the manuscript was put aside to focus on raising my son and two lovely daughters.

Then some fourteen years later with all the advances in technology of computers, smart phones, social media, text messages and more, I dusted-off *Ashes Upon The Snow.* I shared it electronically with a few friends and relatives, and from their interest and encouragement I came to the decision publish in print.

Ashes Upon The Snow in the whole is fiction. However, the accounts of the Snow murders are true just as they happened in 1925, and the accounts of the everyday lives of everyday people are true just as they happened — they just didn't happen in 1925 but spanned different times over a period of 100 years. Many readers will be able to identify themselves as they read this work of fiction.

And finally, one of the reasons for my writing was to document the rural life in Erath County in the early 1900's for my family and yours. My wish is that you have just a fraction of the pleasure in reading *Ashes Upon The Snow* as I did writing and publishing it.

Carroll C. Martin

PROLOGUE

An unexplainable uneasiness drifted over the woman standing, gazing out the window. Watching her son in the old horse drawn wagon — did she know? How could she have known? Death was approaching.

Barely noticing the brown jersey cow meandering about in the tattered pasture, grazing on wilted grass stubs and dried broom weeds, the woman was grateful — finally, she had a place that she could call home.

This day started off just like any other — awakening before sunrise on this winter morning — eating a scanty breakfast and then completing the morning chores.

While his stepfather's sharp axe split the seasoned wood, the boy loaded the firewood onto a horse drawn wagon. Finishing just before noon, the man walked to the old house for a bit of rest.

The boy looked back over his shoulder as he drove the loaded wagon out of the gate. He raised his hand and waved his last goodbye. As the old wagon crept down the narrow lane, the woman at the window looked in the direction of the northern sky. She saw dark clouds approaching on this quite afternoon, a sign that a cold front would soon cover the land, a sign of a disturbance, a sign that a dark day was impending.

Although she wasn't good at it, she prayed that her only child would not suffer the heartaches, the hardships and the loneliness that she had borne during her lifetime. Perhaps, it was a prayer answered — perhaps it was only the boy's carelessness — perhaps it was the beginning of a dark day.

Consumed with a loneliness that she had never known before, she watched the wagon go out of sight beyond a rise in the old gravel road.

She hadn't noticed that the boy failed to close a barbed wire gate, and just as ashes upon the new fallen snow, the aftermath of this oversight would leave its smudge on this small community for years to come.

Then, she heard someone behind her . . .

1

THE HUNTING TRIP

Although the faithful old dog was slowing down a bit, Hootus could still keep up with the boys and this night was no exception. Not as full of life as he had been in the years past, the dog hobbled along, holding up a back leg.

Elvis gave his new puppy that name because Granddad Keller called everybody "Ole Hootus" when he couldn't recollect their name. It was a fitting and proper designation for a dog that looked just like a hootus, whatever that conceivably might be. It wasn't that Hootus was an ugly dog; he just wasn't pretty — he was a hootus. Granddad Keller said so.

A kindly little gentleman, Mr. Swanzy, a neighbor, who lived just up the lane, over the hill and around the corner, gave the khaki-colored puppy to Elvis' daddy. Swanzy declared that the gangly pup was the pick of the litter, even though the litter consisted of only two sickly puppies that didn't seem to have much of a chance of surviving. But that was eleven years ago. Hootus not only survived, the old hunting dog was the perfect companion for Elvis; who had turned seventeen two months ago.

Elvis loved his old dog, part bloodhound, part wolf, and the rest was anyone's guess. He didn't have the distinguishable features of any breed; fuzzy like a wolf, the color of a deer and the dog's long, flopping ears were those of a bloodhound. Overweight and somewhat crippled with arthritis, Hootus, when not begging for table scraps, spent the majority of his day napping in the front of the fireplace during these cool autumn days. The old dog's coat was slowly turning from tan to gray as he was living out his final days. He either just ignored Elvis or was getting hard of hearing. Most of the time, he just paid no attention to Elvis. The lazy days of summer had faded away, and the season of harvest was upon Erath County, Texas in November of 1925. Hunting small game, a sport for the boys, gave them a welcomed break from their school studies and farm work. As an added bonus, the small amount of cash they made from trapping and selling the animal furs provided them with spending money.

Moseying about as he had so many times before in bygone days, sniffing and sorting out the scents, Hootus stayed just ahead of the two boys looking for the wild animals, the raccoons, the opossums and all the other varmints inhabiting the woods.

"This looks like a mighty good spot." Aaron squatted down on his knees to set a trap beside an old hollow log, baiting it and covering it with twigs and new-fallen leaves.

"Hey, Elvis, shine yer light over here, I heard sump'um!"

Elvis Rivers was Aaron Martin's next-door neighbor and his closest friend — wherever you saw Aaron, you would more than likely see Elvis.

Elvis' father, Giles, Irish by descent, purchased a few acres of land from Aaron's father, a little over twelve years ago and built a small frame house among the spreading post oak and live oak trees. Only forty-two years old and during the influenza epidemic of 1918, Giles Rivers passed from this physical life, leaving behind a wife and his only son.

Elvis, only nine years old, left without a father, became the man in the family. It was beyond his youthful understanding why God took his father, just when he needed him the most. Being with Aaron and Hootus in some ways eased the young boy's pain, listening intently anytime he expressed the anger, sorrow and loneliness he felt upon losing his father.

Elvis' mother told him that there were so many people sick and had died during the horrific outbreak that there were scarcely enough people who weren't ailing to bury the dead. His father was laid to rest at Allard Cemetery on a cold, dreary, rainy January day. There wasn't a funeral service — only two men attended the burial. Elvis and his mother were both sick with the murderous disease that day; no other family member or friend was well enough to attend.

Uncle Will and Aunt Florence Savage had a farm near the Rivers, on the east side. Aunt Florence, Elvis' aunt, was his daddy's oldest sister. Uncle Will's first wife, Rose, died many years ago when she was only nineteen years old.

He later courted and married Aunt Florence, twenty years his junior, when he was forty-two years old. Their only child, a son, was a missionary preaching the gospel to the Indians in Arizona. Having no offspring of their own at home, Aunt Florence and Uncle Will supported Mrs. Rivers any way that they could.

"What wuz that?" Aaron whispered.

Elvis shined his flashlight to the right of the boys, searching for the source of the snapping twigs and rustling leaves. The boys saw movement in the darkness as the beam of light captured two glowing, yellowish-orange spheres, reflecting back from the obscurity of the night.

Was it a fox, a coyote or could it be a thing more menacing and dangerous? Aaron stood up and raised his rifle then lowered it — now he could make out the shadowy form in front of him.

"Awe, it's just ole Hootus. Here boy, come here! You skeered me, dang it!"

Aaron, taking a deep breath, was relieved that the shining eyes belonged to Elvis' devoted dog but a bit disappointed that they were not the eyes of a furry animal. It had been over a week since he and Elvis had found a furred varmint with a hide suitable for selling.

Aaron's father, Madison Martin, owned and operated a trading post at Pony Creek, and during this time of the year he bought furs from the trappers in the area. He was a large man at six feet and four inches tall, weighing two hundred and fifty pounds — he was an imposing sight!

He had one son, Aaron and two daughters who would soon be teenagers. He realized that his time of being the most important male in the lives of his two girls was growing short. He knew that with Aaron, he had only one teenage boy to watch after, but with his daughters, he would have to keep an eye on every hormone-charged, teenaged male that might have intentions of courting his daughters.

Aaron and Elvis had been the best of friends ever since that first day they met and started playing together. Meeting at the barbed wire fence that divided their families' farms, they stayed out time and again until they were summoned home, often past dusk. Because of their common interests, they rarely argued with one another.

CARROLL C. MARTIN

The two boys were typical of the adolescents growing up in the rural areas of Central Texas. They once built a tree house from some old discarded lumber that was one time a smoke house that Aaron's family no longer used. High on the boughs of a live oak tree, the tree house served as their retreat, a special place. They knew every niche of the vicinity and found hideouts fit for any bandit in the sloping hills and wooded pastures that were joined to an open prairie.

The boys explored the peacefully haunting woods, searching for flint rocks, grinding stones and arrowheads and on one occasion, they were sure that they had found an Indian burial site in the lower part of Martin's pasture. They dug holes in the hard ground and excavated the area but found no signs of bones, teeth or any other Indian artifacts and after digging for an entire day in the rocky soil, they abandoned the project in pursuit of other adventures.

The two might wander down by a creek that flowed through both farms on the lazy, hot days of summer when the puffs of thunder-heads boiled high, dotting the azure blue sky. Lying on their backs beside the trickling water, they watched the clouds, forming into shapes of pirates, ships and the like. Aaron often dreamed of being able to drift among the billowing clouds, high above the earth, just like a bird.

The boys would often lay down in the soft, green grass at the creek's edge and watch the perch, minnows and the other fish swimming in the crystal clear, shallow water. They waded in the cool, refreshing water, cooling their bare feet that were scorched by the blistering sand on the parched, arid days of the Texas summers.

There were days when the noonday sun cast no shadows; it was hot and the gentle breezes dried the beads of moisture on their faces. After putting a fishing line into the water, there was nothing to do but to wait until a fish nibbled, jerking on the line. A signal of a catch.

When it was so hot that they couldn't stand it a minute longer, they would jump into the almost clear, bluish-green water, stark naked, their pale white flesh gleaming in the sun.

They shoveled out caves in the side of the creek bank, pretending to be cavemen, but the raging waters of the springtime floods had removed all traces of their labors. Cowboys and Indians, Tom and Huck, adventurers and explorers, they played all the parts; they were happy in the peaceful countryside. Those were contented days.

"Elvis, see that hole in that old tree over yonder? Grandpa Keller found a beehive in there last year."

Aaron remembered something about that particular old post oak tree, standing there before him, outlined by the rays of the flashlight. The tree was slowly decaying — broken limbs had fallen to the earth, returning back to the soil. The magnificent tree, once buzzing with activity was quiet and forsaken now — the honeybees had migrated to another location and a spider's glistening web covered the deserted beehive entrance.

Elvis shined the bright beam of the light toward a fork in the branches of a dead tree, pointed out by his friend. "Yeah, I 'member when yore granddaddy got that honey," Elvis said, "He brought a jar full over fer us. It wuz last summer, 'cause I 'member me an' you wuz catchin' crawdads."

Madison Martin raised ducks on his farm and these ducks fancied eating crawdads. The clawed crustaceans, plentiful in the muddy water of a stock tank on the lower part of the farm, lurked near the banks of the pond.

Aaron and Elvis devised a method for catching the shelled critters. First, they needed some string or line that they could tie to the end of a pole made from a willow sapling. They found twine, used for tying feed sacks, and secured it to the ends of their home-made fishing poles. Then using salt pork for bait; the boys tied the enticement to the loose end of the string and threw it into the mucky water.

They usually didn't have to wait for any length of time before a crawdad grabbed hold of the intended meal with its strong gripped claw. The fishermen eased the armored dwellers from the water and put them into a burlap bag, being careful to avoid a pinching from the strong claws of their captured prey.

When twenty to thirty of the squirming critters had been caught and put in the bag, commonly called a tow sack, the boys took them to the waiting, hungry ducks and dumped the crawfish out onto the ground. The quacking ducks waddled up to the boys and devoured the tasty morsels in a feeding frenzy.

"Did you know that honeybees ain't native to America?"

"Naw, I ain't ever thought 'bout it. Where'd they come from?" Aaron asked.

"The early settlers brought 'em from Europe in the sixteen hundreds — that's why they're called European bees."

"I don't call 'em that; they're jest plain ole bees to me." Aaron stepped over a small thorny bush, being careful as to not tear his pants.

Aaron, one year older than Elvis, had long black hair and golden brown eyes, accentuated by his high cheekbones, indicative of his Indian heritage. He spoke slowly and deliberately and rarely appeared to be agitated while Elvis' speech, being more expressive, gave the impression that he was the one with a more pleasing personality. Both boys possessed a Central Texas accent and rarely used proper English, even though they knew better.

Elvis inherited his reddish-blond hair, round face and deep blue eyes from his mother and even though he stood several inches shorter than his tall and lanky friend; he was heavier and more muscular — he was stout.

"Yeah, they're jest bees to me, too, but I thought you'd like to know sump'um like that. Ya never know when it might come in handy. Speaking of knowing, have ya learned that new song yet?"

Aaron's low-pitched voice made him a pretty fair bass singer, when he could be persuaded to sing. He accompanied himself on his guitar with the basic cords, while Elvis picked a guitar as if his fingers were guided by magic. People listened in awe when he plucked the strings of an old guitar, patting their feet in rhythm with the familiar gospel songs.

"I jest 'bout got it down, but I don't know if I'll sang it next Sunday or not. Are ya gonna play the guitar fer me?"

"I guess I might."

The hunters sauntered along, looking into the trees for an opossum, wild turkey or any other wild animal roosting in the branches.

They found animal burrows along the way, but the inhabitants were denned up and well hidden. They walked deeper into the woods, looking in the briar patches, under the bushes and dense undergrowth, but they were having little success in locating any game.

Hootus wandered from place to place, searching out anything of interest to him from animal carcasses to old tree stumps.

The two youths' lives were changing — they were no longer children but not yet men. Aaron had long abandoned the swing under the shade of the trees by the side of their house — the swing that his daddy had built for the eight-year-old boy. Two long ropes tied from a limb of a tall oak tree and a smooth board, fashioned for a seat, was a suitable swing for the country boy who found great pleasure in being alone.

He spent many hours outside, swinging and whistling, as the days of his innocent boyhood passed by. On many nights throughout the years, the nearby neighbors heard the boy whistling in the darkness, long after the sun had set.

Elvis, without a father, had to assume the responsibilities of an adult earlier than most boys. He no longer played under the shade of the trees around his house, building miniature forts and log cabins from the twigs and sticks he found on the ground. He no longer hunted for the tarantulas and horned toads, the doodlebugs and fireflies. He no longer pretended that an old bale of hay was his faithful horse, and neither boy ever climbed up into the tree house, deteriorating with time, the tree house upon which they had worked so hard to build.

The bitter wind howled out of the north, biting the boys' faces, as a new cold front, called a norther, blew in, and Elvis knew that come morning, his kin-folk and neighbors would gather for a hog killing day.

Elvis and Aaron looked forward to these days be-cause of the cheerful mood of the community, and it meant there would be fresh pork to eat.

Now, that it was nearly Christmas, they looked forward to the spirit of the holidays, having no idea that the unrest of this holiday season would linger in their memories, haunting them for the remainder of their lives.

Tall post oak trees towered over the boys like gi-ant beings spreading their huge arms and distorted fingers over the two as they strolled along. A new moon peeked from behind the delicate clouds, ap-pearing as so many wisps of smoke. A hooting owl, watching them from above, seemed to be calling out in harmony with the unnerving howl of the distant coyotes.

"Don't that sound mournful?" Elvis said as he gazed up at ghostly vapors floating across the heav-ens, high above them.

"My Granny Woods told me that when ya hear a coyote and owl sanging together, it means some-body's died an' they wuz so mean and ornery, they's searching fer some peace."

"Do you thank it's so?"

"I don't know; that's jest what Granny told me one time when we heard 'em outside Uncle Will's house.

Sounded like ole death himself, it gave me the willies. I 'spect it is so. I reckon dead ornery people might do jest that," Elvis replied, feeling cold chills creeping up his back as he listened to the haunting cries of the night.

"Was anybody ornery dead that time?" Aaron asked, not sure if he wanted to hear the answer, but too curious not to listen.

"How am I 'posed to know, Aaron, but I thank it wuz when ole Miss Kelly got bit by that big ole black wider spider," Elvis told him, shrugging his shoulders. "She died last year 'bout this time,"

"I reckon that if the coyotes wuz gonna morn fer anybody, it'd be her. She always had a sour look on her face. You 'member when she wuz our school teacher?"

Both boys attended Pony Creek School in the southeastern part of Erath County, Texas. Pony Creek, so named because long before the white man came, the Indians brought their thirsty ponies there to quench their thirst. The refreshing water bubbled up from the abundant natural springs, providing a cool drink for the Indians and their thirsty mounts.

Aaron and Elvis walked to the schoolhouse like most of the other students in the community. From time to time, they caught a ride with their neighbor, Woodrow Lane or Woody as they called him, one of the older boys in school.

When Woody drove the family car to school, a Model T Ford, he picked everyone up waiting beside the road on his way to the small schoolhouse. One by one, the passengers piled into the car, and when loaded to its capacity, others riders clung to the running boards of the vehicle, shouting, laughing and loving country life.

Aaron and Elvis usually enjoyed school and had a good time with their friends and classmates. When attending school, they were freed from the drudgery of working on the farm — pulling cotton, hoeing weeds, hauling hay, picking corn, cutting maize and helping out with the other demanding farm duties.

Elvis excelled in mathematics; Aaron did well in English, and both boys had a passion for American History. They loved their country, and they welcomed the opportunity to learn more about the facts, dates and events that made America a great nation, particularly the stories of the American Revolution, the fall of the Alamo and the settling of the Old West.

On the warm, clear days of spring and early autumn, the boys brought their sack lunches of biscuits with ham or sausage and at lunchtime, they went outside with their classmates to eat under the cool shade of the hovering oak trees. Aaron, Elvis and several other boys had a special place on the banks of the creek where they met, a grassy knoll overlooking the river. While eating their lunches, they talked about the ball games, related hunting stories, spun jokes and yarn and discussed their newest discovery — girls.

Elvis and Aaron both played basketball; the main sport played at Pony Creek School. Aaron was a better player because he was taller than his stocky friend. Teams were formed for both the boys and girls. Pony Creek School played basketball games with the teams from the other communities, usually on Friday afternoons. Parents came to watch their children play, rooting them on, hoping for a victory.

"Yeah, I 'member how Miss Kelly made me dust them 'rasers all by myself when I didn't get my 'rithmetic right that time." Aaron remembered.

"An' how about that time she made fun of pore little Curtis when he couldn't work out that addin' problem on the blackboard? She made him feel awful. Guess she wuz pretty ornery."

"I reckon. I thank she wuz plum mean. She wuz the worst teacher we ever had — I guess she wuz smart, but she wuz jest plain cruel. I shore hope we get Mister Patton again this year," said Elvis, "he's my favorite."

Mathew Patton, the teacher for ninth and tenth grades at Pony Creek School, was the favorite of the students for many reasons. One particular event stood out with the young scholars.

The older, upper classed boys and often times, the girls, started an annual tradition, several years ago on April Fool's day. They cut their classes and left school for the whole day. The teachers seemed powerless to bring the custom to an end. Then, last year, Mr. Patton came up with a solution that suited everyone.

"Study hard and finish your lessons," he told them on the day before, "and tomorrow after lunch, instead of just a few of you kids leaving, we'll all run away from school."

The boys and girls put forth the extra effort necessary to complete their studies and after lunch on the appointed day, the students, along with their teachers, spread out, roaming the woods, over the hills and gullies looking for arrowheads.

They came up to a quiet little stream, and Mr. Patton asked the boys and girls to sit down beside the water while he cut several limbs from a willow tree. He slipped the slippery bark off of a limb and cut a groove in the limb on one edge, just the right size. He cut a notch on one end of the bark and slipped it back onto the grooved limb. He had made a whistle, a Norwegian willow flute, and the students discovered that many of the experiences in life aren't taught in the classroom.

"Yeah, Mister Patton," Aaron agreed, "he's a good un alright — jest listen to 'em coyotes would ye, they're getting louder!"

"Yeah, do you thank somebody's about to die? I shore hope they . . ."

All of a sudden, a sharp crack echoed through the valley above the whistling winds, interrupting the boys' conversation as they neared the edge of the woods. They stopped and listened as a dark cloud spread its shadowy fingers across the sky, covering up the moon.

"What wuz that?" yelled Elvis. "Aaron, did you hear that?"

"Yeah, sounded like somebody's shootin' a gun over that way," Aaron said, pointing toward the south.

The wind suddenly stilled, another echoing report, and then an unnatural silence drifted about the two hunters. Hootus paused and listened, sniffing the cold night air, the hair on the back of his neck bristling. Whimpering, the old dog retreated back to his master with his tail drawn up between his hind legs.

The night had taken on an anomalous sequence of happenings, a sense of a diabolical encountering, the feeling that something evil had just occurred.

"I'll bet ole man Snow's shot some varmint or sump'um," whispered Aaron, "he's always out huntin' or trappin'. Folks say he don't sleep much 'cause he's skeered of sump'um. He burns his coal oil lamp at his house all night long — Bud Stokes told me so, he's seen it many a night."

Aaron stooped down to look under the low hanging trees in the direction from which they heard the unexplained explosions. Hootus stayed close, walking beside Elvis.

"Uncle Will says Snow's part Indian an' he don't have anything to do with nobody," supposed Elvis, "'cept when he's trading horses. He'll talk to you then, but no more than he has to."

Aaron added, "An' he chops wood an' takes it into Stephenville an' sells it to the town folks. He generally pulls that old wagon of his'n into Tate's wagon yard and sometimes he stays there all day, settin' on that wagon of his'n, sharpening his ole axe."

"Does he really carry a Winchester rifle with him all the time?" asked Elvis, looking back behind him, "Uncle Will says he ain't ever see'd 'im without it."

"Yeah, he does, an' nobody's ever see'd fit to ask 'em why. We seen him in town one day when he first showed up 'round here. He had that rifle on the wagon with 'em then an' Daddy told us we shouldn't say anything about it." Not that Aaron ever had any intentions of doing so.

"I heard that Virgil McElroy said sump'um to Snow one day. I thank Virgil was drunk, like he usually is. Him and Snow nearly got into a fight."

Virgil McElroy, being either braver or more foolish than most people, once threatened the mysterious man, the woodchopper. Snow's unblinking eyes narrowed into slits as he looked straight at Virgil, his weak voice quivering as he hinted that, years before, he killed a man who had threatened him.

Thus grew the perception that Snow was a dangerous, treacherous man, and he was to be feared. But people were also afraid of Virgil McElroy, for unlike Snow, his reputation for violence was well known.

"Reckon why Virgil and Snow didn't get into a fight when Virgil said he wuz gonna whoop ole Snow's ass all over the street?" asked Elvis.

"Daddy said they's both mean ole cusses and mean ole cusses have a fearful respect for each other," laughed Aaron.

The boys didn't hear anything more from the direction of the Snow farm and Hootus again was exploring the night. They wandered upon the small creek, rippling in the misty moonlight. The thirsty dog stopped and lapped up the cold water while Aaron knelt down, cupped his hands and took a refreshing drink.

Elvis set down on a small boulder and opened the bag that he carried tied around his shoulder and found his old tin cup. He filled it with the clear water, drank it then offered the cup to Aaron.

Hootus waded around in the shallow water, stirring the sediments on the bottom of the small stream, scattering minnows in all directions.

"Uncle Will said Snow's real good with his axe," Aaron continued to talk about the curious man named Snow, "He can chop a cord of wood in no time flat. He must be a lot stronger than he looks, or that's a real sharp axe!"

"Yeah, I know, an' he keeps that axe with him most the time, too, right there with that gun. Guess he thanks he might find some wood to cut," joked Elvis, "Some folks thank he might of killed somebody with that axe."

With their thirsts quenched, the boys picked up their rifles; Elvis called Hootus, and the hunt continued.

"That reminds me of a story my momma used to read to me about a woodcutter who lived in Russia,"

Elvis began the story. "This here woodcutter an' his wife had seven boys an' they were real poor an' barely had enough to eat. So the woodcutter took 'um out into the woods one day an' left them fer the wolves to eat. The youngest boy wuz real smart an' so he left a trail of white pebbles along the way.

That way, he wuz able to lead his brothers back home. In the meantime, 'fore they got home, his folks found some gold an' wuz able to buy some more food. So when the brothers got home, their folks wuz glad to see 'um."

"What's the name of that story? Are you shore you ain't jest a makin' it up?"

"No, I ain't makin' it up. So anyway, the food ran out in a few weeks so the boys' paw 'cided to take the boys back in the woods an' this time he took 'em further away from home. The ogres found them an' took them home an' put them to bed because they wuz very tired."

"The ogres, who's that?"

"The ogres are these real ugly people an' the man, the daddy, liked to eat little boys — they wuz one of his favoritist foods. So he made a plan to kill the boys while they wuz sleeping, but the smart brother made a plan to save his brothers an' him once again."

"How did he do that?" Aaron asked, stepping over a decaying log.

"The ogres had seven daughters asleep in the house, too. These girls wore a night bonnet or something, so after the ole man ogre passed out from drinking too much ale; the smart brother put the bonnets on his brothers' heads so the ogre couldn't recognize them in the dark."

"This is a real stupid story!" Aaron shook his head and rolled his eyes up.

"I know, I can't believe it wuz in a kid's story book," Elvis continued, "Anyway, the ogre got up an' felt the bonnets in the dark an' he thought the boys wuz his daughters. He went to where his daughters wuz sleeping an' slit their throats with his knife an' only when it got light, he realized what he had done. In the meanwhile, the boys escaped an' took all the ogre's gold an' silver."

"Ain't nobody that mean." Aaron would later remember those words.

"What's the moral of that story? Ain't it got a meaning to it?"

"I reckon it means that . . ."

"Hey, Elvis," Aaron interrupted him, as the boys were crossing over a barbed wire fence, "Ain't this yore Grandpa Rivers' place?"

Grandpa Rivers, hoping to find a better life, brought his family from the Edgefield District in South Carolina to Cherokee County, Texas in the fall of 1847. Shortly after the family arrived in Texas, many of the family members died during a measles epidemic. The family settled in Erath County in the early part of 1880.

A hard-working farmer, proud of his family, he faced a variety of hardships — drought, grasshopper invasions, temperature extremes, sickness and the loss of his wife.

"Yeah," answered Elvis, pointing eastward, "The ole house is right over there."

"Let's go set a trap in that ole cellar. I bet that's a good place fer varmints."

No one had lived in the dilapidated old farmhouse for fifteen years now. Grandpa had lived there by himself after his wife died; Elvis never knew his grandma because she died giving birth to his father. Elvis' aunts and uncles grew up there, in the house that was once a home.

The house caught fire and partly burned four years after Grandpa Rivers departed from this life. Part of the roof had fallen in and the house, now vacant and forlorn, had planks nailed over the windows. Grass was growing up through the boards on the front porch, and where the roses and honeysuckle once flourished, briars grew.

It would be a good place to set a trap, an old cellar, beside the house, partly caved in, a home among the crevices of the logs for the wild things living there in the darkness. Grandpa and Grandma, fearful of the storms, spent considerable time there, times when the lightning and thunder erupted from the violent Texas thunderstorms.

The boys set out their traps for the animals from the last part of October until early April. The furs were worthless during the warmer, summer months when the animals were shedding their coats. Elvis baited several traps and secured them among fallen logs, which at one time were the roof of the old cellar. He was careful not to spring the trap as he withdrew his hand.

The skins from the fur-bearing animals were more valuable when the animals were trapped, rather than being killed with a firearm. Shooting the animals made holes in the furs, as well as plowing furrows along the outer edge of the skin.

Visiting their traps regularly, the boys retrieved the carcasses as soon as practical so that the skins did not become tainted. They scraped off all the excessive tissue and fat, being careful not to trim so deeply as to cut the fibers of the skin. After an animal had been skinned, they stretched the hide and nailed it to the back of a barn door to dry.

"Maybe we'll get something in there. I'll bet Grandpa never thought we'd be settin' traps in his cellar."

"I bet he never thought it would cave in either. Watch out fer snakes," Aaron told Elvis. "They den up for the winter in these ole cellars."

The brisk air aroma was pure and exhilarating but even though the boys were warmly dressed, they were feeling the chill as the Arctic cold front plunged the temperature below freezing. With the traps set in the old cellar, the boys and the dog began their homeward journey.

"Look at the moon!" Elvis shouted. "It looks real weird, like blood or sump'um!"

Appearing as a backward letter C, the crescent moon, peeping through the thin clouds, took on a blood-red glow as it sank low in the sky, just above the horizon.

"And that windmill sounds mournful like a ghost. Did ya ever hear about the Ghost of the McDow Hole?" inquired Aaron.

"They say this here woman ghost named Jenny came stomping som'ers around here one time when the guy who killed her wuz dying."

"Yeah, everybody's heard about that, but it gonna take more than a couple of ghosts to scare me — what's more, I don't believe in no ghost, do you?"

"I don't know," Aaron answered back, "but Granddad Martin believed in 'em. He told me that people used to see Indian ghosts over where he growed up over by Rocky Point. He said he never did see 'em though. He told me how he shore scared his brother one time."

Aaron related about a time, years ago, when Granddad Martin hid behind some bushes along the road from church on the way to the Martin's house. Down by Folly's branch, people claimed to have seen Indian campfires, burning out in the woods, but upon further investigation, no signs of any campfires were ever found by the observers.

Granddad's brother, Strat, attended a party at the Fulbright's place one night in late October, and about the time he thought Strat would be coming home, Granddad hid in some bushes by the road. As Strat passed by his hiding place, Granddad jumped out with a lantern and waved it back and forth. Strat didn't hesitate. He went running, screaming to the top of his lungs all the way home. Strat, positive that he had seen a ghost, was reluctant to travel down the road for years to come. Granddad never told him the difference.

"Jenny Little claims that they have a ghost at their house, "Elvis told Aaron, "She said it wuz a little girl about ten years old with long black hair. Jenny told me her 'n her brother seen the little girl outside like she wuz walking up to the front door an' when they opened the door, no one . . ."

A near-by owl, screeching, interrupted Elvis' story. "Let's stop talking about ghost and scary things, okay?"

"Thought you don't believe in ghosts," snickered Aaron.

"I don't, but I don't want to do anything that'd make 'em mad, jest in case we're in their stomping grounds."

A sudden outburst from Hootus broke the silence of the night. Walking beside Aaron, he gave forth a low snarl, the hair bristling on his back as he ran well ahead of the boys.

"Come on Aaron, he's found something."

The boys ran after the old dog, expecting to find a raccoon, opossum or some varmint that would transform their futile night into a hunting success. They were in the wide-open prairie by this time and the moon had inched down below the horizon. They could see the dim shadow of Hootus running and scurrying about from a fence line to near a big old tree out in the middle of an abandoned cotton field.

Suddenly, the dog stopped and walked back to Aaron. The night became unnaturally quite again — the boys couldn't hear anything except for the moaning wind and the irritating grind of a windmill, far away.

"That's strange," said Elvis, "I thought sure he had something tree'd. This has shore been a strange night. Wonder what he wuz barking at?"

"I don't know," Aaron whispered, looking toward the south again, "I hear sump'um." He paused and cupped his ear. "Is that a wagon over that a way? I guess not; I guess it's jest the wind."

"Hold the light over here an' let me see what time it is. It's almost ten o'clock. We'd better go home." Elvis said, putting his Granddad Keller's old pocket watch back into his pocket.

Elvis motioned for Hootus, and the hunters walked hurriedly toward the sanctuary of home. The dog and boys reached the Rivers' house without any confrontation from a ghost or any other paranormal being. And if the spirits were roaming about that night, nothing even approaching the supernatural made its presence known, and the boys weren't disappointed.

Elvis reminded Aaron that he would see him the following day at the hog killing and went inside the house. Hootus followed behind him and went to his favorite spot in front of the fireplace. Elvis thought about the strangeness of the night, the sound of gunshots, the crimson moon and the wailing of the coyotes, but as soon as he warmed up under the covers of his bed, he drifted off into a peaceful slumber.

Aaron crossed the fence and quickly walked across the dark pasture, being more aware of his surroundings than he normally would be. He pondered about the events that had disturbed the peacefulness of the night, wondering what Hootus had perceived that had excited him. He reasoned that Old Man Snow or some hunter had merely shot a gun and perhaps, Hootus had heard that.

But, something evil had just occurred — a horror that neither Elvis nor Aaron could have imagined.

2

THE MIDNIGHT TRAVELER

Jack Owens, suddenly awakened about midnight, sat up and looked out the window next to his bed. His three dogs, barking feverishly, were warning of an intruder, lurking somewhere outside.

By most people's standards of that day and time, Owens lived in poverty, in the sticks. Bluff Dale, the nearest settlement, was five miles northeast, past Cedar Mountain. Originally called Bluff Spring by the pioneers who settled near the artesian wells of the area, Bluff Dale was located in the northeastern part of Erath County. Nestled among the cedar-covered mountains, the cozy little town is located on the North Paluxy River. Bluff Dale became the official name when the post office was granted in 1877.

Owens' house was on a plot of land, composed of a couple of acres, not even large enough to be called a farm. A small dirt road, close to the front of his home, barely passable and lined with cedar trees, ran northerly to Bluff Dale and southward to Cedar Point.

The old house, built from boxed planking, sat at the base of a scrubby hill, facing eastward toward a valley. Mountain boomers, a lizard-type reptile that ran upright on their hind legs, were plentiful on the steep hill behind the house, as were rattlesnakes and scorpions.

Owens provided for his family, his wife and two daughters, by trapping and doing odd jobs in the area — shearing sheep, hauling hay, clearing timber or any other laborious work. A full beard covered his face, and his long black hair hung down to his shoulders — he fit the stereotype of a mountain-man.

He was tall, stoutly built and muscular. His most striking feature, his piercing blue eyes, revealed nothing about him. Most of the time in cold weather he wore a handmade leather hat or a coonskin cap, a coat made from buffalo hide and tall boots with leather flanges on the back.

He was an isolationist, not by choice, but by a series of tragic circumstances. While studying to be a doctor and attending a medical university, his father was stricken with tuberculosis and after a lengthy illness — he died, leaving behind his mother and younger sister.

A month after his father's passing, Jack quit school and moved back home to find work so that he could help out financially. He became disillusioned with medicine because the doctors were not able to save his father from the ravages of the disease.

A few years later, he found work in the oil fields of West Texas and met his wife-to-be. He married the seventeen-year-old girl four months after they met. He was making more money than he ever had before and had found the love of his life. He worked hard and saved what money he could. He wanted the best for his wife and the family they wanted. Then tragedy struck again.

They were starting their seventh month of marriage when Jack's new wife, Nora, announced to him that they were expecting a child. The happy pair prepared for the new arrival, decorating a room just for the baby. But six months into the pregnancy, Nora went into labor, and they knew something was wrong. The couple's first baby, a girl, was born prematurely with a serious birth defect — an omphalocele, an abdominal wall defect; a defect much too severe to be corrected during this day and time.

Jack was there the night she was born, a brown sack of membrane protruded from the baby's abdomen. The membrane held the baby's liver. The old country doctor had never before encountered such a defect. There was nothing that he could do — the baby died several hours after she was born.

Jack quit working for the oil company and stayed in his room for several weeks, barely eating. He wouldn't talk to Nora — when he wasn't in the bed, he just sat by the window, staring outside. His new bride fought to keep her sanity, losing a baby and husband at the same time. During the second month of his withdrawal from everyone, Jack made a decision — he had to leave the place of his sadness. He moved his wife to the desolate house in the cedar brakes of Central Texas and found a place where he could avoid meeting people, forever giving up his dreams of being a doctor.

He found his happiness in the quietness of the cedar-covered hills and the lonely valleys, thirteen miles east of Stephenville. He and his wife didn't have much, but they started finding peace of mind once again; walking hand and hand, watching the small animals, the brilliant sunrises, the colorful sunsets, the friendly moon and twinkling stars. They were suited for the desolate area in which they were living.

The wind, blowing as the new cold front had arrived, shook the windows of the old house. Owens figured the dogs were barking at the rustlings of the leaves, a varmint or maybe just the wind. He wanted to dismiss it because it was cold out from under the covers, freezing cold in the airy house.

Suddenly, above the whistling wind, he heard something else, the unmistakable screeching of wagon wheels rolling along, somewhere outside on the road. As badly as he wanted to stay in the warmth of his bed beside his wife, he got up and stepped onto the cold floor. He shivered as he found a match and lit a coal oil lamp on a table near the bed. The flickering flame dimly lit the small room, but it was sufficient for him to see. His rifle was near the door, ready.

He could hear the beams of the old house cracking and groaning as the frigid wind assaulted the structure. Quickly, he pulled his pants over his long underwear, put on his boots and coat, opened the door and looked out into the shadows of the night.

A gust blew out the flame in the lamp, immersing him into darkness. As soon as his eyes had adjusted to the darkness of the night, he saw that his dogs, still barking, were out in the middle of the washed out road, north of his old house. Then there was something else, in front of the dogs, the thing that had gotten their attention; the thing of which they were warning.

Off in the distance, he could see it, silhouetted by a swinging lantern — one lone wagon pulled by one lone horse going northerly on the narrow road up toward Cedar Mountain, a distance of about two miles.

The moon, casting its diffused beams down on the mountainside was sinking low in the western sky. Dark shadows fell across the road as the wagon slowly crept along — the irritating pitch of the squealing

wagon wheels was easy to hear in spite of the howling wind.

Owens heard his clock strike twelve times, and he
wondered why anyone would be out in this area in a
wagon on a night like this, especially at this time of
night.

The wagon's driver, too far away for Owens to
make out, occasionally looked back over his shoulder
as the wagon rocked back and forth on the old rub
board road. Owens could see that the midnight rider's hat was tied down with a dark colored scarf that
covered his ears, and the collar of his coat was pulled
up over the back of his neck. The man whipped the
horse, but the old horse's gait remained the same,
slow.

If Owens could have had a better view of the man,
he could have seen that the troubled man was talking to himself, fighting off the demons inside. He
could have seen that the man's eyes had the wild look
of a wounded animal. A lantern, its flame flickering
from the blowing wind, hanging from a pole on the
right side of the wagon, casts eerie shadows, black images over the wagon and its rider. The wind screamed
through the tall trees upon the ghostly hills — the
wind chilled the old man to the bone — the old man
on a midnight mission. It would be several days before
the hideous deeds of the midnight traveler would be
made known.

Owens watched until the wagon disappeared below a row of cedar trees then went back inside the cold house that felt much warmer than the frigid outside. He took off his clothing and got back into his warm bed and drifted back to sleep. He barely heard his dogs when they barked several hours later.

The next morning dawned bright, beautiful and tranquil, in contrast to the previous night. Owens got up from the comfort of his warm bed once again and stirred the shimmering embers in the fireplace. A small flame puffed up as he put on a couple pieces of firewood — he was going to start a fire to warm the cold house. Nora was awake and would cook a filling breakfast as soon as the house warmed a bit. He looked over to the bed on the opposite side of the room, at his two sleeping daughters. He had lost his first born but had been blessed with two more precious girls.

Owens thought about the wagon and its mysterious driver throughout the day because, a couple of hours after the first encounter, he thought he had heard the moaning of the wagon wheels again, as did his dogs. He didn't get up to look this time, choosing to remain in the warmth of his bed. If he had looked, he would have seen the same man, returning from the top of the mountain, carrying with him a macabre secret in the back of the wagon.

Owens decided to do a little hunting before dark, and he took his dogs with him. When he got to the crest of Cedar Mountain, he heard one of his dogs barking high up on the mountain. He thought the dog had merely tree'd some animal — he dismissed it and went back to his house. Perhaps it was the black panther that had been sighted several times on the mountain during the past few years, but not likely, he thought.

Two days later Owens went out with his wagon toward Cedar Mountain, looking for a cedar tree to cut down. Although it was still about a month until Christmas, his two daughters were ready to put up the family Christmas tree, and he had to find one just the right shape and size. Even though Owens was a loner, he adored his two girls, and they wanted a tree.

Owens found a perfectly-shaped tree, cut it and put it into the back of his wagon. Again, he wondered about the mysterious voyager in the wagon two nights ago. He felt sure the lone occupant of the wagon wasn't looking for a Christmas tree — what a stupid thought! But what could he have been up to? He thought about the moonshiners in the area and possibly there could be some connection with the man in the wagon. But he knew the area well, and there were no stills that he knew of in the vicinity of the mountain.

Perhaps the wagon's driver was just a traveler, but it was a strange time to be traveling, especially with the dreadful weather of that night. What undertaking would hold such importance? And why did the wagon driver keep looking back over his shoulder?

Was he looking to see if anyone was following him or was he looking at something in the wagon? Owens wondered if he should have called out to the person or had he done the right thing by remaining silent? Owens did not have answers for his many questions.

The perfectly shaped tree appeared small until he was ready to bring it into the house. It was taller than the door, but his daughters' excitement assured him it was the perfect tree. He made a stand out of a couple of pieces of board and nailed it solidly to the tree. His wife, Nora, popped some popcorn and with the help of the six-year-old, she strung it together with string she had saved from flour sacks — garlands for the girls to put on the tree. The refreshing smell of cedar drifted through the small house as Nora, and the two girls decorated the tree.

On Christmas Eve, the family would gather around the tree, and Owens would read from the second chapter of Luke, the Christmas story, from an old worn Bible that he inherited from his father:

> "And it came to pass, in those days,
> that there went out a decree from

Caesar Augustus, that all the world
should be registered . . ."

Jack never tired of reading Luke's account of Christ's
birth. The story brought back pleasant memories of
his happy childhood and made the present times
more joyous.

The girls, aged five and six, were old enough enjoy
the merriment of the season. They were hoping that
Santa Claus would bring them some play-pretties,
maybe a baby doll for each one of them, and maybe,
a new baby brother that their mother had promised.
But Jack Owens was poor — there wouldn't be any
toys for his little girls this year. The most that they
could expect to find in their Christmas stockings was
an apple or orange, but it was to be a very happy time
for them. For Owens and the rest of the community, it would be a Christmas that they would always
remember.

Earlier, as Owens was carrying the tree into the
house, he looked up toward the north and saw a
wake of buzzards, circling around, hovering and
descending from the sky, up near the top of the
mountain.

The buzzards were scavengers, and he figured
they had found a dead animal's carcass to feed upon.
He didn't suspect that they had found a human

corpse, nor did he realize that his dog had found the same thing last night when he and the dog were out hunting.

Had he put the two events together, the buzzards and the midnight traveler, he might have gone up on the mountain and made a discovery — a naked human body — a body without a head, but he never gave it another thought until ten days later.

3

HOG-KILLING DAY

The day was cold; a brisk breeze was blowing out of the North. The deep blue sky, crystal clear with no hint of a cloud anywhere, shaped a magnificent dome over the land — a perfect day for the task ahead.

Shocks of grain forming hundreds of small tee-pees, straight in a row among the pumpkin vines, lined a field directly north of the River's house. In an adjoining field, encircled by a heavy growth of timber, an ocean of fluffy white cotton was ready to be harvested.

Activity outside Elvis' window woke him early this morning. The men folk, neighbors and friends, were making ready to butcher a hog. Smelling the aroma of brewing coffee, Elvis knew that his breakfast would be ready and waiting for him. It was still frigid cold outside as well as inside his room. A wood burning stove, blazing in the next room, caused condensation, collecting as a frozen puddle at the bottom of the windows.

The folks of this close-knit community helped one another in hard times, rejoiced during the happy times and shared the bounty of the good land. During the slower times of the year when the crops were laid by, most Saturdays would find the people from all around going to Stephenville, the county seat of Erath County. Strolling around the square that surrounded the stately, red and beige three-story courthouse, the people stopped and talked to the others who had gathered for the same reason, visiting with friends.

Elvis and Aaron's families made a day of it when they came from their farms into Stephenville located about eleven miles northwest of the Pony Creek community. They leisurely walked around the square, visiting with others, buying supplies and groceries, getting haircuts, sharing news about their friends and neighbors and most importantly, catching up on the latest gossip.

Occasionally they went to the "picture show" when a good western such as *Go West* with Buster Keaton or *The Lucky Horseshoe* with Tom Mix was showing at the Majestic Theater, located on Belknap Street, just north of the courthouse square in Stephenville.

But today was hog-killing day, a busy day — going to town would have to be put off until next week. Uncle

Will Savage, up before dawn, early by his own stan-
dards, went to call upon Uncle Grover Hammett and
Granddad Dee Keller to help him with butchering the
Rivers' fattened hog.

Uncle Grover and Aunt Nell, Granddad's sister, lived in a two-roomed log cabin, built during
the 1880's, across the fence from the Savage farm.
Granddad and Grandma Keller's farm, about two
hundred acres, was up the lane and across a sandy
field, where, in the summer time, the delicious black-
berries grew.

Uncle Will owned nearly a section of land that
spread out on the east side of Granddad Keller's
farm. His fence line ran down the entire length of
Granddad's place. Trails, in the tall grass, wound
through the live oak trees from the Savage's house to
the Keller's, then on down the lane to the mailboxes,
past the sand field. From there, the trail led across a
creek and through the meadow to Elvis' house.

Elvis' mother, a plump little lady with dark hair
sprinkled with gray, once told him about her trips to
the mailbox when she was a young girl. She would
have walk across a small wooden bridge spanning
a narrow, dry tributary of the Bosque River on the
path from the Keller's house to the mailbox.

"It was only about ten feet across the little bridge;
sometimes when I went to the mailbox by myself, I
ran across the bridge, thinking someone might be

hiding underneath. Most of the time it was just a dry branch, but sometimes after a rain, when the water trickled down over the rocks, I was brave enough to stop an' lean against the rail, watching the water flow by and listening to the birds sing."

Ruth Rivers' Mennonite ancestors, the Kellers and the Kolbs, came from Germany, settling in Pennsylvania in the early 1700's. Her Great-Grandpa Kolb, a Mennonite preacher, brought the family to North Carolina, and then a group of the family traveled westward, settling in Texas. Finding that there were no Mennonites in the area, the majority of the family joined the Baptist Church.

The Kellers settled in Wartrace, Tennessee after migrating from Pennsylvania then on to Texas after the Civil War.

This morning, while she was cooking the family's breakfast, she told Elvis about the time she accidentally lost her little toe while playing at the old home place with her siblings. Elvis treasured hearing these stories his mother told about her childhood.

"One time we were out playing with some old metal wagon wheels. We put an iron rod through the center of 'em, where the axle was supposed to go. Then we would push them up to the top of the hill, sit on the iron rod an' ride down the hill."

She cracked eight brown-shelled eggs, salted and peppered them and scrambled them in a black cast iron skillet. Elvis smelled the smoke from the wood-burning stove, mingling with the aroma of freshly brewed coffee and fluffy biscuits, baking in the oven.

"I was riding on the iron rod when one of the wheels came off and someway cut off my little toe. The blood started shooting from my toe an' Brother saw me an' picked me up an' started running to the house screaming 'Momma, Momma'." Her face lit up when she mentioned Otho, her only brother, who had moved to El Paso to pursue a career in education.

"When Momma got to me, I had so much blood all over me, she thought I was hurt really bad, but they found out that only the end of my little toe was cut off; she cleaned it up and put a poultice of Granny salve on it."

Elvis, sitting at the kitchen table, finished dressing by putting on his thick woolen socks and tying his shoes. He ate an ample breakfast of eggs and gravy that he poured over grits and topped off with a hot, fluffy biscuit. When he had eaten the eggs and grits, he spread a layer of Grandma Keller's blackberry jam and butter on the steaming, hot biscuits and with a glass of fresh milk, he washed it all down and then helped his mother clean off the table.

Elvis's mouth watered thinking about the fresh pork tenderloin and fresh sausage, highly seasoned with sage, he would enjoy for breakfast the next morning.

Under his pants, Elvis had put on a pair of long-legged underwear, called long handles and grabbed his heavy woolen coat and floppy hat. He was ready to join the others outside.

Gathering to help their neighbors with the hog killing was a long-standing tradition with the folks of this community. They shared their meat and labors with one another, and as each family had a hog ready to be butchered, the meat would be shared with all.

"Hey Elvis," Uncle Will called to him as he started out of the house, "Come on out here an' help us gather up some firewood. We're burning daylight."

"Yes sir," Elvis replied as he walked down the back steps of the farmhouse. Ole Hootus, sleeping under the porch, came out and followed Elvis to the woodpile.

Outside a small woodshed, the men folk filled two large cast iron pots with water, built a fire, and waited for the water to get boiling hot. The women, while remaining inside, baked pies and cakes and cooked food for the dinner, the noon meal. They would later join the men to help with processing the meat, when the hog was ready to be butchered.

The water soon came to a boil. Uncle Will shot the hog in the back of the head with his .22-caliber rifle and then stuck it in the throat with a butcher knife so that the blood would flow out of the meat. Elvis saw the bright red blood trickle out onto the sandy ground. He wondered that if a man's throat were cut, would he bleed like that. After the blood had stopped flowing, Uncle Will and Granddad Keller put the hog into a fifty gallon barrel filled with the boiling water and splashed it up and down and turned it until the hair was loosened from the torso.

The old boards creaked as the men lifted the hog's carcass up to the rafters of the woodshed, and then using sharp butcher knives; they scrapped off all the hair. When all the hair had been removed, Uncle Will and Granddad Keller put the hog on a table fabricated from wagon frames and placed across two sawhorses. Then Uncle Will cut the hog open with a huge butcher knife and removed the animal's heart and liver.

Uncle Grover cut off the head using an axe to sever the backbone, and then he split the hog's skull and retrieved the glistening brains. Nothing went to waste — all parts of the hog had some use and value. Elvis shuddered at the sight of the severed head rolling over on one side. Even after watching a hog being butchered year after year, he thought it was gruesome. He felt an unfamiliar sorrow for the hog he had watched grow from a small piglet, this creature that was breathing and had moved just a short time ago.

Ruth Rivers, picking up the organs from the butchered hog, went inside the farmhouse while the other women remained outside, continuing to help with the butchering. After slicing the fresh pork liver and heart, she fried it up in a sizzling hot skillet.

The fresh pork would be eaten for dinner along with more hot biscuits, white gravy and a big pot of hot coffee. She set aside the hog's brains that she would scramble in with the eggs for breakfast the next day. After setting the table, she called to the others outside, informing them that the meal was ready.

There was a knock at the door, and Hootus barked just as Elvis sat down at the dinner table. It was Aaron. Mrs. Rivers said he had a knack for knowing when the food was ready. She opened the door and asked him in.

"Hi, Aaron," said Mrs. Rivers," you're just in time fer dinner. Set yerself down right over there in that empty chair," she insisted, pointing to a well-worn cane-bottom chair.

Aaron readily accepted the invitation, filling a plate with the freshly cooked pork, gravy and biscuits, "Umm boy, is this good!"

"It shore is," Elvis responded, wiping his mouth on his shirtsleeve, "I can't wait to eat some of them sausages."

"I saw ole Virgil McElroy at the feed store the other day," Granddad Keller said, making conversation.

"I'd been talking to him fer quite a spell 'bout this an' that an' out of the blue he asked me why I always seemed to be in a sech good mood and why nothin' ever seemed to bother me. Well sir, I told him it was a gift, an' of course, he asked me what kinda gift. I told him I had the peace that comes from God through the gift of salvation. He told me he used to go to church, a long time ago, and he'd heard about God and Jesus 'an all that religious stuff, but after his wife had fallen an' got killed, he got real bitter and quit going."

Uncle Grover added, "I guess that's why he's so mean."

"Yep," Uncle Will nodded in agreement, "We jest got to keep prayin' fer 'im."

The boys and the others consumed the dinner meal, and the men folk went back outside to finish butchering the hog.

"Granddad, do you need me 'n Aaron right now?" asked Elvis as they walked to the shed.

The boys were anxious to check the traps they had set the night before and were allowed to take a break when there wasn't much they could do to help out.

"Nah," Granddad told Elvis, "Y'all go ahead."

The boys didn't take the time to round up Hootus because they wouldn't have time to do any hunting. Elvis went inside and got his rifle, and a few shells just in case they ran across a rabbit, squirrel or other game.

They walked down the fencerow toward the creek. Passing a small stock tank, Elvis pointed, "Hey

Aaron; this here's that tank where we went swimmin' last summer 'n you got sunburned!"

"An' it wuz a bad'n too," Aaron remembered, "I met Missy the next day over at Willie Stanton's house."

"You liked her, didn't ya?" questioned Elvis.

"Yeah, I did, still do — so the next day, my shoulders were still burnin' like fire, so Daddy said I didn't have to go to work at the store, and nothin' wuz going on in the fields. I went over to Willie's house that afternoon an' that's where I first saw Missy. There were always a bunch of kids hanging around the Stanton's house 'cause you know, Missus Stanton liked all us kids. We all felt welcome an' had a bunch of good clean fun around there."

Aaron gazed up at the sky as he continued reminiscing. "It wuz sometime after lunch. Missus Stanton had made some fried tators an' I didn't eat much 'cause I wuz complaining about my sunburn, so Willie's mother gave me some salve to put on my shoulders. I took my shirt off an' was sittin' in a chair by the door an' 'bout that time, Sally and Missy came in."

A tear came to Aaron's eye as he continued, "She wuz the prettiest of them all, smiling an' full of joy, so it seemed. Her voice wuz like no other that I have heard to this day."

Aaron pulled off his jacket, being warmed by the noontime sun.

"Elvis, she wuz a purty sight, I can still remember them blue eyes, round like a deer's. She had on this purty little ole yellow dress an' her soft brown hair came down to her shoulders."

Elvis nodded his head in agreement.

"Somebody introduced us — I thank it was Willie's sister, Lydia. Well, Missy just walked right over an' started rubbing that salve all over my shoulders. I can't remember much more 'bout that day, 'cept that she smiled at me. Oh yeah, they told me she wuz only sixteen an' here I wuz eighteen, going on nineteen."

Aaron saw several buzzards floating high in the blue sky. "Hum, I wonder what they're after," he asked Elvis as he pointed toward the black dots in the sky.

"No tellin', probably a dead 'coon or sump'um"

Once they were under the shade of the trees, Aaron put his coat back on — the air was cool again. As they neared the creek, Elvis noticed smoke rising up over the trees to the south, toward the Snow farm.

"Guess ole man Snow's really cold today, look at all that smoke," Elvis said, "or maybe he's killin' a hog. I can't tell if the smoke is coming out of his chimney or what."

The boy continued walking for a couple of miles and then reaching the open range; they climbed over the fence to Grandpa River's old place. They noticed some wagon tracks in the dry grass and weeds near the old caved-in cellar. They looked fresh.

"I guess you did hear a wagon last night," Elvis told Aaron as he pulled the empty trap from an opening into the abandoned cellar. "Boy, it's dark down in there, I can't see nothin'." He hadn't brought along his flashlight, and the sunlight didn't illuminate the depths of the cellar.

What the boys did see were several spots of blood on the trap that Elvis had just pulled out of the old cellar. Elvis touched one of the red spots and found it to be sticky wet. The trap had not been sprung, but yet it bore drops of blood.

"Where do you reckon that came from?" Elvis inquired.

"I don't know. Can you see anythang in there?"

Elvis crouched down and looked into one of the dark entrances of the cellar. Aaron squatted down and peered through some fallen timbers into another opening. Neither boy could see anything that may have contributed to the spots of blood on their trap.

"I can't figure that out; the trap ain't sprung, so where'd the blood come from?" Elvis said, looking into another black hole.

"Maybe some varmint got hurt sommers else and was drippin' blood, but I don't see anythang now." Aaron replied.

They left without resetting the trap — they would come back later when they had more time. Had they brought a flashlight and looked more closely, the day would have ended differently.

When the boys returned back to the Rivers' farm, Mr. Savage was cutting the ham shoulders and bacon off the carcass with a razor sharp knife. He and Uncle Grover put the meat into the smokehouse and rubbed the pieces of meat with a homemade curing mix, a mixture of salt, sugar and other spices.

Granddaddy Keller cut the fat meat into manageable pieces, about one-inch square, and put them into a wash pot to cook. Uncle Grover and Uncle Will ground the lean trimmings into sausage, seasoned it, put it into sacks and hung them in the smokehouse.

Granny Keller, who earlier caught the hog's entrails and put them into a tub, sat down and removed the fat from the intestines and put it into a big pot over the open fire. When the grease had separated from the animal's flesh, the women skimmed off the cracklings and strained the lard into cans to be cooled and stored in a cool cellar. This lard would later be used for cooking and seasoning the food.

Putting up the meat from the hog took most of the day. Aaron and Elvis helped out where they were needed. Some of the folks in the area had seen a bobcat a few nights ago, and the boys were anxious to finish their chores so they could go out for another night of hunting and searching for the source of the blood on their trap.

4

THE NEIGHBOR

Ned Gristy didn't kill hogs today. Instead, he was going to Stephenville on this cold, but clear Saturday morning of November 28th.

Ned lived north of the Selden community, a little west of Pony Creek. A friendly, little bald headed man in his late fifties, he was a hard working farmer like most of the people from around there. He always had a pipe in his mouth that he hardly ever lit because it fogged his thick glasses.

He always wore blue overalls, even when attending church, and most of the time, a red handkerchief would be dangling from his back pocket. He wore an old green toboggan pulled down over his ears, especially on a cold day like this day.

The old farmer's spouse, Ida, whom he called, "wife," was typical of the homemakers of the day and time. Today, she was quilting a new bed cover, a Christmas present for her granddaughter. She had set a goal of making a new quilt for all her grandchildren. One by one, she finished the treasured quilts.

"Wife," Ned said as he put on his overcoat, "I'll be back 'fore too long; it's so cold an' I don't 'spect many folks to be in town today. I'll git some flour and coffee."

"Okay, you might ought to git some salt too," Ida replied, "an' oh, if you see Mister Jenkins, let him know I'll have three dozen eggs ready for him at church tomorrow."

The couple raised chickens, milk cows and goats on their small farm from which they sold eggs, butter and milk to the people Ned called "city folks." Income derived from the sales helped out financially, especially in times of crop failure.

Ned always enjoyed visiting and talking to friends and neighbors, and it usually took him over half a day to go to town and back. However, it was too cold for many of the people to meet on the square today, so Ned would not be staying in town for any length of time.

Ned walked to a shed that he had fashioned into a garage for his Model T Ford. After several tries, he was able to crank the old car. Driving down the lane, he noticed two men in conversation by the side of the road, his neighbors.

F. M. Snow's small farm, just about a mile east of the Hico Road, was on Ned's route to Stephenville. A small lane leading from Snow's house intersected the country road at a point where it made a right angle toward the south.

Six mailboxes, attached to a base made from an old wagon wheel, were at this junction. This cluster of mailboxes made it more convenient for the mail carrier because he could stop one time, delivering mail to Luke Johnson, Snow, Ned and three other neighbors rather than having to stop at the separate boxes up and down the road.

The Snow house was on the north side of the road, the Johnson's on the south, and Ned lived down a small lane that approached the road from the east. Snow and Johnson were sitting on a huge rock on the corner, beside the road. Ned stopped to greet his neighbors.

"Hi, how ya'll doin'; shore turned cold last night didn't it?" Ned asked his two neighbors. "Guess lots a folks'll be killin' hog today, its shore a good day fer it."

Snow nodded his head as a greeting, not speaking a word to the neighbor with the high-pitched voice and pleasing smile.

"Tolerable well," replied Luke, "An' how are you an' the misses?"

"We're doin' good an' lookin' forward to a big Christmas — all the kids'll be home — ya'll have a big Thanksgivin'?"

Johnson told him that he and his wife had been down with the flu, but they were feeling better. The farmer cleared his throat, "Guess y'all had a big un?" Johnson was referring to Thanksgiving.

"Yeah, we shore did, had plenty to eat. Ida cooked a fine meal. We killed a fat hen an' she made a batch of dressing, sweet tators, pumkin' pie; umm — that woman of mine shore can cook."

Ned looked at his neighbor. "Snow, you look worried, you feelin' under the weather today? Flu's goin' 'round."

"I wuz up all night," he told the men with a gaze of steel, cold as the day.

Luke Johnson looked over at the hunched man sitting beside him on the rock, noticing that his deep-set eyes were red and moist looking. Snow put his closed hand up to his cheek as he looked away from his two neighbors.

"My ole woman got upset an' said she wanted to leave me, so I hitched up my team and took her an' her ma an' her boy to Iredell. They got on the Waco train. I didn't' get back home till the sun wuz comin' up," his chilling voice revealed nothing more, his eyes revealed his pain. "I didn't thank I'd miss 'em like I do."

"Well, brother, that's too bad, I feel fer ya," said Luke, "y'all ain't been married too long have ya?"

"I ain't yore brother, Mister Johnson,"

Snow's temperament changed from melancholy to hostility, "we took the vows last October the sixth. But, I'm tellin' ya that woman couldn't watch out for a dang thang 'round the house."

Snow clenched his shaking fist and looked around toward his lonely house, mumbling at an undetectable level. He shivered and wrapped a tattered scarf tightly around his neck. His slim face appeared drawn, and a brown stain of chewing tobacco dribbled down and under his chin. He occasionally raked his hands through his long hair, protruding from under his hat.

"She blamed it on the boy though, an' I 'spect she might of been right. I jest couldn't put up with 'er no longer. It had to be done. Weren't no other way. If'n she'd jest seen it my way, it wouldn't of happened." The distraught man rambled on, taking quick breaths.

"That ole hussy just laughed at me. She shouldn't of done that, I don't let anybody laugh at me," Snow hesitated, "I'm glad the ole woman is gone — all she wanted to do is fuss an' fuss at me, but just let me fuss a little bit an' she gets all mad an' says it's over 'tween us."

"Snow, I don't blame ya for gettin' upset, but maybe she'll thank about it an' come back to you," Ned tried to comfort his neighbor, "you know how them women is, they's got their ways."

"Don't 'spect she'll ever be back." His voice trailed off as he spoke. "Her ma an' that spoiled kid of hers."

"I reckon we're all better off now." He looked to the ground, biting his lower lip, accepting the fact that his wife and stepson had departed, leaving him alone once again.

"Changing the subject, I thank I heard some shootin' over your way last night; you hear it?" Ned asked the man who seemed preoccupied, "Thank I heard a couple of shots."

"Uh," Snow hesitated, "yeah, I shot this blamed ole skunk, 'spect that's what you heard if it's concerning ya." Snow's countenance began changing once again as to tell Ned he had said enough about the matter.

"Yeah, reckon so, didn't mean nothin' by it. 'Spect I'd better mosey on to town," Ned nervously shifted his position in the seat of his car and grabbed hold of the floor leaver.

"How long you figure on staying?" asked Snow, squinting his already narrow, dark eyes.

"Weren't planning on staying too long; the wife wants a couple of thangs — ain't planning on staying long a tall."

"Well, I need me some coal oil an' sugar, so ya care if I ride along? But I gotta get back here."

"No, don't mind a tall, it might do ya good," Ned told his neighbor as he put his overcoat into the back seat of his car.

Snow climbed into the front seat of the Model T Ford and set his Winchester rifle between him and Ned. The look on Snow's face convinced Ned that it was best not to make any further conversation about the problems between Snow and his wife.

The two men sat quietly as the Ned drove the car over the narrow, rutted road. When they arrived in Stephenville, Ned let Snow off in front of Minter's Grocery Store. Snow told Ned he appreciated the ride, and that was about the extent of their conversation.

"Snow went an' bought a few thangs but he shore wuz in a hurry. He jest kept on wantin' to leave, so we got in the car an' came back home," Ned later told his wife after returning from Stephenville.

"He shore seemed worried about somethin'. He wuz shakin' his head an' mumblin' to hisself — I guess it's 'cause his wife had left 'em.

5

THE GRUESOME DISCOVERY

Planet earth's warming star had dipped down beneath the western horizon, below the tree line, as one more day came to an end in Erath County. The moon, a beckoning, but mysterious reflection of light, had begun its nightly journey across the spaciousness of the Texas sky as the darkness of evening settled in once again.

The moon was round and full, enchanting the evening sky and casting a magical sort of charm, an awesome, mystical kind of beauty upon the peacefully quiet earth. The land was asleep — only the fur-bearing animals scurried about in the coldness of the wintry nights. The birds, the insects and reptilian creatures had migrated to the warmer climates for the winter or were burrowed deep in the warmth and the safety of the ground.

Beams of moonlight shone through a kitchen window as Millie Martin set the table for the family supper. Today, she had cooked a pot of pinto beans, browned rice and cornbread for dinner, the noon-time meal and tonight, the family would be eating the leftovers for supper. She placed the bowls of food out on the table, poured fresh milk into a pitcher and summoned the family to come to the table. It was time to eat. Aaron's father asked the Lord's blessings upon the supper, and he asked for the Lord's watch care over his family. Aaron crumbled the cornbread into a glass of milk and ate it with the beans, warmed over rice and a slice of onion. He helped himself to a couple of spoonfuls of chow-chow that Millie Martin made from green tomatoes last summer. Millie customarily cooked a desert every day — today it was banana pudding — Aaron finished it off.

Having completed his nightly chores and anxious to go out on the hunt, Elvis and his old dog, Hootus, walked over to the Martins and arrived a little after they finished eating supper. Walking outside the house, Aaron was greeted by Hootus as he put on his coat. He looked up at the brilliant terrestrial globe shining in the eastern sky. He wished every night could be so perfectly beautiful.

A couple of weeks had passed since their families had killed and butchered the hog. All the fresh pork; tenderloin, ribs, heart, liver and brains had been eaten. The scarps were ground into sausage

CARROLL C. MARTIN

and fried into patties. The patties were then stored in large crocks with hot grease poured over them to keep from spoiling. The hams and bacon were rubbed with a mixture of salt and other seasonings for curing. They were then hung in old tow sacks and left to cure in a shed commonly called a smokehouse by the country people. They didn't actually smoke the meat but the shed served as a safe place from the critters of the night, or a stray dog or cat. The hams would be ready to eat before long, and the boys could hardly wait.

After the hams had been cured, the outside of the meat had to be trimmed off before being cooked because the flies laid their eggs on the outside of the ham, and the maggots would be in the outer edges of the meat. Even though this sounds repulsive, the hams were safe to eat — the boys thought the hams were delicious.

"Well, let's get started," said Elvis as he pulled on his coat, "They still ain't found that ole bobcat yet that's been catchin' folk's chickens. I hope we find sump'um — this is gonna be the night."

"Yeah, we'd better get goin' or we'll be late gittin' to Mary's party."

Tonight, Mary Stanton was hosting a party in Selden, and she had invited Aaron and Elvis. The two boys made plans earlier to go to the party, but first they would check the animal traps that they had set out yesterday.

"Maybe Missy will be there," Aaron said.

"I wouldn't count on it," Elvis replied.

"The moon is so bright tonight; we can nearly see without any light," Aaron said, looking outside," but we had better take our flashlight just in case."

The youths went outside into the peaceful, moonlit night, called up Hootus and loaded their rifles. Hootus' ears perked up in anticipation of another splendid adventure. He ran back and forth around the boys, whimpering playfully. Aaron checked the batteries in his flashlight. He put the straps of a canvas bag over his shoulder — it held his ammunition, a knife he used for skinning the animals, some rope and other odds and ends.

The boys walked down into the Martin's pasture, heading toward the creek bottom, talking about nothing of importance. The cold air was so completely still — not even a leaf stirred. The boys' breath, plainly visible, appeared as little puffs of smoke coming from their mouths in the bright moonlight.

"Hey, look at me, I'm smokin'," Aaron said.

"Just like a choo-choo train," laughed Elvis, "rollin' on down the track."

"I wonder what it'd be like to ride a real train," questioned Aaron.

"That would be so much fun; I'll bet they kin go really fast!"

"I thank Uncle Sam got to ride one when he went off to war," added Aaron.

The radiant glow of the round moon in the eastern sky added a touch of elegance to this almost perfect night. The moonbeams slithered through the tree branches, casting fluorescent shadows onto the frosty ground. Thousands of glittering, twinkling stars, looking like brilliant white diamonds high above in the vast, purple-black heavens, disappeared as the overpowering light of the moon washed them away.

Aaron stopped and stooped down to tie his shoelace when he saw an "iron rock" on the ground. Some people thought the rocks were probably meteorites that had fallen to the earth millions of years ago. He and Elvis, a few years ago, found a use for the odd, rust-colored rocks.

They broke them open. Each of the rocks was full of sand, and the sand granules in each rock were of a different color. They poured the multicolored granular silica into jars — each pastel color layered on top of another color until the jar was full. Eventually, the sand metamorphosed into one bland color as people turned and shook the containers, looking at the interesting patterns. Most of the jars of sand were gone now.

"I ain't seen one of these in a while," Aaron said, picking up the rock and putting it into his bag.

"Grandma still has one of our sand jars settin' on a whatnot shelf."

"I'm glad she saved it, I don't have any of mine left," said Elvis.

"Grandma said it was purty, like the colors of the rainbow."

"I wonder where all those rocks came from,"

"Jest one of God's hidden creations, I reckon."

The boys walked down to the trickling creek and ambled along the bank toward Grandpa Rivers' old place. Elvis spotted an inquisitive owl, sitting high in the top of a tree, watching them as they sauntered along.

The grass had withered, and the frozen weeds crackled underneath the weight of the boys' feet, leaving their footprints behind them. Hootus checked out the remains of a rabbit while the boys walked on ahead.

Elvis suddenly sidestepped to avoid stepping on a small dark shape on the ground.

"Man, I thought I wuz about to step on a tran-sler."

It was not a tarantula — they weren't active during this time of year. It was too cold. However, the tarantulas were common in the area throughout the summertime. Aaron and Elvis even hunted for them in the pastures, catching them and preserving them in alcohol. The huge, fuzzy spiders would not decompose for several weeks using this method of preservation.

Aaron shined his flashlight on the dark object that startled Elvis.

"That's jest a cow turd, you know tran-slers ain't out this time of year."

Elvis chuckled, "Yeah, I jest weren't thanking."

"It's a good thang ya didn't step in it anyway!"

"Eww, yuck!"

The night was still and very cold; it was the kind of a night where the sounds travel for miles. The boys heard, far away, coyotes howling at the bright lunar object beaming bright and beautiful in the eastern sky. Although it was cold, the boys were warm in their coats, gloves, boots and toboggans. Hootus led the way through the woods — Elvis continued talking.

"That wuz a real fun party that we had last summer at the Stones'."

"Yeah, boy, it wuz."

"There wuz a whole bunch of kids there."

"I didn't even know three of them girls," said Aaron, "they wuz Herman's cousins from New Mexico."

"I'd seen one of 'em before; the time she came to visit her grandma. Her name was Rebecca. She's the one with the long brown hair and big whatevers." Elvis grinned, making a circling motion over his chest. "Boy, she shore is pretty."

"Yeah, I know, I wanted to go walkin' down the lane with 'er," said Aaron. "But she never wuz behind the door at the right time. I thank they told 'er it wuz me out there an' she didn't want to go walkin' with me."

Aaron was reflecting back on a game that the young people played at the party. The Stones lived down past the Rocky Point Church, east from the town of Stephenville. Their house was at the end of a narrow lane, just wide enough for one vehicle to pass.

Velma Stone hosted a party for the group of teenagers on a Saturday night this past June. Aaron didn't know the name of the game, but he and the others seemed to enjoy playing it.

The boys took turns and came calling, knocking on the front door of Stone's house. The girls had all gathered, giggling, behind the door. The girl, behind the door, at the time the boy knocked, would be that boy's prize and they would go walking, hand and hand down the sunflower-lined lane.

The Stone's house set about a half mile off the main road and the little pathway up to the house was just the thing for the leisure strolls made by the courting couples.

"Missus Stone sure can make good lemonade," remarked Elvis, who seemed more interested in the food than the girls. "Who did you go walking with?"

"Lydia Stanton, Willie's little sister." Aaron had a look of pleasure on his face.

"Oh yeah, why didn't ya ask her to go to the Ole Settler's Reunion in Hico with you?"

"Didn't thank she'd go — she likes John Lawson."

"But you should've asked — now you'll never know — hey, ya know what? I thank she looks a little like Anna Jenkins."

Aaron thought about the time several years ago when he and Elvis were invited to Lester

Powell's house for a church social. Lester lived several miles north of Pony Creek in the Pilot Knob community.

A group of the kids from Lester's church got together one cool night for a hayride that started from Lester's house. Lester's father hitched up his big farm wagon to a pair of his best horses and turned the reins over to Lester. Mr. and Mrs. Powell and two of the other church members went along with the youths to chaperone the group. The kids told the grownups that it wasn't necessary for them to go along, but to no avail.

The twelve teenagers, singing songs, laughing and talking, rode the rocking wagon over the narrow trail through Bill Melton's pasture down to the old caliche pits. During the years, road construction crews had removed vast amounts of the caliche from the ground and covered many of the roads in the region. The white, chalky caliche occurs in abundance in this part of Erath County. The roads were more passable because the vehicles were not apt to get stuck on the caliche topped roads.

The boys and girls, along with their chaperones, stopped at one of the gravel pits to have a weenie roast. The deep pits protected the group from the cold wind blowing out of the south. No one was paired off with anyone else. They were simply a collective group of teenagers, having a joyous time — singing hymns and laughing.

Anna Jenkins was an only child. Although her parents were not rich, they were financially better off than many of the people in this part of Texas. She was a quiet girl who had a beautiful singing voice and was called upon to sing at church quite often. She had naturally curly, brown hair and deep green eyes with long eyelashes. Most thought she looked more like a doll than a fifteen-year-old girl — some even suggested an angel.

Aaron met Anna at a picnic held at the Oak Dale Community Center the spring before, and he had seen her several times since then. When Lester invited him to the hayride, he was hoping Anna would be going on the hayride also. He wasn't disappointed. He wanted to ask her to sit by him on the wagon, but he thought of a hundred reasons she might say no. He watched her perfectly shaped lips when she sang "Amazing Grace" — he thought it must be the voice of a Heavenly spirit.

The kids finished the weenie roast and got back on the wagon for the ride home. They sang more songs and then told ghost stories. Just as they were coming down the crest of a hill before getting back to Powell's house — Anna was singing a folk song that had been passed down from her mother:

> Oh-ohh, Sunday after church we'd go walking in the wheat fields, holding hands and talking . . .

Her strong voice softened and then suddenly she became quiet. A hush fell over the riders on the wagon. The sound of the horses' hooves and the grinding of the wagon wheels seemed amplified. Aaron saw something fall in front of him and heard the screams of excited voices, "Stop! Stop the wagon!"

Anna Jenkins had fallen head-first onto the hard road surface, breaking her neck. Two of the boys and Aaron jumped off the wagon and ran back to where she lay. The adult chaperones on the wagon worked with her and tried to bring her back, but it was evident that she was dying. Aaron watched helplessly as the life flowed out of her. There was nothing that he or anyone could do. A gurgle came deep from her chest as she took her last breath. No one knew why she fell from the wagon. The road was smooth, and the wagon was moving slowly. Dr. Naylor, who pronounced her dead, suspected she might have fainted.

It was cloudy on the day of the funeral. As the six pallbearers laid the casket down into Anna's final resting place, raindrops began to fall — teardrops from Heaven. Then suddenly, the sun found an opening in the clouds and beamed down a silver ray onto the casket, being covered with dirt. It was though the Heavens were mourning the earth's loss while rejoicing the gain of a new angel.

The vision of Anna falling off the wagon haunted Aaron for many nights to come — it was his first experience with death. He thought that if ghosts were real, Anna's spirit might find him and ask him why he hadn't asked her to be by his side on the wagon. If he had asked her, would she have joined him? Would she have died so tragically — so young? He didn't have an answer, yet.

"Yeah, I guess she looks a little like Anna, I don't know. What made you thank about her? I still remember..." his voice trailed off, and he felt a lump in his throat and tears beginning to form in his eyes.

A few weeks after the community grieved over losing Anna, her mother asked Aaron to come by the Jenkins' house. He had only met her parents one time, and that was at the funeral — he couldn't imagine a reason for this unusual request.

He asked Elvis to go along with him to the Jenkins' home, modest but at the same time, elaborate. Mrs. Jenkins looked much older and drawn than she had at the funeral. She invited the boys inside and into the living room. She thanked them for coming by, and she explained when she had been in Anna's room, she had found her diary. She showed Aaron the last entry that Anna wrote in the diary — tears boiled up in his eyes as he read the lines, written in Anna's handwriting, dated September 23, 1923:

"When they began discussing class rings for our class, they told us they would order them if as many as three would get one. I asked Papa if I could get one, and he said I could. But before we got them ordered, Papa saw some of the other parents and found out that only me and two others were getting rings, so he told me he didn't think any of us should get rings unless all of us could. So, I won't be getting a class ring.

We are having a hayride tonight for the kids at church. Lester Powell told me he asked Aaron Martin to go with us. He is the boy that I met at the Oak Dale Community Center. He has beautiful eyes and always seems so nice. Maybe he will finally notice me."

"I'm sorry I brought it up, I jest wasn't thinking." Elvis walked over and put his arms around Aaron's shoulder.

"That's okay; I just never saw anyone dead before, much less watch them die." Not wanting to show how much he cared for the deceased girl, he turned his head away from Elvis.

"I hope I never see anything so awful again. I wish I had another chance to . . ."

Hootus' furious baying interrupted him as they neared the vicinity of Grandpa Rivers' lonely old home place. Hootus was out of sight, but they could hear him, behind the old house, about a half-mile away. The boys picked up their pace, almost running.

"Come on, he's found sump-um!" shouted Elvis.

Bearing toward the ruckus, they crossed over a fence and as they did; they could make out the dim form of Hootus. The loyal dog, running ahead of the boys, was at the in cellar beside the old burned out house.

Closer now, Aaron could see him plainly in the glowing moonlight. Hootus was at the cellar, not going in, but staying just outside. The two boys hurried, expecting to find an animal, hiding in the bowels of the caved in sanctuary. The energized ferocity of Hootus' barking and his frenzied movements told the hunters that something was in there!

Elvis crouched down on his knees, looking under the old logs that were once the top of the storm cellar, shining his flashlight, trying to see inside. He raked back the spider webs spun across the black opening, while he shined the light around, looking for a rat, snake or raccoon; searching for something that had distressed the dog.

A stale, musty odor drifted up from inside the cellar, mixed with a pungency that Elvis could not make out, a faint sickening smell.

"Eww, what's that smell?" Elvis asked. "Ya reckon sump-um's dead?"

He realized that he was looking through a hole at the backside of the cellar, the part with the least access. A jagged log obscured his view, and all he could see was more spider webs in the darkness. Hootus, squirming, tried to get into the hole and then he backed out and ran to the front of the cellar, shaking himself off.

"I don't see anythang."

Elvis sounded bewildered — the dog's actions were anything but normal tonight. Elvis crawled on his knees to another murky opening. Aaron knelt down beside him, holding his rifle, ready to protect his friend. They caught a whiff of the putrid odor again, slight, but it was present. Hootus whimpered and moved back from the dark hole, holding his tail underneath him.

Elvis couldn't understand why his dog was barking so furiously, why was he refusing to enter the dark cavern in the ground. The boys had found game and snakes before, and Hootus hadn't raised such a commotion — maybe it was a big snake, or maybe it was the bobcat, although it was unlikely.

"Elvis, it might be a rattler!" shouted Aaron with eyes opened wide, looking, "watch yourself,

Elvis — watch yourself! Don't take any chances an' don't stick yore hand in there 'till you can see what it is."

Elvis shifted around on the other knee shining the light into the dark crevasses of the cellar's fallen logs as Hootus, yelping, strained to get through an opening into the depths of the black enclosure.

The old dog was too rigid — he couldn't crouch down low enough to enter the opening. Aaron, on his knees, pulled Hootus back from the hole so that Elvis could get a closer look. A coyote howled nearby and Aaron straightened up and looked that direction, seeing nothing but the night. The sound of the cry was too close.

"What in the world's going on here? Dang, this is spooky!" Aaron, a Christian, strong and spiritual was slow to fear anything, but this was unsettling, intimidating.

"I still don't see anythang," Elvis said, lying down on his stomach to shine a ray of light into the dark cavern toward an outline in the empty space.

"Wait a minute! No, it's just a log. I thought I saw something moving."

He shined the beam of the flashlight in the direction of the perceived movement while looking up, over and around the logs and debris. The shift was ever so slight, but it was unmistakable. Still, he could not make out anything in stillness of the frightening hole.

"I know I saw something over there!" Elvis pointed to his left, lowering his head for a better view.

He heard a racket — something was in a tree in front of him and to the right of the cellar. He pulled back from the hole and shined his flashlight up in the tree, first on one limb, then another. Startled, he saw the glow of two eyes watching the goings on from above. He gave out a sigh of relief when he realized it was only a curious owl, nothing more.

Elvis thought that maybe there was nothing to be concerned about — maybe they were only scaring themselves. He had heard that the only thing to fear is fear itself, though it wasn't much reassurance at this moment. He would be courageous; Aaron was. Imagination, he thought, often worse than reality, more frightening than the truth.

But Hootus continued to jump and lurch, yelping and whining, whimpering and growling, trying to get into that black, disturbing, forbidden hole. That was not the boys' imagination, and that was the reality of the night.

"Elvis, what is it? Gosh dang it, why is Hootus actin' like that?"

Aaron moved a little closer to an opening that was at one time, a long time ago, a cellar door. He ducked down, swept back the spider webs with his gloved hand and looked inside. Too dark, he couldn't see anything. He carefully climbed down into the dark opening, a place that once meant safety from the raging storm — a hole now possessing the unknown. Slowly one foot touched the bottom, then the other, he was inside.

He felt unsettled; something was not right. Fearing a snake, he moved sluggishly and cautiously. Through the opening, he could smell the damp and musty odor coming out of the cellar, undisturbed for many years. But he could also smell something else, a scent that shouldn't be there. An odor he had never smelled before. He saw the glow of Elvis' flashlight, reflecting from side to side, and then he saw something wavering, suspended from one of the logs. Something was stuck fast, partially hidden by the log, hanging alone, caught on a timber.

"Elvis, there's something right over there, right below ya. It moves every time ya shift around. It's a sack or sump-um. There, yore 'bout to touch it!"

Elvis instinctively jerked his hand back then slowly and carefully; he reached into the gap between two of the logs with his left hand. He shined his light unto the cold object he was touching, and then he looked at it.

"Oh no!" Elvis, nearly falling, recoiled back from the dark black hole.

"No! It can't be!" screamed Elvis shaking his head and wiping his gloves on the ground, trying to be rid of the substance on them.

"What — what is it? Is it a rattler? Is it the bobcat? Is it a coon?" Aaron climbed back out of the damp hole and saw the terror in Elvis' eyes. He knew that the object that he had seen was much more terrifying than an animal.

Elvis shook his head, indicating no. His lips were tightly closed. His eyes were revealing a horror beyond his words. His heart was pounding. His breathing was shallow and quick. He was finally able to form the words, "Aaron, come on, let's get out of here!"

He got up, turned and then stumbled over a piece of barbed wire that had grabbed his boots. He fell to the ground; as if something from below had grabbed him — the thing in the cellar was trying to pull him into its depths.

"No, let me go!"

"Elvis, what is it? Tell me, Elvis!" Aaron hollered, trying to stay calm, but having little success. He looked at Elvis and saw that all the color had left his face.

"I seen somebody's ear!" He was finally able to say. "It's somebody's ear!"

"Dad gum it, Elvis, yore just trying to spook me!"

Hootus was whimpering and cowering back from the cellar now, "You're jest trying to spook me, an' I ain't skeered — give me the light!"

No, he wasn't scared — he was horrified. Aaron took the dimming flashlight from Elvis' shaking hand and shone it into the pitch-black darkness. He saw, hanging from a beam of rotting wood, a burlap bag — a tow sack, stained dark crimson red.

Protruding from a hole in the sack was what looked like a human ear.

"It can't be!" Aaron shouted to Elvis, trying to diminish what he knew to be real. "Somebody probably threw some cow innards down here, an' it jest looks like a ear poking out."

Aaron felt a shiver run down his spine as he stooped down and grabbed hold of the sack, dragging it from its place of rest and putting it on his knee. He looked at his gloves and saw they were stained with a dark red, sticky substance — he knew it was blood.

The strange and sickening odor that the boys had earlier experienced inundated the air as he opened the sack, exposing the forbidding find, their discovery; the unimaginable. He looked down at the thing inside the bag; he shuttered, and then he pulled back and looked at Elvis whose mouth was wide open in disbelief.

He could feel his heart pounding in his chest, and he felt as if he couldn't get his breath. The terrified teenager looked up into the winter sky, not knowing what to do next.

Elvis had dropped the flashlight, and it fell onto a rock, angling the dim ray of light toward the old house. The movement of the boys and dog cast faint shadows against the house, looking like dark demons, dancing in rhythm with their racing hearts.

Elvis fumbled around, trying to retrieve the light, wanting to run for the safety of home. Even in the darkness with the moon giving the only light, there was no mistaking the horrible thing in the burlap bag.

"It's a head; it's somebody's head!" Elvis screamed as the sack dropped from Aaron's grip to the cold, hard earth with a dull thud.

A sensation of unreality crept over Elvis as he tried to control the panic gripping him. He was able to move, but everything seemed too slow. He picked up the flashlight, but its beam had faded now, the batteries were expended. He found a match in his pocket, struck it and held it above the sack that Aaron had released from his grip. He and Aaron looked at the horrible sight there before them and their dog.

There, staring back from the blood-stained burlap bag were the unblinking eyes of a dead man — a human head. Even in death the eyes had not closed; open eyes, searching into the darkness for someone, anyone, begging for consolation. Frightened, alone and questioning, the wide-opened eyes seemed to be asking, "Who will listen to me? Who will hear how my life has ended so horribly?"

The head, crudely hacked from its body as evidenced by the jagged edges of body tissue at the neck, might belong to a boy about the age of the two standing there. Who or what could be so evil, so deranged as to mutilate a human in such a horrible, despicable, unspeakable manner?

"It's Herman!"

Aaron gasped and felt faint as the blood rushed from his head — fright was overtaking him with a sickness he had felt only once before. He moved back from the horrible discovery and got down on his hands and knees. He couldn't calm his trembling body — the earth was spinning below him. He wanted to run, but where could he go?

Watching the blood spurting and spewing from a hog's neck had not overpowered Elvis to the degree as the sight of this dead person's head. He stared at the questioning eyes in the bag, and then he thought, could the person's slayer be watching, even now? Hoping to awaken from this hideous nightmare, he was able to gather his wits long enough to yell at Aaron.

"Hurry, Aaron, get up! We gotta go get some help!

6

NOTIFYING THE AUTHORITIES

"**S**am, this here's Sheriff Hassler."

Sam Russell, the young district attorney for Erath County, heard a slow-talking, resonant voice on the other end of his telephone.

The familiar caller continued, "Looks like we got us a murder."

§

Sheriff Med Hassler was home, just getting ready to go to bed. A telephone call — a hysterical caller on the other end, "Sheriff, this is Elvis Rivers. Me an' Aaron Martin jest found some feller's head in a tow sack!"

Hassler would be forty-five years old this month — it was his first term as Erath County's

High Sheriff. He was a deputy sheriff for Mont Thomas, and when Thomas decided to retire, Hassler ran for the office. He won the election easily, beating two other opponents.

Hassler's mild disposition, friendliness and reputation for being fair had made him one of the most popular lawmen in the area. He had a slender build and was a little over six feet tall — his dark hair, graying, complimented a handsome, handlebar mustache. His speech was slow and deliberate, and he rarely seemed to be excited.

Hassler wanted to know more details about the unbelievable report he was getting from the excited youth. This was Erath County and things like this, finding the human head without a body; evidently a victim of a grisly murder, just didn't happen here.

"What do you mean, you found a head?" inquired Hassler.

"Me and Aaron wuz out hunting an' we wuz over on Grandpa River's old place an' that's where we found it! It's in a bloody tow sack down there."

"Okay, calm down jest a bit; where is this tow sack?'

"It's out there on the ground. It wuz in the cellar at Grandpa's place. Me 'n Aaron pulled it out."

The sheriff, running his hands through his disheveled hair, remained calm while listening to the distraught boy — the boy reporting an unbelievable narrative.

At first, he thought the boy might be pulling a prank on him; a prank would have been more welcomed, but he soon dismissed that thought. In reality, the two boys had discovered evidence of a brutal killing, a grisly murder.

Hassler asked, "Where are you boys now?"

"We're at the Miller's, Sheriff. Hurry on down here, it's horrible! Me and Aaron thank it's Herman Starnes."

"I'll be on my way — ya'll jest wait there where ya are, and I'll be there as soon as I can an' we'll figure this all out."

Elvis, Aaron and the dog had run past the Otwells' to the Gene Miller's house, the nearest house with a telephone that they could use, about a mile away from the cellar and the gruesome discovery. Mrs. Miller had met the horrified boys at the door.

"Oh my dear Lord," Mrs. Miller gasped as she heard their plea, looking into the darkness of the night, "Oh boys, you two come on in here right now!"

Elvis made his panicked call to Sheriff Hassler and was reassured by a calming voice, "Now we're gonna take care of this; y'all just wait 'til I can get there."

Aaron said a silent prayer, "Lord, protect us, help us make it through this; an' make me strong."

"Oh, Missus Miller," Elvis whimpered, "we seen something dreadful awful. We wuz huntin' an' we found sump'um in a tow sack. Somebody chopped a boy's head clean off! I thank its Herman."

"Oh no, do you really think its Herman?" Mrs. Miller asked, trying to soothe the boy.

"Shore looks like him, ma'am — I can't be fer shore, but his hair is dark an' combed back like Herman does his," Elvis told Mrs. Miller, beginning to calm down just a little bit. "Are you okay Aaron?"

"Yeah, I'm okay, but I'm still shakin' an' I'm still kinda sick at my stomach. Elvis, it's horrible. Who do you thank done it, killed that boy an' cut off his head, I mean."

"I don't know, I sure hope the sheriff gets here soon. What if somebody seen us out there an' they's gonna get us too!"

"Oh, Elvis don't even thank that! Everything will be okay; the sheriff'll be here soon."

A calming peace came over Aaron although his heart was still pounding deep inside his chest — he knew that the Protector, mightier than any killer, was present.

Erath County, located in North Central Texas, sixty-five miles west of Fort Worth did not have any major crime problems. A man murdered his neighbor several years ago over a dispute about some dogs at the Somervell County line. And last summer three convicts broke out of a state prison in Walker County with the intentions of killing the prosecuting attorney, but most of the crimes reported were nothing more than petty theft, cattle rustling, forgery and bootlegging.

Sam Morris Russell, alert and young — forcible and full of vigor, had served as the county's district attorney for a year. His voice was thunderous and persuasive and like most of the men in his family, he didn't seem to have any fear of anyone. Tall and stoutly built, his dark wavy hair and piercing eyes made him handsome.

Russell, born on August 9, 1889, on a farm near Stephenville, went the country schools in Erath County and attended John Tarleton College. He taught school in Erath County from 1913 to 1918, pursued some agriculture interests and during the First World War served as a private in the Forty-sixth Machine Gun Company with the United States Army.

After studying law, he was admitted to the bar in 1919 and began practicing in Stephenville, serving as the county attorney of Erath County before being elected district attorney of the Twenty-ninth Judicial District in 1924. He had his eye on bigger things, perhaps thinking about going to Washington someday.

Russell, a tough prosecutor and a hard-hitting adversary in court, secured life sentences for the three members of the McCall gang who had robbed the State Bank in Meridian. They vowed they would retaliate, threatening Russell as they were led out of the courtroom on their way to the state prison in Huntsville, Texas.

ASHES UPON THE SNOW

Last summer the gang overpowered the a guard and broke out of the state prison. They headed to Stephenville to even the score with Russell — they intended to kill him. The gang murdered several people along the way — two of the women slain by the fugitives were witnesses against them at their trial.

The three escapees eluded the authorities for three days, but the lawmen closed in on the convicts on a cold, rainy night, surrounding and capturing two of the three after a shootout south of Stephenville. The leader of the gang, Buster McCall, was fatally wounded during the short gunfight that ensued — none of the lawmen were injured.

"The Rivers boy just called me an' told me a mighty disturbing thing. They found somebody's head down in the ole cellar on his granddaddy's ole home place," Hassler told the district attorney.

"Deputy Ross is somewhere up in the northern part of the county watchin' fer a pack of wild dogs that's been killin' the farmer's sheep an' goats, so I thought it might be a durn good idea if you went down there with me."

"Do you know anything about who it is?" The inquisitive district attorney asked. He knew there were no reports of anyone missing in the area.

"Naw, the boy said it may be Herman Starnes. I just don't know what to expect, but thought I'd better let you in on it."

"Uh, yeah, I'll get my clothes on an' meet you down at the courthouse in about twenty minutes."

Russell dressed, and since he lived only three blocks west of downtown, he walked to the Erath County Courthouse on the square in Stephenville. He noticed the bright, full moon, now high in the eastern sky, giving its light to the disturbed night. It was crisp, cool and quiet on the city streets; occasionally, he heard the bark of a far away dog.

Then he heard, Dong — Dong — Dong, the courthouse clock bell was chiming out the time as if it were a death call. Dong — Dong . . .

"Eleven times, eleven o'clock," Russell thought to himself, "looks like it could be a long night."

He walked down Washington Street, deserted and still; no one stirred at this time of night and now, even the clock had stopped striking — the only sound to be heard was Russell's own footsteps.

Russell approached the west door of the dark, shadowy courthouse. He unlocked the door, screeching as it opened, and walked into the poorly lit rotunda. Silvery beams of moonlight shined through the windows on the east side of the courthouse as he climbed the stairs up to the second floor — up to the sheriff's office.

Hassler had arrived ahead of the district attorney and was opening the top drawer of his desk as Russell walked in. Hassler hardly ever wore a sidearm, there was no reason to, but tonight was different — he strapped on his holster and .45-Colt revolver. He wasn't sure of what they would find when he got to the ole Rivers' place. An unknown killer was out there somewhere, a killer that might be lurking in the night — a killer that they must find.

Russell asked the tall, lanky lawman, "You found out anything else?"

"Nah, those boys were pretty excited. After the dog had alerted them, they found somebody's head in a ole cellar while they wuz out huntin'."

"Did they find a body?"

"Don't thank so, jest the head, we ain't got no reports of anybody missin' 'round here, so I don't know what we got out there."

The two men left the courthouse and got into Hassler's Model T Ford, the most common type of vehicle found in the area.

Riding down the well-traveled route that lay between Stephenville and Glen Rose, Russell remarked, "I sure wish these things would happen when it was warmer weather an' in the daytime."

The air, cold and frosty, blew in around the doors of the rattling vehicle — Russell pulled his coat up around his neck.

"Yeah, but they never do!"

The night felt peaceful and the moon, in front of them looked welcoming, seemingly unknowing about the terror that lay ahead for many in the small community.

Thirty minutes passed — Hootus, waiting outside, barked, warning that someone was nearing the house. Mrs. Miller saw the headlights of a car coming down the path from the main road.

Apprehension plagued the waiting group until Mrs. Miller saw it was the sheriff and Russell. She too harbored the idea that a killer might be near, watching and waiting to dispose of any witnesses.

"Boys, it's the sheriff." Mrs. Miller felt some relief.

Hassler and Russell met the boys who were waiting anxiously, dreading the foreboding night that was to come, they hadn't asked for this duty. Elvis jumped up from the wooden chair and ran to the door, opening it quickly. The lawmen's arrival, welcoming and reassuring, calmed the discoverers' uncertainties.

"Sheriff, I sure am glad to see you! Me and Aaron has had the wits scared out of us!"

"Okay, Boys, ya'll just calm down an' tell me what happened."

"Me and Aaron wuz out checking our traps at Granddad's place an' ole Hootus wuz barkin' at the cellar, so I went to see what he wuz barkin' at — I thought it was probably some varmint." Elvis' voice had lost some of its quivering. "I was shinin' my light under the logs an' that's when I seen this old bloody tow sack an' I seen a ear sticking out of it!"

"I reached in an' pulled the sack out," Aaron told the sheriff, "an' then I looked in the sack an' I saw this head with its eyes still open."

"Sheriff, it was the awfullest thang I ever saw — I thank it is Herman Starnes," Elvis said, "it' shore looks a lot like him, I thank it's Herman!"

"What makes you think its Herman?" inquired Sam Russell, always suspicious, but always methodical and thorough; he rarely left any stone unturned.

"You know him pretty good?"

"I couldn't tell ya fer sure, sir, but it looks like his hair, an' the way it's combed back, you know, wavy like that."

The boys and lawmen began walking out to Hassler's car. The boys got into the back seat of the vehicle, urging Hootus to lie in the floor, wanting to hug each other, but not daring to.

They were still facing the fact that they would have to view the horror of their find at least one more time. Maybe it would be the final time. The gruesome task still facing Russell and Hassler was viewing the severed head for the first time, the starting point for their investigation.

Hassler's car swayed back and forth on the uneven road as he drove to the old farm with the abandoned storm cellar, the boys pointing out the way.

As they neared the Rivers' farm, a deer jumped out in front, startling everyone; then over the grown up, shabby fencerow, the deer disappeared as soon as it had appeared.

Russell still questioned the boys, "How'd you boys happen to be out here?"

"Like I said," Elvis retorted, "I've told ya this already, me an' Aaron wuz out here checkin' out our traps when ole Hootus started barkin' at that cellar. I thought we probably had caught some varmint."

"Turn right over there," pointing to an open gate leading into his grandfather's old homestead.

Hassler turned down a little lane, overgrown with grass, now brown and brittle, entering an open area that used to be a cotton field and in the middle of the field stood the old burned out house. Fog had formed around it, projecting a menacing aurora through the headlights.

Hassler saw the depression, once the cellar, in the car's headlights and slowed to a stop. He stepped out of the car and shining his flashlight toward the old cellar, he saw it, the bloody tow sack still lying on the ground where Aaron had dropped it.

He slowly and carefully picked up the sack, opened it and shined his flashlight inside. What he saw made him shudder — two human eyes staring at him. The human head appeared to be that of a young teenage boy; it was well preserved, and the color of the skin was almost normal. There were other contents in the bag; a dark colored pin-striped coat, an old checked mackinaw and piece of a white shirt — all there together in the bloody, red stained tow sack. The smell of death was about.

"I don't recognize him," said Hassler, "how about you Sam; look familiar to you?" Hassler held the sack, holding the terrible discovery out for Russell to view.

"No sir, don't look like anybody I've ever seen. Don't think that it's the Starnes boy, but guess we had better go check on 'im." Russell was quiet now.

"Look here, looks like two bullet holes," Hassler said, pulling the coat out of the sack and spreading it out on the ground, "they shot 'im an' cut his head plum off! One hole's in the collar an' the other ones right close to his shoulder blade. That coward shot 'im in the back!"

Hassler noticed a label from an Amarillo tailoring shop sown on the bloody, white shirt. He turned the head over to one side for further examination. His flashlight revealed a wound under the chin, probably made with a knife. He saw abrasions on the face and skull.

"Maybe he was killed somewhere else an' they just cut his head off an' threw it in there," Russell said, looking all around the immediate area. "I think whoever killed him knew this locality an' knew no one lived here. I believe the killer knew the house, knew it had been abandoned an' knew no one would be coming around. There are three other houses around here, and they're all vacant an' I think the bad guy knew that. Do you expect the body's still in the cellar?"

"We didn't see nothin' else in there," Aaron told the officials, believing that if the body were there inside the cellar, they would have seen it.

The officers walked around the area, shining their lights as they searched through the weeds and brush growing in an old field. They looked in the cellar and then through the old house, but failed to find a body, or any signs of a body or any bloodstains on the ground around the house or in the cellar.

Russell's conclusion that the boy must have been slain someplace else, away from the cellar where the boys had found the head, appeared to him to be correct.

"Sam, we want to be as respectful as we can to this poor boy," Hassler said, walking over and picking up the bloody bag. "We shore don't want to treat 'im like a bag of tators."

"The killer sure didn't have much respect when he put the head into that ole tow sack."

Hassler walked over to his Model T Ford, holding the bag that held the head of an unknown young boy. Shining his flashlight, he looked into the back floorboard. Opening the door, he gently placed the bag into floorboard of the car.

"Boys, y'all set over on the other side, an' I'll take ya'll home."

Aaron, shaking his head, "I ain't settin' by that thang!"

"It ain't gonna hurt you," said Elvis, "I'll set next to him; he's a boy, just like us!"

7

THE HEAD IN THE BLOODY SACK

As Elvis was getting out of Sheriff Hassler's car, he saw his mother waiting at the door of the River's home.

"Mother," he yelled, running toward her.

"Elvis, whatever is wrong?" Uneasiness set in as she saw Sheriff Hassler getting out of the Model T Ford, knowing that something was wrong.

"Me an' Aaron wuz out with ole Hootus, checkin' our traps an' we found sump'um awful!"

Hassler told Mrs. Rivers about the horrific, unbelievable events of the night. "I don't thank there's any danger to your boy here, but y'all go on inside an' bolt the door. I'm gonna take the Martin boy on home now."

Aaron, alone in the back seat of the sheriff's sedan, glanced over, seeing the bag with the severed head inside, suddenly felt a wave of nausea. But he composed himself, looked back and waved to Elvis as Hassler drove down the rutted lane toward the Martin farm.

Mrs. Rivers and Elvis went inside the house, bolting the door behind them. Elvis related how a peaceful, moonlit night had turned into a night of terror. Mrs. Rivers, trying to remain calm, listened to her son describe how he and Aaron happened to make the shocking discovery.

Then he remembered; Elvis exclaimed, "I clean fergot about ole Hootus, and I bet Aaron did too!"

Elvis didn't sleep much through the rest of the night; he kept seeing the grotesque sight of the bloody head every time he closed his eyes. He kept seeing those eyes that never blinked and seemed to be calling out, "Help me!"

Elvis was up early the next morning.

"Momma, I wonder who that boy was an' I wonder who killed 'em?" he questioned, "Me and Aaron thanks it looks like Herman, but I ain't too sure."

Elvis always had a pleasant life, and he wondered about the boy that looked about his age who was no longer living. What kind of life did he have? Did he know who had done this awful thing to him? Who could do such a thing? And, even more frightening, where was the killer now? Did the killer know that he and Aaron had found the boy's head? Elvis had many unanswered, apprehensive questions.

Madison Martin, concerned, was waiting for Aaron when the sheriff brought him home. Worried. The boys had never stayed out as late; it was past midnight.

As Sheriff Hassler was talking with Madison, they heard barking, echoing, off in the distance. It was old dog, Hootus, trotting along, down the road and up to the Martin's front yard. The old dog had been left behind with all the turmoil going on during the seriousness of the night after the boys had made the discovery.

"That's the Rivers boy's dog," said Madison, "I'll see to it that he gits back home."

Hassler, along with Russell, drove on into Stephenville and took the severed head to Trewitt's Funeral Home and turned it over to the undertaker, B. I. Trewitt. Hassler asked Trewitt if he recognized the boy whose head was now in his hands.

"No, Sheriff, I don't know this lad, but there's bound to be a mother out there somewhere who's looking for him."

It was now several hours past midnight — everyone was exhausted. Hassler decided to wait until the next day to organize a search party — the specific goal, locating a body.

Sheriff Hassler, before he could retire for the night, had to begin his first step in the tedious, concentrated investigation. Elvis and Aaron thought that the detached head looked like Herman Starnes, their friend. He had to know.

He made the call that he dreaded, knowing there was no alternative, fearing the answer he might find.

"Missus Starnes this here is Sheriff Hassler; ma'am, I need to ask you about Herman."

"Yes sir?" She wondered what was wrong; it was approaching three o'clock in the morning. "Why are you callin' this time of night?"

"Ma'am, is Herman home?" He asked, hoping that he was there but fearful that he wasn't.

"No sir, Mister Hassler, he's been workin' over at the Hatchett's place. I was 'specting him to come home yesterday, but I guess he decided to stay a little longer. Sheriff, what's the matter? Why are you asking 'bout Herman? Is he in some kind of trouble?"

Her concern was now beginning to show in her voice — news is never good at this time of night.

"Now, Missus Starnes, He ain't in no trouble; I don't thank nothing's wrong, I just needed to talk to Herman a bit — where'd you say he wuz?"

"He left a couple of days ago an' he said he wuz going over to Bill Hatchett's house. Him and Bill's goin' to help Mister Hatchett gather in his corn crop. I 'spect they wuz gonna shuck it an' get it ready to grind."

She continued, "Herman an' them wuz supposed to be going to a party at the Bishop's house last night from there. You know where that is, don't ya? I thought he wuz gonna come home last night, but sir, he ain't come in yet — when he gets here, you want me to have him call ya?"

"Please ma'am, if you would, I surely would like to talk to him."

He was becoming uneasy about the possibility that the discoverers of the head might be correct about its identity. The likelihood that Herman was the murdered youth was becoming more plausible all the time.

"Sheriff, why can't you tell me what this is about?"

"Missus Starnes, we found a boy; somebody had killed him — I wuz thanking that Herman might possibly know who it is or give us a clue or somethin'."

"Oh no!" The mother was becoming more upset, "Do you thank it's Herman?"

"Missus Starnes, now don't you worry none, we don't know who it is — I just thought Herman might could help us out tryin' to find out who it is." He had anticipated the question but hadn't prepared the proper response, for there was none.

"What makes you think Herman would know anything about who it is?" her voice trembled.

"We 'spect the boy is 'bout Herman's age an' he knows most the kids in this area."

Sheriff Hassler, becoming more apprehensive, reassured the mother and bidding her good night, got into his car to make the ten-mile trip down to Lem Hatchett's farm, just a few miles from the Rivers' place — too close to the Rivers' place. He had to settle it once and for all, and soon — had Herman merely not come home when he was expected or had he met with an untimely death? The head lying in state at the funeral home, was it his? The drive to the Hatchett's farm seemed to have taken more time than it should have. It would have been a pleasant drive if the sheriff's task wasn't so important, so dismal.

The winter sun was beginning to rise the in the eastern sky as Hassler turned into the gate at the entrance to Hatchett's place. It was clear, cold and looked like it was going to be another beautiful day; the gravity of the circumstances was not being reflected by the splendor of this new day. The sheriff saw Hatchett coming out onto the front porch of this house.

"Hello Sheriff, what brings you out here this early?" Hassler wished that the reason was different. He dreaded the question he must ask — he feared the answer that he might hear.

"Lem, Missus Starnes told me her boy, Herman, was over here, and I shore need to talk to him. Is he here?"

"No, he ain't here; he left for home early yesterday morning."

"Are you sure?" Hassler felt the reality of Hatchett's answer beginning to tighten its grip over him.

"Sheriff, I'm sure, he left here an' said he was going by Andrew Walker's, then home. Why are you asking 'bout Herman for; is he in some kinda trouble?"

"I guess you ain't heard, we found a dead boy over on the ole Rivers' place last night," pointing in that direction, "the head had been cut off his body an' throwed down in a cellar. The Rivers boy thanks it might be Herman. He's pretty sure about it and thangs are shore pointing that way."

Lem was stunned and perplexed by the words the sheriff was telling him, surely this wasn't reality, and he too, began to fear that Herman had met with tragedy while on his way home. Lem tried to remain as composed as possible so he could help the sheriff.

He wanted to remember all he could about the events of the past few days because he feared that he and his son, Bill, may have been the last persons to have seen Herman alive.

"What were Herman's last words?" He couldn't recall.

"What was he wearing?" That too was hazy in his memory. Then he remembered something, it might be important.

"I know how you can tell," Luke told the sheriff, "Herman cut the right side of his face pretty bad. He had it all bandaged up when he left here."

Hassler didn't remember seeing a bandage or cut on the bodiless head. It was so bloody — he just didn't know.

The drive back to town seemed to take even longer than the drive out to the Hatchett's. He drove straight to the funeral home. He needed to look at the face, would he find the identifying cut?

"Sheriff, I'm glad you're here," said B. I. Trewitt, the mortician, "I found something interesting; thought you'd probably like to know."

"What's that," Hassler asked, and dreading the response from the man with the information.

"I'll think this boy's been dead about five to ten days. It's just been so cold, the head stayed well preserved." Hassler began to feel some relief come over him; it was a welcomed statement made by the undertaker.

"May I use your phone?" He would call the Walkers now, believing the report would be good.

"Sure, go right ahead."

Hassler rang the operator and asked if Andrew Walker had telephone service. The operator informed Hassler that the Walkers were telephone subscribers. The sheriff asked the operator to connect him with the Walker house. He heard Mrs. Walker on the other end of the telephone, picking up, as well as several others on the party line. He prayed that they all would receive an affirmative answer to the query that he would be posing.

"Missus Walker, this here's Sheriff Hassler," then he asked the question, "is Herman Starnes over there?"

"Yes he's here; do you want talk to him?" Those were pleasing words, words of jubilation.

"No ma'am, that's just fine; just wanted to know if he was there."

Right away, the sheriff felt relief but at the same time, frustration — he was no closer to knowing the identity of the dead boy than he was last night. But he knew one thing for certain. It was not Herman Starnes because Herman was alive! Hassler later found that Herman got to the Walker house late that night, and because it was late, he decided to stay there. Herman had tried to call his mother Mrs. Starnes, but was not able to get through on the telephone, so he didn't think any more about it.

Sheriff Hassler went back to Trewitt's Funeral Home. The murder victim was not Herman Starnes, but who was it? He went to the back room of the mortuary, where Trewitt had stored the boy's clothing. He picked up the blood-stained shirt. It didn't look like any ordinary shirt; it looked tailor made, and that was unusual in these parts. He looked at the label inside, Williamson Tailors, Amarillo Texas — maybe they could shed some light on the identity of the murdered boy. It was a place to start.

"Operator, get me Williamson Tailors in Amarillo, Texas, please ma'am."

After a long few minutes, the operator connected the call, "This here's Sheriff M. D. Hassler in Stephenville, Texas, and I was a wondering if you might be able to help me out."

Hassler told the reason for his inquiry, but the shop owner was not able to provide any useful information about the wearer of the shirt.

The man told the sheriff, "I have customers throughout the state of Texas and so I make a lot of shirts, but I always monogram the customer's name on the tail of the shirt."

Hassler did not have the benefit of the entire shirt, only a few torn pieces.

"Your murder victim may have bought the shirt from me," the tailor reasoned, "but it's more probable that the boy got hold of it by some other means."

"I'll make two or three hundred shirts a year," he told the sheriff, "and I can't account for them all."

Another dead end. Hassler went to the courthouse and found that Sam Russell was there, already making telephone calls, inquiring about missing boys.

"This is Sam Russell and I'm the district attorney here in Erath County. I want to tell you what we've got here and ask you for any help you might can give us."

He contacted the newspapers in Fort Worth asking for their assistance. He called other police agencies advising them of the murdered boy, finding that there were many youths, teenagers, missing.

He and Hassler received an inundation of telephone calls and telegrams over the next several days.

"I just read the article in the newspaper about finding that boy and the description sounds like my boy," many a heartbroken mothers sobbed over the telephone.

Every lead had to be checked out, but the identity of the slain boy continued to elude them. One family, a needy family residing in Fort Worth's oldest neighborhood, thought it might be their son, Milton. He had been missing from their home for over three months. His mother, Mrs. John Crow, read the account of finding the murder victim in the Fort Worth paper. She was on the verge of a nervous breakdown when she talked to Sheriff Hassler.

"He is a fine boy and although he is but sixteen years old, he is large enough to be taken for eighteen. He stands five feet-eight inches an' weighs one hundred an' thirty pounds. He is one of the nicest behaved boys you ever saw an' would not have run away except that man ten years his elder influenced him to do so."

"Yes ma'am," Hassler said.

She continued, sobbing, pleading, "We have received a stack of letters followin' our efforts to trace him, but we never heard from Milton after he left. After we was forced to take him out of school, he worked for a movie theater. Next, he found work at the Greenwood Florist Company and then went to picking cotton. It was while on his last job that he met the man who induced him to leave home."

The sheriff listened as she told about her boy leaving with the older man.

"We were told that Milton an' the man had gone to Ardmore, but the authorities there could not locate them. We've sought all over the United States for him, in fact."

"I'm mighty sorry to hear that," the sheriff commented.

"Thank you sir, my husband is an invalid an' we were forced to give up our forty-acre farm near Grapevine, for we had no one to work it, an' I obtained work myself in town. I am nearly a wreck from worry."

"What does your boy look like, Missus Crow? Could you describe him for me?" The sheriff asked the anguished woman.

"Milton has a scar below the knee and a slight scar over an eye where he received a cut some months ago. He has brown eyes and wears his hair in a pompadour."

"Missus Crow, I don't believe this is your son 'cause this here boy has blue eyes."

The sheriff heard the thankfulness in her voice, "Oh thank the Lord — now I can still have hopes my Milton will someday come home."

Another prominent Fort Worth citizen went to the funeral home to view the head. His son had also disappeared recently.

"No, thank goodness, that's not my boy," he was relieved to find that the murdered boy was not his son, but still nothing had been answered for him — his son was still missing.

And it was the same for many broken-hearted parents — they came to Stephenville to view the head and left with no answers. No one recognized the head in the casket, and they still hadn't found their missing child.

Russell was astonished to find out how many young boys had drifted away from their homes and had lost touch with their families. He and Hassler checked out every lead, but each one became another dead end in trying to ascertain the identity of the slain youth.

Trewitt embalmed the boy's head and placed it into a wooden casket. The public was permitted to file past and view the head. They tried to give a name to the slain boy because until the identity of the face was known, the search for the slayer could not begin.

Person after person walked by the coffin, looking at the head without a body, but no one recognized the boy, and the discouraged officials could do little more than wait.

"I 'spect that between six and seven hundred people passed by trying to figure out who he was," said Hassler, "it was a terrible thang to see. The boy was probably a handsome feller when he wuz alive."

People came from as far as Wichita Falls, an anxious mother from Sherman, and a father from Brownwood — but no one could put a name to the head lying in the funeral parlor.

Two, then three and finally four days passed and no one had made recognition, and the frustrated lawmen were without a clue as to who was lying in the casket. The identity of the killer was just as elusive.

Then came a glimmer of hope — the authorities received a tip that among the many people viewing the body, one man acted differently, he looked at the head in the casket, looked around, then looked at the head again.

The district attorney located him and point blankly, asked him a question. "Do you know who that is?"

"I know that head, but I'm afraid to speak."

8

TERROR IN THE COMMUNITY

The news of the discovery, a human head found in a bloody burlap bag out in the countryside, had swept throughout the community like a raging wildfire by the next morning. Everyone was talking about it, wondering if the murderer was in their midst, wondering whose head was at Trewitt's Funeral Home, and most of all, wondering about their safety.

The residents of Erath County, accustomed to never locking the doors of their homes at night, were now bolting those doors even in the daytime. The citizenry, always responsive to everyone, now approached every stranger with caution, their neighbors with suspicion — the unknown might be the slayer. Most of the parents, acting out of fear, kept their children out of school, safe within the confines of their houses.

The homeowners loaded their guns, pistols and rifles, and slept with them close to their beds. A dog's barking brought panic to the listener. The usual nighttime sounds became more noticeable as they listened for anything out of the ordinary.

Social events were canceled; no one felt it was safe enough to go to the regularly scheduled Saturday night dance at the Selden School House.

There were only a few courageous souls brave enough to attend Sunday morning services at the community churches. It was the first time that anyone remembered seeing several rifles propped against the back wall of the church.

Uncle Will Savage, doing farm chores, in the past would often leave Aunt Florence alone at their house all during the day, past dark, only coming in to eat lunch.

"Will, I'm afraid to stay here by myself."

After hearing about the black deed, Uncle Will took his wife to the Keller's home where she could spend her days with Grandma Keller. Granddad Keller stayed close by; always in view of the house.

The news that a bodiless head had been prepared for viewing at Trewitt's Funeral Home filtered throughout Erath County. Many folks went attempting to identify the boy; many were just curious.

"Marthie," Granddad Keller said to his wife, Martha, "I'm going into town to see if I know who that boy is."

"Okay, Dee, me an' Florence will be okay here."

Granddad Keller made the trip into Stephenville — a distance of about nine miles in his Model T Coupe. Inside the funeral parlor, he saw there were many others passing by, quietly, to look at the head of the deceased young boy.

Approaching the casket, he saw a face he did not recognize, a young boy with dark brown hair combed back on his head. Granddad Keller noticed some distortion on the right side of the boy's face, but the face was well preserved.

A woman, standing beside Granddad Keller, pointed out the boy's strong chin saying he was probably a handsome boy.

"He's got a strong nose and a pretty mouth," she said.

Virgil McElroy, a strong man, not easily frightened, told Missy to stay indoors and not to go anywhere by herself. He told her he wasn't fearful, but he seemed to be drinking more than his usual.

The inhabitants living in the vicinity of the Old River's place where the head was discovered, having unimaginable fear, didn't stray far from the safety of their homes. Many spent restless nights, listening for every unknown noise.

Fear continued to grow throughout the community and many of the horrified citizens called the sheriff, questioning in a demanding manner as to what was being done to find out the identity of the victim's head and the identity of the slayer.

Who could have done such a horrible deed? Who was the killer? Was it a drunkard with a tarnished reputation or a woodchopper with a mysterious past or was it the black man who had recently arrived in the community?

9

MORDECAI JOHNSON

People began seeing Mordecai Johnson in the Pony Creek area several months before Elvis, Aaron and Hootus found the severed head in the abandoned cellar. A big man, he stood straight and tall and looked younger than his fifty-six years. His short, dark hair showed a hint of gray, and his face was lean and smooth.

His body, a mass of solid muscles, looked imposing on his six feet-three frame. His broad shoulders held up faded blue overall straps that were frayed by the many years of daily wear. Thick lips, a broad nose, wide-set friendly eyes, and ears set close to his head; Mordecai was a handsome, dignified black man.

Mordecai's father, Thomas Johnson, was born a slave on a large plantation near Birmingham, Alabama and by the time he was ten years old, Thomas was working in the fields, making a hand, regularly plowing in the deep, fertile soil. Corn, wheat, cotton and tobacco were raised on the huge southern estate along with the animals that included horses, mules, cattle, hogs and sheep.

The plantation was a beautiful, grandiose place in those days — barns, stables, storehouses, tobacco houses, blacksmith shops, and wheelwright shops. Colonel Sinclair Durham, one of the largest land barons in Alabama, and his family lived in the large plantation home, called the great house.

Superstition, widespread among the slaves, prevailed on the plantation. The Durham family cemetery with its vast granite and marble tombs, stood a short distance from the great house, sheltered beneath the weeping willow and spreading oak trees. The magnificent tombstones told about the generations of the family, as well as their wealth.

Some of the older slaves, while sitting around campfires, told of things seen in the old graveyard. They put into picture, stories of hooded ghosts riding on great black horses and told about frightful sounds heard in the darkness of the night.

Spirituality was a different matter. The people, with Master Sinclair's blessings, built a brush arbor

CARROLL C. MARTIN

in a pecan grove in the big pasture of the plantation and when the weather was fitting, the slaves were "'lowed to meet dar on Sunday fo' preachin'."

Brother Josiah, the preacher, was a slave who could stir up the congregation, preaching hell-fire and brimstone to the assemblage. On different occasions, Brother Jackson, a white preacher from the Baptist church near the farm would visit the plantation to preach the Gospel to the slaves, but Brother Josiah's preaching pleased them more.

Thomas Johnson didn't receive any formal education or schooling. He and some of the other black children went to the white school along with the white children, "to take care of 'em" until the black children were old enough to work in the fields, at which time their education stopped.

Mordecai's mother, Belle, was a small woman with a fair complexion and raven black hair, that always neatly combed and braided at the back of her head. She had told Mordecai about the happy life before the Civil War, before they were freed, before they had to survive — not as a structured workforce, but having to make their own way.

She would smile, reminiscing, "I kin 'member de days when I war one of de house maids. Dere was six of us in de ol' marster's house, me, Sarai, Lou, Hester, Jerry and Jo. My job was lookin' a'ter de corner table whar nothin' but de desserts sat. Jo and Jerry war de table boys, and dey ne'ber touched nothin' wid dere hans', dey used de waiter to pass things wid. We didn't know nothin' but good times bac den."

Even though the Civil War was over and the slaves were now free, many remained on the plantations that were the only home they had ever known. Thomas Johnson and his family remained on the Durham Plantation.

Mordecai often thought about the fun times he had as a boy in Southern Alabama. He and his brother, Moses, were allowed to play with the white boys and girls at the plantation while his mother worked for Master Durham. He remembered that many times; they ate their meals out on the big front porch, and he and his brother would play under the table and torment their little sister by tickling her toes or rubbing flour on her face to "whiten" her up.

Mordecai learned the blacksmith trade from the old "uncles" on the plantation — slaves who were skilled with their hands. There was no actual kinship; the younger boys showed their respect by calling them "uncle." It was just using good manners.

"Uncle" Toney was the blacksmith; "Uncle" Harry repaired the carts and wagons; "Uncle" Abel was the shoemaker, and they all had assistants to help them, learning the skills.

Thomas Johnson eventually was able to save enough to buy his own little farm near the Durham plantation. He was now free in every sense of the word — free to come and go as he pleased, free to raise his own crops, and free to have his entire family living with him.

Mordecai lived on his parent's farm until he was twenty-two years old, and after he had married, rented some land from Elias Stanbury, a landowner. Mordecai hoped to save enough money to buy a place of his own, just as his parents had done.

They were expecting their first child and he was as happy as any man could be. Awakened one cold night, embers had fallen from the fireplace onto the floor and the house with its wood, old and dry, erupted into an instant inferno. Mordecai was startled awake — the front room of the house was fully engulfed in flames; the smoke was so dense he could barely see anything at all.

His wife, sleeping in the bed beside him, overcome by the dense, deadly smoke was not conscious when the flames woke him up. He tried to carry her out through the front door, the only way to escape from the house, but he could not, and the fire consumed his precious mate and his unborn child. His arms were burned so badly that he nearly died from the infection. He would never forget the stench of the burning flesh, the burnt flesh on his own arms and the burning flesh of his dying wife. Both arms were deeply scarred, but the scarring on his arms was not as deep as the scars in his mind.

Shooting a gun up in the air, a custom, a method of notifying the others in the area that there had been a death, started as soon as some of the men heard about the tragic death. First one shot, then another, all through the night until daybreak, gunshots sounding out the mournful summons, giving notice that someone had died.

A heavyhearted group of people assembled at Thomas and Belle's house, dressed in their finest clothing, standing out in the yard, waiting until the one who had the right to touch the dead, arrived. The heavyhearted made the somber walk to the smoldering remains of Mordecai's home. Manuel Davis, the appointed person, drank a mixture called the red root and purged himself before drawing near the house at about ten in the morning. He went into the burnt out dwelling, where the stilled, burnt body, or what remained of a body, lay. Davis continued the custom by preparing the body for burial. After he had finished, he put the body onto a wagon to be carried to the cemetery.

The burial customs passed down from their African heritage influenced funeral ceremonies practiced by the people who, not long ago, were slaves. The people walked, wailing a mournful sound, down to the little burial site, a small graveyard near a river under a big cottonwood tree — the majority of the graves were marked by only a couple of rocks.

Mordecai's friends, both black and white and relatives gathered where many others, mostly slaves, had been buried before. When all of the people had gathered, one man was chosen to shoot a gun toward the north, west, east and south. Mordecai's brother, Moses, knelt down and carefully placed a little bag of parched meal, a small stick with a sharp nail tied on one end and piece of white muslin on the body of Mordecai's beloved wife.

Two of the men placed strips of elm bark over the body, then covered it with dirt, and when the grave was completely covered, everyone clapped their hands and smiled, being careful not to step on the new grave.

Old Brother Lazarus said a few words, "La'wd, de Bible say dat You don't make no 'stakes, but it 'pears to us that You wuz mighty close dis time — it looks like You has taken up sides agin us. Dis precious chile shet her eyes one night and den ole Gabriel sounded his horn. How are You gwine to make us b'lieve dat dis is de best? Though' I pass through de valley of de shadowy o' ole death, I'se fear no evil 'cause Thou art wit me . . ."

A shelter of poles and bark from an Elm tree were fabricated over the grave to keep the cold waters of the rain from soaking the freshly turned soil after the sad possession dispersed, scattering, going to their homes.

Where Mordecai came from was a mystery to the folks in the Pony Creek community — some thought he came west from Alabama, but he never talked about it. Others heard that he came to the region from San Saba County.

He looked for work, any kind of work, wherever he could find it — picking cotton, chopping wood, and occasionally helping the farmers and ranchers in their fence building. He found a little one-room shack near Selden — it had been abandoned ten or fifteen years ago after the last inhabitant, Bud Moore, an old black man died. The owner, Mr. Powers, told Mordecai he could stay in the room as long as he didn't cause any trouble. Mordecai kept to himself and Powers barely knew he was around.

Mordecai carried two awful secrets with him. He had, in fact, lived in San Saba County before coming to Erath County. One day, just before dark, he was leaving the field where he had been picking cotton when he heard two men arguing over behind a row of trees along a fence line.

He heard one of the men yell out at the other as the argument became more heated.

"I'll kill you," and then he heard a gunshot.

He got closer and saw that one of the men laying on the ground and the other, a tall slim man, was standing over him, holding a rifle.

The killer looked over and saw Mordecai, raised his rifle and fired a shot. The bullet came within inches of his head — so close that he heard it sing, buzzing by his ear. Mordecai ran hard and fast and was able to elude the man intent on silencing him.

As far as he knew, the killer had never been caught, because he was the only witness, and he would forever remain silent. He knew that testifying against the white man would mean death for him, too. He left San Saba County that night — he left without his possessions, never to return.

Mordecai also left Alabama in the middle of the night. After the fire had taken the life of his wife, he went to the small town of Talladega to get supplies and foodstuffs. He always walked to town where he bought flour, baking powder, sugar and salt. On this warm spring day, he went to a little general store and bought supplies for his mother, then began walking the seven miles back to the plantation. He had saved his money and found just the axe he wanted when he was in the store. He thought he might clear a little land behind the plantation house, where the land-owner told him he could build a little cabin.

Walking, with the axe over his shoulder, he saw two white men approaching him on the road just as he reached the Waldo Creek Bridge, built at Riddle's Mill; a gristmill operated by the Riddle brothers. He recognized one of the men who he had seen at the plantation several times — a man he saw the night that his dreams had vanished, the night his shack burned.

As the men got closer, the man with a familiar face, the man he had seen before, spoke, "Well, looky here, if it ain't one of the uppity niggers. He's a big one ain't he? Where ye goin' boy?"

The second man, not wanting to cause any trouble turned to his offensive partner and said, "Come on, Marvin, leave him alone, we don't need any trouble."

Marvin ignored the warning of the man walking along with him, "Say, you're the one who had that purty little wife ain't ya?"

The drunken white man's words brought forth a vision Mordecai wanted to forget, the flames, the smoke and his dying wife that he could not save, the vision seared into his memory.

"Marvin, let's leave him be. He weren't bother'n us."

"She was a fine lit'l gal — guess ya know yore kid would have been half white, don't ya? That lit'l wife of yores, us boys were friendly with her — in fact, I wuz over to see her the night yore shack burned."

Mordecai felt the all anger and hurt of a lifetime as he started toward the man who was standing before him. He dropped his sack of supplies on the ground, but held a tight hold on his new axe.

"He don't mean nothing by it — he's just drunk," the second man told Mordecai.

"I do mean something; it taken three of us to hold her down that night — we'd jest left her when you got there, boy."

Rage overtook reason and a crushing blow from Mordecai's big right hand sent this wretched, Alabama sharecropper to the ground. Mordecai looked at the appalling man called Marvin and saw blood flowing from his head. The second man, seeing Mordecai's fury, ran down the road and across the bridge.

Mordecai knelt down on his right knee, and he saw the man's breathing was labored. The man's head struck a sharp stone when he fell backwards, and the blow had knocked him unconscious. Mordecai could hear a gurgling noise as the man struggled for his life. Anger turned into fear.

Mordecai knew that it didn't make any difference that this scoundrel of a man was saying horrible things about his precious wife, things that no man should have to hear. He was a black man, and this man was white. He would never get a chance to explain his actions — even he realized his actions were not justified.

Then fear turned into insanity. He took the axe and held it high over his head. One blow severed the head of this enemy and silenced him forever. He quickly picked up the bleeding head, ran to the old bridge and threw the head into the rushing water.

He knew that the other man could recognize him once his unforgivable deed was discovered.

Then insanity turned into self-preservation. Mordecai left the body where it lay, hurried to his mother's house, packed what little he could call his own, told his mother goodbye, and he was gone, never to return to the place he called home.

After witnessing the murder and leaving San Saba County, Mordecai found the small shack in Erath County. It wasn't much, but he called it home. He became acquainted with the farmers of the area, and they found out that Mordecai was a blacksmith, and they started bringing him work.

He could shoe a horse as quickly as anyone Lucas McCarey had ever seen. McCarey was a farmer-rancher who owned several thousand acres of land just east of the community of Selden, and he found Mordecai to be a hard, steady worker. McCarey, one of the few people who owned a Model T Ford truck in 1925, would pick Mordecai up early in the mornings and take him to work on the farm, and then bring him home at night, often after dark.

Mordecai's shack, located on the same road as Ned Gristy and F. M. Snow, was about a half of a mile from the Snow house. One night, late in the month of November, McCarey was taking Mordecai home, and as they were passing F. M. Snow's house, they saw a large blaze in the fireplace and saw smoke billowing from the chimney. He slowed the truck and rolled down the truck's window. A breeze, blowing from the direction of the house brought an unfamiliar stench.

"Man, what's burning?" McCarey asked the black man on the seat beside him. "You ever smelt anything like that?"

Mordecai recognized the odor he had smelled once before, the stench of burning human flesh.

"Yah-suh Mis'r McCarey", Mordecai's deep voice wavered as he spoke, "I sho' nuff do know dat smell.

10

SUNDAY MORNING

A few months earlier . . .

Aaron awoke to the aroma of chicken, frying, drifting throughout the house and into the room. His mother fried the chicken, the best in this part of the country, in a cast iron skillet until it was deep-golden brown. The crust, extra crispy, cracked up into small pieces, leaving the best part of the chicken to be savored later.

She would make soup tomorrow from the pieces that she didn't fry today, so rich that no Jewish mother could match it.

He turned over in his bed and felt the whispering breeze of the morning blowing cool over him — it was going to be another warm day. The sweet fragrance of the honeysuckle vines just outside his window and the freshness of the morning air mingled with the wonderful aroma of his mother's cooking. The songbirds flitted from tree to tree singing in absolute harmony with nature's perfect Sunday morning choir.

A rooster, strutting about in the back of the house, courting his feathered concubines, crowed a greeting to the hot morning sun; the bright ball of fire rising up in a clear, purplish red sky.

Aaron heard his mother's sweet voice, singing:

> *Some glad morning when this life is o'er,*
> *I'll fly away . . .*

Millie Martin, Aaron's mother, always got up early on Sunday morning and prepared the dinner before she called the family to breakfast. Many times, Aaron heard her singing in the kitchen as she joyfully cooked the noon meal, never complaining. Sundays were a special time for her and at no other time did he hear her singing. She had a beautiful, angelic voice, a pleasing sound of security for Aaron, a sound he loved to hear while waking.

Today, she had fried chicken, cooked some potatoes to be mashed, black-eyed peas, a pan of cornbread and enough biscuits for breakfast and the dinner meal. She had baked a coconut pie, topped with fluffy, egg white meringue, and a lemon chess pie before she had ended her day and went to bed last night. Aaron thought his momma's coconut pie was the best in the country.

Today would be dinner on the ground so when the cooking was finished, she packed vittles into a wooden box to take to church, the pots and bowls inside were protected with a tablecloth.

Aaron looked out the window and saw the fruits of his father's hard work, laboring in the fields and farming the land. Two barns, one larger than the other, painted red with platinum colored sheet-iron roofs were on the west side of the two-story, white frame house. A silo and a water tank, a cistern, and two stacks of golden hay, heaped into rounded piles, were on the side of the larger barn. A windmill was in between the barn and the attractive farmhouse. Farm equipment, a tractor, peanut thresher, plows and cultivators were inside the smaller, though good-sized barn.

Aaron watched the black and white cattle, Holsteins, down near the creek, grazing on the luscious green grass while several of them were resting underneath a mesquite tree, chewing their cud. Beyond the fences along the back of the larger barn, Aaron saw horses, ranging in size, of various colors, nibbling at the tender green blades of oats planted in the field earlier in the spring. A small lane, winding from the road to the house, crossed over large, smooth boulders, a passage across the creek, then on around, up to the house.

Aaron saw his daddy, carrying a milk bucket, walking from the barn. Aaron didn't have to get up early today because it was Sunday, and his daddy took care of the morning chores because he wouldn't be working in the store or the fields today.

Aaron's earliest recollection, the fond memories of Sunday mornings was when he was about four years old — the family lived in an old house built from logs and boxing planks. A room, constructed of logs, off to one side was used for the kitchen — a dividing walkway then one big room warmed by a fireplace made up the other end of the irregular shaped structure. The bodily functions were relieved in an outhouse, down a hill and behind the barn because there weren't facilities in the house. Canned fruits and vegetables, cured meats and dried foods were stored in a shed room off to the side and behind the logged section of the house.

The growing family needed more room, an inside toilet and a kitchen that wasn't so frigid when the cold north wind blew through the slivered cracks in the logged wall. Madison Martin made plans and built a new house for his family, nearer to the well-traveled country road. It was a long siege, but a new, five-room house, facing the east with a porch across the front had finally been completed. Aaron's two sisters shared a room on the northeast side of the new house — he slept in a room on the front of the house that doubled as a living room.

The family lived in that house until a year ago, when Madison Martin bought a farm a couple of miles on down the road, and built the family another new house, a house with three bedrooms. Nestled under two tall trees, the new house was well furnished and comfortable.

"Aaron, Daddy, girls; y'all come on to breakfast; it'll soon be time to get ready for church," Millie shouted.

Aaron yawned, got up, stretched and went to the kitchen where his mother had cooked up bacon and home cured ham, hot biscuits, scrambled eggs and gravy. His sisters, aged nine and eleven, were already up and sitting at the kitchen table — giggling about something, a secret that they vowed not to tell. The family, happy and proud, assembled around the table, holding hands while Madison gave thanks for all that they possessed and asked blessings upon his family and the food, their Sunday morning breakfast.

"Can I go home with Jacob after church?" Aaron asked. "Me, him an' Elvis want to go 'sploring down in Uncle Ira's pasture."

Jacob Martin, Aaron's cousin, was just a couple of months older — both boys were tall, long-legged and lanky. A few years back, William "Uncle Ira" Martin, Madison's older brother, and his wife, Fannie bought a farm on the road to Alexander, south of Stephenville. When the family, Aaron's aunts, uncles and cousins, got together; Uncle Ira's home was the customary gathering place because their grand-mother, Grandma Martin, lived in an adjacent, small house on the farm.

"Oh, I guess so," responded Aaron's mother, "but y'all are goin' to have to get home early, so we can go to church tonight because the revival meeting is starting. Brother Ernest Little is goin' to be doin' the preaching."

"Okay, Momma, Jacob wanted us to stay all night an' go campin', but we'll get back in time to go — pass me that bacon, please."

"Maybe you boys can camp out next week if you've just got to, but I just don't see what y'all get out of sleepin' on the hard ground, fightin' them mosqui-toes and such."

"Momma," sighed Aaron, "all we've done so far this year is work an' go to school an' we want to have a little fun before the plantin' season starts."

"That's enough about it right now, I said we'd thank about it — we still have the whole summer."

"Aaron," asked Lora, his youngest sister, "did you hear them coyotes last night? They sounded mighty close."

"No, I didn't hear 'em, I slept like a log — could I have some more biscuits?"

"They might be lookin' to get into the chicken house," explained their daddy, "there sure seem to be a lot of them coyotes this year."

"I sure hope ya'll got that chicken pen fence patched up, we can't stand to lose any more chickens, t'aint hardly enough eggs now."

"Momma," Aaron told his mother, "Me an' Elvis got it fixed a couple of days ago, so don't go frettin' none."

"I weren't frettin, it just seem to me that there's always somethin' around here that needs fixin'. Son, you'd better take you a change of clothes if you're goin' to Jacob's."

"Yes ma'am."

Madison Martin finished breakfast; polished his Sunday, "go to meetin'" boots and then went to get ready for the Sunday Church services. Aaron liked the scent of the lotion that his father put on his face after he shaved; the aroma of the *Aqua Velva* would conjure up pleasant memories for Aaron in years to come.

Aaron dressed in a fresh pair of denim overalls and a white cotton shirt, and then went out to the larger barn, and hitched up the horses to the wagon. Then he pulled the wagon in front of the house while his mother and sisters finished getting ready. He heard the geese honking down by the stock tank and watched the chickens as they chased grasshoppers, buzzing all around. He felt fortunate to have a loving family, a hard working mother and father, all on the picture perfect farm that he called home.

The trip to church took the family about an hour. The one-roomed schoolhouse served as a meeting place for Rocky Point Baptist Church on Sunday mornings and the place of schooling during the week. The white painted frame building was at the bottom of a rocky hill, surrounded by cedar scrubs and an occasional live oak tree. Windows, on the south and north sides of the building, were raised to keep the congregation as comfortable as possible when the beaming sun warmed the morning air. Fans, the kind that were made of cardboard attached to a wooden handle, were on all the pews, because most of the time during the summertime in Texas, the wind doesn't blow. Today, the cooling breezes hesitantly blew, sporadically stopping and then puffing the white curtains through the wide, opened windows.

Aaron could hear the singing as they got closer to the church — beautiful, country harmony flowing out of the open windows:

> *Bringing in the sheaves, bringing in the sheaves,*
> *We shall come rejoicing, bringing in the sheaves.*

Aaron remembered hearing the song when he was much younger, thinking the words to the hymn were "We shall come see Joyce an' bringing in the sheets."

It was not going to be just a weekend revival, the one starting today, but it would last two or three weeks, depending on the lost souls that needed saving.

Aaron became a Christian earlier in the year, accepting Christ as his personal Savior. It was during an earlier revival meeting. Upon hearing the message, a story about the rich man in hell, begging Lazarus for just a sip of water, Aaron knew that he didn't want to go to that place of eternal torment where the fires burned forever. He heard the preacher, pounding his fist on the brown, wooden pulpit, giving the fearful warning,

"If you died tonight, where would you spend eternity? Would you burn forever in the lake of fire? Would your soul be separated from God an' your loved ones from now on?"

He listened closely to Brother Ernest Little, the visiting preacher, who was also a carpenter. The sermon, the plan of salvation, the message was nothing new, he had heard it all his life, "for all have sinned and come short of the glory of God."

He understood that all even meant him, and that's what frightened him. Even though he tried to live a good life by obeying his parents and treating everyone with respect, the preacher said that wasn't enough — a man couldn't be saved by his good works. A man must accept God's free gift, the Gift of Salvation. It sounded simple to Aaron, almost too easy.

"It is yours for the taking," the preacher said.

But that's where it didn't make much sense to the boy. How can you receive something that you can't see?

Madison Martin tied the horses to the hitching rail behind the building after the rest of the family got out of the wagon and went inside. Aaron found a seat by Cousin Jacob, and as they usually did, they sat toward the back of the one-roomed building. Frank Miller, Aaron's friend and classmate, arriving a short time later, came and sat down beside him and Jacob. Frank was one grade below Aaron and about the same size as Elvis Rivers — both were short, a little over five feet tall. Frank's mother was a little woman, about four feet and nine inches tall, and of German descent.

"Hey."

"Hey," Aaron whispered quietly.

The Millers moved into the Old Beck place, down the lane and across the road from the Martin farm, having come from Kansas a couple of years earlier. Frank's father, Gene, built a large chicken house. A large structure, fifty feet wide and seventy-five feet long, was the domicile for over fifteen hundred laying chickens. The Miller's livelihood came from the sale of the eggs to a merchant in Fort Worth.

The Millers went back to visit relatives in Kansas last spring and needed someone to feed the chickens and gather the eggs. Aaron and his daddy volunteered for the assignment. Going to the chicken house early in the mornings and again in the afternoons, they gathered the eggs and put out feed and water for the white hens, housed in the facility reeking from the overpowering odor of ammonia, emitting from the manure.

On the second day, while gathering the eggs, Aaron found one that was in a peculiar shape. It was small and looked more like a long-necked gourd than anything else, but it didn't really look much like of anything, much less an egg. The Millers held the record for chickens that produced freak eggs, according to the local newspaper, *The Empire Tribune.* Aaron found another one of the oddities — bolstering the unbroken record.

"Turn with me to the fourteenth chapter of Acts," Brother Bays began his sermon this morning with his slow Texas drawl, "where we find the Apostle Paul, who is about to be stoned, telling the people at Antioch . . ."

"It takes Brother Bays about an hour to preach a ten minute sermon," Aaron thought as his mind drifted off, daydreaming, looking over the congregation, not thinking about much of anything — it was getting warmer inside the small church building.

He spied Mr. Allison, a balding little man with white hair, pushing his tiny, gold-rimmed glasses higher up on his short nose. The round eyes of the old deacon watched the messenger in the pulpit intently, and his round friendly face glistened with perspiration as the temperature warmed in the meeting place. Aaron studied Mr. Allison's face, thinking that he might look like the apostle Paul if he only had longer hair and a beard.

He looked out and saw a big yellow grasshopper climbing up the screen of the open window and heard many more of the buzzing insects outside — a lazy sound, he yawned. The gentle breeze, already warm, carried an aroma into his nostrils, the cedar trees, plentiful on the landscape, flourished up the hill and then all the way down to the creek behind and north of the building. Aaron ran his fingers up and down, over the grooves in the handmade pews, then opened his Bible and read:

> "To Aaron
> From Mother and Daddy
> Christmas 1919"

It brought back memories of the Christmas, about six years ago, right after the big influenza epidemic; right after Elvis' daddy had died. The church members always assembled at the church on the Sunday before Christmas day to celebrate Christ's birth with a Christmas play. This Christmas, many of the church members were still feeling the effects of the terrible sickness, but they made a decision to stay with tradition and go on with the play.

Deacons Carpenter and Moseley cut a large cedar tree and brought it to the church and set it up in the back corner of the one-roomed house of worship, near the stove. Several of the women decorated the tree with stringed popcorn and homemade tinsels, thrilling all the younger children who were expecting a visit from Santa Claus.

Aaron and his family sat in front of the wood-burning stove that was large enough to warm the entire room on this cold night. Aaron, in proper costume, played the part of one of the wise men from the East, the Magi, seeking the Newborn Child, the Savior. After a successful performance, they heard a knock at the door and in walked the man in the red suit. Santa handed out the presents, and Aaron opened his gift, the Bible.

Aaron often wondered about that custom for celebrating Christmas, especially in church. From the time children are old enough to comprehend, they are told to believe in Santa Claus and to believe in Jesus and God. Then, one day, the realization comes that Santa Claus is not real — there is no such person. Now that he was seventeen, Aaron wondered, would the day come, was it still before him that he would be told that God and Jesus are not real? Just like Santa? No, he knew better, he knew God was real even though he couldn't see him. He felt God's presence within his heart. But what about the children who aren't brought up in a Christian home? Does God stay real to them? Perhaps someday, after he acquired more understanding, he would know the answer.

Aaron looked over at the old man, who was known only by his initials, F. M. Snow. Such gloomy, angry eyes — he looked as though he had sunk into unconquerable sadness. He sat, hunkered over, less than an imposing sight, on the end of a pew, not revealing the meanness within. Aaron reckoned that Old Man Snow was as likely as anyone needing salvation because of his reputation around the community. Aaron would never have dreamed as he watched the woodchopper that the quiet man staring straight at the preacher would soon touch his life and his sense of well-being.

"It is through many trial and tribulations," continued Brother Bays, "that we, by only the grace of God enter into his Kingdom."

F. M. Snow continued staring straight ahead and thinking about the time a little over five years ago when he was living in San Saba County; the time that he had to leave.

"He shouldn't have done that to me," he thought, "I showed him some tribulations," knowing that he had done away with all the evidence of his dark deed, all evidence but for one thing.

"That man that wuz out there, he might have saw me," worried Snow, "but I don't thank he seen me good a 'nuff; I couldn't tell much 'bout him."

Snow laughed quietly to himself, "He ran like a skeered jackrabbit when I shot at 'im; besides, nobody knows where I am."

Aaron, looking around, became aware of some visitors in the congregation that morning, a lady, maybe she was about forty or forty-five years old, an older woman and a boy who was most likely in his late teens. The older woman's gray hair was covered with a bonnet, and Aaron could see a brown stained twig in her mouth — he knew it was her snuff stick. He could see the tell-tale evidence oozing down her chin. Many of the women in those days would find a stick, twirl it around in their can of *Garrett's Snuff* and then place the twig between their cheek and gums to achieve the effects of the nicotine.

The boy's dark brown hair was combed straight back in a manner that Aaron combed his own hair. He guessed the boy with a dark complexion to be about eighteen or nineteen years old, and he supposed the woman sitting beside him was his mother. He was wearing a white shirt and gray pants that were too short. The Sunday visitors, sitting on the front row by the piano, also came to the attention of F. M. Snow.

"Shall we stand for a word of prayer," the preacher said, ending the morning service.

Today was the fifth Sunday dinner on the ground at Rocky Point Baptist Church.

"I wonder why they call it dinner on the ground," Elvis thought, "It's always on the tables, 'course I set on the ground sometimes to eat."

As soon as the closing prayer had been offered to the Almighty, the women began putting the noontime meal out on the tables. Each woman brought their "special" dish; meats, vegetables, breads and desserts. The men had set up tables outside the church under the shade of the live oak trees on the east side of the church building, in front of the brush arbor.

Elvis, looking over the bountiful selections of home cooked dishes, spoke up, "I shore hope Missus Allison made some of that tator salad of hers."

Frank Miller asked Aaron as they walked outside, "Did you hear about Sheriff Hassler arrestin' Virgil McElroy an' puttin' him in the jailhouse last night?"

"Nah, what'd he do this time?" Aaron shook his head, disgustingly, but not surprised.

"He got drunk and pulled a knife on Jed Reid because Jed wouldn't give him any more beer — they wuz over at Jed's house, all of 'em drunk as a skunk."

"He's gonna kill somebody one of the days, wonder he ain't already. He's just plum mean."

Virgil McElroy, Missy's father, wasn't always bad-tempered and vicious. A little over twenty years ago, he married Patsy Williams, one of the prettiest girls around, his childhood sweetheart.

One night, a couple of years after they had been married, he and Patsy were going home, down a little country road that led to her mother's house. Virgil was driving a horse and wagon. Their new baby girl, Missy, four months old, was on the seat between them.

Virgil told the sheriff that his wife went to sleep and was leaning over next to him when the wheel of the wagon hit a huge rock. Patsy fell from the wagon, headfirst, striking the ground hard enough to break her neck, killing her instantly. The sheriff never quite believed Virgil's story and he suspected that Virgil may have pushed his wife out of the wagon, but he could never prove it. Virgil maintained his story that it was an accident; that it happened just as he said — there was no reason to believe differently.

The tragedy of his wife's death and being left with a four-month-old daughter dealt a hard blow to Virgil, and he began drinking more and more, and it was rare that he would be seen sober. Once, an immaculate dresser, he wore the same, filthy clothing day after day, usually until they were worn out, and if he ever bathed, it was a rare occasion. His beard, his long hair and a patch over his left eye made him appear to be as wretched as the reputation he had gained.

Patsy's parents took his daughter, Missy, and raised her without any help from Virgil — he was bitter at them, the world and God. Virgil was never able to keep steady work after Patsy's death, so he began stealing and was sent to prison for fifteen years after robbing a grocery store near Glen Rose. He became a pitiful excuse for a human being, drinking, vulgar language, fighting, robbing, and cursing God — he did it all.

Virgil, now forty-seven years old, continued to drink after he was released from prison and got into fight after fight. He always carried a three blade pocketknife he called "Old Bertha" and once stabbed Pete Coleman during a fight but Coleman refused to have him prosecuted. It was told that Virgil threatened to kill him if the prosecution proceeded.

Many people wondered if it was the tragedy or Virgil's guilt that caused him to change into a bitter, dangerous man, an angry alcoholic.

"Daddy thanks he killed his wife 'cause she wuz running 'round on him," Aaron told Frank, "she wuz pretty an' she knew it. Daddy said she flirted with all the men, and when Virgil found out about her and Jake Hughes, he almost went crazy."

"I don't know if he killed her or not, but he shore is mean now — I'm scared of 'im cause he always wants to start something. Do you know his daughter?"

"Nah, don't reckon I've ever seen her — don't she live in town with her grandparents?" Aaron didn't know the girl that would change his life, but he would soon meet her.

"Yeah, thank so," Frank looked toward the tables, abounding with food, "I thank they're 'bout ready to eat."

The ladies had finished spreading the lunch out on the tables, and all the church members assembled around as Brother Allison, the hot sun bearing down on his bald head, gave the blessing.

"Our most gracious Heavenly Father — we just want to take this time to thank Thee for all the bountiful blessings that Thou have bestowed upon us, your faithful flock, and we humbly give Thee thanks for this food we are about to receive . . ."

Aaron wondered if God could understand plain English as well as he could understand the Old English, Biblical talking that the old Baptist deacon was presenting to the Lord. Brother Allison was a schoolteacher in his working days, but his language, as well as most of the prayer givers, was filled with thee, thou and thy when they communicated with the Almighty.

"Amen."

The tables had been set with an abundance of food, black-eyed peas, roasting ears, fried and boiled okra, corn on the cob, fresh tomatoes, cucumbers, fried chicken, sausage, roast beef, potatoes and all sorts of bread and deserts.

Baptists are known for their dinners on the ground; the abundance of the food and the large amount consumed. The members of Rocky Point Baptist were no exception. Aaron, Jacob, Frank and the other boys filled their plates and went inside the church building, putting their plates of food on the pews, which served as their tables.

"Aaron," asked Jacob, "Are y'all coming over this afternoon?"

"Yeah, we kin stay fer awhile, but Momma said we'll have to come home early so we kin go to the revival meeting."

"Okay, I wuz hoping you could stay all night."

"Maybe we kin come over in a week or so," replied Aaron, "or maybe Momma will let me go with you after church tonight."

F. M. Snow avoided talking to anyone as he filled his plate until he got near the lady visitor and without making eye contact he spoke, "My name is Francis Snow, but I like to be called F. M."

"Well, hello Mister Snow, I'm Maggie Poston and this is my mother, Annie Olds an' this here's my boy, Bernie Connally."

"Please to meet y'all," Snow touched the brim of his old dirty felt hat, "yes ma'am, shore am. Y'all are kinda new round here, ain't ya?"

"We just came up last week from Waco to look fer work. We thought Bernie might be able to hoe pea-nuts, chop cotton an' me and Ma thought we would take on some housework if we could find someone needing any help. Then too, I could pull some cotton when it's ready."

"Where y'all staying?"

"We came up here in our covered wagon and we'll stay in it 'till we can find us a place to live. Bernie is a strong boy, and he is a good, honest worker — do you know of anyone looking for help?"

"No Ma'am, I don't keep up with sech — I just do for myself."

"My late departed husband, bless his poor soul, was the same way — you know, you kind of put me in mind of him, the way you talk an' all."

"So you're a wider lady?"

"Yes I am; I lost Bernie's father some years ago an' then several years later, I remarried Mister Poston, and now he's gone, God rest his soul."

"I've never been hitched myself, never found me a woman an' as old as I am now, guess I never will tie the knot. I never saw much use in gittin' tied down to some woman."

"Now, don't say that Mister Snow, you just ain't met the right one, an' you've still got some good years left."

"Tell us about you," Mrs. Olds said to Snow as she was serving her plate with peas.

"Taint too much to tell; I've lived all around — Palo Pinto an' San Saba an' here. I like to trade horses, an' I chop a little wood to put food on the table.

I'll be plantin' me a little cotton over at my place 'fore long."

"Oh, you got a place?" quizzed Mrs. Olds.

"Yeah, I got me a little place rented over by Selden if you know where that is; let's set down over here," Snow, pointed to a rock under a small shade tree.

Taking a bite of fried chicken, Maggie remarked, "I guess we're in fer a hot summer; tweren't cold 'nuff this winter to kill all the bugs."

Snow nodded in agreement, "The heat shore takes it out of me."

They continued making small talk about the weather, the upcoming elections and "this and that" while eating their food. The other church members finished the noon meal, and many stayed for a Sunday afternoon singing while others went home to do their chores before the nighttime service began.

"Are y'all staying fer the sanging?" asked Snow.

"Oh, we ain't thought much about it, are you?"

"No, I got to get back to the farm."

"I thank we'll just go on and find a place to park the wagon fer tonight."

Snow's smile turned back to his usual frown as he watched his new acquaintances leave, going up the road toward town in their covered wagon, their home. He went on back to his lonely farm and spent the rest of the afternoon resting up for the next day when he would start planting his cotton. He lit a coal oil lamp as night approached; a ritual he performed every night. He would not blow out the flickering flame of the lamp until sunrise on Monday morning.

The next day, Monday morning, the last day of school had finally arrived. It was the day that all the children had been waiting for — not only was school out for the summer, but tonight, they would present their traditional end of the year programs. A few days ago, the men of the community, most of them parents, had taken time off from their farming duties and congregated at the small schoolhouse to build an outside stage for the performances. Cedar posts, stripped of their stringy bark, were nailed to the edges of the makeshift stage and the men strung wire from the posts to hang curtains around the stage.

After school was over for the day, some of the men moved pews out of the school building for the seating of those attending the performance of the play that night. The crowd tonight was expected to be large, so a number of the men drove their wagons to nearby Methodist and Baptist churches and moved in more seating. The ongoing revival at the Baptist church would take up again tomorrow night after they returned the church pews.

Aaron Martin's younger sister and Elvis' younger brother, in the third grade, were the stars of the play,

Red Bird and White Fawn, to be presented tonight. Madison Martin built a small canoe to put on the stage in front of the "white-man" fashioned teepees where the young actors were to present the entertainment. Millie Martin made a little Indian suit out of a burlap bag as costume for Lora to wear.

The play started on schedule at about eight o'clock in the evening — being the last part of May, it was nearly dark when the curtains opened.

Lora Martin was cast as White Fawn and the part of Redbird was played by Joel Rivers. Redbird walked out on the stage on a pair of stilts in front of White Fawn, trying to gain her affections.

He walked back and forth, but little White Fawn, her nose held high, ignored his courting gestures for a while, then, hand in hand, they walked together around the stage through the enchanted forest. The play climaxed when all of the little Indians grouped around the stage, holding hands, singing Indian songs while Redbird and White Fawn paddled down the make-believe river in their canoe.

No one paid any attention to the old man lurking in the dark shadows of the bushes, but why should they? Nothing bad ever happened in Erath County.

11

THE CAMP OUT

"It shore is purty out here tonight," Elvis gazed up into the vastness of the nighttime sky, stroking and scratching Hootus' head. It was a warm July night in Erath County. The boys were caught up with their farm work, and they had a free night. The season had transitioned to summer — too warm for trapping or hunting fur-bearing animals that now had their less valuable summer coats. Elvis, Aaron, Willie Stanton, Frank Miller and Jacob had gotten together earlier in the week and made plans to go on an overnight camp-out. They had congregated a little before a turquoise sky faded into darkness at the Martin farm.

They carried some old quilts, tattered with years of use, and a tarpaulin down to the lower part of the farm, near a stock tank. The water in the tank, painted with red and orange streaks, tinted by the sinking sun, was low because of the lack of rainfall this year. They found a smooth grassy area close to the water that was free from rocks and grass burr stickers — they deemed it would be a good spot to set up their camp.

The sun that had parched the arid earth drifted behind the tree-lined horizon as the boys spread the tarpaulin on the ground. Frank and Aaron fashioned a crude tent by using tree branches as poles, putting them under the ends of the tarp to hold it up. They anchored the limbs with ropes that were staked to the ground with sharpened sticks. The boys put their sleeping quilts inside their makeshift tent.

Elvis, gathering firewood to build a campfire, saw a cottontail rabbit scurrying away to safety into a clump of underbrush. By the time it was completely dark, Elvis had a good blaze burning in the middle of the chosen campsite.

Hootus ambled down to the banks of the watering hole, spooking several frightened grasshoppers into the water, soon to be consumed by the frogs and fish in the pond. Hearing the rippling water, his ears perked up and then continuing his business of exploring, he trotted along the water's edge, sniffing and tasting the water. Spotting a clump of grass, he hiked up a hind leg and put his mark on it.

Aaron sat down in front of the fire, eating some boiled eggs that his mother had cooked. Elvis and

Frank shared several biscuits and slices of bacon that Mrs. Rivers had cooked earlier in the day.

"I wonder why stuff always tastes better when we're out here like this." Jacob, eating a sausage, asked an unanswered question.

The stars, blue-white, twinkling sprinkles of light overhead in the dark sky emerged one by one in uncountable numbers. A cool breeze, blowing out of the south, welcome after the hot, scorching day, meandered through the tall whispering trees, lining the western side of their campsite. A sad whip-poor-will, weeping in the distance, added a touch of mystic to the night as the silvery disc began its ascent into the wide, velvety sky. The campfire flames, warm and beckoning as the night became cooler, danced around waving back and forth like a flag of fire. Gray puffs of smoke spiraled up into nothingness, and small embers rose out of the flames, flickering and then vanishing forever into the darkness.

The boys and the old dog gathered in a circle around the friendly fire — a protective barrier against whatever creatures lurked in the blackness of the night. An owl, camouflaged deep into the summer night, eyes glowing, screeched, calling out to the night while fireflies flickered about.

Aaron remembered when he and Elvis, being just a little mischievous, caught the fireflies, lightning bugs as they called them, and put them into fruit jars. The flashing bugs were later turned loose inside an unsuspecting victim's house or on a sleeping dog. He always wondered how they were able to produce their light as he watched and studied them for hours.

A bullfrog croaked, and then jumped into the water as Hootus walked near the edge of the tank. Elvis shined a flashlight toward the splashing sound, and the boys saw the water rippling into widening circles where the frog had leaped into the murky pond. A water bug swam in erratic patterns on the surface of the water before becoming a meal for a lucky fish, more than likely, a bass. More ripples broke the stillness of the muddy water reminding Elvis of a familiar tale.

"Hey Aaron, why don't you tell us that story about Jenny's Ghost?" Elvis asked because the boys liked to tell ghost stories on their campouts to show how brave they were.

And Aaron was the story teller, and he began the story as he always told it, the same way his daddy told it to him.

"Well, it goes something like this. Once upon a time, in the late eighteen hundreds, this here family named Papworth moved to Greens Creek close't to the McDow Hole an' they setup housekeeping. They came from Missouri or sommers like that. There wuz Charlie, Jenny an' their son, I thank his name wuz Temple; I ain't fer shore. Charlie built 'em a fine log cabin, and they hadn't lived there too long till they had another kid on the way."

Aaron shifted position on the hard ground and continued telling his story.

"Well sir, ole Charlie had to go back to where they came from to pick up some furniture an' other thangs that he inherited from his momma and papa. He left Jenny, the boy an' his newborn baby behind 'cause he wuz gonna take the train an' he 'spected he'd be back real soon. Some of the neighbors said they'd watch out fer Jenny an' the kids, an' they checked on 'em every day, but one day she couldn't be found anywhere 'round."

Aaron spoke more quietly, "The neighbors found the little boy underneath the bed in the cabin, but they never found Jenny. The boy was skeered to death an' couldn't tell 'em nothing. He wuz jest blabbering about this an' about that an' didn't make no since a tall."

The boys were listening in anticipation as to what Aaron would tell next although they had heard the story time and again, their eyes were wide with excitement as they drew closer to the protective flame. The frogs, in a nocturnal melody, joined the chirping crickets and the whip-poor-will as an occasional mosquito buzzed around the boys' ears. The rustling leaves, tickled by the gentle breezes, added a backdrop of mystery to the storyteller's tale.

"They searched the countryside fer an' wide but they didn't come up with nothin', nobody, nothin'. All the boy could tell 'em wuz some bad men got his momma and the baby. They thought maybe the Indians had killed 'er but the Indians wuz Charlie's friends, so that weren't the answer. This here feller named Brownlow wuz in the area an' he wuz a cattle rustler an' come to find out, he wuz the one who killed Jenny an' her baby an' after he had killed both of 'em, he throwed 'em into a well."

The moon, rising in the eastern sky, splashed down its watery white-silver beams on the campsite, giving it a ghostly glow between the shadows of the trees. A brooding mist forming on the banks of the water some distance away attracted Aaron's attention as he looked around, as if he was searching for some wayward spirit, then he continued his story — Elvis pulled Hootus nearer to him.

"The reason he killed Jenny wuz this. She overheard his rustling plans an' he had to git rid of her so she wouldn't talk. Well, ole Charlie got back an' found out what happened an' him an' the boy lived by themselves in the cabin after that. He had his suspicions an' he started telling the folks that ole Brownlow wuz a rustler an' Brownlow didn't cotton to that a tall. It made him madder 'n all git out. One night Brownlow an' some of his gang, when there weren't no moon, came to even thangs with Charlie. They hung Charlie from this big old tree that wuz out in the front yard. Then when they wuz gone, his boy came out of hidin' an' cut 'em down. Charlie was a gasping for air an' pert' nert' dead."

"I thought you said this wuz a ghost story," Willie said, "where's the ghost part?"

"I'm gittin' to it; I'm gittin' to it. So, Charlie an' the boy had enough of the outlaws' shenanigans an' they left the territory. Later on, this feller Keith an' his boy wuz out an' decided to stay in the old cabin one night, to save them a ride home in the night, 'cause it were powerful dark. They tied their horses outside an' went in the cabin an' after they ate some dried meat, they blowed out the lantern an' went to bed. It wuz the first night that they wuz there, after they'd gone to sleep, along 'bout midnight; they heard a knocking at the door. Tap, tap, knock. At first, they thought it were nothing, but then a knock came agin. Tap, tap, knock, knock. Well, sir, Mister Keith got up out of the bed an' opened the door an' what he seen wuz Jenny, holding her baby. As they watched her, she looked like some smoke floating 'round there an' they wuz skeered to death, then all of a sudden, she vanished without a sound. I mean she wuz gone in a instant."

"Now you're gittin' somewhere!" Willie said approvingly as he looked into the shimmering, golden flame, reflecting off the boy's faces.

"They thought they wuz dreaming, 'cause they knowed Jenny wuz dead, so they decided to give it another try the next night. This time, after they'd gone to sleep, they heard a awful, mournful sound an' it woke 'em up an' then there she wuz. She came gliding in through the wall an' Keith, who had been sleepin', still thought he wuz dreamin' when he seen 'er."

Elvis and Frank moved a little closer to one another as the ghostly tale was taking on a little more mysterious excitement. They wouldn't admit that they were feeling a little skirmish, but they kept glancing out into the shadows. Hootus would perk up from time to time, and then he would lay his head back down, next to Elvis' leg.

"And then, on the third night," Aaron started talking more slowly, "he an' the boy wuz wide awake. He felt sump' um cold 'round his neck. It wuz a hot night, but the boy an' his daddy wuz shivering cold; cold around their necks. They pulled up the covers, but it wuz still cold. Keith got up an' opened the door an' there she wuz again, so real he could have reached out an' touched her. He asked if it wuz truly her, 'Jenny is it you'? She screamed out like a panther, a banshee, then into the twilight; she wuz gone. From then on, Keith stayed away from the Papworth cabin."

Aaron spoke with more volume now, "After that, she wuz seen traipsing all over the countryside. She'd appear, holding her baby down by the railroad tracks, an' at times, she'd be on the track. She'd just stand there an' the engineer'd throw on the brakes of the train, but it'd be too late, the train would run over her 'fore they could git it stopped. The train people would git out to look for who they'd run over, but they never found any trace of Jenny or her baby or anythang else."

"One night, ole Brownlow; he lay dying when all of a sudden, he started screaming an' thrashing around, Don't let her touch me! Then he'd yell, over an' over again; her blood, see her blood! Boys, that happened just right over there." Aaron pointed to the northwest, as the others remained completely still and quite.

"Then they wuz this coffin maker who tried to stay in the cabin. They found him one morning an' he wuz dead. He had a horrified look on his face an' his black hair had turned white, overnight. He'd been writing a letter an' the letter stopped, right in the middle of a word. One man used to see Jenny, floatin' over the water, down at the McDow watering hole, when he wuz watering his hogs. They say the creek changed its course over the years an' sometimes later, some human bones wuz found where the cabin once stood. It was probably in a old well. I heard my grandpa say that these wuz the mortal remains of Jenny and her baby."

"So, this here ghost is still roamin' around sommers. I heard that jest last year; some boys went out there to swim in McDow's hole one hot summer day. A mist 'peared an' a chill, a feelin' of something bein' there, suddenly came over the watering hole. The boys got out an' built a fire, but it scattered and went out quick like the wind had blowed on it. They never figured it out, what happened to the fire an' why the water got so cold that day. Wuz it Jenny?"

Aaron had captivated his audience completely by now; the fog forming over the water of the pond, the moonlight illuminating it, the rustling leaves and the familiar nightly sounds only added an air of spookiness to his ghostly yarn.

He spoke softly, almost whispering; Hootus cocked his head to one side watching him inquiringly. "Reckon where is Jenny's ghost now? Does anybody know? Reckon how long she'll be drifting around, looking for justice? She could be out there, with her baby, all alone in the dark! Listen, an' you jest might hear her screams."

The boys moved closer together; looking around them. The nightly sounds seemed to grow louder; the chirping crickets, the croaking frogs and coyotes howling at the silent moon, high up in the sky.

"Don't turn around, but she might be right over there," Aaron pointed, "Or she might be right behind you. Better not look."

The boys were quiet now, listening in the darkness of the night, hoping not to hear anything out of the ordinary but imagining that something, spirits, might be hiding just beyond the flicker of their waning campfire.

The southern breeze was picking up a bit causing the leaves to make a haunting rustling that added more mystery to the story. Elvis could feel icy cold chills covering him — it was only the puffs of wind unnerving him and trying to rationalize the feeling he thought, "It was only a ghost story."

"Getting' sorta cold out here, ain't it fellers?" Aaron started talking quietly and deliberately slow, "We'd better stir up our fire a bit 'cause it's bout to burn down an' we don't want it to go plum out. We couldn't see much then. Y'all feel that? You thank its jest the wind, don't ya? It jest might be poor little lost Jenny's ghost wanderin' 'round out there all alone with her baby in the dark. Is she out there? She could be, right out there."

Frank shifted around on the hard ground and looked at the trees that were to the west of them, wondering if Jenny's spirit was out there in the darkness, just waiting for him to go to sleep. Was she out there, rustling the leaves or was it just the wind? He wasn't sure. He swallowed and took a deep breath.

"I ain't skeered," Frank told the rest, "but, I thank we need to take turns keeping watch while the rest of us sleep."

"Good idea," seconded Willie and Elvis.

"Look over yonder," Willie said, pointing toward the southwest. "I kin see a light."

The faint glow that the boys saw, coming from the direction of the Snow farm, was the flames of a kerosene lamp.

"Let's go check it out," suggested Elvis.

"No, I ain't going," replied Jacob, "I'm staying here, might be that ghost."

With that, Elvis' enthusiasm had been dampened, and the boys decided to remain within the safety of their campfire.

$\mathcal{Q}$

The old two-room house on the Snow farm was just a stone throw from where the boys were having their campout. Snow rented the farm from a family estate, and the house was probably as old as he was and hadn't been cared for any better. The sagging roof leaked, and the chinking between the logs had fallen out in several spots, allowing small animals, spiders and insects to sneak into the house. It was impossible to keep warm when the cold winds of winter blew through those cracks. The house was nearly inhabitable at times during the winter, but to F. M. Snow, it was home.

Maybe the old man was afraid of a ghost, too — or something — no one knew why, but as soon as a day began to fade into darkness, as soon as nighttime arrived, he always lit a lantern or kerosene lamp and let it burn throughout the night. The lamp always burned every night; Snow's rifle was always by his side. What was he afraid of — no one knew. The loneliness, it could have been, his poor health, maybe, but perhaps it was the evil demons from his dark past.

Tonight was no exception. Snow lit the kerosene lantern before sitting down at a flimsy, dirty kitchen table and eating a plateful of leftover pinto beans; commonly called red beans by Southerners. Satisfying his hunger, he scraped the remaining beans out the back door, for the dogs and then wiping the plate with a soiled red rag that he used for a handkerchief, he put the plate back on the old table.

He sat down in an old cane-bottom chair and using his pocket knife; he picked food particles from his rotting teeth. He looked out the window and saw the moon, a bright lunar ball, rising in the east; it was hot inside; he picked up his rifle and went outside the old house.

Sitting on his porch, whittling an old piece of wood, he glanced up every once in a while, watching his two old dogs wander about in tall, brown grass he called a yard. He thought about taking the dogs and going down to the creek to look for raccoons, but he soon dismissed the thought — he was too tired.

He noticed the flickering flame from the boys' campfire but didn't give it much thought. He could see in the bright moonlight and the field where he recently finished planting his cotton. Noticing the gate was down, he walked over and closed the gate.

He didn't want his old cow to wonder into the newly planted cotton field — the cow that soon would
be the cause of unspeakable terror in this peaceful
community.

12

THE KISS

aron glanced at the calendar — August 15, 1925 — one of the several dates that would forever be etched into his memory. After enjoying a hearty breakfast — fried ham with scrambled eggs, biscuits and gravy, he walked to his daddy's General Store in Johnsville, about a mile from the Martin farm. He worked at the store during the summertime while his daddy worked around the farm; fixing fences, mending the barns, tending the livestock and the many other tasks required to keep the farm running smoothly. Aaron felt it was a pretty fair trade.

The warming star of August had already made an appearance in the eastern sky by the time he arrived at the store, a little after seven o'clock on this Saturday morning. He could not see a cloud anywhere in the cerulean blue sky and he knew it was going to be another hot day. The earth was powder dry, parched by the unrelenting sun, and the lack of rain had browned the dry grass.

The aroma of the spices, coffee and other foodstuffs flowed forth when he opened the front door of the store. He unlocked and propped open the back door so the gentle breezes would blow through the store. He enjoyed visiting with the customers — many would stop by just to visit this time of year as they were in between their farm work.

The crops had been planted; it was the growing season for the cotton and peanuts. The next chore, hoeing the weeds out of the crops, would commence very soon. Many of the farmers had already started the unpleasant toil. The August days were so hot that most of the workers went to the fields for a few hours early in the morning and again late in the afternoon.

Doc Hamilton was the first customer of the day, if he could be called a customer — he never bought anything because he never had any money. Doc fell off a horse, striking his head when he was a five-year-old boy. The blow caused Doc to never be quite right — unable to read, and some said he had the mind of a nine-year-old. He had no concept of figures such as counting money, but he had a way with the livestock and people.

He had an old black mule he called Osrow that he rode to Johnsville on occasion — no one else had ever been able to mount the animal, much less ride him. Doc's mother died when he was in his teens and since he wasn't able to care for himself, a neighbor lady, Mrs. Stone, took him in. Mrs. Stone was a widow, and Doc helped her around her farm doing easy tasks such as feeding the livestock, gathering the eggs and doing simple fieldwork.

Doc introduced himself to Aaron several years ago when one day he just seemed to wander into the store; wearing a pair of tattered blue overalls that were several sizes too big, a dirty yellow shirt and western boots that were well worn. He rolled-up the cuffs of the overalls because they were too long, and his shirt was several sizes too large. He never wore socks or underwear — he didn't know he was supposed to.

Doc couldn't tell time, but he always had two or three watches with him and a large brown coin purse where he kept his "things" that consisted of two pocket knives, a spoon, a straight razor, two .22-caliber shells and a couple of quarters.

He was five feet-six inches tall and weighed about one hundred and forty pounds. He had straight, gray hair that was always long. Aaron didn't know how old Doc was, but he judged him to be in his early fifties.

"My big name is Dee Hubbard Hamilton, but I'm called Doc. That's my nickname," he told Aaron as he rolled his eyes up and grinned a toothless smile. Never calling anyone by their correct name, he always called a person by the name he gave to him or her the first time he encountered them. He never forgot it.

"Say, Walter," talking to Aaron, "You got any 'em nanners that you wuz going to throw away?"

If he wanted it, Doc always asked for food and other items in the store, saying that the item needed to be thrown away.

"You bet, Doc, I thank these are getting too ripe, don't you?" Aaron put some of the more ripe bananas into a paper sack, "Do you thank Miss Stone will make you some nanner puddin'?"

"Uh huh," Doc closed his eyes as he rolled them up, "Say, ya got any of them cans of sardines back there? Let's go check 'fore that old man gits here."

Doc referred to Giles Martin, Aaron's grandfather, as that old man. Doc didn't like Giles because the old man always pretended that he disapproved of giving good merchandise to the little man. Aaron found a couple of dented cans of sardines and put them into the sack.

Alvie Hope, Aaron's neighbor, came in the opened door. Hope moved to Texas about fifty years ago from Louisiana and still had his Cajun accent.

"Hi, how y'all are?" He said when he saw Doc and Aaron, "May, I gone told you, it gone be a hot one today."

Mr. Hope hung around the store to pass the time of day. He was eighty-nine years old and wasn't physically able to work all day out in the field as he once could. His wife, Effie, had completely lost her sense of hearing, and it was difficult for him to communicate with her. Therefore, he enjoyed talking with the customers of the store.

"I'm gonna have me some sardines fer supper," Doc said, grinning, showing the older man his sack of goods.

"I'm gonna told you, we was so po, I seen the time my momma had to feed us five childrun wit just one sardine. Tied slicks string to it and we all gots to swallow dat li'l fish one times den momma would pull it out an' the next one would gets to swallow it. Den papa gots to et it."

The Old Cajun laughed. He had more tall stories than most men had true ones. His ruddy face became even redder when he laughed. He walked over to a counter at the front of the store and picked up a container of Carter's Little Liver Pills — the ones in a little red bottle with a cork on top.

"When my daddy was libin' he use to take a handful of dem liver pills mose every day. Why, he tooks so many of dem liver pills, dat when he died, dey had to beat his liver to death wit dis big o' stick."

"That ain't true," admonished Aaron, "that's just another one of yore tall tales."

"Uh nuh, dats true. I ain't making dis up, no." He grinned.

Mr. Hope walked outside to the front of the store and sat on a bench, whittling on a piece of soft pine-wood. He always had a penny for the small children coming with their parents to the store, and every once in awhile; he parted with one of his whittlings. He carved miniature figures, dogs, horses and other animals. Each time that he completed a carving, he would give it away.

"Walter, let's get us some of them crackers," Doc pointed to the cracker barrel, "don't ya want some?"

"I ain't hungry right now; you go ahead an' help yourself. How old are you Doc?" Aaron asked him in a teasing manner.

"I'll be thirty-two my next birthday," wiping the perspiration from his face with the same handker-chief he had just used to blow his nose.

"What time is it, Doc?" Aaron asked, giving no indication of what he had just witnessed.

"One-thirty," replied Doc, looking at an old bro-ken wristwatch on his left arm.

"What time does this one say?" asked Aaron, pointing to another broken wristwatch on his right arm.

"Four o'clock."

"Which one's right?"

"Both of 'em."

Aaron waited on several regular store customers while entertaining Doc, who talked to all of them. Doc was well known throughout the community, and everyone enjoyed hearing him tell his stories about fighting in the war and living in Mexico, of course, he had not done either. The little man had a dream of owning a farm that he could call his own and a pair of mules someday — a pipe dream that would never materialize for him. Aaron believed that Doc was content all the time because he had the dream.

Doc strolled toward the back of the store when he saw F. M. Snow and Maggie Poston walk in — he didn't want to talk to them. Snow told Aaron that he and Maggie were laboring in Mrs. Stone's field. He made it known to Aaron that he wouldn't mind try-ing to kindle a romance with Maggie. Snow saw Doc and asked him if he wanted a ride back home. Doc shook his head, no.

Aaron asked Doc after Snow and Maggie left, "Why didn't you want to go with them?"

"Cause, he's a sum-bitch."

"I gone tell ya, he no count," agreed Mr. Hope.

Doc and Mr. Hope wandered in and out of the store while Aaron waited on more customers and put out new merchandise in the store. Doc examined tools that were in the back of a storage shed behind the store — a hoe, rake, file and some posthole diggers. Aaron watched him through the back door of the store, making certain he didn't take any of the tools out of the shed to hide in the tall grass, later to be retrieved.

Aaron wasn't sure if Doc knew any better, but he would steal things he wanted if he found he wasn't being watched. Doc found a couple of washers and put them into his pocket. He seemed to sense that it was getting close to dinnertime, and he knew Mrs. Stone would have a meal ready for him.

Virgil McElroy walked into the store, talking loudly, as usual and smelling of alcohol, "Hi boys, shore is a hot day, ain't it? Well, hey Doc, here; let me see here what I got."

Virgil reached into his pocket and pulled out a nickel and a dollar bill. He held out the coin and bill and said, "Doc, which one of these do ya want?"

Doc didn't hesitate, reaching out and taking the nickel from Virgil's hand, he smiled and put it into his coin purse; Virgil, laughing, slapped his knee. He and many others played the little trick on Doc and no matter how many timed the game was played,

Doc always took the nickel. Mr. Hope just grinned and shook his head.

Aaron always despised the way those men treated Doc, making fun of him; until one day, he visited Doc at Mrs. Stone's farm, down on the Bosque river. Doc had a room on the southeast corner of the house and on this occasion; Aaron and Doc were in the room looking for a pair of gloves so that Doc could help haul some brush for Aaron. Aaron saw can after can in the room, coffee cans, baking powder cans, soup cans and syrup cans — each can was full of nickels. Then Aaron knew. If Doc had ever taken the dollar bill, the game would have been over. It made Aaron wonder, who was really the fool.

"Walter," Doc called as he was leaving, "brang yore .22 rifle with ya next time an' we'll go fishing."

"Well, Martin boy, I gone a go home," Mr. Hope waved as he walked out the door. It was also his lunchtime.

A little after lunch, another one of the local, colorful characters, Chief Geronimo Wilson, came into the store. Chief, about sixty-five years old, always wore a khaki shirt, khaki pants and a straw hat that covered his gray hair. Chief, a stoutly built white man with a full face, believed he was, or at least he claimed to be a full blood Indian.

And the peculiarities didn't end there. Chief, like Doc Hamilton, was a little more than mildly retarded and the brunt of the men's jokes. Chief maintained he was an Indian and his teasers made the most of it. They coaxed him into performing his "Indian dances" and "war hoops" right on Stephenville's downtown square, or anywhere people might be gathered. It was all in fun, and Chief probably enjoyed the attention, but lately, the joking had gone too far and Chief, a big man, had the potential of being dangerous.

A group of the men had told Chief that a motion picture company had filmed him with a "moving Kodak camera", and had taken the motion picture to Hollywood where he was in a movie starring Tom Mix. The men jokingly told him he would be paid a great deal of money for his fine job of acting in the movies. Of course, when Chief didn't receive any money, his mockers took it further. They told Chief that somebody, probably his neighbors, was stealing his money from his mailbox.

One of the neighbors, living about a half mile south of the self-proclaimed Indian, was F. M. Snow. Chief would go out of his way to avoid the man. Whenever he saw Snow, who frequently offered him a ride in his wagon, Chief most often looked straight ahead and ignored him.

"I ain't gittin' yore money, you ignorant fool, yore jest a crazy sum-bitch if you thank I got it!" Snow told him one day. Chief just looked straight ahead and said nothing.

Aaron, like the rest of the people, went along with the teasing of the snaggle-toothed man.

"What kind of Indian are ya, Chief?"

"Uh, well I'm, uh; I'm Cherokee, Choctaw an' Apache," he said, grinning and clapping his hands together.

"Hey, Indian, I heard ya made another movie." Aaron continued the teasing.

"Yeah, they put me in front of that movin' Kodak camera an' took my picture. Uh huh, yeah."

"Oh yeah, where wuz that?"

"Over there in Fort Worth, Texas, over there at that movie show in Fort Worth, Texas. Up an' down the streets there in Fort Worth, Texas."

One of the men had, in fact, taken Chief to Fort Worth and took him to a movie theater where *Riders of the Purple Sage* starring Tom Mix was showing. Albert Cox had taken the opportunity to further the charade and told Chief that he was Tom Mix. From that point on, Chief was a movie star in his own mind.

"What part did you play?"

"I wuz the 'Little Joe.'"

"What did you do?"

"I gave 'em that old Indian war dance an' did the hoochie coochie."

"Chief, do you know what that means?"

"Yeah, it's a old Indian war dance."

"I don't thank that's what it means, but if ya say so. Say Indian, do you know any Indian songs?" Aaron asked him as two older ladies entered the store.

Chief thought for a second then began singing:

On the lon-n-g Pay-cos, where the bears and terry pine fowls wake us up in the midnight.

"That's a ole Indian song, yes sir, a ole Indian song my momma used to sang."

The women looked at him and shook their head in disgust. One whispered something to the other. Self righteously, they ignored the loud man.

"How much did ya get paid when ya wuz in that movie?"

"I ain't got a penny out of it; the blamed mail thieves stoled all my money, yes sir, every dime, yes sir," his voice trailed off, nearly to a whisper.

Aaron sensed that Chief was becoming agitated. "I 'spect they'll catch 'em an' get all your money for you."

Chief saw one of his neighbors pass by in a wagon. It wasn't F. M. Snow. He walked out of the store and flagged the man down, got into the wagon, securing a ride home.

Cecil Ray Dumas dropped by the store around four o'clock in the afternoon. He came to the community every summer to stay with his grandmother, Mrs. Thompson. His mother and father were separated, and he lived with his father in Cleburne. He was nineteen years old and owned a car — a 1921

Chevy coupe with a rumble seat. Aaron met Cecil
Ray earlier in the summer, through his friend, Willie
Stanton, Mrs. Thompson's neighbor.

"Hey Aaron, you want to go out spooning tonight?" Cecil Ray asked, smiling.

"I don't know, why?" Aaron knew not to give an
affirmative answer immediately — it was always wise
to check out the facts before entering into an agreement with the grinning redhead.

"I'm gonna go pick up Sally after dark, an' her
cousin, Missy, is gonna be over at her house, an' she
wants to go out with you."

Aaron had met Missy earlier in the summer — it was
a few days after the camp out, about the middle of July,
when he was at Willie Stanton's house in Stephenville.
He and Willie had gone swimming the day before in the
Martin's tank and had gotten sunburned. Mrs. Stanton
gave Aaron a poultice she called "Granny Salve" to rub
on his red, blistered shoulders — the salve, so called
because Mrs. Stanton's Great-Grandmother Daniels
mixed it up every year and divided it out among all the
relatives. Aaron had pulled off his shirt and was just getting ready to apply the potion when he saw her. It would
be a day that he would remember forever.

A young lady, sixteen years old with smooth,
chestnut brown hair flowing gently down her back,
came into the room. She was a pretty girl, born
by a blunder of nature, into a family less desirable
than most. Although she was charming, she had no

expectations of being understood or loved. She suffered inside; she wanted to be loved, but felt incapable of giving love because she despised herself so much. But on the outside, she sparkled, full of energy and life. She laughed, giggled and made people feel good.

"Aaron, this is Missy." Willie's sister, Lydia, introduced them.

"Hi."

"Hi."

Aaron thought he must have seen an angel. Missy, with ocean blue eyes, apple cheeks and a little upturned nose, had the face of a girl in between childhood and womanhood. Her hair, flowing like a waterfall, caressed her shoulders and her sky-blue cotton dress highlighted her olive, tanned skin. Missy gently applied the "Granny Salve" to Aaron's back while he looked up into her wide blue eyes.

"What makes you think she wants to go with me?" Aaron asked Cecil Ray, "She barely talked to me that day I met her."

Aaron had not seen Missy again since that day, although he thought about her often.

"I'm telling you; she wants to be with you, Sally told me so."

"Okay, I'll be real nervous, but okay," he was already nervous.

Cecil Ray told Aaron he would pick him up about seven o'clock and they would meet the girls at Sally's house. Aaron left the store and went home and got cleaned up — ready for a rendezvous with Missy. Cecil Ray was a practical joker and Aaron thought he was probably trying to pull one on him, but he got ready just in case. Sure enough, Cecil Ray arrived at his house at seven o'clock as he said he would.

"Hi there, are ya ready fer yore date?" Cecil Ray asked.

"Yeah, I guess so, but I'm awful nervous — that Missy is shore purty."

Cecil Ray had dark red hair that stood up all over a head that seemed to be too large for his small body. He wore thick glasses that were always slipping down his nose. His freckled face was long and slim, and his ears poked out like a couple of saucers. Cecil Ray's personality overcame his not so handsome features. He was always happy, laughing, and no one was a stranger to him. All the teenagers in the area liked him, although he was several years older.

He and Aaron drove to the Lowe's house — a distance of about four miles. Sally watched Cecil Ray while he parked his car in front of the house. The boys walked up, and Cecil Ray knocked on the front door. Aaron was now beginning to feel that his mouth was full of cotton, and his tongue was sticking to the roof of his mouth. He could feel his heart pounding in his chest — his knees were weak and shaking. Cecil Ray was as calm as if he were merely walking up to his grandmother's house.

"Look at that!" Cecil Ray pointed to the August moon making its appearance in the eastern sky.

Sally opened the door and invited the boys into the front room of the house, a room that served as a living room and sleeping quarters for Sally's little brother, Patrick. Aaron saw Missy, sitting on a couch, her hands folded in her lap.

"H-h-hi," he stuttered wondering what to say next, "Cecil Ray and me were jest . . . we just wuz thanking. Is it alright if I set down?" He sat down in a chair across the room from Missy.

"Hi, Aaron, Yes, it's okay to set down," Missy said, her almond shaped blue eyes looking straight at Aaron who couldn't think of anything else to say.

"Me an' Aaron would of been here sooner, 'cept I drove my car off the end of a bridge that washed out the other day when it rained so hard. We wondered what we wuz going to do because the front wheels wuz hanging off the end of the bridge. Aaron gets out an' holds the front of the car up while I backed the car back on the road." Another one of Cecil Ray's stories broke the tension, and everyone started laughing.

"You're lying! Y'all didn't do that." Sally was beginning to feel more at ease with the funny boy with the red hair.

"We dang shore did, tell 'em Aaron. You had to hold the car up an' got yore hands all dirty didn't ya?

"I reckon — I mean, ya know I 'spect we shouldn't brag too much." Aaron was not a jokester and was not as quick witted as Cecil Ray.

Cecil Ray walked over to a painting of a landscape, "This shore is a pretty picture; who painted it?"

"I don't know," replied Sally, "it's been in the house for as long as I can remember."

Missy asked Aaron, "Did your back get well after you got that sunburn?"

"Uh, yeah. It didn't hurt very long." Aaron was feeling more relaxed. "I guess it wuz that slave you rubbed on me."

"Would y'all like some lemon-aide of somethin' to drink," Sally asked.

"No thank you," Aaron said.

"Yeah, I'll take a glass," Cecil Ray told her.

"Me too!" Said Missy.

"Well, if everybody's gonna drink some, I will too." Aaron walked over to Sally, who was pouring the lemon-aide into glasses. He picked up two glasses of the refreshments and took one and handed it to Missy.

"Thank you," Missy smiled.

"Hey, why don't we go ridin' in my car," Cecil Ray suggested after they all had finished their drinks.

"Okay."

Sally closed the front door of the house, and the two couples walked out to the car. Cecil Ray and Sally sat in the front seat, and Aaron and Missy sat in the back rumble seat.

"Have y'all ever heard of Gentry's Bridge? Let's go there," suggested Missy.

"No, I ain't, what is it?" asked Cecil Ray.

"I don't know what happened out there, but if ya stop on top of the bridge, you're supposed to hear this woman scream," Missy said, relating the story as it had been told to her. "A bunch of the kids has heard it."

"Shore, let's go — how do we get there?"

Missy gave the directions to an old wooden bridge that crossed over the Bosque River about five miles due south of Stephenville.

"There's ole man Snow an' that lady who was with him in the store this morning," Aaron said pointing to a couple passing by in a wagon. "Doc Hamilton shore don't like him for some reason."

"He don't look like much to me," Cecil Ray said, "I'll bet he couldn't even whoop me, and I'm a little feller."

"Well, let's don't find out," replied Sally, glancing over at the old man who was directing two old, scrawny horses, cursing as he whipped them.

The young people, arriving at the destination, crossed a wooden bridge spanning over the Bosque River. Cecil Ray parked the car on the east side of the rickety bridge, behind a riverbank, nestled among a canopy of tall oak trees. The couples got out of the car and talked as they watched earth's glowing satellite, the moon, leisurely rise over the towering trees.

"I wonder who's staring at the moon like we are tonight?" Cecil Ray asked.

"I don't know, but it's beautiful," replied Sally.

"I love a moon-lit night," Missy said.

"Me, too," agreed Aaron, "it's like God's flashlight shining down on us."

"Missy, I thought you had a boy you were keeping company with," Cecil Ray said.

"Oh, he is just a good friend from church; we aren't together anymore."

"Hum, this is lookin' better all the time," thought Aaron.

The tranquil chirping of the serenading crickets playing their nighttime melodies, the gentle rustling of leaves and the occasional advertisement call from a nearby bullfrog filled the nighttime air. The wind, only a breeze, cool and gently blowing over the water, was welcome after the heat of the long summer day.

Further, down the river, a coyote's mournful cry echoed back on this warm summer night. An owl, somewhere high in one of the trees, gave forth a mysterious trill. Noises that wouldn't be noticed in the daylight were all about. Was it only a coyote and owl, or was it the lady that haunted this bridge?

"It's scary out here," Sally whispered, "Let's git back in the car."

"Okay, scaredy cat!"

Aaron took Missy's hand and helped her up onto the rumble seat of Cecil's Chevy.

"I can't believe you're scared, Sally," Missy said in disgust, "nothin's out here."

Aaron got up into the rumble seat and sat next to Missy, continuing to hold her hand. Cecil Ray opened the passenger door, bowed and motioned to Sally to get into the old Chevy's front seat. He got into the car and scooted over next to Sally.

"Well, what are we gonna do now that miss scaredy cat don't want to go strollin' down the river?" Cecil Ray asked.

"I'm sorry."

"If I'd brought my guitar, we could sang," Aaron said.

"That would shore be better than jest sittin' here. Come on; let's git out agin an' walk down the river," Cecil Ray suggested.

"No!" shouted Sally.

"Okay then, Sally, give me a kiss," Cecil Ray said, puckering up.

"No!" Not really meaning it, Sally pretended to be offended.

"It's going to be like a bull chasing a cow down through the pasture if you don't give me a kiss."

"You're so silly," Sally giggled, "you don't deserve a kiss."

"Uh huh; will you kiss me if Missy kisses Aaron?"

He didn't wait for Sally's reply, "Aaron, why don't ya kiss Missy?"

Aaron still holding Missy's soft hand, looked into her heavenly eyes, "May I kiss you?"

Missy looked up at Aaron beside her. The moonlight sparkled in her wide and friendly eyes. Smiling at the boy, she gave her reply, nodding her head in an affirmative manner.

"Yes! But you're not supposed to ask."

Aaron lifted her chin; Missy closed her eyes. Their lips met — a kiss as tender and light as a summer breeze. Aaron shivered; it was nothing like he had ever experienced before. A blush crept up Missy's face. Twice and then three times — each kiss held a little longer than the previous one. The kiss by which Aaron would judge all other kisses.

"Aw, dang it Sally, they beat us." Cecil Ray never had any intention of kissing Sally anyhow.

The woman at the bridge didn't scream on this night, a perfect night — the seeds of love were being planted. It was over much too soon for Aaron; the moment passed quickly — soon it was time to take the two girls back home.

Trying to sleep, Aaron thought about the softness of Missy's velvety lips, the delicate scent of her hair and her funny little giggle. He felt a strange something that he had never experienced. He barely knew her and he was missing her. Was this love?

Two days later, much-needed rain, thunderously loud but refreshing, came during the night and Monday morning's red sky reminded Aaron of the old adage:

> "Red sky in morning, sailors take warning — red sky at night, sailors' delight."

He had heard the old-timers quote this time and time again; he supposed it to be true, and the day would probably bring another afternoon thunderstorm.

For now, a once cool breeze blowing into his window quickly warmed as the sun rose higher in the eastern sky. Aaron's thoughts turned to Missy and their first kiss, two days ago, and how he had hoped to see her at church yesterday, but it was not to be.

"She's gone with her grandmother to visit her uncle in Walnut Springs," Sally had told him, "but she'll probably be at the party at my house this coming Saturday night.

"Why don't you come," she invited, "and bring some of your friends?"

Aaron would be with Missy once again before school started, but this romance was never to be. Missy was Virgil McCoy's only daughter; a young girl growing up without having the love of a mother or father. A young girl, always reaching out for true love, but never finding it.

Aaron would forget many things during his lifetime, but he would never forget their first kiss — the kiss from which he would never be free.

13

THE LORD TAKETH

A flash of lightening and then darkness. A loud clap of thunder and then quietness. Cecil Ray was awakened by an early morning rain shower. He hoped it would dampen the soil sufficiently so that he wouldn't have to help his Grandpa Thompson in the field today. His hopes were quickly dashed when he heard Grandpa call out to him.

"Cecil Ray, git up, it's gonna be dry enough to go git in the field 'fore long."

"Okay Grandpa, I'm gittin' up now — shore thought it'd be wet enough that I wouldn't have to work today," he laughed, "I'm gonna pray fer a little more rain."

"Yeah, I'll bet ya wuz hopin' fer it to be just wet enough so we couldn't work, so you could go run 'round in that automobile of yores. Them thangs are gonna be the ruination of us. All you kids want to do is go fer a ride. I'm tellin' ya, my pappy'd never stood fer all this foolishness."

"Yeah, I know, Grandpa, but thangs are a changin', I'll bet someday, we'll be able to drive as fer as El Paso in one day."

"Ah, hush yore mouth, boy, that's jest plain foolishness."

"You oughta get you a car, Grandpa. You an' Grandma could go visit yore brother more often."

"I ain't had one of them new-fangled contraptions in my eighty years an' got by alright. I shore don't need one of 'em now."

Grandma Thompson, a spry little woman for her seventy-eight years, had finished cooking breakfast when Cecil Ray came into the kitchen.

"Yum, yum, that's shore smells good!"

He ate hot biscuits, honey and butter before filling his plate with scrambled eggs and gravy. Grandpa didn't have any teeth and hadn't had for over twenty years, but he could gum his food as well as most people could chew with a good set of teeth. He finished his last biscuit, sopping with blackberry jam and butter, wiped his hands on a dishcloth and sipped the last of his black, hot coffee.

"If yore finished, go hitch up the team." Grandpa's decrees had always sounded stern for as long as Cecil Ray could remember.

Cecil Ray slipped on an old pair of boots, put on a straw hat and walked to the old barn. He took the rigging off a hook and went to the back of the barn, caught the horses and hitched up the team. He and Grandpa rode the wagon over the damp road to a farm for a distance of three miles — the farm that belonged to Thompson's neighbor, Louis Savage.

As they pulled into the gate, Grandpa Thompson waved to Louis, who already was in the field with his team of three horses, plowing the weeds out of his peanut crop. Grandpa glanced at his pocket watch and thought, "It's only seven-thirty in the mornin' and that Louis's already hard at it."

"Mornin', Mister Savage," Cecil Ray called out.

"Mornin' Cecil Ray."

"Looks like it's gonna be another hot one, don't it?" Cecil Ray asked.

"Yes siree, it shore does, shore wish't we'd got 'little more rain. The stock tanks are beginnin' to dry up an' this ground's soon gonna be hard as a rock. If we don't get a good rain soon, we're liable to lose our crop."

Louis Savage, an Erath County native, was forty-two years old last June. His dark complexion and black hair was characteristic of the Savage family. He was a quiet man and always treated his fellow man with dignity. People remarked that unlike many people, his moods never changed, and his mood was always good.

He was a model citizen of Erath County, always honorable, upright and fair with everyone. Louis, a family man who had been blessed with a beautiful singing voice, loved to sing; especially he loved to sing hymns.

"How's your wife an' babies?" Grandpa asked. "Guess they're gittin' 'bout big enough to walk."

"They's all doin' good. They wuz a year old last May. I 'spect I'm a mighty lucky man. Who'd a thought I'd have me some twins? They wuz still sleeping when I left this morning — I kinda wanted to wake them up to tell 'em bye, but I'll see 'em tonight if nothin' don't happen."

Louis did not take a bride until he was thirty-nine years old and had he been a lady, he would have been called an old maid. Most of his neighbors and family thought he was a confirmed bachelor who would never marry, but to their amazement, he married a woman from Fort Worth. He had, unbeknownst to his friends, been courting the lady for some time. When asked why he didn't ever tell anyone about his courtship he replied, "I never wuz one of those gabby kinda folks."

Louis Savage's family, who had settled in Erath County in the 1880's, was highly respected in the community. Louis was a fine neighbor who lived up to the Golden Rule; taking care of his neighbor's needs even before he attended his own. He and his wife were the proud parents of twin babies, a boy and a girl.

Thunderheads started boiling up in the summer sky about ten o'clock. The air, the soil, and the earth were heating up under the scorching sun. The humidity, caused by last night's rain, beat down upon the three field hands making the heat feel even hotter than the ninety-two degrees. Cecil Ray took turns with his grandfather behind the plow. Very little breeze was blowing; the sweat trickled off the workers soaking their clothing.

"Man, it's sultry," Cecil Ray took off his hat and wiped his red face, "Those clouds look like it's gonna rain again. I shore am hot!"

"Take ye a drank of water and sit fer a spell," Grandpa told the boy who was not used to being under the Texas sun, "You'll be alright, drec'ly."

Cecil Ray took a drink from a water bag that Grandpa filled before leaving for the field. The water gradually seeped between the fibers of the material, and the evaporation helped cool the water.

The clouds continued to build up and by eleven o'clock; Cecil Ray saw a storm approaching from the northwest and soon it was sprinkling rain. The men continued to work, thinking perhaps as some of the people did in the days of Noah that the shower might be over quickly. But soon, the storm clouds opened up, and the torrential rain began to pour from the heavens. They knew that this was going to be a hard, drenching rain and that the plowing for this day was over until another time.

Cecil Ray and Louis unhooked their plows and hitched their teams back to their wagons to return home. The lightning was flashing and getting closer as the rain fell in sheets — blown by a fierce wind. Thunder was rumbling through the sky, sounding like a stampede of frightened cattle being chased by ghostly riders.

"We'd better get out of this lightning and git on to the house Cecil Ray," Grandpa shouted, his face showing his concern. He was afraid of storms and lightning, just as his parents had been. He remembered a tornado on a day about like this several years earlier that killed a man who lived close to Stephenville. He desired the safety of a storm cellar.

"There is about as much danger in one place as another," Louis told the old gentleman as they climbed up onto Louis' wagon while Cecil Ray climbed onto the other wagon.

"We gotta go now!" shouted Cecil Ray pulling his wagon around and in front of Louis' wagon.

Grandpa Thompson was standing about three feet behind Louis, leading an extra horse by the reins. He saw that Cecil Ray was directly in front of them, motioning for them to come around him and lead the way out of the field.

Louis standing up in the wagon, sang out with his strong voice:

> *Shall we gather at the river?*
> *Where bright angel feet have trod;*
> *With its crystal tide forever*
> *Flowing by the throne of God.*

He, popped the reins as his team pulled the wagon around Cecil Ray and then directed his horses toward shelter. The cold rain poured down on the men, soaking their clothing.

> *Yes, we'll gather at the river,*
> *The beautiful, the beautiful . . .*

Suddenly, without any warning, a mighty bolt of lightning flashed forth from the dark clouds, striking Louis Savage near the top center of his head.

The bolt descended down the left side of his face around his chin, then down to his chest, splattering flesh all around — in the wagon and on the ground. The highly charged bolt of lightning split into two bolts at Louis' waist. One passed down his left leg, tearing off three toes, then through the bed of the wagon, burning a hole the size of a quarter. The other bolt traveled down his right side and through the wagon, burning another hole. The force of the lightning bolt tore the man's clothing to shreds. His new pair of striped overalls and shirt was completely gone, and except for his belt, his body bore no clothing.

Two animals lay dead among the shredded pieces of clothing — about thirty feet in front of the wagon. The forces of the lightning bolt traveled like a ball of fire through the wet plow lines that Louis Savage was holding, killing both the mule and horse that were hitched to his wagon.

Grandpa Thompson was thrown off his feet onto the bed of his drenched wagon. He was shaken, and the wind was knocked out of him, but he was unharmed. When he had recovered from the force of the deadly bolt and the deafening explosion, a sweet, pungent odor flooded his nostrils — ozone. He saw the horse that he had been leading as it galloped wildly across the field. Then he saw the mangled body of Louis Savage lying across the front wheel of the wagon.

Cecil Ray, stunned by the explosion of the thunder and the brilliant blaze that descended from the sky, was now directly behind the wagon where Louis Savage lay mortally wounded — a victim of the brutal forces of nature, the tremendous, destructive energy of a lightning bolt. As Cecil Ray began to regain his senses, he saw the bits of torn clothing lying all around him — he smelled the coppery fumes and felt the cold rain that was falling like sheets of water.

He felt as though he has lost some time. He couldn't remember coming into the field, but he was there. He couldn't remember anything about the morning. He quieted the horses that were hitched to the wagon upon which he was sitting, and he was finally able to speak, "Grandpa, are ye okay? I couldn't stop it!"

"Yes son, I'm okay, go get us some help, I'm 'fraid the lightening took Mister Savage an' he's dead, I'll stay with the body while you get some help. Tell Grandma to go stay with Missus Savage 'til she hears from us, she'll know what to do."

"Okay, Grandpa, if you're shore yer alright, I'll be on my way."

"I'm okay; it jest knocked the wind out of me fer a minute, now go on, do what I tell ya."

"Giddy up," he yelled, slapping the reins against the horses' necks, "I'll hurry, Grandpa!"

Madison Martin's farm, the closest to the field where Louis Savage lay dead, was two and a half miles away. The rain continued pouring from the rolling, dark clouds, and the thunder was rolling through the heavens when Cecil Ray jumped out of the wagon and ran to the door of the Martin's house. Madison and Aaron met him at the door.

"What's wrong, boy?" Madison could see the terror on Cecil Ray's face. "Come on in and git out of the rain!"

"We need some help, me an' my grandpa need some help! A man's been struck by lightnin' and he's dead! Grandpa's out there with 'im!"

"Who is it?" Madison asked the shaking boy.

"It's Mister Savage, sir." Cecil Ray told the Martins that his grandfather wanted someone to notify his grandmother and ask her to go be with Mrs. Savage when the news of the tragedy was made known to her.

Madison and Aaron went to the field with Cecil Ray — Millie Martin went to deliver the tragic news to Grandma Thompson. Expecting to find a body with no visible injuries, as is usual when lightning electrocutes a person — the Martins were stunned at the gruesome sight of Louis Savage's corpse. Grandpa Thompson was picking up a piece of hat that he found about thirty feet from the body when Madison first saw him.

Madison and Aaron walked up to the front of Louis' wagon and saw the body — it had been thrown onto the wagon wheel. The body was missing all its clothing. The victim of nature's fury was laying with his eyes wide open, but unblinking. The man died instantly. His heart stopped immediately and the only blood visible was a small amount oozing from his mouth and ears.

For the second time in his young life, Aaron had seen the tragedy of death. Anna Jenkins was the first, having died after she fell from the wagon at the church hayride. She was so young, so beautiful and so full of life. And Mr. Savage, he had a new wife and two little babies. Why, Aaron wondered, did they die before their time? Was this God's over-all plan? How was He glorified by the death of these two precious souls?

Aaron saw that pieces of flesh were missing from the man's chest, and his lower torso was dark red, mingled with purple. He found the man's pocket watch lying on the ground next to the right side of Louis's body — the hands of the watch were fused by the savage fury of the electrical bolt. Aaron was sick; the smell and sight of another death had overcome him.

The rain stopped as suddenly as it began, and the sun was beginning to peak through the breaks in the storm clouds a short time after Aaron and his daddy got to the field. A cool breeze was blowing from the storm clouds. It would have been a beautiful day had not tragedy struck so quickly.

Another neighbor, Wes Reid, had been summoned to the scene of Louis's untimely death. Mr. Reid helped Madison and Aaron put Louis Savage's corpse onto the wagon, and they readied him for his last ride home. Madison covered the body with a tarpaulin, which Louis had in the wagon, used to protect his cargo when necessary. Madison saw a part of a shoe in the bed of the wagon and was mystified that the bolt of lightning had such awesome force. The men quietly picked up pieces of garments that were once the clothing of Louis Savage, a man so full of life and energy just an hour ago.

The slow ride back to Louis's home gave Aaron time to reflect about the uncertainty of life and wondered if Louis Savage had said goodbye. He wondered why a good man, who had two babies, was taken when someone as vicious as Virgil McElroy was know to be or as wicked as F. M. Snow was thought to be were allowed to live.

Grandpa Thompson thought about Louis's words spoken earlier in the day. Did he have a premonition about his death? Is that why he had wanted to wake his sleeping babies?

Aaron lay in bed, thinking of the day and the mutilated human corpse that he had witnessed. Nothing, he thought, could be as violent as this catastrophic death. He remembered seeing Mrs. Savage's anguish when they brought Louis home. He thought about the two twins, yet too young to understand. He hoped that he would never again see such a sight. But soon, he would encounter something even more disturbing.

14

F. M. AND MAGGIE SNOW

October 6, 1925 . . .

" I want to give you a home," F. M. Snow told Maggie Poston as they walked up the steps of the Erath County courthouse and into the county clerk's office.

The courthouse building, constructed from native limestone and red sandstone, had been completed in 1893 — a majestic structure, it could be seen from any direction when approaching the town, Stephenville.

Maggie and Mister Snow, as she called him, had been working together in the neighboring cotton fields near his small farm. People of the community had been seeing them together since they first met at the dinner on the ground at church. They came to work in the fields together and left at night together. They even shared their snuff — a romance was blooming.

Snow, forty-six years old, had moved to a little farm south of Stephenville in Erath County a couple of years earlier from Palo Pinto County, Texas. He apparently had fallen from the sky because no one knew anything about his past, only that he made it clear to Virgil McElroy that he would not be threatened. He was a tall, slender man with thin lips set in a straight line, deep-set brown eyes and high cheekbones, indicating that he might be part Indian. Never smiling and always staying to himself, he frightened people. The rifle, always within his reach, gave to speculations that this eccentric man was menacing.

Snow and Maggie Poston walked into the county clerk's office at about ten o'clock in the morning, and Snow made their intentions known, "Me an' Missus Maggie want to get us a marriage license."

Coleman D. Nichols, the clerk, issued the license to the couple and wished them luck and happiness.

"I know we'll be happy, I love this here woman," smiling at his bride-to-be.

The prospective newlyweds ate lunch at a little café in Stephenville, then rode Snow's wagon to Rocky Point Church, about five miles east of Stephenville. Brother Bays, the minister, who also was a farmer and carpenter, met the couple at the church at two o'clock. He told Snow he would unite them in marriage. They called upon Deacon Hook and his wife, Wilma, to be their witnesses.

"We have gathered here today to join this man and this woman into the bonds of holy matrimony," Brother Bays slowly began the ceremony.

"We find that the Lord saw that it was not good for a man to live alone in this world," then concluding, "I now pronounce you man and wife; you may kiss your bride."

Snow gave Mrs. Snow a little peck on her cheek and said, "Now we gotta be goin' 'cause we got work to do." And they were off to start their life together.

Snow's seventeen-acre farm was down a little country road in the Indian Creek Community, about eight miles southeast of Stephenville. The old two-room house, much in need of repair, had a fireplace, but very little in the way of furnishings. Several out-buildings including an old barn, were as much in disrepair as the house. A windmill, standing like a sentinel guarding the farm, provided water for drinking, cooking, bathing and Snow's livestock — a couple of horses and one old cow. Snow's plans were to do some farming and cut wood to provide for his new wife.

The newly wedded couple returned to Snow's farm, fed and watered the cow and horses, and penned them up for the night. Snow opened the front door of the house for his new bride.

"I've been doing most of my cooking here on the fireplace, but I've got me a coal oil stove that I'll bring in if you want me to," Snow told Maggie, "Now, why don't you get us sump'um ready for supper."

"Mister Snow, you just leave it to me, I'm gonna fix you up a fine meal."

Snow wiped off an old homemade table, in the northern room, "I call this my eating table."

Maggie saw the table and two cane-bottom chairs in the room used for the kitchen. It wasn't much, but it was better than living in the covered wagon. The only other furniture in the house, in the room with a fireplace, was an old iron bedstead with a well-worn feather mattress.

"When we get settled, we can send back to Waco and get my furniture."

Maggie was beginning to realize that her new husband had very little worldly goods that he could bring into their union. Still, it was better than living in a wagon — she didn't have many possessions of her own.

After they had finished their first meal together as a married couple, a pot of potatoes, Mr. and Mrs. Snow took the two cane-bottom chairs out on the front porch. Although it was October, the temperature had been in the nineties during the day. The sun was sinking down below the trees in the western sky, and the first stars began to awaken for the night.

Snow pulled out a plug of tobacco that he kept wrapped in a rag in his back pocket. He cut him a plug to chew, and put it into his mouth.

"Maggie, I've been so unhappy for a whole year since I moved here, an' even before. I'm plum glad ya came along."

"I know, Mister Snow, I know. You're a fine man an' I'll try to make you a good wife. My other three husbands thought the world of me."

"And I'll shore try to be a good husband fer ya," Snow squinted his eyes, "but I understood that you'd been married only once."

"Well, I've only known you fer a couple of months now an' we still don't know much about each other. I never said one way or the other — it jest never came up. I didn't mean no deceit. I jest despise deceitfulness, don't you, Mister Snow?"

"It might be better to just let some thangs go unsaid," Snow commented, "I've always sorta stayed to myself an' tried to mind my own business. So I 'spect it's best to let the past be."

"Oh-h-h," she held the word, "that's just like my Sid. He was Bernie's papa ya know. He was a quiet sort of a man. He never had much to say 'bout nothin. I had to coax 'em an' coax him to git him to talk to me."

"Well, I ain't prying, but how long were y'all married? Did he pass natural?"

"No, he wuz robbed and killed by some Negro men when Bernie wuz twelve years old. It was hard on the boy; I don't thank he ever got over it. He still talks 'bout his papa. I know he misses 'im. It was hard on me too; I'm subject to nervous spells, ya know."

"Woman, I'm shore sorry, I didn't know, did they catch 'em, the ones who done it?"

"Yes sir, they found him an' his Negro sidekicks. I told the law they wuz the ones that done it. It wuz jest like they didn't want to catch nobody, asking me all those questions an' sech. The laws kept on asking me about Sid's insurance an' thangs like that. Why, they even made out it was me, puttin' them Negroes up to killin' my Sid."

"How did you know it was a Nigger?" Snow questioned.

"I seen 'em, Mister Snow; I watched it all with my own eyes! That big, fat, ugly one shot my Sid right in the chest an' I couldn't do anythang about it."

Maggie looked off toward the twilight at the sinking sun, "We wuz coming back from town one night, an' that bunch of Negro boys stopped us right there on the road."

Maggie continued, "That big one — he took Mister Connally's wallet an' pocket watch, an' all that time, he was holding that gun on me an' I wuz scared to death! Now, ya know, I didn't put 'em up to that."

"Oh, honey," Snow took her hand, "you had to be so scared." He didn't ever remember using a pet name like "honey" before — he surprised himself.

"I wuz. Them Negro boys took off up the highway, an' that's the last time we ever saw 'em."

Snow, wondering who the "we" was that Maggie was talking about, rubbed the back of his neck.

"Well, that's too bad, but now, it's all in the past." Snow wanted to change the subject.

"An' do you know what they did to them boys?"

"No, ma'am." Snow knew she was going to tell him.

"Well, there wuz a trial an' I gave my testimony, I stated, under oath, that they wuz the Negroes that did it. They put two of 'em in prison fer life — one of 'em died in jail, so I heared. Them two boys in prison still claim they didn't kill my Sid, but I know different, I seen 'em. I know I weren't mistaken when I picked 'em out. They should of killed them all; them murderers. I never got a penny of Sid's money 'cause they said we wuz separated when it happened. We wuz separated fer awhile, but we had gotten back together."

"Yes 'um."

"If somebody killed your loved ones, shoot 'em right before your eyes, you'd want 'em to be hung wouldn't ya? You thank about it."

"Yes 'um, I reckon so." Snow spit tobacco juice over the side of the porch, "I reckon so."

"I ain't never forgave 'em either. Me an' Bernie has had a hard row to hoe, I'm tellin' ya, 'fore Mister Poston came along, ya know, I lost him tragically, too."

"Yes 'um."

"I met Bernie's papa when I wuz twenty-seven years old, married him an' we moved to Texas. Bernie wuz born when I wuz twenty-nine years old, most people considered me to be too old."

Snow, showing irritation, nodded his head.

"Bernie's my boy; we been through thick an' thin."

Maggie wed two more times after Connally's death, and both of these husbands had died, but not naturally.

"After Bernie's daddy got killed, I married Clem Anderson."

Snow nodded again.

"An' he wuz killed when a runaway wagon run 'em down. They claimed it wuz a accident, but I know better. Mister Anderson loved his poker games an' he lost what little money we had. He didn't have no insurance either. So that left me an' Bernie without a place to stay an' no money to speak of."

Snow, spitting out more tobacco juice, shook his head.

"An' then I met Andrew Poston, oh, he wuz my sweetheart." Maggie smiled to herself.

"He wuz sleeping outside the house one day an' a brick fell off the fireplace an' stuck 'im in the head. Now can ya jest imagine that?"

"No ma'am."

Maggie was born in Georgia in 1878 to a poor sharecropper's family. She was a heavyset woman, contrasting F. M. Snow's slim build. She always wore a dress, even when working in the fields — crawling on her knees, picking cotton. She wore her dark brown hair braided, pinned in a circle on the back of her head. A big straw hat protected her pale face, round and puffy, anytime she was outside. Her gold-rimmed glasses, used for reading, were usually found on the top of her head.

She and Snow were different in every way — Snow's nose was long, hers was short — his lips were thin, hers were full — he was quiet, she was talkative — his voice was soft, hers was annoyingly loud — he was dangerous — perhaps she was also. She was critical of everything and everybody — her lot was to complain.

Snow's two old hound dogs, Maude and Claude, were stretched out on the porch in front of Snow's feet. He loved those dogs, and he kept them with him all the time; they were a comfort to him. In fact, he was quickly coming to the realization that they were just as much company as Maggie, and they didn't talk all the time.

"Mister Snow, did you ever read about that monkey trial they had in Tennessee?"

"No ma'am."

"Well, sir, they's a teacher over there who was teaching that a human bean came from a monkey over six hundred thousand years ago. He called it a revolution or something like that. I read 'bout it in the paper; he said that ever thang is still changing. It's all a pack of lies. If my late husband wuz here, it'd jest kill 'em. He was a very religious man, Mister Snow. He knowed the Bible back an' forth."

Snow nodded his head, looking away.

"Everybody knows that God created a man six thousand years ago; it's in the Bible, jest as plain as day. Right after He said that there should be a light, He made all the animals an' then He made a man in His own image; that's how the Bible reads and its God's word. He wrote it His-self."

"Yes 'um."

"I think that ole teacher's name is Scopes — he wuz a teachin' that blasphemy to the little children. He was tryin' to make them believe it, the heathen. They put him in jail; ya know."

"They did?"

"Yes sir, that old infidel lawyer of his died, praise the Lord," Maggie smiled in satisfaction.

Snow, uneasy, went into the house, rolled up the wick in the kerosene lamp and lit it. Darkness had descended as the couple; Maggie was talking, and even though Snow wasn't alone tonight, he still needed his light.

"You don't partake of that intoxicating liquor do you Mister Snow?" Maggie inquired as he walked back outside.

"No ma'am."

"I sure wouldn't live with a man who dranks. Bernie's papa, rest his soul, used to drank 'til I showed him in the Good Book that drankin' is a abomination to the Lord. Then he saw the light an' became a Godly man — he quit that drankin' an' Lawsy — that man could pray. That's 'bout the only time he ever spoke a word; he was a quiet man, jest like you. You'd liked him, Mister Snow; he was a good listener, jest like you."

Snow nodded his head and petted Maude, lying beside him.

"Mister Snow, tell be 'bout yourself. You've been awful quiet."

"Well, hun, I wuz jest . . ."

"Mister Snow, I'm gonna see to it that we start goin' to church regular, jest like me an' Sid. Mister Poston never went to church with me — he wasn't a churchgoer like Bernie's papa. I kept after him, though. You know what it says in the Good Book; if ye are unevenly yoked, keep on at the one who's strayed. But Mister Poston would never hear of it. It's better for a camel to go through the eye of a needle than to be like that. Ya know, they say I talk too much, but I'm not like some folks — I like to say what's on my mind."

"Maggie, I'm gonna go out an' ride 'Ole Joe' fer awhile."

F. M. Snow had several idiosyncrasies — riding "Old Joe," one of his two old, spindly horses, was one of them. Whenever the man became bored or frustrated, he would put a saddle his old horse and mount him.

Snow, mumbling quietly, walked slowly out to the pen where "Old Joe" was corralled for the night, threw the saddle on the horse's back, and led the horse out into the pasture. Snow began his angry ride. He whipped the horse's flanks with two long pieces of rawhide, fashioned into a whip. The sorrel whinnied, leaped and began galloping, twisting.

The relentless whipping continued, the gelding ran and bucked, trying to throw the rider off, but the man held on, yelling obscenities. After about fifteen minutes, it was over — the horse, lathered with sweat and breathing heavily, stood humbly and still. Snow took the saddle off and walked back to the porch and sat down in the cane-bottom chair, not speaking a word. The newlyweds sat quietly and listened to the night until their bedtime, nine o'clock.

The marriage was not consummated that first night. The excitement and intensity of riding and whipping the horse, the smell of the horse perspiring

in the night, the agonizing neighs, and the conclusion for Snow was as always. He relished the feeling
of being able to control the animal, the feeling of
power it brought him. His frustration had been relieved for the moment.

The next morning, Maggie was up early, and she
saw Snow was already outside.

"Mister Snow, what do you want for breakfast?"

"Oh, just some hot coffee an' some eggs — I 'spect
that'd be fine, don't make no fuss over me."

"Mister Snow, don't be expecting me to make a
fuss over ya. I want a man who can do fer his-self. You
'spectin' me to have to do all the thankin' fer us?"

Snow shook his head, wondering what brought
forth that comment, "Alright, Maggie, jest tryin' to
git along with ya, I 'spect I need some practice bein'
a husband."

Maggie thought to herself, "I've been down this
road before an' I ain't gonna make the same mis-
takes again, not with this one."

She went about getting the breakfast prepared,
eggs and water gravy — nothing elaborate, but it was
all they had. She poured more water into the coffee
grounds from the brew last night; it would be weak,
but it was coffee. She strolled through the room,
thinking it needed a woman's touch, and then she
thought about her mother and Bernie who were still
living out of the covered wagon. She knew it would

be getting cold soon, and they would need better shelter. It wouldn't hurt to ask.

"Mister Snow," as they sat down to the table, "I wuz just thanking — maybe Ma and Bernie could move in here with us."

Snow quickly finished his breakfast, went outside and saddled "Old Joe."

15

THE HARVEST

I t was that time of year, time for beginning the work that the farmers dreaded the most — picking cotton. It was an essential job and early October found the area farmers in preparation for the task facing them. The boll weevil hadn't yet invaded the land so the farmers had planted as much cotton as they could cultivate. King Cotton was selling for a good price this year.

Everything had to be made ready before the field hands started picking cotton. The farmers put wooden frames on the sides of their wagons; the wagons needed to hold enough cotton to produce a bale — approximately fifteen hundred pounds of the picked, fluffy cotton. The farmers wanted the bales to weigh roughly five hundred pounds after ginning.

After the cotton had been picked, the farmers hauled it to the nearest cotton gin. There, the trash and burrs were removed from the cotton and blown out as debris — gin trash. The cottonseed dropped back into their wagon to be brought back to the farm and used for cow feed. Most of the farmers had a cottonseed bin near their cow pen. While the cows were being milked, the farmers fed a bucket of the cottonseed to each cow.

F. M. Snow and his new bride were planning to be working in the fields this fall. He had checked over the cotton sacks looking for holes, several days before he and Maggie were to start picking cotton. One of his sacks was so badly worn that he ripped it up and kept the best pieces to be used to patch the other sacks that were torn from being pulled over the rough ground and cotton stalks. He planned to buy a new sack on his first trip to town.

Snow took the scraps from the torn up sack and folded the soft material into several layers, making protective pads that they could tie over their knees. When their backs got tired from stooping, they would crawl on their knees picking the cotton until their backs were rested, and this process was repeated over and over throughout the long day.

Snow and Maggie learned Ned Gristy's cotton crop was ready to be picked. Snow hitched "Old Joe" to his wagon, and they rode to the Gristy farm, just east of Snow's place and started picking the cotton early one morning in the early part of October. It was still cold when they arrived at the field — the dark, brown soil looked like icing for a chocolate cake. Maggie had made dinner for them before they left for the field — a big pot of beans, bread, biscuit and jelly for them to eat in picnic fashion.

By the end of the first day, the workers, who were paid one-half cent for each pound of cotton they picked, had picked a sufficient amount of cotton for a bale. The next morning Maggie, Snow and the other field hands continued picking the fluffy crop; Ned took the wagon, nearly overflowing, to Gentry's cotton gin. It took most of the day for Ned to get his wagon emptied — there were many other farmers lined up waiting for the same thing; to have their cotton processed.

During the time that Ned was making his trip to the gin and back, Snow and Maggie weighed their sacks full of cotton on scales that were fastened to three poles that were wired together in a teepee like fashion and then they emptied the cotton onto the ground. When the wagon was in the field, the wagon tongue was propped up, and the scales were attached to it.

When the Snows had finished picking cotton for Ned, there was still one more field to be picked — the cotton growing in Snow's own field. Snow had made a good crop this year, and he was counting on making enough money to buy supplies and food staples for the winter. That was his plan, but his cotton would go unpicked.

When the farmers of the community had finished picking their cotton, the school trustees met to set a day for school to commence. Pony Creek School did not take up until the middle October in the fall of 1925. The older children, living on the farms, helped their parents with the harvesting of the crops. As a result, school did not start until most of the crops were gathered.

When all the crops were harvested at last, the first day of school rolled around. Children of all ages met in the one-roomed school house and to help them get acquainted, the teacher asked the students to give a speech that would chronicle some aspect of their home life, sharing a part of their personality with the other students. Mr. Patton, the teacher, found that the speeches, although not elaborate, helped the children establish new friendships.

Aaron Martin was the first; he gave an oration about the harvesting season, and the first crop to be harvested was the corn. He glanced over and saw Missy and began his speech nervously, his mouth feeling as dry as the cotton he had picked a few days earlier. He looked at the other students, knowing that they were just as apprehensive as he was.

"When our corn wuz ready to gather, Daddy hitched up the mules, ole Pete an' Moe, to the wagon an' we headed fer the corn patch. We gathered five rows at a time; the wagon ran over one row an' knocked the stalks over on the ground. Daddy called that row the down row. I had to gather the corn on the down row an' then my sisters gathered two rows on one side an' Daddy gathered two rows on the other side."

Some of the students were gazing out the schoolhouse window, but Aaron continued his speech, his hands were not as clammy and he was gaining more confidence.

"After the wagon wuz filled, we rode the wagon to the barn an' Daddy took a scoop an' threw the corn in the corncrib. Me an' my sisters got to rest while he wuz unloading the corn. We had to watch 'til he wuz finished an' when he drove the wagon away from the barn door, me an' my sisters picked up the ears of corn that fell to the ground an' put 'em in the barn."

"The next crop that got ready was the maize. Me an' uh, my daddy took our pocketknives an' went down 'tween two rows of the maize at a time. We called the maize hi-gear most of the time, but sometimes we still called it maize. Then we cut the hi-gear stalks an' all, an' tied 'em into bundles." Aaron told the class that the shocks of hegira looked like little teepees all over the field.

"We left it in the field until it dried; then Daddy hauled it to the big red barn fer winter feed fer the cows an' horses."

Aaron continued to tell about his farming experiences; although most of his classmates were children of farmers, some of the children had no idea about life on a farm. Aaron told his classmate that working on a farm wasn't entirely unpleasant.

"Sometimes in the summertime, Daddy went to the house an' got a cool watermelon an' took it out under the shade of the tree an' cut it before we went back to the field. There's nothin' better than a juicy watermelon on a hot day."

Aaron looked over at Missy, who was smiling, as he sat down.

Mary Lou Lane was the next speaker. A tenth grader, she had a soft, pleasing voice, and her brown eyes twinkled as she spoke. She helped Mr. Patton with the young students after she finished her own work. She gave a speech that touched on farm life and getting ready for school.

"Before we started gathering our crops this year, Momma took us to town an' bought enough cotton print material to make us two new dresses apiece for school. While she was sewing our dresses, my sisters an' me did the cooking an' dish washing, an' we fed the chickens an' gathered the eggs. We have a large flock of white leghorn chickens. Sometimes we gather the eggs twice a day to keep the chickens from breaking so many of them. Then we put the eggs in a crate an' wash the dirty ones an' get them ready to take to town an' sell on Saturday."

Mary Lou told the class about the other chores that she and her sisters, Nancy and Omah, were required to perform around the farm — she only had one brother.

"We round up our cows an' milk them by hand, an' we take the milk to the house an' strain it into a big tank on the separator. Then somebody has to turn the handle an' the cream goes into one jar an' the milk into another jar. The milk that we don't use at the house is fed to the pigs. We take the cream to town an' sell it when we take the eggs."

After a cheese plant was built in Stephenville, the farmers quit separating the cream from the milk an' started selling the whole milk. Mary Lou told how her family prepared the milk to be sold to the Triangle Cheese Company.

"We strain the milk into ten-gallon milk cans an' a truck comes by an' picks it up, takes it into town an' returns with the empty cans. The milk hauler also delivers ice, so Papa bought us an icebox. It has a big storage compartment on top that holds a hundred-pound block of ice. Underneath is space for food — there is a pipe running from the ice compartment to the bottom of the box an' we have to keep a pan underneath it to catch the ice drippings. It sure is nice to have cool milk an' butter that's firm enough to cut it with a knife."

Mary Lou continued telling about this first day of school, "My sisters, Nancy, Omah an' me got ready an' put on our new print dresses, got our pencils an' tablets an' lunch bucket an' started out for school. We walked all the way. We live about two miles north of here. We walked past where the old school house once stood, past the cemetery, through Mr. Steven's pasture, then into the lane that leads to the main road to school."

"Last year, when we walked home from the school, there was a large bunch of us kids most every day. There would be a lot of talking an' laughing an' teasing an' a little fightin'; but no one was mad, they was just playing. When we got to the Walton's place, they left us, an' then the Lanes, then the Millers, then Woods an' finally, we walked the last stretch by ourselves."

She continued her speech, "Since we have to walk quite a ways, Momma thinks we should be prepared for it. So she bought us some long underwear an' some overshoes that come up to our knees. When we had our first, real blue norther, she'll made us put on that long underwear, then pulled our stockings up over it. I had just about as soon to freeze as to wear them, but if the other kids are wearing them, I guess it won't be so bad."

Frank Miller, Aaron's friend, didn't like making speeches. Listening to Mary Lou, he was reminded about one particularly cold day when he lived in Kansas. This was the topic of his story.

"I remember one day when we lived in Kansas, I had to walk to school through the snow. It had drifted up in places where I had to walk — it was so deep that the snow came up over the tops of my over-shoes. But when I got to school, the room was nice an' warm. There was a big wood burning, pot-bellied stove that had a steel jacket around it."

Elvis Rivers nodded his head; the stove was most likely similar to the one in their schoolhouse.

"After I had warmed up an' before the classes took up, I went outside with some of the other kids to play in the snow an' ice. One man brought his two children to school on horseback. When he saw all of us playing outside, he asked our teacher if he thought the kids should be out in this weather. The teacher told the man that the children had sense enough to know when to get out of the cold."

Frank grinned as he recalled an incident, "But one boy didn't have sense enough to judge how thick the ice was. There was this ole pond down in one corner of the schoolyard. This boy was having a good time sliding on the ice when it broke an' he fell in an' got wet up to his knees. The teacher told him to pull off his shoes, socks an' overalls an' put on his sister's coat an' then the teacher hung his wet clothes an' shoes over the steel jacket of the stove to dry."

Frank was through talking.

The outdoor toilets behind the school building were extremely cold in the winter an' hot during the sultry days of springtime. Many times the students had to kill spiders and fight off the swarming yellow jackets that made a home in the toilets. Mary Stanton remembered an occurrence at the outdoor toilet.

"Mister Patton, you'll remember this. One day, Missy McElroy an' I went to the outhouse an' when we got close to the door, the yellow jackets were flying around an' we were afraid to go in. So we went around behind, thinking no one could see us. But two of the boys had crawled over in the pasture. They saw us an' started laughing an' clapping their hands. We were almost too embarrassed to go back to the schoolhouse, 'cause the kids kept laughing at us."

"You asked what all the laughing was about, but no one would talk, so you called Judith to come talk to you an' she told you what happened."

Mr. Patton remembered the day he quizzed his niece, Judith.

Mary continued, "You rang the bell for everybody to come inside the schoolhouse. I remember you called the two boys an' made them go tear down the yellow jackets nest from the outhouse. They were not laughing when they came back. I think that was a fair punishment."

By the end of the week, the children were weary of being in school. Mr. Patton made an announcement that if all the students finish their lessons by noon on Friday, there would be a spelling bee or ciphering match after lunch — then all the students would be allowed to go home a little early. The children were dismissed early on Friday.

As October marched into November; F. M. Snow, Maggie and her family were at a turning point in their lives, and each day brought them closer to the doomed end. Bernie's carelessness, Annie Olds' questioning and Maggie's incessant chatter was wearing on the man named Snow.

16

THE BLACK DAY

November 27, 1925 . . .

Bernie Connally, a slender, clean-shaven nineteen-year-old boy, combed his dark brown hair straight back. His full, dark eyebrows arched over his piercing green eyes. He had a Roman nose, small lips and noticeable ears. He was as his mother said, "sort of handsome." He was soft spoken and seldom mingled with others his age; in fact, he wasn't comfortable with people of any age.

Although many young boys his age were already out of the house, living on their own, he preferred the closeness of his mother. Bernie and his grandmother, Annie Olds, moved into the ancient house with his mother and stepfather, the newlyweds, twelve days ago. Life in the covered wagon was difficult for them at best. Although by no means perfect, crowding into the small house was a situation by which they could adjust.

Bernie helped Snow around the tiny farm, gathering the timber for firewood, feeding the horses and milking the one cow. Granny Olds helped with the cooking so Maggie and Snow would have more time to work in the field. The newly formed family was among the poorest in Erath County.

Granny Olds and Maggie hung up print flour sacks for window curtains and put a worn cloth on the table. They cleaned the house thoroughly — it was beginning look like a home. Snow and Maggie slept in the south room, the kitchen, while Bernie and his grandmother slept in a room at the back of the house. A fireplace on the north end of the back room barely provided any warmth for the old house.

On this morning, November 27th, Bernie woke up and dressed in a dirty white shirt; a nice shirt at one time, and slipped a pair of old overalls over his long underwear. Maggie had cooked eggs for the family's meager breakfast. He ate a couple of the scrambled eggs and drank a cup of coffee, brewed from coffee grounds of the previous day. Putting on a brown mackinaw coat, he went out behind the house, to help his stepfather, F. M. Snow.

"Mornin' Bernie, it's gonna be a little cool, but I thank it's gonna be a purdy day." Snow was already splitting up firewood.

Bernie nodded his reply. He hitched Snow's old horse to a wagon and began loading it with firewood while Snow was splitting it into usable pieces. Snow was intent on Bernie hauling the firewood into Stephenville with expectations of selling it.

"Take it over on that vacant lot on the south side of the square," Snow told him as he finished splitting the firewood.

Then laying his sharp axe into the wagon, "You might need this in case somebody complains 'bout some pieces bein' too big.".

Mid-morning was cool but pleasant. Maggie and Granny Olds planned a day of washing the clothing for the family. It was the first tolerable day to be outside in several weeks; the weather had been too cold. Maggie found a suitable place behind the house, filled a cast-iron wash pot with rainwater from the cistern and built a fire around it. Granny Olds went to the covered wagon and retrieved two old washtubs that she and Maggie had accumulated over the years.

Feeling her arthritis after years of bending over in the fields, Granny Olds sat down in a cane-bottom chair. While the two women waited for the water to get hot, Maggie put their few pieces of white clothing into one of the tubs and poured cold water over the pieces — covering them. Soon the blazing fire heated the water in the cast-iron pot to boiling.

"Bernie's wearing that old shirt I bought fer him in Waco; its gettin' dirty," Maggie remarked, "I ought to git him to change it 'fore he leaves."

Maggie filled the second tub, mixing boiling water with the cold to make it warm. With a rubbing board and a bar of lye soap, Maggie began the drudgery of loosening the soil and stains from the clothing. She scrubbed the garments on the rubbing board until the pieces looked to be clean, and then dropped them into the pot of boiling water where the bar of lye soap had dissolved.

The white articles of clothing simmered in the hot, boiling water; Granny Olds stirred the garments occasionally with a rounded wooden, punching stick. Maggie began the washing process once again, putting the colored clothing into the tub after she filled it with fresh, cold water.

The women, together, after the clothing had been pre-washed, dumped the water from the tubs and filled them with clean rinse water. Using the punching stick, Maggie took the articles from the hot water and put them into the clean water and rinsed them. Both women wrung the water out of the articles of clothing and put them on the fence to dry. The washday was completed when Maggie used the wash water to mop the floor of the kitchen and to clean the cane-bottom chairs.

Maggie couldn't shake the uneasiness she had felt since awakening — something was wrong. She finished mopping the floor while Granny Olds peeled potatoes to cook for the noon meal. Looking outside the window, Maggie saw that Bernie had almost finished loading the wagon with the firewood and her Mister Snow had walked down to the barn.

"Mister Snow didn't sleep a wink last night; he tossed an' turned an' kept me awake," Maggie told her mother.

"He's full of meanness, girl; I don't know why you can't see that."

"Now, Momma, we ought to be glad we got this place; we ain't had no place to call home since Mister Poston left us," Maggie told her mother, "jest 'member how cold it'd be in that ole wagon. 'Fore long, we'll sell the cotton an' be able to buy some niceties for the house."

Snow had planted cotton earlier in the year, and it was a good crop — just about ready to be picked. A good crop assured there would be enough money to buy the food staples for the winter; flour, meal, salt, sugar and pinto beans. He had fenced off the cotton field to keep the cow out, and he reminded the family daily to keep the gate closed.

Having finished loading the firewood onto the wagon, Bernie went inside the house and got his

.32-caliber pistol his father had given him for his fourteenth birthday. He wanted to take the gun in case he saw any game along the way, and he felt more protected when he had the gun, especially if darkness overtook him; which was likely today; he was starting late.

"Momma, I'm gone," he told his mother, "I love you." She never tired of hearing those words from him and today, they seemed very special — they were the last words she would ever hear him speak.

"Bye, Bye, my darling! You be careful."

She hugged him and kissed his cheek. He went out and climbed onto the old wagon and drove it out of the first gate. She felt an unexplained sadness as she watched him go. She didn't understand why; she wanted to call him back, but she didn't. Calling him back might have changed the outcome of this tragic day — this black day.

Snow, in order to keep his one old milk cow out of his cotton crop, had fenced off the old Jersey that pastured in a meadow at the farm. The cotton patch was in a field nearer to the house through which one had to pass to access the road to Stephenville.

Bernie drove the wagon out to the road and turned toward town. He closed the gate next to the road, never realizing he left the gate open between the cow's pasture and the cotton patch. This oversight would be a fatal one — an oversight that would forever change this small community.

The young boy's mother watched him as he turned, raising his hand and waving to her; his last goodbye. The wagon crept on down the old gravel road, over a small rise in the road, then out of sight.

Later, Snow awoke from a short nap — he was sleepy because he had been restless during the night; it was mid-afternoon. He decided it would be a good day to walk down on the creek and hunt for some squirrels that were numerous in this part of the country or perhaps a wild turkey. The afternoon was still and pleasant, but he noticed that the northern sky was beginning to darken with clouds, and he suspected a norther would be arriving in the afternoon or later in the evening.

The family scarcely had fresh meat this time of year, or in fact, any time of year. Snow thought, "If I can find some squirrels, Maggie can fry 'em an' make some gravy; we will have a fine supper."

But a turkey would be the prize, a peace offering to Granny Olds, who constantly criticized him to Maggie.

Snow took his dogs, Maude and Claude, and Maggie's .22-caliber rifle, the one she inherited from Mr. Poston, and walked south of the house and climbed over a fence onto Ned Gristy's place. He didn't ask Ned for permission to hunt on his creek, but he knew there was no need. The landowners in these parts didn't care if hunters came onto their property because the hunters respected the other person's property, and they would not cause any damage.

Snow walked along the creek bank. He stepped over a broken tree limb as he gazed up into the trees looking for a squirrel that would become the staple of his family's meal tonight. He saw the squirrels had made many nests in the branches of the tall cottonwood trees that lined the creek. He thought that he could poke into a nest and run the mother squirrel out and shoot her, but that would leave the tiny orphans with no way to protect themselves. He knew they would die in a few days for lack of food. He preferred to shoot a squirrel that was away from the nest because the chances were good it would be a male squirrel.

The woods were quiet today — the occasional whistle of a bobwhite and the chattering of the squirrels were about the only sounds breaking the tranquil silence. He walked into a grove of pecan trees and saw several squirrels frolicking through the branches. The crack of his rifle startled them as the shot felled one of the small furry animals from the tall tree. Then the angry echo of another shot reverberated through the once quiet hollow. He picked up the two squirrel carcasses, put them into a leather pouch slung over his left shoulder and walked on.

The nameless creek was about six feet wide and ran all the time because it was fed from springs further up the watershed. He saw perch and minnows swimming around in the ice cold water, and he wished he had brought a fishing pole because perch would be just about as good as a squirrel. He waited as Maude lapped up the cold water — Claude lifted a hind leg and marked a nearby tree.

Walking along, he pondered the past month since he had married Maggie Mae. He had been very lonely in life and had seen hard times. He loved Maggie deeply and thought that his life with her was the stability he had searched for over the years. He wanted to make a home for her, her mother and son; however, he was troubled by her incessant wordiness — talking most of the time, as it seemed to him. But the loneliness was much worse; he vowed to himself that nothing would ever separate them. This vow would be broken in just a few short hours.

He pondered the new members of his household as he strolled along in a peaceful wooded area. He thought Bernie to be a quiet lad who did as he was told. The boy dropped out of school a couple of years ago so he could help support his mother and grandmother. Snow noticed the boy was very possessive of his mother and the only time Snow ever saw any anger in the boy was when he perceived that someone was trying to take advantage of his mother.

Granny Olds was about seventy-five years old. Her yellow tinged, gray hair was always tied in a bun on the back of her head. Her plump features and round face mirrored Maggie, nearly an exact copy

— only older. Her eyesight was failing — she could no longer sew and mend the clothing as she once could. She had a pair of old reading glasses, but they were of little use to her. Her hearing also was failing. She could discern Maggie's high-pitched, loud voice at times, but F. M. Snow's soft mumbling was unintelligible to her.

The grandmother's back ached most of the time. Her back was humped because of rheumatoid arthritis. The years of hard work added to her misery. She and Maggie dipped snuff and shared with Snow on occasion. She kept her snuff in a small, round tin can with a tight fitting lid. When she got ready for a dip, she found a twig and chewed the end to make a soft, pliable brush to dip into her little can. Granny Olds helped with cooking the meals and taking care of the house the best she could. Although she wasn't as vocal as the overbearing Maggie, she was opinionated, and her opinion of F. M. Snow was not good.

"He's got the devil in him girl!"

Daily, she begged Maggie to leave that man, "He's no count. Me, you an' Bernie — we could make it on our own again," she told Maggie again today.

Not that she really believed Snow was all that bad, but she resented sharing Maggie with him. It was the same with Mr. Connally and Mr. Poston.

Snow looked at the sun's position in the sky and determined it to be about four o'clock in the afternoon. He had shot six squirrels and feeling they would be sufficient for a good meal, he began walking up to the house, and as he approached, he saw it — the open gate! The old jersey cow was in the cotton patch! The cow wasn't supposed to be there! The cow looked up at the old man, and then lowered her head to continue devouring the cotton stalks. Snow ran up to the field and saw that the cow had trampled most of the cotton stalks that she had not eaten. He propped the hunting rifle against the fence and laid the squirrels down and picked up a tree branch from the ground.

"GET OUT OF HERE!" He yelled with all his might, hammering the fence with the tree limb. "Shoo, get out of here you blasted cow! Look at this durn mess! You sum-bitch!"

He felt rage take him over instantly — his trembling voice screamed. "Maggie Mae, git out here an' help me git this danged cow out of my cotton! Woman, get out here! Now!"

Maggie was putting the last piece of clean clothing into a cedar chest when she was startled by footsteps behind her. She turned to see Snow with the tree branch raised high in the air coming toward her. Thinking he was going to strike her with it, she ducked down.

"Mister Snow, what's wrong?"

"You've let the danged cow get into my cotton; that's what's wrong," he screamed. "What in the heck have y'all been doing in there? Why ain't ya been payin' attention? Been in there gabbin' with yore ma again, I 'spect. Come help me drive this dang cow out of the field! Damn it! Damn it! Damn it!"

Snow, with Maggie following along behind, went outside to the field where the brown jersey was still eating and demolishing the cotton stalks. Snow pointed to the left and yelled, "Git over there an' start helpin' me!"

Maggie threw up her hands, waving them in the air. Snow, cursing and screaming, picked up a small limb and began whipping the old cow and in a short time, they managed to drive her out of the field.

Snow walked around in the field with a blank stare examining the damaged cotton crop. He saw that there was nothing that could be salvaged.

"Come on, let's go. There's nothin' we kin do here. It's all ruint," he muttered.

As they walked back to the house, Snow again inquired, "Why didn't you see that the gate wuz not closed? Why didn't you see that the cow wuz in my cotton? Why?"

Maggie told him she was busy inside the house taking care of the chores, ironing the clothes, when in reality — she knew she had been asleep. Her mother, if she wasn't napping, could neither see nor hear well enough to have noticed the old Jersey cow wandering through the cotton field; causing the deadly destruction.

"Mister Snow, now don't get so upset." She looked into his glaring eyes. "Jest calm down now."

"Look, woman, look at this field, its ruint." His hand made a sweeping motion in the direction of the fallen cotton. "Who left the dad-blamed gate open?"

"I guess Bernie fergot to close it when he left for town."

"Well, we've lost our cotton! Jest how do you thank we are going to be able to get by this winter without the money we could of got from the cotton?"

Snow' red face was distorted by an all-consuming rage, his nostrils were flaring, and his mouth was quivering and drooling as he shook his tightly closed fists.

"I don't know how, please calm down." She had seen Snow's anger before when Maude, his dog, had caught one of the neighbor's chickens. The neighbor confronted Snow and told him that he would kill the dog the next time. Snow's anger beamed from his face when he told the man that he, too, would die if he laid a hand to the dog. The neighbor left, believing Snow would keep his word.

"Yeah, you don't know — you don't know a durn thang do you, 'cept talking. You can shore do plenty of that!" Snow's eyes, closing into slits, revealed the explosive fury boiling up inside him. His voice broke and quivered as he yelled.

Becoming more fearful, Maggie crept her way toward her .22-caliber rifle that was still leaning on the fence. She looked back at the old house for her mother, but the old woman was nowhere in sight. She wished that Bernie was home and even more, she wished he had not chosen to take the wood to town today. She wondered why he failed to close the gate, but most of all; she wondered why she had not noticed it.

"Why the heck didn't that boy close the dang gate? I told y'all to watch it an' keep it closed. I told ya an' told ya!" Snow yelled, "Wuz that too much to expect? All that kid ever does is jest cause me misery! Got no responsibility!"

"I don't know why he didn't shut it, maybe he . . ."

"Maybe he, maybe he — yore always taking up fer him!"

Maggie backed slowly, inching toward her rifle. Snow, thinking that Maggie might shoot him, yelled, "Get away from that blasted gun, you bitch!"

"I've got to protect myself," he thought, "She's gonna git 'er gun an' kill me!"

Was he really afraid of her? Perhaps, or maybe it was just his rage that persuaded him to escalate his assault. He picked up a two-by-four piece of wood, about four feet long.

"Don't you touch that gun, Maggie Mae, I'm warning ya! I'll knock yore blooming head off."

"Mister Snow, you shan't be talking to me like that, I'm a lady an' you ain't gonna talk to me in that manner. You hear me! Don't ya git no closer to me."

She reached down, touching the rifle, trying to get a hold on it, but she was too shaken — she dropped the gun. Snow ran toward her with the timber of wood, yelling, screaming, and cursing. Again, bending down to get a hold of the rifle, Maggie turned away from Snow. With all his strength, the angry man raised the timber and struck her at the base of her skull.

The blow, a dull, hollow thud, knocked the woman to the ground instantly, face-first. She lay there for a few seconds — stunned — she couldn't see anything, and there was an unrecognized ringing in her head. The pain, the throbbing — uncontrollable shaking. She lifted her head; her vision cleared a bit — she staggered up and then fell back down to the firm earth. Up again, she staggered toward the rifle, blood dripping out of her nose and mouth. Snow backed away toward his wagon, shocked that she was able to get back up.

"Oh, Maggie, what have I done?" His anger changed to concern. "Maggie, I'm so sorry."

Then Maggie turned away from him, stumbling toward the house, leaving the rifle where it lay.

"I've got to git back to the house; I got to git my momma, she'll help me — you hear me!" Maggie cried faintly.

Weakness overtook her, and she fell on the ground, but managing to get up again, she pulled herself up onto the porch.

"Mister Snow, you'll pay for this. We's leavin' you, all of us, an' we's leavin' today, jest as soon as Bernie gits back here."

She opened the door and went inside the place she had come to know as home. She felt faint, dizzy as the bright crimson blood from her nose trickled down — staining her dress. She remembered the time, that terrible time, long years ago when her father had beaten her; she had vowed to herself that it wouldn't happen again. Two of her husbands had paid the consequences — The man she called Mr. Snow was much smaller.

Snow, still outside the house, remembered the .32-caliber pistol that Bernie always kept near his bed. Not realizing that Bernie had taken the gun to town with him, Snow walked to his wagon and got his Winchester rifle. He would be ready to defend himself. This horrible day was running through his mind like a nightmare that he wanted to bring to an end.

"What have I done? Why can't I control myself? I've got to go calm Maggie."

Snow walked toward the house watching the front door for any sign of movement; his rifle held up — ready. Maggie opened the front door of the house holding a butcher knife in one hand and the door facing in the other. She staggered out onto the porch. Raising the knife, she ambled toward the man holding the rifle. One shot rang out. The bullet from Snow's rifle hit Maggie in the breast, through her heart; she clutched her chest and fell to the floor of the porch. Snow walked up to her and saw blood pouring from her mouth and heard a gurgling in her throat. She took two or three labored breaths then she was still, her eyes wide open, staring at her slayer — her husband.

Then, thinking about the old woman inside the house, his mother-in-law, Snow walked out to his wagon and picked up his razor-sharp axe, then back to the house. He knew that his Maggie was dead by his own hand and now, the old woman must die.

"There's no other way," he thought.

Snow opened the door and saw her, sitting with her back to him. She was humming and sitting in a rocking chair, one of her few pieces of furniture — unaware that he was there.

She had not heard the awful sounds outside. Maggie's killer slowly walked up behind her. It only took one blow to the back of her head. Then a chopping, hacking to the back of her neck, again and again until her head fell to the floor, rolling off to the right side of her feet. The force of Snow's blows caused the feeble old body to sink slowly out of the chair.

Snow found an old rag and wiped the blood off his axe, and then he walked quietly to his wagon and put the axe down by the seat. He calmly walked up to the porch and dragged Maggie's stilled, bleeding body into the house and laid the body of his wife beside her mother. Blood, the crimson life fluid, was splattered all over the room, puddling on the floor and trickling down the wall.

Snow's calmness turned into horror as he stared at the two bodies lying on the floor. Granny Old's severed head, still laying beside the rocking chair, had been horribly disfigured by the impact of the killer's axe. Maggie's body was lying on the floor in a pool of her own blood. The sickening smell of death flooded the room — Snow ran outside and began to vomit. His heart rate was accelerating; he felt as though he was smothering, sweating, trembling, shaking — he sat on the ground.

Then he remembered, Bernie was gone — he realized his next quandary. The old woman and Maggie were dead. The boy would have to die. He couldn't let the boy come home and discover the dead bodies of his mother and grandmother.

"There's no other way."

17

THE BLACK NIGHT

Snow scarcely noticed that nightfall was almost upon him, that the fluttering eyes of death were watching from a distance. His attention was elsewhere, "I'm goin' to town after that blamed kid!"

Saddling "Old Joe," he rode out the gate turning the old horse toward town — he was shivering, looking back at all the damage and destruction that had occurred during the afternoon, and once again, he began to heave, vomiting. He was only thinking about the task facing him; he had to find the boy and bring him home to be with his mother and grandmother.

"They need to be together at a time like this. Giddy up! Come on ya danged ole horse, let's go," the whip stung the horse's rump, "oh, what was I thanking — I've done it now!"

"Thangs'll be fine as soon as they're all together," Snow whispered to himself, whipping the horse to make him trot faster.

"That boy should of closed the gate an' none uh this would of happened." He looked back at the gate that he had just closed. "That's all I asked of 'em, jest keep the blamed gate closed."

The road from Snow's house ran past several farmhouses before getting to the main road — the route from Stephenville to Hico. He saw that lamps were burning in these homes — the families were most likely sitting down to eat a warm supper. He had not eaten — he had to get the boy first.

The dark clouds from the cold front were floating, rolling nearer, and he felt the wind changing directions; puffing from the north, suddenly becoming much cooler. Snow had traveled on the main road, but for a short time, when he came upon the boy and the wagon, just north of the intersection of two roads. Snow directed "Old Joe" toward Bernie; returning home with his empty wagon.

"Boy, come on, your ma's sick an' needs you at the house." He dismounted his horse and tied it to the back of the wagon. Climbing up onto the wagon, he sat down beside Bernie.

"What's wrong with 'er? Why'd you come to meet me out here for?" Bernie asked, his voice showing his concern.

"She's-uh-uh, got a bad headache; she's took real sick. I thank maybe she's coming down with the flu or sump'um. She wanted me to brang you home as soon as I could."

Bernie nervously slapped the reins against the old horse's neck, urging the horse to pick up its slow pace. The ride back to the house was somber, without speaking. This was not unusual because Bernie and Snow rarely talked to each other — Bernie resented the man because he was not his father and Snow just didn't like him. The boy reminded Snow of the person he would never be; quiet and even-tempered.

The wind, now moaning out of the north, was suddenly becoming colder as it howled through the leafless trees. The crescent moon, glimmering between the branches, watched the man and boy down below.

Reaching the Snow farm, the boy stopped the wagon and Snow, taking his rifle with him, got off the wagon to open the gate. The boy guided the wagon though the opening in the fence and past Snow, who was raising his rifle, aiming it at Bernie's back.

"Hey, boy!" Bernie turned and looked at his step-father, putting his hand on his pistol.

"What?"

"You left the durn gate wide open when you left an' the old brown cow has ruint the cotton!"

"No, sir, I closed it. I'm sure of it."

"Yer ma said you left it down, an' I thank you did, 'cause you don't pay no 'tention to nothin'."

"Where's Ma? She'll tell ya." Bernie thought he had closed the gate, but now, he wasn't that sure.

Snow, still pointing the rifle at Bernie, "She in the house, but she can't help you now; this is 'tween me an' you."

Bernie turned back and whipped the horse. The wagon began inching frontward, toward the house, toward his mother. Fear gripped him; he would be safe with her. He always had been.

The gunshot from behind startled him. He didn't feel the pain, just a sharp jolt to his backside, pressing him forward. Looking down at his chest, he saw the red blood, his blood, oozing out from under his coat; he felt its warmth on his stomach. Laboring to breathe, he coughed, blood exploding from his mouth — his life was flowing away.

No pain, darkness swept over him — sounds were no longer making any sense to him, sounds of another gunshot, but not so loud — he didn't feel the bullet piercing his back. He could see a light; a bright light in the darkness — wait, now he could hear it; his mother calling out to him. There she was in the bright light, and his father was standing there too, motioning him to follow.

The two shots rang out, echoing through the woods, further and further into the deepness — then it was silent; too quiet. The boy fell forward, looking back at his stepfather, his eyes questioning the man holding the rifle. Why? Fatally wounded, his eyes remained unclosed. Bernie slumped down into the seat of the wagon.

"None uh this would uh happened if you'd closed that gate — none uh this."

Snow walked up to the wagon, shaking the boy's limp, motionless body. He saw the river of blood, draining from Bernie's wounds, trickling over the side of the wagon — down onto the hard ground. Bernie was dead. He pulled the lifeless, bleeding corpse into the bed of the wagon. Climbing up on the wagon seat, he put his rifle down and took the horse's reins. He could hear the mournful howl of coyotes in the distance, the occasional screech of an owl and saw the eerie glow coming forth from the sinking moon; suddenly, it appeared red as if tainted with blood — Bernie's blood.

"I must be mad," he thought, "I wuz a hoping this would turn out different. Now, what will your ma thank? How am I 'sposed to 'splain it to her."

As the wagon rocked over the rocky road, he kept looking back at Bernie's corpse, knowing he had to dispose of the boy's body. But where?

He turned the wagon back out the gate, eastward until he started getting closer to the settlement of Duffau. Then turning back, he went to the road that leads to Bluff Dale, a little town thirteen miles northeast of his farm. In the vicinity of Bluff Dale, the hills and mountains were sparsely populated, and Snow thought he could travel to this locale without being discovered. He would find a suitable place to dispose of the body of the boy whose life he had taken — a hiding place in the remote area.

"He wasn't a bad boy. Yes he wuz — he didn't close the gate. They wuz gonna kill me, I know they wuz. He left that gate open jest to make me mad. That's it. They had it all planned out. That's why he took his pistol. But it didn't work out fer 'em. They didn't git ole Snow."

Snow rocked back and forth as the wagon rolled over the ruts in the road. He hunkered in the wagon seat, holding his head down so that his hat would partially block the blustering wind. He pulled his coat up more tightly around his neck to keep the cold from stinging his neck.

"Gee-haw," the somber figure yelled at the horse, "come on, gee-haw, let's go."

The old wagon wheels groaned mournfully, turning slowly below the man and his gruesome cargo. "Oh, what wuz I thanking?"

"I've got to figure out what I can do with Maggie an' her momma — something's got to be done. Maybe they all should be together. I had to do it; this here boy would of shot me. I know he would of. The ole woman was causing trouble 'tween me an' Maggie Mae — just like the last time."

"I'd have me a good woman now if it hadn't uh been fer that ole boy down in San Saba. I kin still hear 'em laughin' at me, him an' his ma. Well, they never caught me then an' they won't this time. I'm too smart fer 'em. ole Snow kin take up fer his self."

After Snow was traveling toward Cedar Mountain — he judged it to be past midnight, he heard dogs barking as he trudged up the road. He saw that someone was opening a front door on the house he had just passed about a quarter of a mile back. A man stepped out onto the porch and looked his direction.

"I see ya lookin' at me but yore too fer away to git a good look. I ain't gonna worry 'bout ya."

Snow pulled his hat down and continued on his journey to a non-determined destination. He traveled another couple of miles onto Cedar Mountain. The cold north wind had chilled him to the bone and he wished for the comfort of his warm bed. He would not see sleep this dark night. He looked at his pocket watch; it was one thirty in the morning.

The moon, low in the clearing western sky, highlighted the wagon's shadowy silhouette. Snow heard the gusty wind whistling through the cedar trees,

casting their ghostly shadows over the roadway; barely passable in the old wagon.

"This here'll be a good place."

Snow stopped on the top of a hill, slowly got off
the wagon and looked around — out into the darkness. He thought that someone was watching him,
just as they had been in San Saba County.

"What is that over there? Hey! I know you're
over there!" He shot a couple of rounds into the
air. "I hear ya talking over there. Why did you foller
me out here?" Was that the wind calling his name?
Sno-o-o-ow.

He realized that no one was there — it was just
his imagination. He walked around to the back of
the wagon and with some effort, pulled the boy's
body out. The body had stiffened and fell onto the
hard ground with a deadened timbre.

"I've got to make sure that if somebody finds
him, they won't know who he is."

Snow dragged the cold, stiff corpse under a fence
and away from the road finally stopping under a
gnarled mesquite tree. Snow couldn't drag the boy's
body any further; he had expended all his energy.
Snow went back to the wagon and found a burlap bag.

"Yeah, this tow sack'll do."

He walked back to the body, removing all of
Bernie's clothing except for his long handled underwear; he stuffed the mackinaw coat and shirt into the
burlap bag. Then he trudged back to the wagon and

retrieved his sharp axe and walked up to the cold corpse, his stepson, lying on the ground.

"I guess I should say some words over him now … it's got to be done."

Snow raised the sharp axe over his head. One sharp blow, the sickening sounds of crushing bone — another, and then another forceful blow to the back of the boy's neck, severing the head completely from the boy's torso. Blood, oozing, flowed forth now. Using his old pocketknife, in a sawing motion, he cut the remaining sinews of flesh free of the boy's body. Showing no remorse; he could have just as easily been butchering a hog, instead of dismembering the body of his stepson.

"There, you an' yore grandma are the cause of my misery — I'm gonna lose everything on account of you two! May you rest in peace 'til the buzzards pick your bones clean, you little sum-bitch."

Snow, picking up the detached head by the boy's hair, put it into the burlap bag with Bernie's clothing and slung it into the back of the wagon. A dull thud echoed through the night as the severed head fell onto the wagon bed and rolled out of the sack. Snow looked at the head and saw its non-blinking eyes were open and staring straight at him.

"No, No! Yore dead. You can't touch me — no, leave me alone. I ain't listenin' to ya."

The murderer put the head back into the sack, wiped the sticky substance, Bernie's blood, off his hands with Bernie's shirt then returned it into the bag with the rest of the clothing. Snow pulled himself up onto the wagon, took the reins and began his solitary journey home.

The wind, now screaming like a ghostly spirit, cut through the driver of the blood stained wagon, making him shiver uncontrollably. It was dark now, real dark, pitch black. A lone wolf was howling somewhere down the forlorn mountainside, and each dark shadow cast by his dim lantern seemed to be watching him as he continued his gruesome undertaking — going home.

Snow, feeling the effects of the day and hours without sleep gradually drifted out of reality, "I've got to get back an' take care of Maggie. I know she's wondering what happened — I had to leave 'er to get the boy — she'll understand. Her ma's with 'er, so she ain't alone."

Then reality of his plight was now before him.

"I've gotta thank an' work all this out. If somebody finds the boy's body, they'll never know who it is. I've jest gotta thank up some good story to tell 'em. Maggie blamed it on the Niggers; I can too, but I don't believe a word of what she told me, not after today. I gotta get me some sleep."

"This ole horse is shore gettin' tard. It's gonna take me the rest of the night to git back to the house where Maggie is waitin'. It shore is cold an' I bet the fire's gone out by now. Maggie an' her ma is shore gonna be cold 'til I get there. That's it; I'll start a good fire, there in the fireplace and get down to business. But first, I'm gonna cook me some eggs to eat. I 'spect Maggie an' 'er ma kin wait."

Snow faded back into the moment realizing he still had the head of the murdered boy in the burlap bag. He looked back at the tow sack, glistening with the blood that had oozed out, and he contemplated on another dilemma —disposing of the bag holding the boy's head. Then he saw it; an abandoned cellar, partially caved in. "This will be a good place," he thought.

Snow stopped the horse, got out of the wagon and picked up the bag. Walking toward the abandoned cellar, he threw the tow sack into the bowels of the cellar — not noticing that the bag, swinging in the darkness, had gotten hung on a jutting piece timber.

18

THE FOLLOWING DAYS

The populace of Erath County went about their dealings as usual on this Saturday morning, unaware of the unspeakable that had taken place on the Snow farm. Why shouldn't they? The inhabitants of Erath County believed they were untouched by the crimes that plagued the larger cities. Neighbors helped their fellow neighbors. They shared food with ones that might be hungry. They helped with doing odd jobs and loaned their tools. Everyone trusted their neighbors and strangers were welcomed.

Ned Gristy, waking at five o'clock this cold morning as he always did, put logs into the fireplace, and soon, he had a roaring, warming fire. The cook stove was next. He had a morning routine — lighting the coal oil lamps, starting the fires in the fireplace and cook stove, replenishing the firewood supply and then going outside to the outdoor toilet — the outhouse.

Ned wasn't aware of the horrifying events that occurred at the Snow farm yesterday. Not yet. Looking over toward Snow's house, and seeing billowing smoke rising from the chimney, he thought, "Snow must of really been cold 'cause he's shore got a big fire a goin' over there."

He had gotten acquainted with his neighbors, F. M. Snow and his wife, Maggie and Snow's stepson, Bernie Connally when they picked cotton for him earlier this fall. Even though Snow always seemed cordial, he wasn't particularly friendly. Ned always felt uneasy around him; an uneasiness brought about by Snow's disposition and the fact he always kept his rifle handy. The Gristy grandchildren, while visiting, evidently sensed something sinister about the man because they would be found hiding under the bed if by chance Snow entered the Gristy's home — the Gristy's didn't give it much thought until later.

Ned, on occasion, had watched Snow ride his old horse, "Old Joe." Snow looked like old satan himself, a wild man, riding the horse, if that was what it could be called — he yelled, screaming and beating the horse until the aged horse was completely worn down.

Ned's wife, Ida Gristy, staying in the warmth of her bed until the chill was out of the house, got up to cook their breakfast. She was the perfect match for her husband — a little woman that put her hair up in a bun on the back of her head; the style of that period of time. She kept her glasses on top of her head until she needed them to read or when she was doing other close work such as piecing together the quilt she was making for of her grandchildren.

She hung the quilting frames in a spare room, just off the kitchen. Other ladies of the community, friends, often congregated at her house for a quilting get-together. The ladies had made quilt pieces for her — a friendship quilt would be her next project. A girlish design, wearing a bonnet, commonly referred to as a "Little Dutch Girl Quilt," was the pattern used by the piece maker. Each contributor would stitch their signature — Bessie Swanzy, Grandma Keller, Flora Sikes and many others — a signature of pride on the piece they sewed.

Ida Gristy, being neighborly, took bread and deserts that she baked to the Snows several times after Snow and Maggie were married. Baking came easy to her, and she took pleasure in sharing her wares with her neighbors. She often commented to her husband that Snow was quiet, even to the point of being shy. To her amazement, but very seldom, the mysterious man would tell a joke. She felt ill at ease whenever she looked into his face; his eyes — she perceived something evil. It was just something she felt, but she rarely mentioned it to her husband or anyone.

She cut slices of home-cured ham that Ned brought into the house last night from a shed he called a smokehouse. Putting the sliced ham into a cast-iron skillet, she set it on an already hot stove. Beginning to sizzle in the hot skillet, various shades of blue and green tinted the home-cured meat as it fried. Ida used the dripping that fried out of the ham, mixed with boiling-hot coffee, to make red-eye gravy when hominy grits were on the breakfast menu.

Ned came back into the house after taking care of his morning call from nature. He poured water out of a jar into a coffee pot, put in the coffee and put it on the hot stove. While he was waiting for the coffee to perk, he continued his morning routine. He took his well-worn Bible from the shelf and began reading in the book of Samuel — where Saul had requested the services of a witch.

After he had finished reading God's Word, he walked over to the window, wiped the condensation off and looked outside; toward Snow's farm.

"I thank I heard a wagon over at Snow's this morning before I got up," Ned told his wife, "An' he's got a big fire goin', reckon what he's up to?"

"I haven't the foggiest notion. T'wouldn't surprise me a bit if he was up to no good. Mrs. Fulbright told me she bet he was in with 'em moonshiners down by Glen Rose. Looks like the laws would put a stop that foolishness."

Prohibition, in effect throughout the nation and the demand for liquor, created a profitable opportunity for the backwoods populace of eastern Erath County and the adjoining county — Somervell. The tall cedar trees on the rocky, snaky mountains provided an excellent camouflage for their numerous stills. It was wise to stay out of that area at nighttime. Traveling alone in the daylight often brought a harsh warning from an armed, bearded mountain man, "Stay on the traveled path and keep on moving!"

The Federal Prohibition Enforcement Officers made an early morning raid on a mountain shack a couple of months ago in the eastern part of Erath County. The officers found two, sixty-gallon stills and about fifteen hundred gallons of corn-and-raisin mash. The officials destroyed all the mash and took the stills to prohibition headquarters in Fort Worth. They found scores of bottles and jars in the floor of the shack; waiting to be filled with the intoxicating moonshine. When the police officers conducted the raid, they found no one in the shack, so no arrests were made — although the stills were still warm. The talk was that Virgil McElroy and a Mexican, Jose Ortega, departed just before the officers arrived and conducted the raid.

Ned doubted that Snow associated with the brewers of white lightening — he didn't think Snow had the intelligence, but who was to say. He just didn't know much about his strange neighbor — he heard he had come to the area from Palo Pinto County. All Ned knew for certain was that Snow showed up a little over a year ago in an old wagon pulled by two pitiful old horses. He rented a farm from a family estate — adjacent to Ned. It wasn't much of a farm, seventeen acres, an old house nearly past inhabiting and a few unstable out buildings.

Snow had moved all his worldly processions to the farm in an old wagon a few months ago. Inside the wagon were what the man called his things — a rifle, a double-bladed axe, a couple of hound dogs, some worn out furniture and a coal oil stove. Behind the wagon was another poor horse with a worn-out saddle on his back, and one old Jersey cow.

Ned walked to the small farm to welcome his new neighbor several days after he moved into the neglected house. Snow told Ned that he was going to make a crop and cut a little wood. Snow made mention that he had lived in San Saba County at one time — leaving because the black men were getting all the work in the fields.

"I ain't gonna work along beside them," Snow told Ned, "I showed one ole boy that got in my way, who was boss."

Snow, shaking his fist, "He won't ever talk to a white man like that again."

Ned saw that Snow kept a coal oil lamp burning almost every night, and he thought it was extremely curious. Asking Snow about the night-light, he was told to mind his own affairs, which made Ned wonder even more about the mystifying man. Perhaps Snow merely couldn't see well in the dark but Ned suspected that his neighbor feared something in the darkness of the night — something more menacing than he could ever imagine.

When he wasn't working and when the weather was warm and fitting, Snow spent his hours at home sitting on the front porch of his old house in one of his cane-bottom chairs; his dogs beside him. In cooler weather, he stayed in front of the fireplace, sitting there all alone.

Snow's lifestyle had been changed a little over a month ago. Ned saw that the man who seemed to be a loner had taken a wife — not only did he have a new bride, Snow moved his mother-in-law and stepson into the rundown house.

Ida Gristy finished frying the ham, cracked four eggs and put them into the hot cast-iron skillet, frying them in the grease that cooked out of the ham. Today, she didn't make the red-eye gravy — she didn't cook grits. The aroma of the perking coffee filled the room and blended with the freshly cooked ham and eggs that were steaming on the table. Ned set the table for his wife while she took hot biscuits from the wood-burning oven. The couple, sitting down to eat their country breakfast, finished eating long before the winter sun came up.

Dawn broke as quietly as a sleeping baby. He was glad that the weather had cleared after the onset of a cold front. The wind had stilled; the cloudless sky was uncommonly blue and the brisk air was refreshing. It was going to be a good day.

Ned went out to tend to his livestock after he finished breakfast. Throwing hay out for his cattle, he noticed that the smoke was still boiling up from Snow's chimney, more smoke than usual. "I guess it's sure cold in his old house."

Luke Johnson, Ned's neighbor, up early this morning, gave little thought to the smoke puffing from Snow's chimney as he walked to his barn to begin his chore of milking. Living farther away from the Snow farm, he had not heard Snow's early morning return from Cedar Mountain.

Johnson, his wife and two daughters, just as others in the area, didn't know much about F. M. Snow, but they found him to be strange — unfriendly. A few days after Snow moved into the old house, Johnson went to introduce himself to Snow and to welcome the old man. Snow, looked up, then continued whittling on an old stick, then ignoring Johnson's presence, he got up and went inside his shack without says a word, leaving Johnson outside.

Bernie Connally, with the intentions of courting Johnson's oldest daughter, Alva, came to the house during the early part of November and gently knocked on the front door. Alva came to the door — Bernie had hardly made his introduction when the stepfather, Snow, came running up the lane, screaming.

"Git yore self back to the house, an' don't ever let me catch ya over here agin."

The Johnsons were a poor family who moved to the Selden area ten years ago. Although they didn't have much in the way of money, they resided in a well-kept farmhouse, and they had sufficient furnishings. Mrs. Johnson made all the family garments on her *Singer* sewing machine that she inherited from a wealthy aunt. She mended socks and sewed patches over torn holes in their clothes. The family always appeared neatly dressed. Clothing made from feed and flour sacks which came in various prints and patterns were fashioned into clothing by Mrs. Johnson's skillful hands.

Like Snow, Johnson paid rent to the land owner by sharing a portion of the crops that they raised on the farm. This system worked well; the tenants and landowners shared the risks of the harvest as well as any profit produced on the rented land. The Johnsons grew a variety of crops in the fields, vegetables in the garden and fruit in an orchard.

Johnson finished his milking chore and went to his warm house where his wife, had cooked a country breakfast of eggs, biscuits and gravy. Johnson mentioned to his wife that he had heard gunshots toward the Snow farm yesterday, just before nightfall. Again, he gave this little thought.

The Rivers family, up early, was making preparations for hog killing day. Elvis recalled the events of the night before; the hunting trip with his old dog, Hootus, and Aaron Martin. He wondered again about the strange happenings of the night, the gunshots, the noise that sounded like a wagon, the squeaking windmill.

"Oh well," he thought, "it was jest a weird night."

He forgot all about it when he heard his mother call him for breakfast. He was hungry; he sat down at the kitchen table and looked out the window, seeing the men folk who were already assembled.

"Aren't you going to that party at Mary Stanton's house tonight?" Mrs. Rivers asked.

"No ma'am, that ain't fer a couple of weeks yet, on December tenth."

"Well, I was wrong about that. I guess I was thinking about that Saturday night dance at the Millers."

"Yeah, me an' Aaron probably won't go to that."

Aaron woke up early, and as usual, he was thinking about Missy. He pictured her in his mind; he could see her smile, hear her funny little giggle. He could imagine them walking down by the river — hand and hand. "Why couldn't it be," he thought.

He dressed. He knew that this was a hog-killing day at the Rivers' farm, and there would be fresh pork to eat. He wasn't going to miss out on that!

Ned finished his morning chores around the farm. He changed clothes and was ready to leave for town a little after eight o'clock.

"I'm going into Stephenville today — make me out a list of what all ya need me to git for ya," Ned told his wife. "I 'spect I'll be back here 'fore noon if the old car makes it."

He started the old Ford car and drove out of the driveway and turned west, toward town.

He saw F. M. Snow and Luke Johnson standing out by the mailbox. Not being in any hurry, he stopped to visit with the two men. One of the men carried a dark secret.

19

THE PARTY

December 9, 1925 . . .

Aaron Martin sat alone in his room, just after dark, reading the letter once more, just as he had dozens of times before. A letter from Missy, a letter she had written last August, a couple of weeks after the kiss:

> "Dear Aaron,
> I have heard that some people think that a girl as young as I am cannot know about love. Though I've only been with you several times since we met, I can truly say that I love you. I

know what love is, and this is love. I
will always be yours, and I will never
forsake you or hurt you. If you love me
as I love you, I beg you to wait for me.

Love Missy"

For the first time in his young life, he had feelings
that he couldn't understand. Day and night, his
thoughts were of Missy — the tenderness of her kisses, the scent of her hair and the happiness of her
little giggle.

Missy lived in Stephenville now. Her grandparents moved into town after her grandfather could no
longer take care of the cattle at his farm. Aaron, in
the twelfth grade at Pony Creek this year, couldn't
understand the change he had seen in Missy. She
had become standoffish and seemed to avoid him;
ignoring him when others were around.

Aaron saw her several times after he received the
letter — the letter declaring her love for him. He was
with her after church services a few days after their
first kiss. She was still his Missy, happy and loving —
holding his hand, sweet, gentle kisses and the words
she said, "I love you."

He saw her once more at Willie Stanton's house;
she was more reserved, but still Aaron believed he
had found true love.

Then came the night that she said goodbye. The night his dreams were shattered. It was still August, that night seemed so long ago now; that night it happened. Aaron had worked at the store that day, and on his way home, walking down the road, he saw them together. Missy and her old beau, Richard Fagan, were in front of Willie Stanton's house, holding hands, and Missy was laughing. Richard was known for his wild ways, drinking and fighting; the things Missy told Aaron she detested.

Sleep didn't come for several nights after that terrible night; he would see Missy and Richard together in his dreams. He remembered what Missy told him that night; she would see anyone she wanted — she wanted to have some fun. He wasn't hungry; his parents noticed that he didn't want to talk about anything. Aaron loved his parents but this matter, a heartache; he didn't feel comfortable discussing it with them. How could they understand his feelings? His hurt? His mother and father were happily married. He never saw them exchange even a cross word. They wouldn't understand his loss.

The hot days of August drifted by like the lazy white clouds and all too soon it was September, then October. Missy's bubbling personality made her popular in school, and she started dating others, most of them were, in Aaron's opinion, not deserving of her. Missy's indifference crushed Aaron. It was as though the night of the kiss never happened. How could she write such a letter declaring her love for him, only to cast him aside? He never recognized the influence of having Virgil McElroy as a father. Missy, although she wasn't aware of it, was in search of a boy that was just like her father; someone with no responsibility, someone who would leave her. She tried to find love with many boys, and she tried to find love with many older men — each relationship would become unfulfilling and would end in a short time.

Still, Aaron didn't understand. He read the letter over and over — surely she truly loved him at the time, or she wouldn't have written the letter to him. Or, was she too young to know about life and love? Sally Lowe, whose true motive was to put more of a wedge between Missy and Aaron told him, "Missy always wants a boy who she can't get or one who don't like her."

If her newest suitor began showing more than a passing interest, she would end the relationship and pursue someone else and with her charming personality; it wouldn't be long before she had another "victim" in her snare.

Aaron and Willie Stanton drove into Stephenville on several occasions. Aaron wanted to see Missy; he wanted to talk to her. He wanted to feel the warmth of her lips again. Willie gave him moral support, but Aaron believed that if Cecil Ray were still around, he would be more likely to help him have another chance to be with Missy.

Cecil Ray had left suddenly one day without telling anyone goodbye. Was it because he witnessed Louis Savage's death? Or was it because of some unknown secret? No one knew the reason for his hasty departure. Those last few days he was in town, he acted differently; he no longer joked or tried to make the other kids laugh. He looked as though he was carrying a huge burden that plunged him down into deep darkness.

"I can't figure out why Cecil Ray jest up an' left that day," Aaron told Willie as they rode around Stephenville one night a couple of weeks ago. "He shore looked at me funny, like he'd seen a ghost or sump'um,"

That night, the boys had driven by Missy's grandparents' house several times. Aaron was in hopes of getting to see her. But it was not to be, and Aaron couldn't build up the courage to stop by the house where she lived. He did build up the courage to leave a note, a poem, in her mailbox — a note that made no sense to anyone but him — and maybe to her:

> "There's the house where you live,
> Gonna pass it one more time,
> But I guess you're not home

'Cause I've lost what once was mine.

Been trying hard to pretend
that I no longer care,
But just seeing you is
more than I can bear.

Knowing I can't be with you,
I feel so all alone,
And I just can't forget,
the only love I've ever known.

Aaron"

December 10, 1925 . . .

Mary Stanton lived in the small town of Selden — located just over a mile west of the Snow farm. Tonight, she was hosting a party at her house. Mary, Willie Stanton's cousin, had short hair the color of the midnight sky. Long, brown eyelashes framed her chocolate eyes, and a tiny birthmark on her right cheek accented her flawless olive complexion.

Aaron and Elvis were planning to go to the party. Aaron would try to have a good time, but he knew that the one he wanted, Missy, would be out with someone else.

They had set out animal traps the day before, and before going to Mary's party, they needed check their traps. That was the plan on this moon-lit night.

Mary's best girlfriend, Mattie, would be at the party. Mattie and Aaron were in the same grade. Mattie was fond of Aaron, but he wasn't interested because of his feelings for Missy, and he found Mary to be the more attractive of the two girls.

Richard Foreman, another boy, was invited to the party. He lived between Johnsville and Selden, south of the Martin farm in a house that his grandfather built in the 1870's, three and a half miles from Mary's house. He began walking to her house about an hour after the sun had disappeared in the winter sky. Looking toward the east, he saw the huge, full moon rising in the eastern sky. He stopped by Daniel McCarey's house, and Daniel walked the rest of the way with him to the Stanton's house.

Dexter Stanton, Mary's father, built a small, four-roomed, frame house a couple of years after he and Mary's mother married. The house, located a block from downtown Selden, was just across from the Yancy Cotton Gin where Dexter worked during the ginning season. During the rest of the year, he found different odd jobs in and around Selden. He dug graves for the funeral home, cleared timber for the neighboring farmers, worked with the road crews and did all sorts of hard labor — he could barely make ends meet, but he always made sure his family had enough to eat. Mary's mother took in washing and ironing from some of the most affluent citizens of the community to help her family endure the economic hardships facing them.

Willie Stanton and his sister, Lydia; Sally Lowe and Jeffery Carroll were already at the party when Daniel and Richard walked in.

"Are Elvis an' Aaron coming?" Daniel asked as he sat down on a cane-bottom chair in Mary's room.

"I thank they are," Mary said, "but they said they were going by to check on some of their traps first."

"They sure do like to go huntin' — I don't mind going every once in a while, but I'd get tired of it every night. I'd rather listen to the radio, or I've been thinking about writing a book."

"That's interesting. What would you write about?" asked Mattie.

"I don't know. I think a good murder mystery would be fun to write, but since nothing ever happens around here, I don't know where to start."

"Why don't ya just start writin' about stuff you know and just go from there?"

"I could do that an' jest make up some murder stuff."

"Yes, have ya been listenin' to your new radio lately?"

"Yeah, the other night, I listened to that radio station in Dallas an' they had a brand new show called *The Grand Ole Opry*."

"What was that about?" asked Mary.

"It wuz from Nashville, Tennessee. They had a bunch of sangers an' guitar pickers an' stuff like that. It wuz purty good. This here one guy, Jimmie Rogers; boy could he yodel."

Mary replied, "Mattie an' me went to her uncle's house the other day an' they had one of 'em new Victrola talking machines."

"What's that?" Daniel asked.

Richard answered, "It's a machine that plays these thin round thangs called phonograph records. It has a thang called a arm that has a needle in it. The record goes on a round thang that turns. I don't know how it works, but when somebody puts that needle on the turnin' record, it makes the sound like sanging or sump'um."

"Oh yeah, I've heard of 'em."

"It sure is pretty outside tonight," commented Daniel, looking out through the window, "the moon's so bright, it's nearly as light as day. I wonder where Elvis an' Aaron are? I thought they'd be here by now."

"I don't have any idea," Jeffery said, looking at his pocket watch, "maybe they found somethin' an' they ain't payin' no attention to the time."

Richard picked up an Ouija Board sitting under a table and showed it to Daniel. Mary told them the board used to belong to a fortuneteller that her grandpa met in Germany. She said she was afraid to play with the board because her mother said it was evil.

"Come on, it'll be fun," said Daniel.

"How is it supposed to work?" asked Richard who didn't like messing with the unknowns of the spiritual world.

"It's supposed to have a spirit trapped inside. You can ask whatever you want an' it will be answered," Mary told him.

"Want to try it?" Daniel asked Richard, "You might find out if you're really gonna get rich."

"I don't believe in that stuff, but I've heard that ya ain't supposed to mess with Ouija Boards."

"Come on, you're skeered, ain't you," Daniel taunted.

Richard gave in and put his fingers on the prongs along with Daniel. "You ask it the first question," Daniel told Richard.

"What is Mary's middle name?"

The planchette moving slowly on the board pointed to and spelled out "A-N-N-E."

"You already knew that an' you pushed it," Richard said sternly.

"Yeah, but I didn't push it; you did! I'll ask it a question."

"Where is Elvis an' Aaron?"

The pointer quivered then slowly began to spell out a word. Richard jerked his hand off the pointer, watching the mysterious talking board as the tear drop shaped planchette predicted out an ominous message, "M-U-R-D-E-R."

The disturbing message quickly brought an end to their dabbling with the unknown. Was it a predictor of something horrible? The kids didn't know, but they felt it best to leave such things alone. It might be a harmless game, but why tempt the demons? But what should they make of the ominous communication? The boys and girls would find out, in a short time that the unspeakable had already happened.

"Maybe we'd better quit playing with that. Hey Jeffrey, tell us one of your famous stories," said Richard.

Jeffrey Carroll was known for his ability to weave a scary story.

"Ok, y'all gather 'round."

Carroll and the rest of the party sat down in the middle of the floor and made a circle. He spoke softly, beginning his tale.

"This here's is a very scary story that I heard a long time ago — it's hard to believe, but I'm tellin' ya, it's the truth.

There's a house that's at the end of a road in Carthage, this little town in the Pineywoods of East Texas. This house wuz built before the Civil War an' folks says it's hainted. It's got tall grass all 'round it. The man that built it died when he was on a trip to Africa. Some people thought that a African witch doctor had probably put a voodoo spell on 'im. Anyway, he died. Almost as soon as they found out that he died, people began to say the house wuz hainted."

The storyteller looked around the room at the flickering shadows cast by the lamp and cupped his ear as though he was listening for something; then he continued his account of the story.

"Several of his kin-folks came to stay at the old house an' after awhile they said the house was hainted. Windows an' doors would open by themselves an' they'd hear weird sounds, both day an' night. They heard footsteps going up an' down the stairs in broad daylight, but they didn't see nothin'. Pieces of furniture got piled up during the night."

Richard glanced out the window to make sure nothing was peeping in at them from the darkness of the outside. Daniel nervously cleared his throat and crossed his arms in front of him. Aaron and Elvis still had not made an appearance; they were overdue as Jeffrey was spinning this frightening tale.

"The kin-folks couldn't take it any longer an' they left. Nobody lived in the house for about ten years. Several people wanted to buy the old house — but somehow, before the deal was closed, they heard that it wuz haunted. No one wanted the house until one day this old lady by the name of Missus King bought the house. She wuz gonna rent it out to people.

Pretty soon, several people were rentin' out rooms from her. There wuz a old banker, three widder ladies, an' several students from a college that wuz close by. They wuz happy to be livin' there; even after hearing that the house was haunted."

The attentive listeners spoke not a word while Jeffery wove the threads of his haunting story. The girls held one another for comfort and safety — the boys stood their ground. Aaron and Elvis still hadn't made their appearance.

"Two of the boys went out on the porch to smoke their pipes. It wuz a hot day in the middle of August, an' it was just turning dark. They filled their pipes with tobacco, lit them an' started puffin' and talkin'. They talked about fishin' an' travelin' to far off places an' stuff like that. One of the boys named Robert asked the other boy what he thought wuz scary.

The other boy wuz named Leonard. He thought that stumblin' over a dead body in the dark wuz pretty scary. Robert said that seein' a body floatin' in a river would scare him. Leonard said he would be scared if'n he saw a ghost.

After awhile, they finished smokin' their pipes. They decided to quit talkin' about scary thangs an' they said goodnight to each other. Leonard went to his room; an' then he went to bed. He started readin' a book before he went to sleep. He turned down the lamp in his room until there wuz just a small flame burnin'. The room was in total darkness except for the small flame that wuz glowin'.

Then something terrible happened! He wuz la-yin' in bed with his eyes closed. Somethin' crawled out from under his bed an' jumped on his chest, an' then suddenly it grabbed him by the throat, an' tried to choke him. Whatever it wuz, it had real boney fee-lin' fingers.

Leonard wuz very strong an' he wasn't a coward, but this thang took him by surprise. In an instant he grabbed the thang, an' held on to it as hard as he could. In a few seconds, the bony hands that had grabbed his throat turned loose an' he could breathe again. Then the fight wuz on!

He held the creature down with his knee an' fi-nally, he had the thang under control usin' all his strength. He rested for a moment to get his breath, an' then remembered that before he went to bed, he had put a large red handkerchief under his pillow. He reached for it an' after another few minutes of scufflin'; he managed to tie the creature's arms. He heard the thang puffin' in the darkness an' he could feel its heart beatin'.

He felt fairly safe now, so he turned up the lamp to see what had attacked 'im. He couldn't describe how the when he turned on the lamp. He screamed real loud an' in less than a minute the other people came runnin' to his room."

Jeffery dramatically put his hands over his face and shook his head. He looked over at Mary and continued. Elvis and Aaron still had not arrived.

"Leonard looked at the thang an' didn't see nothin'! It felt warm an' it wuz apparently flesh. Leonard wuz holding on to somethin', but the people in the room couldn't see a thang! Not even an outline of anythang! The thang wuz invisible!

Just then Robert came into the room an' as soon as he saw the look on Leonard's face, he hollered, 'Holy cow Leonard! What happened'?"

Jeffery paused. He looked around the room and saw all the party goers were waiting, in anticipation of the answer.

"I don't know what it is," Jeffrey whispered, "but . . ."

A loud, interrupting knock on the door startled Jeffrey and his listeners. Mary screamed, reaching for Daniel's arm while he cautiously opened the front door. It was Willie Stanton's father, Emmett. The man's distressed countenance expressed his horror. Something was dreadfully wrong.

"Kids, something terrible has happened — Aaron and Elvis has found somebody's head down on the River's place when they wuz out there checkin' their traps."

"What do ya mean that they found a head, what are ya talkin' about?" Daniel asked.

"They found a boy's head that's been chopped plum off. No one knows who it is or anythin' about it. We came to take you home."

F. M. Snow, unaware that the two boys had discovered Bernie's head, woke up early after one more restless night — one of many facing this wicked old man. He barely noticed the lingering stench left by the decomposing bodies; the bodies of his wife and mother-in-law that he had burned to ashes.

He thought that he had destroyed all evidence of his horrific crime. He had explained the disappearance of his family — they were in Waco. He had disposed of Bernie's body in a remote area, and if anyone found it, there was nothing to identify the corpse. He had removed the clothing, and although he would have preferred an old well as a place to hide Bernie's head, he felt the abandoned cellar was just as good.

There was one unforeseen setback to his "perfect crime" that he hadn't counted on — two teenage boys and a dog.

20

THE ARREST

Monday, December 14, 1925 . . .

"Hey, good mornin'. Where ya headed?" Ned asked, stopping his car.

He saw F. M. Snow, walking down the country road toward town and as usual, Snow was carrying his rifle with him

"I wuz goin' to town to get a few thangs. I need some coal oil an' sugar," Snow told him, "how fer are ye going?"

"I'm going into town; gotta go do some business at the bank."

"Wonder if you'd mind if I ride along?"

"Nah, I don't mind, I'd like yore company, git in. How ye been doin'?"

"Awe, I ain't been doing no good, been feeling sickly an' can't sleep a' tall."

"A man shore needs his sleep. I sleep pretty well most the time."

The putrid odor from the dead, although faint, had saturated into Snow's clothing.

Ned sniffed, "What's that smell?"

"I don't smell nothin'!" Snow retorted.

"It's 'bout gone away now; I guess it wuz my imagination. Say, you heered anythang from yore wife?"

Snow's eyes squinted, and he tightened his lips. "No, an' I don't keer to talk about it."

Ned decided it would be best to honor Snow's wishes, talking about the weather and non-controversial subjects on the remainder of their trip into town.

Once into Stephenville, Snow got out on the square; Ned telling him they would meet on the north side of the courthouse in about an hour. Snow again assured Ned he wouldn't be long and he needed to head back home soon and would be waiting for Ned's return.

After leaving Ned, F. M. Snow walked across the street to Minter's Grocery Store on the north side of the courthouse square. He was surprised to hear the shoppers talking about the macabre finding of the boy's head that was now being viewed at the funeral home. How had his dark deed been discovered?

Alarmed, Snow heard one man report that the identity of the dead boy remained unknown.

Snow had to see for himself; he quickly left the store and walked over to the funeral home to look at the head of the boy. He was stunned to find the head in such a good condition. He looked around, spotted the sheriff and quietly walked out the back door of the funeral home, knowing it would be just a matter of time before someone recognized his murdered stepson.

As it was once before, that time in San Saba County, he would have to leave the locale before the officials linked him to the gruesome murder. Then he saw Ned, entering the front door of the funeral home — yes, it was just a matter of time.

Ned had gone to Farmer's First National bank to make a deposit and noticed everyone was talking about Elvis and Aaron's frightening discovery from a few nights before. Finishing his business at the bank, he drove to the funeral home to view the unidentified head. He didn't notice that F. M. Snow was going out the backdoor of the funeral home as he entered the front. He walked up to the casket and looked at the face; a face he had seen before. He knew it was Bernie Connally. He felt himself shaking when Sam Russell approached him.

"Do you know who that is?" The district attorney asked him gruffly.

"I know that head, but I'm afraid to speak."

"You're gonna speak an' you're gonna tell us who it is!"

"I think I know whose head that is, but I won't say because it would be dangerous unless I know," he said at last in a whisper. "It looks like Bernie Connally, my neighbor's step-boy. My wife knows the boy better than I do — she can probably tell us fer sure."

"Which one of your neighbors? I think I know most folks around here."

"F. M. Snow. . ." His voice trailed off.

"Well, we need to go talk to that ole boy; you say he lives by you?"

"Yes sir, but . . . Uh . . . he rode into town with me — I just let him off awhile ago."

"Where at?" The district attorney motioned for the sheriff.

"I let him out on the square about thirty minutes ago. He told me he had to pick up a few thangs. He acted real upset when I asked him 'bout his wife."

"What does he look like?" asked Sheriff Hassler. "Can you describe him?"

"Uh, he's 'bout forty-five or fifty, tall feller, pretty skinny. I don't pay much attention to thangs like that. I know he's wearing a old black hat an' a dirty old brown coat. An' he got that rifle with 'im."

"I've heard of that man an' his reputation, an' I saw him in here no more than five minutes ago," said Hassler, "He left out the back way. If he's our killer, he knows that we know."

"Mister Gristy, you go on up to my office an' wait fer us, while we go look fer Snow," the sheriff instructed.

Trewitt's Funeral Home was located in a white house on Graham Street at the intersection of Tarleton Street, three blocks north of the square. Hassler and Russell walked toward the courthouse, looking for the man called Snow. They did not see the suspected killer anywhere in sight around the courthouse square.

Having not seen anyone suspicious, the sheriff and Russell went to the sheriff's office and notified his deputy, Ross Pearcy, to be watching for the man, a suspect.

"Be careful if ya make contact with 'im because I've heard Snow's a crack shot with his rifle," the sheriff warned.

Hassler and Russell once again questioned a waiting Ned, who reluctantly gave them more information.

"A few days after Thanksgiving, I came by Snow's house in my car," he said. "I was on my way to Stephenville. Snow an' another man, Luke Johnson, were at the mail box an' I stopped an' talked with 'em."

"Who is Luke Johnson," asked Russell.

"He's my neighbor that lives to the south of me," Ned, pointing southward.

"Okay, I follow ya. What was so unusual about that?" quizzed Russell.

"Well, Snow looked worried," Ned continued, "Told me he wuz up all night. Ya know; I thank I smelt somethin' dead this mornin' when he got in the car."

Russell looked at the sheriff, "Go on."

"Well, he told me that his wife had quit 'im, so he hooked up his team an' took her, his mother-in-law an' Bernie to Iredell. He said he put 'em on the train to Waco, an' didn't' get back home till daylight."

"Do you remember anythang else about that day?" asked Hassler.

"Well, you know it wuz nearly a month ago but the best I can remember, I asked 'im to come to town with me an' that's when he asked me how long I was going to stay. I told him it wouldn't be long. He said he needed some coal oil an' sugar. He didn't talk much then, just like today while we wuz riding into town. After he got his thangs, he jest kept on worryin' me about leavin'. Pretty soon, we got into the car an' I drove 'im back to his place. When we got there, I asked 'im if he needed any help with his stuff an' he told me jest to leave it by the gate, so I did. Now I'm glad I did."

"Probably a good thing," agreed Russell, "Let's go get your wife."

"Alright, but I shore thank I smelt somethin' dead when he got in the car with me."

Sheriff Hassler asked Pearcy to continue searching the town for Snow while he, along with Russell and Ned, got into the car and went to the Gristy home.

"Oh Ned, what's wrong?" seeing her husband with the sheriff.

"Wife, they's found a young man's head an' it's over at the funeral home. They don't know who it is, but I looked at him an' I thank it's Bernie Connally. They want you to go look at it an' see what you thank."

Ned's wife, Ida, was hesitant to get involved in the identification of the mysterious head because she was afraid of Snow, but she knew that if he were the killer, he couldn't be allowed to go free. Ida nervously changed into a clean dress, put on a bonnet and shortly, they were in route to Trewitt's Funeral Home.

"You go on up there an' look an' if ya recognize him, don't let on, an' don't say nothin' to nobody," Sheriff Hassler warned Ida.

Ida walked slowly past the coffin where the boy's head was at rest. She looked at the face, a face that she immediately recognized and felt her heart pounding with fear. She felt dizzy and thought she might faint. She knew, without a doubt, it was the head of Bernie Connally, her neighbor's son. After viewing the head, Ida went back to the rear of the funeral home and talked to Sam Russell and Sheriff D. M. Hassler.

"I'm jest real shore it's Bernie Connally, our neighbor's stepson," she whispered to the sheriff, "if it is him, he will have a white scar just over the right eyebrow an' a extra long dog tooth in his right upper jaw. That poor boy is just about sixteen; I thank."

The head bore those particular markings, and she told them she was sure it was Connally, and she gave a detailed description of the clothing that he usually wore, a white shirt and a brown mackinaw coat.

"Where's his mother, Mister Snow's wife, Miss Maggie? Have you talked to her?" Ida asked the lawmen and then she thought about it; she realized that she had not seen her neighbors for several days.

"No ma'am, we ain't talked to her, yet. Your husband wuz the first to recognize the boy jest a while ago." Hassler wondered why Mrs. Snow hadn't reported her son to be missing. That was a question that needed an answer — had something befallen her also?

Hassler, Russell and Pearcy, after a quick search, didn't find Snow anywhere around town. It was imperative; they needed to locate and talk to Snow as soon as they could.

Captain Tom Hickman, of the Texas Rangers, had assigned Ranger Stewart Stanley to assist with the gruesome murder case. Stanley had arrived shortly before noon and was waiting at the sheriff's office for the return of the local lawmen.

"Let me fill ya in on what we know so far," Hassler told the ranger.

Hassler briefed Stanley on the facts of the investigation, and soon the three lawmen and the district attorney were on their way to Snow' farm.

Hassler had gotten directions to the farm from Ned. The lawmen found the old house and getting out of the car; they walked cautiously up to Snow's front door. Hassler knocked on the door, his right hand on his pistol. Stanley and Pearcy kept back, one on each side of the door with their firearms ready. Russell, unarmed, waited further back. Snow came to the door, holding a plate and dishtowel in his hand. He wiped his nose with the dish-towel.

"Hello boys," he spoke calmly, "What can I do fer ya?"

"We need to ask you some questions," Hassler told him, "would you mind stepping outside?"

"Shore, I'd be glad to." Snow replied politely.

"We're looking for a boy named Bernie Connally, is he your step-son?" Hassler asked the man who was now leaning against a post supporting the porch.

"Yes sir."

"Where is he now?"

"Uh, I took him, his ma an' his grandma to Iredell last night, so they could go visit some of their folks down there."

Hassler, noticing the discrepancies in Snow's account of the Iredell trip, recalled the fact that Ned had told him that Snow took his family to Iredell over a week ago to catch the train to Waco.

"You were in town today, weren't you?"

Snow looked off and put his hand over his mouth, then looked back, "Yes sir, I rode in with my neighbor. I didn't stay long."

"What did you do when you were in town?" Sam Russell asked Snow. "Who did you talk to?"

"I went an' bought me a little dab of groceries at Minter's, then got me some coal oil an' came home. I couldn't find my neighbor, so jest I walked on home." Snow remained calm while talking to the officers.

Hassler asked, "You say you took your family to Iredell last night?"

"Yes sir, I shore did." Snow shifted onto another foot.

"What time did you leave?"

"We left just a little 'fore dark. I wuz gone all night."

"An' you're saying they went to visit some folks in Iredell?"

"Uh, no sir, I took them down there to catch the train to go to Waco. It weren't last night; it wuz a few days ago. I must of misunderstood what you said. Yeah, they were goin' down there to visit some of their folks. Me an' the wife had us a argument, so I 'spect they might stay there fer awhile."

"A few days ago, or last night?"

"It wuz a few days ago, last Thursday to be exact, I thank."

'Well then, what time did you get to Iredell? What time did the train leave for Waco?" Stanley asked noticing that Snow seemed to be enjoying the questioning.

"We got there 'bout one o'clock in the morning an' the train came shortly after that."

"Mister Snow, do you own a rifle?" Hassler asked the question that he already knew the answer to.

"Yes sir, a Winchester — it's sitting right over there." Snow pointed to his rifle leaning against a wall just inside the house.

Russell asked the next question, "Did you go to the funeral home this morning?"

"Uh, no — no sir, I ain't been to no funeral home, why ya asking?" The smile left Snow's face as he cleared his throat. "What business would I have at a funeral home?"

"You tell me. I saw you there this morning. You were wearing that coat hanging right over there."

"No Sir! It weren't me. If y'all don't have any further business, I'm asking you to leave."

The four officials turned and walked off the porch as Snow ambled back inside the house and closed the door. The officers watched to be sure that Snow didn't come back out with his rifle.

While they were getting into the sheriff's car, Hassler asked the men, "Did y'all notice he never asked why we were out here? I thank he's our killer fer sure."

"Yeah," Pearcy added, "An' there's no way them two old horses of his could of made that trip to Iredell in one night, whether it was last night or a few nights ago. That's about a forty-five mile round trip."

The lawmen went back into Stephenville. Hassler asked Pearcy to inquire around town to find out what he could about Snow, while he and Stanley went to Iredell to the Texas Central Railroad Station. They were going to check out Snow's claim that he took his wife and mother-in-law there to catch the train to Waco — they knew he didn't take Bernie Connally.

Iredell, Texas is located fifty-nine miles northwest of Waco in northwestern Bosque County, twelve miles east of Hico and thirty-one miles southeast of Stephenville. In the 1850s, Ward Keeler and Ranse Walker settled in the region and named the small community after Keeler's son, Ire. The United States Post Office opened at Iredell in 1870.

The settlement moved from its original location near the Walker homestead in 1880 to the south bank of the Bosque River near the Texas Central Railroad Station. Later that year, Iredell was destroyed by a flood and rebuilt on higher ground. In 1884, the population was estimated to be thirty, and by 1892, it had grown to six hundred people. Iredell was a retail and service center for the people in the surrounding countryside.

Texas Central Railroad had a total of three hundred and nine miles of the main track including the track that ran from Iredell to Waco.

Hassler and Stanley located the railroad depot and the man inside greeted them.

"Hi, how y'all doin'?" Bud Howard asked the lawmen. "Could I hep ya?"

"Yes sir, I'm Sheriff D. M. Hassler from Stephenville an' this here's Ranger Stewart," Hassler told the station operator.

"Pleased to me ya," Howard shook the men's hands. "We don't see much of the law in these parts."

"We looking fer a little information about some people who may have caught a train sometime yesterday,"

"Nobody caught the train yesterday — the train didn't even stop."

"So, you didn't see no boy an' a couple of women who were going to Waco?"

"No sir, nobody like that was here yesterday or anytime last week. What's this about? Y'all looking for somebody?"

"We are investigating a murder in Erath County an' we need to talk to a couple of ladies if we can find them. You're saying that no one caught the train anytime last week?"

"Yes sir, that's what I'm saying — I've been here the whole time, and nobody rode the train from here either last night or last week."

"We shore appreciate yore help in this matter."

"Well sir, shore sorry I can't help y'all out none. Y'all want me to contact you if they show up around here?"

"Yes sir, but I 'spect you probably won't be seeing 'em."

Hassler, using the railroad station's payphone, called back to Stephenville and talked to Deputy Pearcy, who was finding out more damning facts about F. M. Snow's recent activities. His investigation found that Bernie had driven into the county seat on the afternoon of November 27 with a wagonload of wood. That same day Snow had been seen buying rifle cartridges from a store in Stephenville. About five-thirty that day, Snow stopped and asked Bud Lucas, his neighbor if he had seen Bernie pass by on his way from town. Later, Lucas saw Bernie driving back toward the Snow farm with Snow sitting in the back of the wagon, leading a horse.

Hassler now had more information about the man called Snow. He and Stanley drove down to Waco and met with the authorities there. They could not find any trace of the missing women. The Erath County officers were certain that they knew the identity of the slayer who had hacked off the head of his stepson and disposed of it in the old cellar.

Hassler instructed the deputy to sign a complaint and get a warrant for the arrest of F. M. Snow. Pearcy went to the courthouse and before J. S. Watson, the Justice of Peace, swore out a complaint:

> "Ross Pearcy has reason to believe and does believe that on or about the 5th day of December, 1925, F. M. Snow, with malice and aforethought did kill Bernie Connally by shooting him with a gun and by cutting the said Bernie Connally's head off of his body."

The Justice of Peace drew up warrant number 745 for the arrest of F. M. Snow.

Snow loaded his old wagon with his few possessions, then went and got his cow; the cow that had, in his mind, caused all the trouble. Tying the cow to the back of his wagon, he started on his journey to a yet undecided destination. He looked back at the old house for the last time. He would never be back.

"As shore as the world, they knowed I done it." He thought. "I'd got clean away if I weren't fer those two boys. Damn their souls to hell!"

Mrs. Buck Hill had earlier told Snow that she was interested in buying some second-hand furniture. He drove his rickety old wagon to the Hill's house and made the sale — a beat up kitchen table, a couple of cane-bottom chairs, two iron bedsteads and an old wood burning cook stove. Altogether it brought him seven dollars.

Mrs. Hill asked him, "Mister Snow, why're you pullin' up stakes an' leavin' without any furniture? Ain't you gonna be keepin' house somers? Don't ya think ya might be coming back sometime?"

"Tain't likely," Snow told the woman, "I 'spect that since its jest me, I'll jest move from place to place an' live out of the wagon."

"But s'pose your wife comes back to ya?"

"Tain't likely," Snow said softly.

"By the way, ya thank yore man would wanna buy these guns?" pointing at his rifle and Bernie's pistol.

"I don't know, but he's right in there; why don't ya ask 'im?"

After he had made his sales, riding down the road in his old wagon, Snow thought back on the black day that led to his being alone. He and Bernie had cut the firewood and loaded it on the wagon so that the boy could take it to town to be sold. That was the plan. He remembered taking a nap — squirrel hunting and upon returning to the house, there she was — the old cow, grazing in the cotton patch. Yes, that's how it was — now it came to mind, he was enraged — the confrontation. The boy did not close the gate!

About the same time, near dusk, the sheriff and the ranger were returning from Waco to Stephenville. They dreaded their next task knowing Pearcy had secured a murder warrant for Snow's arrest.

"We gotta be careful when we find 'im, we just don't know how he's gonna react!"

"He must be one crazy sum-bitch to of done what he did to that boy!"

And then suddenly, in the twilight, they saw a wagon, drawn by two old horses approaching them about a mile west of Snow's house. Maggie's horse was tied to the side of the wagon and a cow brought up the rear. As the officer's car drew nearer, the wagon approached a bridge just before getting to the main road — close enough for Hassler to make a positive identification.

"That's Snow," said Hassler softly, peering through the twilight.

Hassler quickly stopped the car and the officers jumped out; their firearms drawn. Then suddenly, as though it was a Divine Act, a small boy appeared from behind some bushes lining the old road. Running up to the back of the wagon, he untied the rope haltering the old milk cow. Then just as suddenly, as the boy appeared, he disappeared back into the bushes.

Snow looked back and saw his wandering cow. He got down off the wagon, leaving his deadly rifle, and went to chase down the cow, which he believed had broken loose.

"You're under arrest, Snow!"

The man's constant companion, his rifle, was on the wagon seat in plain sight but was too far away to be of any use. He offered no resistance while Hassler put the handcuffs on his bony wrist, whispering under his breath, "Damned cow, if I could of got to my rifle . . ."

Snow objected to the fact that he had to leave his wagon and horses with a neighbor but offered no further resistance.

Hassler and Stanley drove the three-mile trip back into Stephenville and placed the suspected killer in a dark, cold jail cell, arriving just after the sun had set somberly in the western sky.

The Erath County Jail, located a block southwest of the courthouse, looked like a small-scale castle nestled under the large, leafless oak trees. Its dark red brick, barred windows, and steep front steps gave the old building a forbidding appearance. A hangman's rope hung just inside the entrance as a reminder to those incarcerated there, that Erath County believed in the severest of punishments for those who chose to break the law. It was evident that some condemned individual had once broken the rope — the frayed ends were tied into a knot, just above the noose.

Russell, Hassler and Stanley questioned the man who now seemed as meek as a lamb; sitting on the cell bunk, shivering from the cold. Snow stayed with this story that he had taken his wife, his mother-in-law and stepson to Iredell and left them at the train station.

Hassler looked at Snow and in a quiet voice said, "We know that ain't the truth 'cause we talked to the station agent. Snow, we found Bernie's head."

"What do you mean you found his head, what happened to him? What are you talking about?"

"Some boys found the boy's head in a ole cellar an' some witnesses have positively identified 'im. We know it's Bernie's head."

"Bernie's dead?" Snow asked calmly.

"Yeah, he's dead," said Russell, "you know he's dead, and you killed him, didn't you?"

"I didn't kill him; I told ya; I took him to Iredell. I took him, his ma an' grandma. If he's dead, that nigger did it!" His calmness erupted into agitation as he jumped up, dropping the blanket to the floor he had wrapped around him.

Hassler had a perplexed look on his face. "What are you talking about, Snow? Ye ain't makin' no sense."

"I'm telling ya that if the boy's passed on, that blooming nigger must of did it. He wuz always walking by our place an' nosing around. I knowed he wuz up to no good. Ya know, in fact, I heared 'im tell the boy he'd kill 'im. I seen 'em hangin' round the house jest a few days ago. Yes sir, he's the one all right. Y'all go find that nigger."

It wasn't' long before the news of Snow's arrest spread through the town and the outlying regions. Knowing that the brutal murderer had been captured brought a great sense of relief to the populace and anger began to displace the people's fears. A crowd of people began to gather around the little country jail — some of them carried torches that cast dark images, ghostly images on the front of the building and out into the street. The roar of the crowd, becoming louder and louder, was mingled with shouts of "Killer!" "Murderer!" and "String 'em up!"

Snow cowered back into a corner, pulling the musty smelling blanket over him.

"Listen to 'em," he said, "They's a lynch party. Y'all gotta take keer of me. I ain't gonna get lynched fer somethin' I didn't do. Y'all ain't got no right to do this to me."

Hassler looked out through the barred windows and saw that the gathering was beginning to take on the personality of a mob. After about thirty minutes, he instructed Pearcy to get the prisoner ready to travel — they were going to move him to the Tarrant County Jail in Fort Worth.

Snow, whimpering, urinated in his pants and began to shiver uncontrollably. Hassler unlocked the cell and brought the inmate to the front of the jail and allowed him to warm in front of the only stove in the jail. Pearcy found some dry trousers that belonged to a man who had died while in the jail. He gave them to Snow and told him to get ready to travel.

Snow changed his pants, and Hassler put the handcuffs and shackles back on him. Stanley and Hassler, holding shotguns, led Snow through the crowd to the sheriff's car. Virgil McElroy stepped aside when the Ranger nodded his head, motioning him to move out of the way. Virgil felt it would be best not to test the patience of the big man carrying the shotgun.

Stanley stood six feet and five inches tall and weighed close to two hundred and eighty-five pounds. As large as he was, he could kick up his foot as high as his head. His wrists were enormous, and he had never been beaten in an arm wrestling match.

As Snow passed by him, Virgil yelled, "I knowed they'd get ya, old man. Threaten me will ya? Ole Virgil ain't forgittin' that! Yore lucky that you didn't get to meet 'Ole Bertha.'"

Mordecai Johnson, curious, had come to the jail. He stood back in the shadows and in the darkness;

only the whites of his wide eyes could be easily seen. Mordecai didn't know that this was the man who lived in the house on the road he traveled so often, because he had never seen him up close until now. He didn't know this was the man who lived in the house — the house where he and Mr. McCarey saw the flaming fireplace and smelled the odor of burning human flesh. The man being led to the car looked over to his direction and then quickly turned his head. Mordecai had seen the face before, in San Saba County. Then he remembered.

21

THE SEARCH WARRANT

The rattling of keys — the mournful creaking of metal hinges in need of oil — then the clanking of a closing metal door echoing through the halls of the Tarrant County Jail greeted Snow into a dimly lit cell as the jailer locked the prisoner into solitary confinement.

Sheriff Hassler and Ranger Stanley, concerned for Snow's safety, had made the sixty some odd mile trip to Fort Worth with the accused slayer. Seeing that Snow was now secured, the sheriff and Stanley met Texas Ranger Captain Tom Hickman, who was awaiting their arrival in one of the jail's offices.

"This is Sheriff Med Hassler from Stephenville," Stanley introduced Hassler to Hickman.

"It's my pleasure," Hickman said, shaking Hassler's hand, "long trip from Stephenville?"

"Yes sir, it was," responded Hassler.

"Capt 'n, he ain't told us a thang about where we can find the victim's body," Stanley reported, "he keeps claiming he took the boy an' his family to Iredell so's they could catch a train to Waco."

"Stickin' to that story is he?" the Capitan looked towards the prisoner's cell.

"Yes sir an' he keeps claimin' a Negro killed the boy."

"Is that right? I'll see what he has to tell me after he's settled in there awhile."

"Well then, we're gonna leave 'im with you," the sheriff told Hickman, "We gotta git back to Stephenville. We still gotta try to find the boy's body an' locate those two women."

"We're gittin' a search warrant for Snow's farm," Stanley added, "we'll let ya know if we find anything."

The journey back to Stephenville was still facing the two lawmen, already exhausted from their lack of sleep. But there would be little rest tonight — a search of the Snow farm was planned for early the next morning — a search to look for the boy's body and anything that might lead them to the missing women.

Back at the jail, Snow shrunk back in horror as he looked at a sketch now before him; a drawing made by another prisoner, the likeness of a woman on the cell wall.

"Cover it up," he screamed to the jailer, "I can't stand to look at it."

"I've got this terrible headache, can't ya git me something fer it?" the accused man complained.

Snow began to feel an uneasiness creep over his body. He had known the feeling before. Locked up in the small cell, he felt the walls closing in on him.

"Oh, no, not now," he thought, "I can't stand it." He was experiencing what he called his smothering spells, and no one was there to help him.

"If only Maggie wuz here, she'd know what to do. Oh, my darlin' Maggie."

His arms and fingers began to feel numb, and he became aware of strange, tingling sensations in his feet. He was breathing hard and fast, feeling he could not get his breath, as if someone were holding a pillow over his face, suffocating him and drawing the life out of him. His heart, pounding faster and harder with each passing second, brought a new fear; he was afraid that his heart would beat so rapidly that it could no longer function then it would finally stop. A dark cloud of fear settled over him. He thought that he would die at any moment.

"Help me, somethin's wrong with me! I can't stand it in here, please let me out of here!"

A cup of water — he tried to pick it up to take a drink. Maybe that would help him. His arms trembled. He drew the cup to his lips — his tongue felt the water; then he lost control his fingers. The tin vessel fell to the floor with a clank, spilling the water on him and his bunk bed. Even though it was cold in the cell, he began sweating and wiped his face with an old dirty rag he used for a handkerchief. Then the panic gradually subsided, and he began to breath slower and the pounding deep inside his chest subsided.

Capitan Hickman wanted to question Snow and walking up to the cell he held out a photo of the decapitated head of Snow's stepson.

"What do you know about this?" Hickman inquired, pointing to the grisly photo.

"I ain't guilty of anythang," Snow declared, turning his back on the Ranger Capitan, "an' that ain't Bernie in that picture! Leave me along, I'm too damn sick to talk to you anymore!"

A disgusted Hickman left the prisoner. He would await tomorrow's results of the search of Snow's farm before questioning of the suspected killer any further. He would have more leverage in questioning the suspected killer if the Stephenville lawmen found damning evidence.

Hassler and Stanley, returning to Stephenville, arrived about midnight. After another fretful night of sleep, Hassler was up early so he would be ready to go to Snow's farm by daybreak.

Deputy Pearcy had been instructed to obtain a search warrant, and Justice of the Peace, J. S. Watson issued such a warrant. The Erath County lawmen would be probing the house and outlying property, looking for the torso of the young man now identified as Bernie Connally, and perhaps a clue as to the whereabouts of his mother, Maggie Poston and his grandmother, Annie Olds.

"Man, why did I ever want this sheriff's job?" he wondered to himself.

Hassler went to the courthouse, and there met with Deputy Pearcy, Sam Russell, and Ranger Stanley. It was still the dead of night when they drove to the farm; abandoned except for a few chickens wandering around in the yard. A dog barked in the distance.

Saturday morning dawned dreary as a blanket of gray enclosed the ground — fog. A gently falling mist would make the cold search even more unpleasant. As the men got out of the car, they heard the mournful wail of Snow's two old hound dogs, tied to a tree in the back of the unnaturally calm house.

"He went off an' left his old dogs; jest left 'em to starve to death," Stanley said.

The search party decided first to give a quick swing around the perimeter of the property, before investigating inside the house.

Deputy Pearcy walked into the woods, north of the old house and found a wagon hidden by a cedar bush.

"Hey," he hollered out, "I've found a axe back here in this old wagon!"

He picked up the axe and saw that the handle had been recently scraped, and seeing traces of something, dark red he said, "I think this might be blood here on the axe handle."

Hassler walked over to the old wagon and helped Pearcy unload the few remaining pieces of firewood.

"Look there," Pearcy said, pointing to dark reddish stains that had been revealed between the boards of the wagon floor.

"That shore looks like blood to me," the sheriff said, "an' I'll bet ya it's that boy's blood. Well men, let's go see what's in the house."

The old weather-beaten house, one of the oldest in the county, looked too dilapidated for anyone to be living in it. The chinking was falling out from between the logs and holes in the wall were large enough for small animals to crawl through.

"How in the world do you reckon anybody could live in here, especially as cold as it has been?" asked Russell, "look at those cracks over there."

Stepping up on the porch and being careful not to walk on a rotting board, Russell saw a discoloration of the wood that caught his attention, "Look here on the front porch. Here's a spot that appears to have been freshly scrubbed."

Kneeling down and looking between the cracks, Russell spoke again, "I can see somethin' what looks like blood."

The porch flooring groaned and cracked as Russell and the sheriff walked up to peer into the small window on the front of the house, but darkness concealed anything that might be inside. Nothing but silence. The silence of death and the whispers of the four investigators — nothing more.

Hassler turned the cold doorknob, slowly opening the door; not knowing what to expect. The door scraped the floor as it opened, making an unsettling sound like that of a hurt dog. The sheriff shined his flashlight inside and saw a big stone fireplace as they entered the room. Watching the intruders was a black cat; sitting quietly in a far corner of the room. Suddenly the cat hissed, jumped up and crawled through a large crack in the wall, startling the sheriff who was unsure of what he was going to find inside.

"Look at that!" Hassler said shining the light at the wall, "that dadgum cat crawled out through that hole in the wall. Scared the dickens out of me!"

"Come on boys, let's go in," the sheriff told the others, "Let's git this over with."

Hassler walked further into the room, and there in front of the fireplace; he made out another discolored spot on the floor that appeared to have been recently scrubbed. Hassler got down on his knees to look more closely.

"Here are some more spots that shore look like blood to me," Hassler said. "Y'all smell that?"

The stench of decomposing flesh was about. Deputy Pearcy walked into an adjacent room — the kitchen, cold and unlit. He shined his flashlight onto the old wooden floor and saw cockroaches running from the beam of light. Looking at a place near the center of the room, he could see flies swarming about.

"Hey fellers, I may have found somethin' in here," he called out, "it looks like some boards may have been pulled up and nailed back down. The body may be under there! We need something to pry up these boards."

Hassler looked around the room, and finding nothing to use as a pry bar; he went outside and retrieved the engine crank handle from his Model T Ford.

Hassler returned to the kitchen area of the house and pried on one of the boards that appeared to have been recently nailed. As Pearcy pulled up one of the boards, the malodor that swept forth almost overpowered the search party. There was no mistaking that odor — decomposing human flesh.

The searchers felt they were about to find the body of the murdered boy, Bernie Connally, but what they saw only added to the mystery — a hole beneath the ripped up flooring that was more than large enough for the body, but it was empty.

"It looks like there may of been two bodies down here," Hassler said, looking at the impressions in the dirt.

He dug down into the soil with the iron crank handle exposing dirt that had been soaked with blood to a depth of about six inches.

The investigators were looking for the body of Bernie Connally, but now there was evidence that there were two bodies. The investigation was becoming more gruesome and puzzling as the lawmen found more evidence that something more horrible than they first believed had taken place in the house.

"Why would he put a body under there just to remove it later?" questioned Pearcy.

Stanley went over to the fireplace and raked around in the huge pile of ashes. His fingers came in contact with a hard substance and he pulled it out of the ashes — the reality of what had happened here was becoming more apparent.

"I'm pretty sure that this is a piece of bone," holding up the fragment for the others to see.

"Damn, he must of burned the boy in the fireplace!" surmised Pearcy.

"That sorry sum-bitch!"

Pearcy began helping Stanley sift through the pile of ashes and one by one; they found more pieces of bone fragments and what appeared to be human teeth.

Russell made the apparent observation, "Well, they can't be the boy's. His teeth are in the funeral home!"

Finding what appeared to be human teeth — teeth that could not be those of Bernie Connally added more mystery; more questions to this already gruesome search.

Stanley and Russell went outside and to the back of the house, which still had more ominous secrets to give up. Some thirty yards from the house they spotted something on the ground — another pile of fresh ashes. Stanley and Russell sifted through the wet ashes and discovered more pieces of bone. On the porch, Stanley found a small wooden box, about the size of a shoebox. He picked up the fragments of bone and teeth that Stanley and Russell had left in piles and put them into the box.

"We need to know if these are the remains of a human, so I suggest we go into town an' let a doctor take a look at them," Russell said. "I expect Doc Naylor is at his office about now."

Returning to Stephenville, Hassler and Russell took the pieces of charred bone to Dr. S. N. Naylor, whose office was on the second story of a building on the north side of the square. The young doctor examined the charred bones and said, "The bones are human; there's no question about it."

The questions now facing the lawmen — had Snow destroyed his stepson's body in the flames of the old fireplace? What could explain the finding of human teeth? And what about the evidence that there was a second body?

Sheriff Hassler called Capitan Hickman in Fort Worth, "Capt 'n, this is Sheriff Hassler, I wanted to let you know what we found at the Snow farm.

22

THE MYSTERIOUS TRIP

Throughout the long history of the Texas Rangers, Captain Thomas R. Hickman, was one of the bravest and most courageous. The oldest law enforcement agency in the United States was first formed in 1823 when Stephen F. Austin called for men to act as rangers in the common defense.

Well-known for his ability to cause men to give up their guilt-laden secrets, Hickman had what he needed — evidence that a human body had been burned in the fireplace — the fireplace belonging to the inmate lodged in the Tarrant County Jail.

"Saturday afternoon, another long week," thought Hickman, walking up the steps of the jail.

Once inside, he requested that the jailer get Snow and bring him to a holding cell used for interrogation on the second floor of the jail. Sitting at a table, Hickman asked Snow to sit across from him, offering him a cigarette.

"No thank ya," Snow held up his hand, "but I shore could use a chaw."

"Go get us some chewin' tobacco," the ranger instructed the jailer.

"How about a piece of homemade peanut brittle?"

"No thank ya; I ain't got the teeth fer it."

The jailer, returning a short time later, gave Hickman a pouch of *Red Man*, which Hickman laid on the table.

"How are you feeling today?" the ranger asked.

"Purdy poorly, I ain't slept much."

Offering Snow the chewing tobacco, the Ranger Captain began his questioning of Snow, asking general questions to put the accused killer at ease. He found that Snow had moved around the state quite a bit; never staying in one place very long. He was fond of animals, especially his two dogs — the two dogs he left behind.

Snow even joked with Hickman a bit, "My ole cow laughed so hard one time that milk came out her nose."

"Are they feeding you okay?"

"Nah, they can't even cook water in here without burning it," Snow grinned.

"Yeah, it's not your momma's home cooking," then Hickman spoke more seriously, "but Snow, the reason we're here — the men down in Stephenville; they found some bones in your fireplace."

"Found some bones?" Snow's grin faded away.

"Yes sir, they sure did, an' my question is this, it's your house, your fireplace, so tell me where did those bones come from and whose are they?"

"Well sir, come to thank about it, I cooked me some hog meat a ways back, it's probably them hog bones," Snow answered arrogantly.

Hickman shook his head, "No, I don't think so; those Stephenville boys; they're pretty sharp. They had the bones examined, and do you know what?"

"No, I guess I don't see what you're gittin' at."

"Snow, you know dern good an' well what they found," Hickman said slowly, pointing his finger at Snow, "they wuz human bones."

Snow slowly lowered his head, knowing that the evidence against him was mounting up, began his admission to Hickman.

"Snow has confessed to killin' the boy," Hickman later reported to Russell. "Meet me tonight a little before midnight in Bluff Dale and we'll go get the body. I'll bring Snow along 'cause he said he'd lead us to it."

Hassler, Pearcy and Russell driving to the tiny town of Bluff Dale, twelve miles east of Stephenville, saw the winter moon climbing above the horizon, just as they entered the peaceful village.

Hickman, his handcuffed prisoner and W. D. Van Blarcom, a crime reporter for the *Fort Worth Star-Telegram*, who had come alone in hopes of getting a story, met the Stephenville authorities who had been waiting for some time on the outskirts of Bluff Dale.

"We had us some car trouble just out of Granbury," Hickman explained.

"Gas line got clogged up. Snow says we need to go down that road." Hickman pointed southward to a dirt road — the Cedar Point Road.

Driving over rutted roads, almost impassable, and after traveling about three miles south of the settlement of Cedar Point, Snow motioned for Hickman to stop.

"This is the place, boys, up that way," Snow pointed westward.

They had reached the point at the base of Cedar Mountain where the automobiles could not be driven any further up the steep incline. The difficult ascent would have to be made on foot.

Hickman, removing the handcuffs from Snow's boney arms, told the prisoner, "We've got this far along without a fuss, so let's keep it that way."

Snow nodded his head in affirmation. "It's up that way."

It was midnight; clouds floated over the moon, blotting out its light. The beams from Hassler and Pearcy's flashlights illuminated the path for the others. Snow led the way with Hickman and Hassler on each side, holding him by his arms. They followed an old road that snaked its way up the mountain; overrun with bushes and washed out by the torrential rains. A lone wolf's howl, somewhere in the distance, contributed to this eerie trip as an owl, watching the midnight visitors, screeched an unwelcome warning.

"How much further is it, Snow?" Pearcy asked the man who was wiping the tears from his eyes. Snow, making no reply, just kept walking.

Higher up the mountain with each step, Snow continued leading the searchers on to a still unknown destination. The prisoner stopped abruptly, held up a skinny forefinger and pointed to a spot nearby, "Only a little further now — I'll show you where the body is."

The men tighten their grip on the prisoner just in case he tried to make a leap for liberty into the trees and boulders that lined the road.

"Why did you cut off the boy's head?" Russell asked the killer.

"I don't know why. I can't explain how I felt at the time. I must have been crazy. I jest couldn't thank straight."

Snow started walking once more; one hundred, then two hundred paces further, he stopped and pointed again.

"Boys, the body is right over there," pointing to his right toward a wire fence that separated the road from a pasture.

"About ten foot over there."

Cautiously approaching the fence, not knowing what to expect, W. D. Van Blarcom, the reporter, was the first to see the body.

"Here it is, over here by this mesquite tree."

The clouds floating away from the face of the midnight moon, shined down through the leafless tree onto the naked body, partially covered with cedar branches. Blarcom knelt down for a closer look, motioning to the others.

Sheriff Hassler and Ranger Stanley walked over to look at the body, and shining a flashlight, Stanley saw the ground was stained dark red with Bernie's blood. He pointed his light toward the naked body.

"An' look here," Stanley said, pointing to torn flesh, "the animals have been at it."

"Yeah, probably coyotes an' buzzards an' such," agreed Hassler.

The two officers turned over the lifeless, stiff body. Further examination revealed a bullet wound between the shoulder blades.

"Ya shot 'em in the back, didn't ya?" Hassler spoke, glaring at the suspected murderer.

"Ok, Snow," Hickman said to the man who did not approach the body. He sat quietly on a nearby rock, "We've come this far; it's time to make this right. We know you killed the boy, now where's your wife an' her mother?"

A panther's scream, echoing through the valley below, seemed to unnerve Snow, as well as the lawmen. Curious eyes, reflecting the light back from the flashlights dotted the surrounding bushes. And the body, lying there without a head, added to the gruesomeness of the night.

Snow insisted, among those bizarre surroundings, "I tell ya, I put 'em on the train to Waco. As far as I know, they're okay."

Ranger Hickman said, "It's no use pretending any longer, Snow. You murdered your wife an' her mother. We found their bones."

"I'm tired — will you please see that I get a square deal if I tell it all?" The prisoner asked, climbing down from the rock.

"It's my duty to prosecute you an' I'll make no promises," was Russell's reply, "but we will find out anyway, so you might as well tell us."

"What about my dogs?" Snow asked, squatting down and sitting on the ground, "What's gonna happen to my dogs? I luv them dogs. Will ye see that they're taken keer of?"

"You ran off an' left 'em, but we'll see that they're attended to," responded Russell.

Snow looked over at the naked body, lying there on the cold ground, then he remembered his cow — the cow he felt was the cause of all his troubles, the cause his insaneness, the cause of the tragic deaths.

"Sheriff, will you sell my cow fer me?"

"Yes, we'll do that."

"I want a fair trial, an' I do not want my neck broken jest to please y'all. Kin ya give me ya word that it'll be a fair trial?" Snow said, standing up and becoming more defiant.

"A fair trial you will get, I'll guarantee you that," Russell told the old farmer.

And with that, Snow confessed that he killed Maggie and Annie Olds, as well as Bernie Connally.

"I had a quarrel in which Bernie attacked me with a pistol an' my wife fired on me with a small rifle," Snow uttered.

"It wuz self-defense," he declared, "that's why I killed both of um. The old woman got in the line of fire an' so she got killed."

With that confession, the men started their trek back down the mountain. Hassler would make arraignments for removing the body from its temporary resting place on the ridge.

"Okay, let's get back to Fort Worth," Hickman said as they turned and started the journey back down the mountain to their cars.

Hickman took Snow back to the Tarrant County Jail and once again, the clanking of the metal door locked Snow back into his small jail cell. It was early, almost daybreak.

Sunday morning found Tarrant County Assistant District Attorney William H. Tolbert getting ready for church, when he heard his telephone ringing.

"Bill, this is Tom Hickman, I'd like to meet you at your office as soon as we can — I need to get a confession from a man from Erath County, who murdered his family."

Hickman, with his prisoner Snow, met Tolbert at his office a little before lunch time. The three sat down at a table, Snow on the left side of Hickman facing Tolbert, who would type the confessional statement.

Tolbert began, "I need to warn that you don't have to give us a confession, an' what you tell us today will be used against you at your trial. Do you understand that?"

"Yes sir. I done it, so I'll tell ya about it. Where do you want me to start?"

"Just tell us what happened, like you did last night —start at the first," Hickman told him.

"Well, I've been a farmer all my life," Snow began as Tolbert typed out the statement.

Snow held his head down and began sobbing, "Madness jest came over me."

Snow continued, telling his account of the black day as Tolbert reduced the statement to writing. When the statement was completed, Captain Hickman read it back to Snow, and Snow, agreeing it was factual, signed the confession.

Word that Snow had been moved to the jail in Fort Worth became known to the newspaper reporters throughout the State of Texas. One by one, they came to the jail in hopes of getting a picture, and an interview with the old farmer accused of a horrible crime. And one by one they left disappointed while Snow was being held incommunicado and no reporter was allowed to see him.

Snow, sitting in his cell a few days later, became upset when a new prisoner was moved into the cell with him. Snow looked at the drawing of the woman on the wall of the cell. Again, he pleaded with the jailer to cover the drawing because he couldn't bear to look at the image before him. He was not a model prisoner.

The new prisoner, Ralph Vance, looked at the man huddled in the corner of the cell. "I'll be gittin' out of here tomorrow 'cause they reversed my conviction."

"Good fer you," Snow replied sarcastically, "What'd ya do to get in here?"

"They said I killed my baby, but they couldn't prove it — something to do with corpus delicti."

The man had been charged with slaying his eight-day-old boy. A constable and his deputies were on a stakeout near Lake Worth when they noticed Vance, a young man in his twenties, burning something in the road. The officers went to the fire and saw the man burning baby clothes. Later in the night, he led the officers down a country road to a shallow grave where he had buried his son. Vance maintained his innocence and told the officers the baby died of natural causes — he buried him secretly one dark night to save paying a funeral bill.

"So, just don't admit to nothin' an' they can't touch ya," Vance told Snow.

"A little too late fer me; I already told 'em about it."

"Then tell 'em you're crazy an' plead insanity."

"That might be sound advice, but tell me, did ya kill yore baby?"

"Like I said, don't admit to nothing," Vance said with a smirk on his face.

"You're a baby killer! Jailer, get this man out of my sight.

23

CHRISTMAS DAY — 1925

It had finally arrived, the day for the yearly Martin get-together — Christmas. This year, Grandma Martin, Madison's brothers and sister, and Aaron's cousins would all gather at the Madison Martin home to celebrate the birth of our Lord. The Martins, a close-knit family, decided several years ago for all of the family to meet around Christmas time, and it had become an annual affair. Instead of burdening one family as the host each year, they also had decided to rotate among the brothers. This year was Brother Madison's turn.

Millie Martin was up early; chicken and dressing would be her contribution to the noontime Christmas dinner. Looking out the kitchen window as she crumbled up cornbread, she saw the sun was beginning its daily journey across a cloudless sky; its beams flickering through the leafless tree limbs. It would almost be a perfect day.

It had only been two weeks since F.M. Snow was arrested for murdering his family. The people of the community were relieved that the killer had finally been identified and arrested, and most were able to go back to their daily routines. The exceptions were the Martins, the Rivers and the Gristy families. They would be witnesses at Snow's upcoming murder trial.

Aaron, rubbing his eyes, wandered into the kitchen.

"Good mornin'," Millie greeted Aaron, "how'd you sleep?"

"I had another bad dream, Momma."

"Oh no, was it the same one?"

"No, I dreamed that I wuz floatin' high over the top of the farm. I could see the top of the house, the barns an' everything. Then I came up to the windmill an' the blades turned into that head that we found."

"Oh, honey, I know that was awful," Millie said, stirring a cup of chicken broth into the crumbled cornbread, "Go wash your hands an' get ready to eat breakfast."

Aaron poured water into the washbasin and washed his hands and face. Madison, finishing the morning chores, came in the house, washed his hands and sat at the kitchen table. Millie, giving

Madison a spoonful of the dressing, asked, "How does it taste?"

"Needs more sage."

Victoria, Aaron's oldest sister, soon to be twelve, was helping Millie cook the family breakfast. Ann, the younger sister, set the table while the cooks finished cooking a skillet full of scrambled eggs, a plate of fried pork sausages, hot biscuits and gravy. After the family had sat down at the table, Madison offered a prayer.

"Lord, thank you for another beautiful day, an' thank you for this food, Amen."

"You kids can open your present before everybody gits here," Madison said as they finished the breakfast.

Aaron, Ann, and Victoria broke and ran to the largest room in the house; the one with the decorated Christmas tree. Madison and Millie followed them into the room. They were anxious to see the beaming smiles on their children's faces as they ripped open their presents. Three wrapped presents, one for Aaron and one for each of his sisters, lay to one side under the aromatic cedar tree. Piled on the other side of the tree were five small presents to be opened at the Martin Family Christmas tree later that day.

"I know what this is! Thanks, Momma," Victoria, opening her gift — a new Sunday dress that Millie fashioned for her.

"What did you get, Aaron?" asked Ann, opening her present, "Look, I got two new baby dolls!"

Aaron tore the wrapping paper, revealing a box — a camera — an *Autographic Kodak Junior Camera* and two rolls of film. This model of camera was unique in that the photographer could enter text on the roll of film with a stylus. The written information would appear in the margin of the processed film.

"Oh, thanks, Momma and Daddy; I've been wantin' one of these forever. I'm gonna do some kodakin' today!"

Aaron sat down in the big easy chair in the living room and started reading over the instructions for his new camera:

> "Pull up on the rewind knob on the left side of the Kodak camera. This will open up the back of the camera. Be sure you pull up far enough. If the back does not open, it means . . ."

Aaron's mind began to wander as he thought of a Christmas years ago when he was only six. That year, a long, slender, heavy box had lain under the tree for days. He remembered going to the tree, in secret, every day and shaking the long box trying to surmise what was in the mysterious box and finally on Christmas morning he opened his present and found a brand new .22 single shot rifle.

Lately, Aaron had often wondered if the rifle was a present just for him or did his daddy need a rifle to end the fatted hog's life on hog killing day? "It's probably a little of both," Aaron thought to himself.

Millie returned to the kitchen where she put the chicken and dressing into the oven of her new cook stove, the Chambers Fireless Gas Range.

Madison had made a bountiful harvest this year, and as it was his custom upon making a good crop, Madison would purchase something nice for his wife. This year it was the latest model cook stove.

"Ann, come help me with the dishes," Millie requested, "you can clean off the table for me."

"What's Victoria gonna have to do?"

"She is goin' to straighten up the front room before the company gets here," then, speaking to her oldest, "Victoria, make sure the bed is made; that's where they're gonna be puttin' their coats."

A short time later, a knock on the door, the first of the kinfolks were arriving. Uncle Lum and Aunt Lois drove in from Fort Worth late yesterday evening and had stayed the night with Uncle Ira and Aunt Fannie.

Uncle Lum, the oldest of the brothers, had tried his luck at being a cowboy in the West, among other things, but finally settled as a barber in Ft. Worth.

"We've been readin' in the paper about Aaron and that other boy finding that head," Aunt Lois said handing Millie a bowl of mashed potatoes, "I'm sure glad they caught that awful man."

"Yes, we'll just be glad when it's all behind us. There's still the trial comin' up."

Uncle Lum, carrying a coconut pie not far behind asked, "Where do you want me to set this thang?"

"Just set it there on the cabinet, y'all just make yourselves at home while I finish up here in the kitchen."

Madison said, shaking his head, "That woman; she's in hog heaven. She's cooked enough for Coxey's Army."

"I heard that," replied Millie, "You know I'd rather have a barrel full left over than be a spoonful short."

"Yeah, I know it," grinned Madison, "did ya put more sage put in the dressin'?"

Then under his breath, as he walked away, "Can't get that woman to put enough sage in anythang."

Uncle Jack and Aunt Harriet were the next to arrive for the family reunion. Uncle Jack had left the farm for the oil fields of west Texas when he was twenty-one. The mass production of the Model T Ford, "The Tin Lizzie", made the car affordable for the middle-class family and with more automobiles traveling the roads, the demand for oil was increasing, creating jobs for many farm boys.

One by one the Martin family's uncles, aunts and cousins continued to trickle into the house, each family bringing a dish or two of food.

"Hi Grandma," Aaron greeted his eighty-four old grandmother, "come on an' set down in yore favorite chair, who brung you today?"

"Uncle Lum."

Grandma in fact, suffering from what the doctors called, "hardening of the arteries" came to the reunion with Uncle Ira and Aunt Fannie. The Martin brothers had gotten together several years ago and built a small two-room house at Uncle Ira's farm; handy for her to be cared for, but still able to have a house she could call her own.

It was time to eat the dinner; the table overflowed with a Christmas buffet — chicken and dressing with giblet gravy, mashed potatoes, fried ham, corn, a chicken pot pie, green beans, sweet potatoes and hot rolls. And in addition, there were desserts; cakes and pies and Millie's famous fried apricot pies.

"I want one of those," exclaimed Uncle Jack pointing to a dish of the fried pies.

Everybody wanted one of Millie's delicious apricot pies; the plate was emptied before most had started eating.

"Jack, just take one," scolded Aunt Harriet as he wrapped a pie into a clean handkerchief he had brought just for this occasion.

"Earl, will you ask the blessings on our food?" Madison asked his brother-in-law.

The custom of the day dictated that the grown-ups ate their meal first and then the children were served their Christmas dinner. Today would be a special one for Aaron; a passage from boyhood to manhood — he would get to eat this Christmas dinner with the grown-ups. He could hear Ann talking behind his back. "Aaron thinks he's so big settin' with the big folks; just makes me want to puke."

"You hush up," scolded Millie, "your time will come."

Aaron filled his plate and sat down by his cousin, Katherine. Katie, as nicknamed by the family, was an only child, sixteen years old — she had twinkling blue eyes, sparklingly golden hair, a perfect shade of blond and a mischievous smile. Being close, she and Aaron were best friends, sharing their hopes and dreams as well as their disappointments and heartaches.

Katie wiping her mouth with a napkin asked, "Were ya scared when ya found that boy's head?"

"I shore wuz, me an' Elvis thought we might be next 'cause we thought whoever killed him might be watchin' us."

"I'll bet y'all were because we were scared; I didn't sleep at all that night we heard about it. What's gonna happen next? What will they do to 'im?"

Aaron, taking a bite of chicken pot pie, "They's gonna be a trial, probably sometime next month. The sheriff told me that I'd have to tell about findin' the boy's head. I shore do dread it. I hope they never turn that man loose!"

"You'll do okay; just think about something pleasant while you're waiting."

"I guess I can think about being with Missy last summer. That wuz pretty pleasant!"

"I know you're sweet on her, but you got more class than she does; you'll find someone that you'll like just as much as you like her."

Jacob came over and sat down by his two cousins who were already eating. He said, setting a plate full of food on the table, "Hey Aaron, let's go down in the pasture after we have the Christmas tree. I want to try out my new bow an' arrow."

"I don't know; I'm still kinda spooked. I'd rather stay here. I think we're going to sang after awhile an' we can play some dominos."

Aaron took a sip of tea, then another bite of Millie's dressing.

"An' besides, I want to do some kodakin' with my new camera."

"Okay, but it shore is a purty day out there."

"Did y'all listen to the *WSM Barn Dance* last Saturday night?" asked Katie, "it comes on every week ya know."

"Yeah," said Jacob, "that Uncle Jimmy Thompson shore can play the fiddle. Did you know he is seventy-seven years old?"

"Nah, I didn't know that, really?"

"Yeah, I seen his picture in one of them magazines down at the barber shop. Must've been an old picture 'cause he didn't look that old. But the thing said he was that old."

Madison called from the front room, "Y'all come on in here when you've finished eatin' an' we'll give out the presents.

Each person brought one gift. It was traditional. The family drew names at the Christmas get-togethers, and the drawn name was to remain secret until the following Christmas. A limit of no more than fifty cents was the agreed amount for a present, and many of the gifts were handmade. As the family members finished eating, they took a place in the front room, called the living room, although Madison's family "lived" in a room at the back of the house, next to the kitchen.

Aaron's sisters handed out the gifts to the lucky recipients. Aunt Rachel held up a bonnet that Aunt Fannie made for her. Uncle Sam thanked Aaron for a handkerchief.

"I can use this," Madison said, holding up a fob for his pocket watch, "Thank you, Lois."

One by one the presents were handed out until the Christmas tree was barren of gifts. Now it was time for visiting, playing forty-two and singing. Some of the older cousins gathered around the upright piano to sing some old gospel songs mixed in with Christmas carols; the younger cousins spread out on the bare floor and played with their new Christmas toys.

But, not all stayed in the house on this pleasant Christmas afternoon. Another Christmas tradition, when the weather permitted, was to go squirrel hunting down on Duffau Creek. Tall trees, cottonwoods, lining the creek banks were the domicile of the medium-sized rodents. Besides being a sport, hunting the squirrels provided fresh meat — they could be fried or used for meat to make stew.

Aaron, Jacob and some of the uncles eased their way down to the creek, about a half mile behind the hay barn. Wandering along the creek bank, they heard chattering somewhere in the distance — a warning that something wasn't quite right.

"There he is," Uncle Ira shouted, pointing to the squirrel that had flattened himself out against a tree limb.

He eased his .22-caliber rifle up to his shoulder, and the prey scooted around to the other side of the limb. Uncle Ira, not to be defeated, eased around to the other side of the tree. One shot was all it took. Uncle Ira had a knack for spotting the squirrels, and his aim was deadly.

Uncle Jack brought along his new Christmas present; a present that he bought for himself, a

Remington Model 24 semi-automatic .22 rifle. Another tree, another squirrel — Uncle Jack took aim — two rapid shots; bang-bang — the target was hit and as it was falling to the ground, three more rapid shots; bang-bang-bang!

"Boy, I gotta have one of them," Aaron said, amazed by the rapid firing rifle, "I gotta tell Elvis about it! Man, we could kill every coon an' possum in this country!"

"Yeah, but it took 'em five shots; I could uh got five of 'em with that many shots," whispered Uncle Ira.

Today, Ned and Ida would be going to Ned's brothers' home in Duffau. They were also having Christmas dinner, although this Christmas wasn't very cheerful for them. Living next to the Snow farm was a constant reminder of the terrible deed committed by the man called Snow. Ida, looking over toward the Snow farm couldn't help but think about the horrible murders; remembering Bernie's lifeless head, the head of a boy that she had identified at the funeral home. She too would be subpoenaed to testify at Snow's murder trial.

"Now wife, don't worry so much about havin' to go to that trial, jest listen to what them lawyers say an' answer 'em the best ya can," Ned told his worried wife.

"I know, but it still makes me nervous thinkin' about all those people that will be there." She placed a big platter of fried chicken into a food basket.

"Now, Now."

"How could that horrible man just chop up his family like that?"

"All I can say is old satan's got a holt on him. Come on, let's go," Ned said, carrying the basket of food out the door.

Ned easily cranked his car. He and Ida began their short journey to Duffau. Trees that had shed their leaves lined the country road; the golden globe in the sky shined down through the leafless branches, warming the Christmas day.

Passing by the abandoned Snow farm, the sight of the terrible massacre, they saw that all was calm and serene today.

"I jest can't believe all this has happened," Ida told her husband, "that poor boy an' his family."

"Yep, it wuz terrible, you might hear about sump'um like that in a big city, but not here in Erath County."

"An' it happened so close to Christmas, it jest ruins my Christmas spirit."

"I know, wife, I know."

The car chugged on down the road, leaving a small cloud of dust behind. Fallen leaves swirled as the car made its journey down the country road.

"It shore is dry," Ned complained, trying to change the subject, "We shore need a good soaking rain. That would help everybody's spirits."

"I sure could use a spirit lifter. I knew that ole man was mean, but Lord, who'd thought this?"

Still trying to change the subject, Ned said, pointing, "I see McCarey's got a new bull."

The Rivers' Christmas became even more dismal when the bad news came from El Paso. Mrs. Rivers' only brother, Calvin, died during a surgical procedure.

"Uncle Will an' Aunt Florence will take care of things around here," Mrs. Rivers mourned, "we gotta be in El Paso by Monday."

"I wanted to see Raymond an' Oliver, but not this way," Elvis said, mentioning his cousins.

Grandpa Harris, Elvis' grandfather, was confident that his new Chevrolet Superior would make the long trip. After loading the car, they began their westward journey. Getting a late start, they would only travel to Abilene today, where they would stay the night with Mrs. Rivers' sister, Mary.

"Who'd a thought we could of made it over a hunerd miles in a single day?" Grandpa Harris bragged on his new Chevrolet as they neared Abilene.

"Yep, Grandpa that shore is a fine piece of an automobile," Elvis answered back, "an' we didn't leave 'til ten in this morning. Jest thank what we could er done if we wuz to get a good start."

"Yes sirree, tomorrow we'll hit some of that straight road where that new thirty-five mile a hour is legal. Gonna try to make it to Odessie so's we can make it on into El Pasy the next day. That is if yore granny don't fuss at me too loud fer a driving so fast."

The next day's ride to Odessa wasn't any more pleasant than the day before with the exception that Mary's family following along on the burial trip, and that gave some comfort and peace of mind should trouble arise. Grandma Harris was taking the death exceptionally hard. She would be fine for a few miles and then cry for a few miles, more than once lamenting, "I never thought I'd have to bury one of my own."

Later, telling Aaron about the trip, Elvis said, "I've always heard of something called wailing but never really seen it, but I seen it on that trip. Grandma would be all right for a while an' then she'd wail a spell, she'd be all right for a while, an' then she'd wail a spell. That wuz the longest trip of my life."

Traveling from Odessa to El Paso the following day was about the same except Grandma Harris was about smoked out.

"Pa," she said to Grandpa Harris, "I know it's freezing cold outside but couldn't you crack that winder just a little an' let some of this cigarette smoke out? This is the third day we've had a constant dose of it — thank the Lord Elvis don't smoke, we'd have a double dose then."

"Sorry Ma," Grandpa Harris said opening the front vent window slightly, "I'm so nervous I just keep firing up one right after the other."

Elvis thinking to himself, "I don't know which is worse, having the winder up in the winter an' my eyes burning from all that smoke; or having the winders down in the summer time an' having ashes from them cigarettes blowed back in my eyes."

F. M. Snow, the accused murderer, still lodged in the Tarrant County Jail, cursing at times, and then weeping at other times, sat in the corner of his cell waiting for his Christmas meal. The jailer brought it — today it was chicken soup and crackers.

Oh, I miss my Maggie," he cried, "I wuz wantin' us to have a Christmas together. I'd druther be where she is."

His murder trial was scheduled to begin in January. Maybe he suspected, perhaps not; this would be his last Christmas to spend on this earth.

24

THE TRIAL

The Erath County Courthouse, a majestic building, can be seen from all directions when entering Stephenville, Texas. It is the third courthouse that has been the home of justice for Erath County. The first courthouse, a wooden building, in a blaze that could be seen for miles around, burned to the ground in 1866. When the county commissioners planned the second courthouse, they elected to build a stone structure, but by 1887, the new building was beginning to deteriorate.

The second building's fate was determined and in 1891, the block style building was torn down and the commissioners, once again, completed plans to construct the courthouse that is in use today. The cornerstone was laid, and construction began in December 1891.

The three-story building, constructed from native limestone from the Leon River and red sandstone from the Pecos River, is different from many of the other courthouses in Texas. The tower is in the center of the complex rather than being on one side. Syrian columns support the north entrance arch, and many years after the courthouse's completion, a Howard clock was installed in the central tower.

Imported marble was selected to cover floors of the majestic three story building, and East Texas Pine makes up the woodwork inside the building. Stairs, on the east and west side of the building, were built from wrought iron and cast iron.

A visitor from Philadelphia once made the comment to some of the local residents that the first thing that came in sight when he got to Stephenville was that monstrosity of a courthouse. This statement did not set well with the Erath County citizens who were very proud of their courthouse.

The Grand Jury met in the courthouse on Monday; December 21st, 1925 to determine if there was enough evidence to bind F. M. Snow over for a jury trial. Henry Belcher was the foreman of the twelve-man Grand Jury.

The main clue in unraveling the gruesome mystery was Ned's recognition of the head that he viewed at the funeral home. He and his wife, Ida, gave testimony to the jury panel that they made the positive identification that the murdered boy was

Bernie Connally. Aaron Martin and Elvis Rivers told about finding the head in a tow sack in the old abandoned cellar. Sam Russell read Snow's confession to the members of the jury, where Snow admitted to the slaying and cremation of the women's bodies.

The Grand Jury handed over the indictment:

> "F. M. Snow did with malice and afore-
> thought kill Bernie Connally by shoot-
> ing him with a pistol and a gun."

And with that indictment, there would be a murder trial. It began on January 18, 1926 at the Erath County Courthouse in the Twenty-ninth District courtroom. Judge J. B. Keith was the presiding Judge. Sitting at a table in front of the judge's bench leading the prosecution, was the district attorney, Sam Russell. He was assisted by the prosecuting attorney from Palo Pinto, Oscar Herring. Herring was well known for his delivery of prosecutorial speeches. Defending Snow at the table to the left of the prosecution was E. W. Crowell from Farmersville, M. L. Munday from Fort Worth and Wallace Scott from Dublin.

Judge Keith rapped his gavel and began, "I have before me two motions made by the defense. The first is a motion for a change of venue stating that the defendant, F. M. Snow will be unable to get a fair trial here in Erath County. I overrule and deny this motion."

Snow lowered his head and put his hands under his chin. Pearcy, guarding Snow, stayed close to him. Snow coughed as the judge continued.

"The second motion is for a delay of the trial so that the defendant can be taken back to the Tarrant County Jail where there he can be examined by doctors to determine if he is mentally unbalanced. This motion is also overruled and denied."

Snow looked over in the direction of his lawyers. The defense attorneys immediately prepared another motion — Munday stood up, presenting his motion, "Your Honor, I ask that a continuance be granted on the grounds that we defense attorneys have not had sufficient time to prepare our case to defend Mister Snow."

Judge Keith denied this third request to delay the murder trial for the woodchopper accused of slaying his wife, stepson and mother-in-law.

"You've had more than sufficient time to prepare this case. I overrule and deny this motion. Are there any more motions to be brought before the court?"

"Not at this time, Your Honor."

The courtroom was packed to capacity as the picking of the jury began. A circus tent was set up on the East Side of the courthouse to take care of the people who could not get a seat in the crowded courtroom. One hundred and fifty people were summoned for the jury panel. Sam Russell, standing and leaning forward with both hands on the table, was the first to address the prospective jurors.

"Ladies an' Gentlemen, good morning. My name is Sam Russell an' I am the district attorney for Erath County. Here to my right is Oscar Herring, who will be assisting me with the prosecution of this case."

Russell straightened up and pointed to Herring with an open hand. Herring nodded his head as a greeting. Russell adjusted his glasses and walked from behind the table and walked closer to the prospective jurors, and continued.

"This is an opportunity for us attorneys to get to know a little about you an' for you to know a few details about this case. I think you will find that there is evidence to show, beyond a doubt, that the defendant, Francis Marion Snow, that man sitting right over there, on the evening of November twenty-seventh, nineteen hundred an' twenty-five, did kill his step-son, Bernie Connally."

Russell pointed to Snow, who was sitting at the table to his left. Snow, staring straight ahead, didn't acknowledge the district attorney's statement.

"First, I would like to know how many of you here know the defendant — may I see a show of hands."

Snow looked around and saw that Luke Johnson and four other people held up their hands.

"Yes sir, Mister Johnson, you know the defendant?"

"Yes sir, he's my neighbor."

"Is there anything about being his neighbor that would cause you to not be able to listen to the all the evidence that will be presented here an' render a fair verdict?"

"Yes sir, there is, the morning after he . . ."

The district attorney interrupted him and asked him to approach the bench before Judge Keith. Two of the defense attorneys, along with the district attorney, stood in front of the judge as Johnson spoke, just above a whisper.

"It was about the morning after this all wuz supposed to have happened — he told me he had a fight with his wife an' he told me he took 'em to Iredell to catch a train — I could tell he wuz upset. An' I jest thank he did it."

Judge Keith made his ruling, "Mister Johnson, I'm going to excuse you from serving on this jury; however, I understand you may be called as a witness in these proceedings, so I'll ask you to leave this courtroom and remain outside this courtroom until you are dismissed."

Johnson left the courtroom where he waited in the rotunda with the other witnesses. He would not be allowed to hear any of the trial's testimony.

The other three people who knew Snow did not know any of the detail of the murder and only knew Snow by sight but had never talked to him. The questioning of the jury panel continued and only two jurors had been selected when court adjourned Monday afternoon.

The following day, Tuesday, January 19th, there were only six people chosen when court recessed. Many were disqualified because of their objection to the death penalty. The judge made it plain that no one would be allowed to sit on the jury if they had viewed the boy's head at the funeral home. Hundreds of people were disqualified because they had gone to the funeral home in an attempt to identify the youth whose head had been severed from the body. Hoping that a jury could be seated by Wednesday, Judge Keith summoned one hundred and fifty more men since the original panel was nearly exhausted. Snow was growing weary of the selection process and the disqualification of many one the panel of prospective jurors.

"Why don't they jest put a bunch of Negroes on the jury?" he said with a disgusted look on his face as several more men left the courtroom after being disqualified, "I told 'em I did it! Let's jest get it over with! It don't make a bit of difference to me 'cause I'm gonna hang anyway."

Snow was returned to his cell a little after dark on Tuesday afternoon. A black man, Leroy Phillips, was in the cell beside him when he returned. Snow ate a few bites of stew that had been cooked for the prisoners, occasionally glancing over at the new inmate. The black man was the first to speak.

"What ya in here fer?"

Snow remained silent and turned away from his cellmate.

"I stolt a sack of tators fer my kids. Don't know what'll come of um now," Phillips lamented.

"I killed my wife and hacked 'er to pieces," Snow told the man coldly. He looked outside the jail and saw that another crowd was beginning to form around the building.

One by one, the crowd began chanting, "Snow! Throw on another leg — Snow! Throw on another leg, Snow . . ."

Snow crouched down in the corner of his cell and began weeping and crying out for his Maggie. Suddenly he sprang up toward Phillips, banging on the cell bars, "They want to kill me! Listen to 'em out there!"

Phillips backed away from the man who was now screaming at the top of his voice. "Sur-Sur, I don't mean ya no harm, please don't hurt me."

Snow began sobbing again and told Phillips he was sorry he frightened him. "These mad spells jest come over me. I killed 'em all, my Maggie an' her boy an' the old woman. I'm a mad man, I tell ya. I burned 'em an' now I'm gonna burn in hell!"

"They wuz a man over in San Saba County a couple years back. He told me he wuz gonna whoop my ass, so I jest shot 'em an' chopped off his head. I throwed it down into a ole well down there," Snow said, making a throwing motion.

"They never found out I done it," he told the man who was shaking in his cell, "You'd best not tell anyone what I told ya, 'cause I'll git you!"

"Naw Suh, I shore ain't gonna do that."

Two more inmates were in the jail on this night. Shivering from the cold, one of the men took his cue from the noisy gathering outside, "Yeah, Snow, throw on another leg, its cold in here."

Wednesday morning found Snow sick in his cold cell. Sheriff Hassler notified Judge Keith, who ordered Dr. T. M. Gordon to examine Snow.

"He's in a highly nervous state," the doctor reported to the court.

A short time later, Snow, feeling well enough to continue, was brought to the courtroom. He took little interest in the questions that were being asked by the attorneys. He sat quietly, looking down at the table while holding his head in his hands. The Wednesday morning session failed to seat any more jurors and having questioned nearly three hundred people by Wednesday afternoon, one hundred more citizens were ordered to appear in court for the Thursday session.

After four long and trying days, a jury was sworn in late Thursday afternoon. Turning toward Snow, Judge Keith asked him to enter his plea. Snow jumped up and promptly answered, "I'm guilty!"

His attorney, Wallace Scott, with a surprised look on his face, told the court that the plea was not guilty.

The judge accepted the not guilty plea and excused the jurors for the day — admonishing them not talk to anyone about the case.

A cold front blew into the area overnight, and on Friday morning; the temperature fell to four below zero with snow and ice covering the ground. Many of the stock tanks had solidly frozen over during the night, and the farmers had to use an axe to chop a hole in the ice so their livestock could have access to drinking water. Many of the courtroom spectators had to leave some of the proceedings in order to feed their cattle and horses.

The courtroom was extremely cold as the testimony began. A coal oil stove was passed around to help to keep the juror's feet warm. The prosecutor from Palo Pinto County, Oscar Herring, began his opening statement to the all male jury.

"Your Honor, may it please the court — Gentlemen of the jury, we want to thank you for your service here. This is a case about a horrible murder an' we know it's going to be hard for you to listen to all the testimony that will be presented. There are some gruesome details that we will have to put before you. The burden is on the state of Texas to prove that F. M. Snow killed his step-son, Bernie Connally, an' after he had killed him, he cut his head off his body."

Herring walked nearer the jury box, "We believe the evidence will show that on November the twenty-seventh of last year, F. M. Snow blowed his wife's brains out with a Winchester rifle, an' then he killed his mother-in-law by severing her head with an axe. There will be evidence to show that he hacked up those two women's bodies an' methodically cremated them in an attempt to hide this hideous crime."

Herring heard several sighs and noticed the reaction of the jury as he continued, "An' after he had brutally murdered his wife an' her mother, he wasn't finished with his killing! No, we are going to present evidence that the same F. M. Snow rode his horse to town with only one purpose — to find Bernie Connally. An', what did he do when he found him? He got on the wagon with the boy an' they rode to the Snow farm an' just as they got there, F. M. Snow shot Bernie in the back an' killed him."

The courtroom was as quiet as a grave, and no one moved. Herring walked over and picked up an axe that was propped up against a table in front of the judge's bench.

"The testimony is going to show you beyond a reasonable doubt that F. M. Snow took Bernie Connally's body to a location over ten miles from his house where he discarded it like a piece of trash. But that wasn't enough for this evil killer, he took his axe an' chopped the head off the boy's body an' disposed of it in a different location. You will hear evidence that two boys found Bernie's head in a ole cellar where this cold blooded killer had tried to hide it."

More gasps came from the spectators sitting in the cold courthouse. Herring concluded by asking the jury members to listen carefully to all the evidence and to find the defendant, F. M. Snow guilty of murder. Herring thanked the jury again and sat down at the prosecution's table. Snow's defense attorney, Matt Munday, made an opening statement to the twelve men sitting in judgment of his client.

"Your Honor, members of the jury — I, too, want to thank you for your service here on this cold, cold day. I know you all had rather be somewhere else, but you are a vital part in this process of our legal system. You have heard Mister Herring give a fine speech an' what a fine speech it was about how horrendous this crime was. But I ask you to listen to the all the evidence that will be presented in this trial. Mister Herring is a fine speaker, but everything Mister Herring told you is not evidence so none of it can be considered . . ."

"Objection," Herring rose to his feet, "Your honor, when the evidence is entered, they must consider it."

"Objection overruled," the judge said calmly, "Gentlemen, you will only consider the evidence that is presented to you, an' nothing more. The attorneys are laying out their case for you at this time, but what they are telling you is not evidence. Continue Mister Munday."

Snow stared straight ahead showing no emotion. He was drawn and shivering from the cold. His pathetic form made one wonder how he could have committed such a dark deed.

"Thank you, Your Honor; Gentlemen of the jury, I believe that when you hear all the evidence, an' when you weigh that evidence, you will find this man is innocent of the charge of murder. No matter what you have heard, an' no matter what you believe, you must listen to only the evidence," Munday admonished the jurors.

"The prosecution is prepared to tell you some awful things, some gruesome things — they want to paint Frank Snow as being an evil man, however, I believe the evidence will show that Frank Snow married Maggie Poston, an' out of kindness, he took her son an' his mother-in-law into his home. She was the love of his life, an' he wanted to make a home for them. Then, we are going ask you to examine the defendant's wife Maggie Connally Poston Snow. You will find that before she married Frank, she had several husbands an' each one of them died in mysterious fashions. An' that young man, Bernie Connally, he outweighed Mister Snow by at least forty pounds. He was strong an' healthy, an' we intend to show that Frank Snow feared him. I think that evidence is going to show that Mister Snow acted only in self-defense. An' evidence will show that a person has the right to defend his life, an' F. M. Snow had no other choice other than being killed himself. When all the evidence is heard, I believe you will render a true an' fair verdict, an' that verdict will be that Frank Snow is not guilty of murder."

Munday returned to his table and sat next to his client. The prosecution called Aaron Martin as the first witness. The judge swore him in and Sam Russell began the questioning.

"It's cold in here isn't it?" Aaron shook his head indicating yes. "Would you state your name for the record, please?"

"A-A Aaron Martin," he replied in a quiet voice.

"Speak just a little louder, Aaron, how old are you?"

"Eighteen, sir."

"Please tell the jury where you live."

"I live in the Pony Creek community, sir."

Russell established the fact that he was a resident of Erath County and had lived in the county all his life. Aaron, sitting on his hands to keep them warm, quickly glanced around the courtroom.

"Aaron, do you remember your where-a-bouts on the night of December the tenth last year?"

"Yes Sir, me an' Elvis wuz out huntin' an' checkin' our traps over to his grandpa's place."

"An' did anything out of the ordinary happen that night?" Russell stood up and walked toward Aaron.

"Yes sir."

"An' would you tell the jury about that, Aaron?"

"Me an' Elvis heard his dog barking by this old burned out house. There's this here ole cellar next to the ole house an' we went up there an' looked in that there cellar an' Elvis saw a tow sack a hangin' from a nail or sump'um."

Aaron paused and took a breath and rubbed his face with his left hand.

"Okay, after you saw the sack, explain what happened next."

"Elvis pulled the sack out from the cellar," Aaron said, shaking, his voice quivering.

"Okay, you're doing fine, did you find out the contents of that bag?"

"Yes sir."

"What was in that bag, son?"

"It wuz a boy's head."

The courtroom was very quite as the district attorney picked up a photograph and showed it to the boy, "I want you to look at this photo. Can you tell me what is in this picture?"

The boy looking pale shook his head indicating a positive answer. He swallowed.

"It's that boy's head," his voice was barely audible.

"No more questions for this young man." The district attorney introduced the photograph of the head into evidence under the objection of the defense and passed it around for the jury to view.

Matt Munday, Snow's attorney, was twenty-nine years old; just out of law school and ready to make a name for himself. A heavy dark green coat covered his dark gray suit. He parted his black hair in the middle, and his gold-rimmed glasses accented his slender face. He had a few questions for the boy who had rather be anywhere than in that freezing courtroom.

"My name is Matt Munday; did you take that picture?" He asked sternly.

"No sir."

"Then, do you know who took the picture?"

"No sir."

"Well then, how can you set there an' identify this picture for the jury?"

"It looks like the head we found."

"An' I guess it looked just like that when you found it, is that right?"

"No sir, it was all bloody an' everything, but . . ." Munday stopped him.

"So it doesn't look the same does it? But you're telling this jury that you're sure it's what you an' the Rivers boy found? No more questions." The cocky defense attorney turned his back to Aaron and walked back to Snow's table.

Russell stood up, "You know, if it was a photo of a cow, it might be difficult to identify, but we don't see many heads that don't have a body in these parts, and Mister Munday you know that! Aaron, you've looked at this photograph very carefully haven't you?" The boy nodded when Russell asked the question.

"An' even though the photograph was taken after the head was cleaned up — you can still identify it, can't you?" Russell asked the boy calmly.

"Yes sir, I'll never forget it."

"A thing like that would be hard to forget. We pass the witness an' call K .N. Baxley."

Russell questioned Baxley, the photography studio owner. Handing the photograph to him, he asked, "Can you identify this photograph and do you know who made it?"

"Yes sir, it's a photo that I took after I was called to the funeral home by Sheriff Hassler."

"And how can you be sure that it is the same photo that's marked as state's exhibit one?"

"It's because I placed my initials and date on the back of the photo."

"Turn the photo over; what do you see there?"

"I see my initials, 'KNB' and the date of 'December 11, 1925.'"

"No further questions; the state calls Elvis Rivers to the stand."

The boy looked around and walked slowly to the witness chair. He looked over at the jury and took a deep breath. Russell questioned him about finding the head in the abandoned cellar. Elvis' testimony confirmed the statements made by his friend, Aaron.

"Elvis, I want to ask you one more thing, do you remember a night, several nights before you discovered the boy's head. It was a night or so after Thanksgiving; do you remember anything unusual about that night?"

"Aaron an' me were out huntin' an' we heard somebody shootin' over t'ward Snow's place."

Munday, on cross examination asked, "So you heard shooting. Do you know who was doing the shooting?"

"No sir."

"Do you know what they were shooting at?"

"No sir."

"So, somebody, who we don't know, was shooting at something. Is that correct?"

"I guess so."

"Could that somebody be shooting a fox or a raccoon, or some other varmint?"

"I guess so."

"No more questions."

Sam Russell called Ned Gristy to the witness stand next.

"Mister Gristy, when you went to the funeral home to view the boy's head, did you know who it was?" Russell questioned.

"I thought I recognized him."

"An' who did you think it was?"

"It looked like our neighbor's boy, Bernie Connally, but I wasn't sure though."

Ida Gristy testified next. She told about going to the funeral home and identifying the bodiless head as being that of their neighbor, Bernie Connally.

Connally's uncle and another neighbor, Mrs. Lou Hill, testified that they also recognized the boy after viewing the head in the casket at Trewitt's Funeral Home.

Russell called Sheriff M. D. Hassler as the state's next witness. Hassler was sworn in, and Russell established the fact that Hassler was the sheriff of Erath County and that the murder had occurred in Erath County and that Hassler had jurisdiction in the case. Russell began his examination of his main witness. Hassler told of his experience in law enforcement and that he was qualified to testify as an expert on firearms.

"On or about December tenth, did you receive a telephone call, an' if so, what was the nature of that call?"

"The call wuz from the River's boy; he was pretty excited."

"And why was he excited?"

"He told me that he an' the Martin boy had found a human head in a ole cellar."

"An' where was this cellar located?"

"On the ole Rivers farm five about miles out t'wards Glen Rose."

Hassler related to the jury that the boys thought the head was Herman Starnes, but Starnes was found to be alive and well.

Hassler told the jury about the steps he had taken to identify the slain victim and how the identification led to the arrest of F. M. Snow. He gave an account of going to the murder suspect's house with his deputy, the Texas Ranger and the district attorney, and it was there that they discovered bones in the fireplace. Hassler gave details about the eerie trip with Snow's guiding them up Cedar Mountain where they located Connally's body.

"An' did you examine the body?"

"Yes sir, I did."

"Would you tell the jury what you saw?"

"I carefully examined the coat an' shirt that the boys found in the sack with the head. I examined the deceased boy's body an' I found two bullet holes."

"An' based upon your experience as a law enforcement officer, was the victim shot from the front or back?"

"He was shot in the back." Gasps came from the spectators in the courtroom. The judge rapped his gavel and warned them to remain silent through the rest of the proceedings.

Russell continued, "The defendant's attorneys are going to argue that this murder was self-defense. Can you explain to this jury how shooting a boy in the back two times can be called self-defense?"

"Objection, calls for speculation an' there is no evidence that victim was shot in the back, an' there is absolutely no evidence tying my client to any kind of a shooting," Munday shouted, jumping from his chair.

"Objection sustained, let's stick to the evidence Mister Russell," the judge cautioned the attorney.

"Yes your Honor, but the court has recognized Sheriff Hassler as an expert on firearms. It is his opinion that the boy was shot in the back. His opinion is not speculation. Anyone using any reason at all knows that shooting someone in the back is not self-defense, it was not then, an' it will never be."

"Mister Russell, the jury can decide that, please continue."

"Yes your Honor, in your opinion as an expert, was the victim, Bernie Connally, approaching Snow when he was shot, or was he going back as if retreating?"

"It's my opinion that the victim was not approaching the defendant when he was shot in the back."

"No more questions."

Wallace Scott, representing Snow, tried to discredit Hassler as an expert witness, but the calm sheriff would not be compromised. Scott asked Hassler further questions about Snow's arrest.

"When you arrested my client, he told you about some threats made against Bernie Connally by a Negro man didn't he?"

Hassler responded to the attempt by the defense attorney to raise a doubt in the jurors' minds, "Yes sir, he made mention of such a threat."

"An' I'm sure you followed up on this information an' questioned that Negro man?"

"No sir, We identified him as being one Mordecai Johnson, but we never did find him — however, I felt there was no need to question the Negro since your client confessed . . ." The defense attorney stopped him from speaking further.

Mordecai Johnson in fact, would not have been found. As soon as he realized that he had seen this killer before, Mordecai, once again, pulled up and left everything behind. Not so much that he feared the man accused of murder — he did not want to have any contact with the law officers. He was still wanted for a murder in Alabama. Mordecai Johnson would never be seen again in this area.

The defense attorney continued to ask questions, "An' did my client not tell you that he only was acting in self-defense — that he had to wrestle with the boy an' he barely escaped with his own life? Isn't that what he told you?"

"Yes sir, that's what he said, but . . ." Scott cut him off.

"An' didn't he tell you that the boy had a gun, a .32 pistol?"

"Yes. He said that an' . . ."

"An' didn't he tell you the boy pointed that pistol at 'em? An' didn't he tell you he thought the boy was gonna shoot him?"

"Yes, he said that."

"In fact, he told you that he was barely able to over-power the boy an' take the gun away from him — isn't that what he told you?" The lawyer didn't wait for the sheriff to answer.

"No more questions."

"Snow told you how he disposed of that gun, didn't he?" Russell asked the sheriff in rebuttal.

"Yes sir, he told me he sold the gun to Buck Hill."

"An' in the course of your investigation, you veri-fied that Buck Hill had indeed bought that pistol for a sum of two dollars — isn't that correct sheriff?"

"Yes sir, that's correct. Buck Hill also told me something else."

"Objection, this is hearsay because . . ."

Scott knew what Hassler was going to say, and he didn't want the jury to hear it — the objection was overruled and Russell remained quiet as the sheriff continued.

"Hill told me that he went to Snow's house one night an' it was late, so he decided to stay all night with Snow. He said Snow had a big fire going in the fireplace although the night was not that cold. He told me that Snow asked him if he could smell any-thing dead."

"An' what do you think Snow would have done if Hill had smelled the dead bodies?"

"Objection! Your Honor, I adamantly object! That calls for speculation on the part of the good sheriff."

Russell withdrew his question, "We can only surmise what would have happened to Mister Hill if he had detected the smell of death."

"Sheriff Hassler, were you present at the farm rented by the defendant the day after the head of Bernie Connally was identified?" Russell asked.

"Yes sir."

"About what time of day did you arrive there?"

"We got there just before the sun come up, I 'spect it was 'bout seven."

"Would you tell this jury what you found?"

"We found evidence of blood on the front porch an' inside the house.

"Did you find anything else?"

"Yes sir, I went over to the fireplace an' began diggin' 'round in there. I found something that . . ."

Scott jumped up, "Your Honor, I object to this line of questioning because it tends to infer that there might have been another crime committed."

Russell responded, "Your Honor, the body of Bernie Connally had not been found and the officers were merely searching the house, looking for the boy's body. Mister Scott is the only one who has mentioned any other crime up to this point."

"I'll allow you continue, however I don't expect you to make any sort of reference to any other crime, whatsoever," Keith told the attorneys, "Sheriff Hassler, you may continue."

"I found somethin' hard in the fireplace. I pulled it out an' looked at it an' I thought it wuz human bone. Then I found a tooth an' I wuz purty shore I wuz right."

"An' did you take these particles as evidence?"

"Yes sir."

"An' had the body of Bernie Connally been found at that time?"

"No Sir."

"In fact, you didn't find the body of Bernie Connally at the Snow farm, did you?"

"Your Honor," Scott jumped up again.

"Ah, you can set back down. I have no further questions for the good sheriff.

25

THE TRIAL CONTINUES

"Mister Scott, do you have any questions for this witness?" Judge Keith asked.

"No, Your Honor, no questions for this witness at this time." Attorney Scott didn't want to expand on this damaging information presented by Sheriff Hassler as the trial continued.

The district attorney called Jack Sloan, a clerk at the Higginbotham Brothers store in Stephenville.

"Mister Sloan, I want you to recall the afternoon of November twenty-seventh of last year. Do you remember seeing the defendant?"

"Yes, he came in the store late that afternoon. He wanted to buy some rifle shells. He told me some varmints had been killing his chickens, an' he was going to put a stop to it."

"Do you recall what kind of bullets he wanted?"

"Yes sir, they were .44-caliber cartridges for that Winchester rifle he had with him."

"An', how can you be sure of the exact date?"

"I'd better remember it — it was my anniversary."

"No more questions."

"Mister Sloan, did you work all day on the twenty-seventh of November," Attorney Scott asked.

"Yes, I did."

"How many customers did you wait on that day?"

"Oh, thirty; maybe forty."

"And you can remember everything that every customer bought?"

"Probably not."

"No further questions."

Russell asked Sloan, "How are you sure that the defendant bought cartridges from you that day?"

"He wanted to put them on his account. I have the charge ticket right here in my pocket."

Russell smiled, and then called Buck Hill as a witness.

"Buck, do you know that man sitting right over there?" pointing to the defendant Snow.

"Yes sir, it's Mister Snow."

"Fine, now sometime in late November, did you talk to the defendant?"

"Yes, I did."

"At that time, did he make mention of his wife?"

"Yes sir, he said she was in Waco."

"Did he make mention of the where-a-bouts of Bernie Connally?"

"He told me that both he an' Missus Olds were also in Waco."

"In Waco, did he tell you why they were in Waco?"

"What he told me wuz that he had quarreled with his wife an' she had left him."

"Now, did you have an occasion to go to the defendant's house sometime after November the twenty-seventh?"

"Yes sir. Dark caught me one night, an' I stopped by his place and asked if I could stay the night at his place."

"And did you stay?"

"Yes sir."

"And on this particular night, did the defendant ask you a rather strange question?"

"He asked me if I could smell sump'um dead. I told him that I couldn't smell nothin' cause I had a bad cold."

"Then, on another occasion, did you make a purchase from the defendant?"

"Yes sir, he sold me a .32-caliber pistol."

Buck's wife was called to testify next.

"Missus Hill, in the days that followed November the twenty-seventh, did you have an encounter with the defendant?"

"Yes, I bought some furnishing from him, a table an' a couple of chairs an' a few other odds an' ends."

"Did he say why he was selling those items?"

"He told me that he was moving an' didn't have any further need of the furniture. When I asked him about his wife, he told me that she had left 'im an' wouldn't be back."

"No other questions for Missus Hill."

"Does the defense wish to cross examine?" asked the Judge.

"No, Your Honor."

"Mister Russell, do you wish to introduce any further witnesses?"

"Yes Your Honor, we call Ernest Cork," Russell announced.

After being sworn, the district attorney began his questioning,

"Where do you live Mister Cork?"

"On the road from Stephenville to Hico, about five miles south of here."

"Is that anywhere near where the defendant resided?"

"Yes sir, the turn-off to his place is about a quarter of a mile south of me toward Hico."

"On or about November the twenty-seventh of last year, did you see the defendant?"

"Yes sir."

"What time of day was it?"

"About sundown."

"An' what was he doing?"

"He was riding on the back of a wagon with a boy. The boy was in the front seat."

"Did you notice anything else?"

"He had a horse tied behind the wagon an' he had a rifle across his lap."

"Is there anything else about that evening that stands out in your mind?"

"Yes sir, oh . . . I guess it was about fifteen to twenty minutes later, I heard two gunshots," Cork replied.

William Tolbert, the Assistant District Attorney from Fort Worth, testified that he took a statement from Snow after he gave a legal warning to Snow that the statement would be used against him at his trial.

Munday objected, "Your honor, once more, I object to the admissibility of this statement, because my client makes references to other crimes that he may have committed."

Judge Keith recessed the trial for the morning and stated that he would give his ruling in the afternoon. It was near the noon hour and Snow was returned to his jail cell to await the judge's decision.

Once again, he grieved over the slaying of his family to a cellmate, "If there had only been another man there to help me quiet 'em, it would of never happened."

He continued, moaning, "I ain't been able to sleep any since the killing. If jest I hadn't shot the ole

woman, my wife's mother, who happened to be behind my wife when I shot her. I wish I hadn't married
her; she jest weren't the woman I thought she wuz.
I never wuz in trouble before, I wish I had another
chance."

"I shore would like to know how her other two
husbands got killed," Snow continued, "I jest met
her a couple months ago an' she didn't tell me 'bout
them 'til later on. The boy's daddy got killed by some
robbers in Waco. An' the one before me wuz beat to
death."

Snow was returned to the courtroom and the afternoon session of the trial began with Judge Keith's
ruling,

"The evidence in this case disclosed the fact that
the defendant made statements to Buck Hill and others in the community that his wife and mother-in-law
had gone to Waco. The evidence further disclosed
that the defendant sold property to Missus Hill near
the same time. The last time that Bernie Connally
was seen alive, a little before dark on the evening of
the 27th day of November, 1925, he was seen driving
the wagon back toward the Snow home, and Snow
was in the back of the wagon holding his Winchester
across his lap."

The Judge adjusted his glasses and continued, "In
his statement, Snow admitted to the effect that he
killed Bernie Connally, hid his body on a mountain,
cut his head off with an axe, an' placed the severed

head in a cellar on the ole Rivers' place where it was found an' afterwards was identified by witnesses who knew Bernie Connally during his lifetime. Snow admitted killing an' burning the bodies of his wife an' mother-in-law. Inferable from these facts, the Court thinks that the defendant slew his wife an' mother-in-law before he came to town after Bernie Connally. Snow shot Connally to death to keep him from finding out that Snow had slain his mother an' grandmother. He carried his body away to the mountain to avoid detection. That is the intent an' motive in question."

Judge Keith cleared his throat, "Moreover, inferable from all the facts and circumstances in the case, Connally, his mother and grandmother were killed by the defendant at the same time an' place. The admission of the other slayings is Res gestae. The confession is admitted an' would not be objectionable on the grounds that it involved other crimes."

"Mister Tolbert, you are still under oath, Mister Russell, you may continue."

"Describe the defendant's attitude the night there in Fort Worth when you took his statement."

"Sometimes, he would break down in tears an' at other times, he would become very defiant. He said that when he saw the bodies laying there on the ground, he became a madman. And it was at that point that Snow jumped up out of his chair, an' said he was still mad. 'God, I'm still mad,' I believe were his exact words."

"Did you ask him why he killed his wife?" asked Russell.

"Yes sir, he told me that his wife wasn't afraid of him — he had to kill her."

"And what was his attitude when he was making his confession?

"He was unusually calm."

"Do you know who typed up this statement?"

"Yes sir, I typed it up as he narrated it to me."

"Mister Tolbert, now, would you please read the statement to the jury." Russell told the man holding the confession that was now in evidence.

"Objection," Scott tried once more.

"Objection overruled, Mister Tolbert you may continue."

Tolbert began reading:

> "Before I start, I want to say that Mister Tolbert, Mister Morris, Captain Hickman an' the other officers have treated me with the kindest of courtesies. I'm going to tell my story because I know I am going to meet my Maker soon an' I want to tell the truth.
>
> I have been a farmer all my life. Two years ago, I went to Stephenville. For one year, I was unhappy. I did not

want to live alone. This year Maggie came to pick cotton near where I lived. She had her mother an' her son. I fell in love with her an' on October 6th, I asked her to become my wife. That day I obtained a marriage license in Stephenville, an' we were married a few hours later by a minister in a little country church near where I was living. I wanted to give her a home, also her mother an' son.

On November twenty-seventh, I came home in the afternoon an' found that my wife had let the cow get into the cotton patch. We had words about it because I was perplexed because I did not want the stock to destroy the crop that I had toiled to make. Bernie told me, 'I'll end you now,' an' he took up the argument for his mother. He had a five-shooter pistol pointed at me an' I knocked his arm up, an' he fired a shot up into the ceiling, then there was a terrific struggle an' Bernie fired three shots. Before that time, no unfriendly relations prevailed between me an' Bernie.

I first shot to death my stepson, Bernie Connally, an', then I fired one shot from a rifle that went through my wife, Maggie, then it struck her mother an' killed her. I carried Bernie's body to Cedar Mountain where I decapitated it. It required me all night to carry the body to the mountain. I took the head an' wrapped it in some clothing an' placed it in a cellar at the old River's place.

The next night at about nine o'clock was when I destroyed the other bodies by fire. I mean the bodies of my wife an' mother-in-law in the fireplace in the house where we lived. I destroyed both bodies the same night in the same way, an' it taken me until about four o'clock in the morning. I put the ashes just outside the back of the house."

The coldness of the courtroom only accentuated the silence when Tolbert finished reading the statement. No one spoke, and no one moved. Mr. Munday, Snow's attorney, was allowed to cross-examine the witness, and he challenged Tolbert as to whether the statement in fact, was given voluntarily.

"When you took this so called confession from Frank, he was still grieving over the loss of his family, wasn't he?"

"I guess he could have been, but like I said earlier, he was unusually calm."

"Unusually calm, now wouldn't that seem a little odd especially since he was surrounded by police officers?"

"I'm just telling you what I observed."

"Well, since he was calm, an' since he had to be grieving, wouldn't you think that he didn't fully realize the consequences of making a written statement?"

"Mister Munday, he was fully aware of making such a statement. No less than four times, he was warned that anything he admitted to could be used against him at his trial. Captain Hickman read his confession back to him, an' Snow interrupted him several times, saying he wanted to make it right."

"What did he want to make right?"

"Once was when he corrected the initials in his name an' another time he said the pistol was a five-shooter instead of a six-shooter."

"Didn't you promise him a square deal?" Munday asked.

"No sir, I told him it was our duty to prosecute him an' I wouldn't promise him anything."

Munday continued to build a case that Snow acted out of self-defense when he took his stepson's life,

"Do you read anything in that statement that would indicate that my client acted in any other way except in self-defense?"

"What do you mean, I don't know . . ."

"Didn't my client state that the boy took up the argument for his mother, isn't that what he said?"

"Yes." Tolbert remained calm as the red-faced attorney raised his voice.

"And didn't he say there was an awful struggle?"

"Yes sir, he said that."

"My client was in fear of his life, wasn't he?"

"I don't know what your client was feeling. I can't say whether he was afraid or not."

"If you were wrestling around out there on the ground with a strong twenty-year-old boy who had a gun, wouldn't you be in fear of your life?" shouted Scott.

"Objection, calls for speculation, an' there is no evidence they were wrestling on the ground or anywhere else." shouted Russell.

"No more questions." Scott returned to his chair, pulled it out and sat down and began making himself notes.

Drs. Samuel Naylor and Edward Lankford examined Connally's body the day after Snow led the lawmen to the mountain, showing them where it rested. They both gave testimony that it was their opinion that the boy had been shot in the back because both bullets made exit holes from the front side of his torso. Their findings did not coincide with Snow's confession that he shot the boy in self-defense.

Russell produced a box, about the size of a shoe-box. He asked Dr. Naylor to identify the contents of the box.

"It's bone fragments."

"Objection, your Honor," Munday protested, "My client is on trial an' is indicted for the murder of Bernie Connally. Mister Russell's evidence has not been admitted, an' it is tending to establish the commission of another an' different crime. This evidence does not shed any light on the issue here before us today. The only purpose of this evidence is to inflame the minds of the jury against my client."

Munday walked over to the witness stand and touched the box.

"These fragments, if they are indeed bones, are not admissible for any purpose other than to prejudice the jury. Now, here they are, being displayed in plain view of the jury. I object to any testimony whatsoever about these fragments. The district attorney is putting before the jury, indirectly, some prejudicial matter which cannot be introduced to the jury. The contents on this box have not been introduced as evidence, an' I strenuously object to the district attorney's producing such a box an' suggesting that the contents are evidence. The very idea of having the good doctor to identify the same."

Russell stood up and walked toward the defendant's table.

"It is the theory of the State that this defendant murdered Bernie Connally, an' at another time an' place he also murdered the two women. The State's theory is that the defendant's motive for murdering the boy was to prevent him from discovering that his mother an' grandmother had been murdered. It is the State's theory that these fragments are the remains of the women, who the defendant admits to killing. Therefore, identification of the bones establishes the State's theory for motive, your Honor."

"Snow has made a confession," said the Judge, "that he first shot to death his stepson, Bernie Connally, an' then fired one shot from a rifle that went through his wife and then struck her mother an' killed her. In the confession, Snow told of the cremation of Missus Olds and his wife, and during a search of the fireplace, many bone fragments were found and preserved and brought to Court in the box. I overrule your objection, Mister Munday, but I will not permit the introduction of the bones as evidence. The witnesses may only identify this particular box of bones and character of the same, whether they are human or not."

Russell continued, "Doctor Naylor, are these bones human or just some animal that strayed into that fireplace?"

"They are human bones."

"What else is in that box?"

"Objection, your Honor has stated that this box is not evidence, an' I object to any further testimony regarding the box or its contents." Scott pounded his fist on the table.

"Overruled, I'll permit the doctor to identify the contents of the container."

Russell asked again, "Doctor Langford, what else is in the box?"

"There are human teeth an' fragments of flesh that I believe is human."

"And the bones are not from a dog or cat or horse or any other kind of animal, are they?"

"No sir, they are human bones."

"No further questions for this witness, your Honor."

"I have no questions for the doctor," Scott said. He didn't want the jury's thoughts to be focused on the damning box.

Deputy Sheriff Pearcy and Ranger Stanley identified the bones as being the same as the ones discovered during the search of Snow's property. Pearcy testified that the bones were found in the fireplace of the old house and in a pile of ashes behind the house. Ranger Stanley identified the box by his initials written on top of the box and dated December 11, 1925.

Russell recalled Sheriff Hassler to the stand.

"Sheriff Hassler, once the identity of Bernie Connally had been made, what was your next step?"

"I located the defendant because I needed to question him."

"And, what did he tell you?"

"He told me an' Deputy Pearcy that he took his family to Iredell to catch a train to Waco."

"And did he later tell you a different story when you confronted him with the fact that Bernie Connally had been murdered?"

"Yes sir, he blamed it on a black man."

"Do you think the defendant would have conjured of that story if it had truly been self-defense?"

"Objection!"

"I'll withdraw the question."

The defense began their arguments on January twentieth of 1926. They put Snow on the stand, but they didn't ask him any questions. The defense merely wanted the jury to observe a meek, little man who would be incapable to committing such a crime. Snow, about five feet and nine inches tall, stooped and frail of frame, appeared to be almost an invalid. His weak eyes, red and watery, seemed to be pleading for mercy, revealing nothing of his aggressiveness.

Snow wore heavy earth-worn shoes of a Texas farmer. He wore grey trousers, a dirty sweater and a coat fastened up with a safety pin. The coat once belonged to his-stepson, Bernie Connally.

Attorney Scott wanted the jury to observe his demeanor and appearance because Snow hoped to escape the electric chair by his plea of temporary insanity and self-defense. Snow returned to his chair and slumped down, cowering before the gaze of the courtroom spectators.

Munday called Mrs. Jean Sheppard to the stand.

"What is your occupation, Missus Sheppard?"

"I am a psychologist an' social worker in the Dallas Public Schools."

"Your honor, we object to this witness, she is not an expert." Russell said, rising to his feet.

"I will allow you to testify as a psychologist, but you are not to give testimony inferring that you are a brain expert. Continue Mister Scott."

"Missus Sheppard, we asked you to examine our client, Frank Snow. What experience do you have as far as your work in psychology?

"I made mental tests for the state of California before the juvenile courts. I so enjoyed working with those sweet boys."

"I see, when did you examine my client?"

"It was five days ago. Or maybe it was six; it was the day that you brought him to my office. I just can't be for sure. You know how time flies by."

Scott asked, "After your examination of Frank Snow, what are your findings?

"He is feeble minded an' has the mind of a nine-year-old child," she told the jury, "This man is one of the sweetest men that I have ever tested. He seems like a peace lovin' creature. I have worked with many people in my home state an' found they . . ."

The defense attorney, Wallace, held up his hand in an effort to get her to cease talking. Russell objected several times to her volunteering information; to her failure to directly answer Scott's questions.

The defense attorney asked her, "Are such mental test as you state you made for the juvenile courts in California used by the courts in that state?" to which Mr. Russell made an objection that was sustained by the judge.

Mrs. Shepherd continued, "They are standard tests, they are used all over the country, an' I have used them in courts an' they are accepted."

At which point the judge interrupted and told her, "Young lady, can you stop talking? And if you can't stop, I will have the sheriff take charge of you".

Then the judge declared, "You will not content yourself with answering the question propounded to you by counsel. But you seemingly want to tell the jury of the wonderful effect that your psychological theories have wrought upon the legal procedures in the courts of the country, and this was over the objection of the district attorney. Mister Russell, do you have any questions for this witness?"

"Yes your honor, we do have several questions — Missus Sheppard, you testified that the defendant has a mind of a nine-year-old, is that not correct?"

"Yes sir, just like a sweet little boy."

"In your expert opinion, could a man with the brain of a nine-year-old be capable of building a steamship, or an airplane or maybe even a radio?"

"I guess it would be possible."

"And would that man with the brain of a nine-year-old be capable of committing a brutal murder?"

"Objection!" Scott jumped up from his chair.

"You may answer as an expert, Missus Sheppard," the Judge said.

"I guess that would also be possible, but . . ."

Russell interrupted the expert, "If this man is so feeble minded, how do you think he was able to live by himself an' get by all these years? And how in the world, did he figure out he needed to cover up this terrible crime by hacking the boy's head off?"

The defense objected, and then they called as their next witness, a farmer by the name of Leonard Young.

"He's not too bright," Young stated, "I once saw Snow talking to his horse as if he were trying to persuade the animal to run him a race. Before Snow started to run the horse, he poured conversation into the horse's ear, but the horse refused to budge. The race became a one-sided affair."

Russell cross examined the witness, "It is highly probable that many of the farmers around here talk to their animals — although it might look strange, does talking to a horse mean that you're crazy?"

"No sir, I don't guess it does."

"When was the last time that you saw the defendant?"

"It's been several years now."

"Several years, so how could you know his state of mind an' sanity on the day be murdered his family?"

"I don't guess I could."

"He's absent-minded," testified Bob Gaines from Millsap. "I've seen Snow make the horse run up an' down the road at a fast rate. He would work for any wages without questioning the amount. I once paid him only one dollar an' twenty-five cents for one day's work."

Russell asked Gaines, "Well, you've done the same work for seventy-five cents a day, haven't you?"

"Yes sir."

"Is being absent-minded an excuse for committing murder?'

"No sir. I reckon not."

"Do you know anything about the events of November the twenty-seventh?"

"No sir."

Snow's cousin, Jake Snow from Palo Pinto County, testified next for the defense,

"Jake," Munday asked, "What can you tell us about your cousin?"

"Sir, he was slow in school, an' he quit when he wuz in the sixth grade. He thought that the older boys were out to git him, an' he always seemed to be afraid. One thing that always worried me wuz he like to kill small animals an' he wuz always starting fires."

"Would you say he was obsessed with fires?"

"Yes sir, I thank he wuz. Many times, he would be out in the woods with a fire burning," Jake testified, "he would be dancing around the fire an' making all kinds of strange sounds."

"And what do you think he was doing on these occasions?" The defense attorney asked.

"I don't have any idea, but I thank he was crazy."

Russell objected, "Your Honor, Jake Snow is not qualified to determine the soundness of anyone's mind, much less his cousin's mind."

Having presented all their evidence, the defense rested its case on Saturday, January 23, 1926. After the State rested, Munday, the attorney for the defendant stated to the court,

"Your Honor, the defense has not had the opportunity to have our client examined by competent analysts because the defendant is without funds to procure the services of an analyst. In attendance today are two competent analysts, Doctor Wilmer L. Allison and Doctor J. D. Bozeman, neither of which has had an opportunity to examine the defendant."

The Court ruled that the defense had ample opportunity and time to have their client examined. Munday then requested that the Court to permit a private and confidential examination of the defendant by these two analysts.

The judge overruled this request and stated that Snow would be examined in the presence of Sam Russell and Oscar Herring, the attorneys representing the state in this case. The defense attorneys objected to this ruling stating that such action was highly prejudicial because Snow should have the legal right to have confidential communication with the physician of his own choosing.

Munday protested that the presence of officers who were prosecuting his client, seeking to obtain the death penalty against him in the presence of the sheriff, and the other officers would tend to intimidate and embarrass and prevent him from having a full, fair, impartial and complete examination.

The judge instructed the district attorney and other officers not to take part in the examination and not to interfere in any way with those making the examination. Thus, the two doctors examined Snow, but the results were never made known.

The lawyers made their summations before the jury. Russell began first and step-by-step, he laid out the events of that horrible day and then concluded, "The evidence before you shows beyond a reasonable doubt that the defendant, F. M. Snow, on or about November 27th, 1925, did murder Bernie Connally."

Munday approached the jury. "You have heard testimony given in this courtroom the past few days that prove beyond any doubt that the beheading of the defendant's stepson an' the burning of the bodies of his wife an' mother-in-law were the acts of a crazy man. You have heard testimony that Mister Snow, upon finding the cattle in his crop, argued with his wife an' stepson.

You heard his own words, 'When I saw the bodies there, I became a madman.' Gentlemen of the jury, these are the acts of a madman. No sane man would brutally chop up the bodies of two women, one of which he loved so intensely. No sane man would burn those bodies in a fireplace in his own house. No sane man would eat his meals in the same house where the bodies lay. No sane man would sever a head from its body."

Munday now spoke softly, "Gentlemen, you must weigh the evidence an' when you do, you will find that Francis Marion Snow is not guilty of the murder of Bernie Connally by reason of insanity."

Munday turned and slowly returned to his chair at the defense table. Judge Keith closed the trial with a charge to the jury:

"You are to determine the guilt or innocence of the defendant, Francis Marion Snow. You and you alone, will render that verdict. You will only consider testimony as it relates to the death of Bernie Connally and nothing more. The state must have proved beyond a reasonable doubt that Bernie Connally is dead.

If you believe beyond a reasonable doubt that it was necessary for F. M. Snow to kill Bernie Connally as an act of self-defense, that he had to protect himself from harm, you must acquit the defendant.

If you have reasonable doubt about the defendant's confession, that any promise was made to the defendant to obtain that confession, or that the defendant was threatened in any way, you must disregard that confession and base you verdict solely on the evidence presented to you.

If you believe that the defendant was suffering from a mental disorder that rendered him unable to choose right from wrong at the time of the killing, you must give him an acquittal.

If you believe that the defendant killed Bernie Connally after consciously deciding to do so and that decision was present at the time of the killing, you must find him guilty of murder and access his punishment anywhere from five years in the state prison to the punishment of death. Gentlemen of the jury, you may begin your deliberation.

26

THE VERDICT

The attorneys had presented their case, and both sides had rested; no further evidence would be presented to the jury Judge Keith had given his instructions to the jury late in the afternoon of Wednesday, January 27, 1926 and they had retired to the jury room to begin their deliberations. The first charge given to the jury was to determine on the first ballot, the guilt or innocence of F. M. Snow. If the defendant was found to be guilty, the second ballot was to set the punishment.

"This court is in recess until the jury has reached a verdict," the Judge rapped his gavel.

It took the jury only fifteen minutes to reach their verdict, but due to the lateness of the evening the decision would not be announced until the next morning.

The courthouse was packed Thursday morning; all were waiting for the verdict to be read. The foreman of the jury, L. L. Hammond, handed the verdict, written on a sheet of yellow paper, to the Judge. The judge read the written verdict then asked the foreman of the jury,

"Is this your unanimous verdict?"

"It is your Honor."

"Please read your verdict aloud," handing the yellow note back to Hammond:

> "We the jury find the defendant guilty
> of . . ."

He was interrupted by cheering in the courtroom. Rapping his gavel on the bench, the judge brought the court to order and stated there would be no further display of any type while the proceedings were going on. He asked the jury foreman to continue:

> "We the jury find the defendant guilty
> of murder, and under the second
> count in the indictment, assess his
> punishment at death."

M. L. Munday, the defense attorney, immediately filed a motion for a new trial and was given ninety days to set forth reasons for requesting one more trial.

Snow told Sheriff Hassler, as he returned Snow to the county jail, "We are going to fight this to the last ditch."

The sheriff told waiting newspaper reporters that Snow wasn't surprised by the verdict, in fact, "He seemed to expect it. He seemed to be relieved that his trial was over. He didn't seem too concerned about the sentence he was given."

A few minutes after Snow was returned to his cell, his attorneys went to the county jail to visit him. They talked to him for over an hour.

"Snow had very little to say about the verdict," Munday told newspaper reporters from Fort Worth, "he did not seem to be surprised — he seemed to be expecting it. He did tell us he has always told the truth about how the three slayings took place. He said two witnesses for the State lied about him. We left him in as good spirits as could be expected under the circumstances. He believes he will be granted a new trial that will be fair."

Brother Bays, making his jail rounds, visited with Snow a few days after the trial had ended. Snow gave a different version of the horrific murders. Snow told the preacher that he and his wife had quarreled and in a fit of anger; he hit her with a scantling board, causing her death.

"I decided that I had to dispose of her," Snow admitted to the preacher, "so I went to get my axe an' that's when I saw the ole woman sitting next to the fireplace with 'er back to me."

A tear came to Snow's eye, "I swung my axe an' almost severed her head from her body. Then I got my wife's body an' carried it into the house."

The murderer continued his confession, "I locked the door an' went to town to look fer the boy. I told him that his mother wuz sick an' I rode home with 'im. I shot 'im twice in the back. I changed teams an' hauled the boy's body to the mountain."

Snow wiped the tears from his eyes, "I hid the women's bodies under the floor, but after they found the boy's head, I took 'em out an' burned 'em in the fireplace."

Snow looked at the preacher then bowed his head — he spoke just above a whisper, "I know I'm gonna meet my Maker soon, an' I jest want to make it right."

The murder trial was finally over, and the people of the community were ready to put the horrible events of the past few months behind them and move on with their lives. Another trial held in Judge Keith's courtroom a few weeks after the Snow trial, brought quite a bit of attention, but was not as dramatic, and the jury reached a quick verdict. A civil lawsuit grew out of the death of a two and one-half-year-old baby that died the preceding September. The baby's father brought accusations that a medicine, Coco-quinine, bought at Hardin Drug Store was responsible for the baby's death. The jury's verdict was for the defendant and did not award the twenty thousand dollars asked by the child's father.

Erath County grew steadily in 1925 and by the middle of 1926, the population was crowding the ten thousand mark. Much of the growth was attributed to families moving into Stephenville to take advantage of the excellent educational facilities at John Tarleton College and Stephenville High School. John Tarleton College was the second largest junior college in the United States. The college officials were planning to start construction on a new dining hall in the fall.

New homes were springing up throughout the city, and many building projects were underway and there was not an idle carpenter or painter to be found. The main street through town, Washington Street, was paved during the year. Dr. J. C. Terrell and his wife Ellen founded a new hospital in the Stephenville Langdon Hotel.

The first flowers of spring were beginning to blossom in the fields and meadows with splashes of reds, blues, yellows, whites and many other colors. The trees were putting on a fresh coat of green. Birds, sparrows, wrens, robins and many more were singing their melodious songs throughout the countryside; building their nest and welcoming the first warm days after a very cold winter. Honeybees, wasps, butterflies and insects of all varieties were beginning to make their appearance; buzzing from plant to plant, and pollinating the colorful flowers. Small animals, the rabbits, squirrels, raccoons, and opossums were scurrying about — it was that time of year, the time for romance.

With the trial behind him, Aaron Martin slept late on this beautiful April morning — it was Saturday and there was no school today. Aaron stretched and yawned, then got out of bed and dressed. He went to the kitchen where his mother, Millie, outside planting green beans in the freshly turned soil, had left sausages and biscuits on the kitchen table for him. He leisurely ate his breakfast and then stepped out on the back porch and stretched again.

"Mornin' Momma, I'm gonna go to Daddy's store."

"Okay, I'll see you later."

As he strolled along to the store, Aaron looked at the freshness of the morning. The aroma of the blooming flowers, the blue sky and songbirds made for a beautiful beginning of a new day.

"Hi, Daddy," he said, walking into the store.

"Mornin,' Son, how'd ya sleep?"

"I slept real good; I don't ever thank I woke up all night long."

"You must of slept good; the coyotes wuz yelpin' an' kept wakin' me up. There must of been a pack of 'em down by the river; I could hear 'em most of the night."

"I didn't hear 'em, reckon I slept good. Daddy, can I take the car out tonight?"

Aaron's father, Madison, having made a bountiful harvest, not only was he able to buy a new cook stove for Mille, but he also purchased the family a new vehicle, a shiny black 1925 Chrysler Sedan.

"Maybe so, whatcha gonna do?"

"I thought I'd go over to git Willie, an' we'd jest mess 'round."

"Well, I reckon if you'll be careful an' be back home by nine. An' no drankin' you hear?"

"Okay, thank you, I'm ready to watch the store fer ya."

Aaron would be allowed to take the car out tonight. He was going to "go run around" with Willie Stanton. It had been a gorgeous springtime day and in the spring, it is said that a young man's fancy turn to love. He thought they might go into Stephenville and meet some girls at the ice cream parlor — that's what he thought he should do, but Missy still played upon his mind.

He hadn't seen Missy for several months, but thinking about her often, he wondered why she was such a mystery to him, and then, was she happy? Realizing that time was marching on, he would soon be graduating from high school and preparing to go to college. Missy would be in the eleventh grade at Stephenville High School. Almost a year had passed since that day he was sunburned, that day when he first saw her, and he couldn't forget that magical night of their first kiss. And tonight, as so many nights before, he had the same wish,

"Maybe tonight, when I drive by her house, I'll see her and maybe tonight, she will want to see me."

Aaron finished his work at the store, ate supper and picked up Willie in the new Chrysler. The sun had finished its daily task as Aaron drove to the courthouse square, but the boys didn't see anyone they knew. They heard the courthouse clock striking.

"Seven o'clock," Willie said.

Aaron drove past the Majestic Theatre and saw that *Three Faces East*, staring Jeta Condal and Huey Nathal, was showing.

"Do ya want to go see the picture show?" Aaron asked.

"Naw, I ain't got 'nuff money," Willie replied.

"That's okay; we ain't got much time anyway; I gotta be home by nine. Let's go drive by Missy's house."

"Whatcha gonna do if ya see her?"

"I'll see if she'll talk to me."

"Yeah, sure ya will!"

And as luck would have it, Aaron saw Missy and her cousin Sally, sitting on the front porch steps as they neared the house. Aaron waved then drove on past the house; Missy returned the wave.

"Why didn't you stop?" Willie questioned.

"I don't know, I feel all shaky inside. I'll go 'round the block an' see if they are still sittin' there."

The second time, approaching Missy's house, Aaron was thinking to himself, "I'm gonna do it — no, better not — what if she gets mad at me — this is worse than having to tell the jury 'bout finding that boy's head — okay, here's the house, I'm gonna stop."

He found the courage and stopped the car in front of the house and waved again, "now what should I do?"

Before he could make a plan of action, Missy and Sally began walking up to the car; Missy came around to Aaron's side. Aaron could feel his heart thumping in his chest.

"Hi, I was wonderin' if you were gonna stop," Missy, smiling, spoke first, "is this your car?"

"No, it, it's m — my daddy's," he finally was able to speak, "what're y'all doing."

"We're just been sittin' out here; it's such a pretty night."

Aaron's mouth was as dry as if he were chewing on a piece of cotton. He took a deep breath.

"Uh, okay, uh, I wuz jest wonderin'. Would y'all like to go ridin' 'round?"

Missy looked at Sally over the top of the car, whispering something that Aaron couldn't understand, and then said, "Sure!"

"Well git in."

"Just a minute," Missy turned and ran back up on the porch, "Granny, we'll be back before too long."

Missy came back to the car, opening the back door of the vehicle; she sat in the back seat. She scooted across the seat behind Aaron, and Sally got in and closed the car door. Aaron drove to Washington Street, which had recently been paved; then east, past the courthouse and across the Bosque River bridge with very little conversation — except the two girls. They were whispering and giggling.

Willie looked back at the girls, and Missy who quit whispering and smiling, "Oh, Hi!"

"Hi, what are y'all whispering about?"

"Oh, nothing," they both grinned.

Aaron, wanting to sit with Missy, said, "Willie, would you like to drive my daddy's car?"

"You bet I would!"

Aaron pulled over to the side and stopped the car. He got out and opened the back door, suggesting, "Sally, why don't you ride in the front with Willie."

"Okay."

Aaron sat in the back seat beside Missy, who was smiling at him.

"Whatcha been doin'?" he asked.

"Nothin' much, just goin' to school. I broke up with Richard."

"You did?"

"Yep, I kept thinkin' 'bout you, an' wonderin' what you were doin'"

"I had to go to that trial in January."

"Yes, I know, we read about it in the paper. Wuz you scared?"

"Oh, no, it weren't bad at all," Aaron trying to show his braveness, "I jest told um what happened."

"Are you sure you wuzn't just a little scared?"

"Naw," trying to change the subject, "I'm gonna start to John Tarleton College this fall."

"I don't guess I'll get to go to college, an' I really don't want to."

"Where do y'all want to go?" Willie inquired.

"Let's go down to that li'l road by Uncle Ira's place," Aaron recommended, "It's not too far from here."

"Okay, that sounds good to me."

Sally asked, "What have you been up to Willie?"

"Uh, jest goin' to school an' helpin' Mister Doshier on the weekends."

"Is that the man you worked for last summer?"

"Yeah, same one," Willie acknowledged, "he's staying busy with the way Stephenville is growin'."

"What do you do for him?"

"Oh, jest carry bricks an' mix up the mud."

Soon, they neared the turn-off, and Willie drove down the small tree-lined lane that meandered around, and as they approached a hilltop, Aaron asked Willie to park the car. The moon had popped up above the horizon, full and bright. The moonlight sparkled in Missy's eyes as she looked up at it.

"Ain't it purdy out here?" Willie said, rolling down the car window, "It ain't cold a tall."

"Yeah boy," agreed Aaron, reaching for Missy's hand.

Missy then smiled and moved closer to him and gazed up into his eyes. Aaron put his hand under Missy's chin and tilted her head up. Slowly, their lips touched, a soft tender kiss. They smiled, and Missy laid her head back onto the seat of the car.

Willie broke the silence, "This shore is a nice car."

"Yes," agreed Sally, "You're a pretty good driver, Willie."

"Thanks, Sally."

Sally looked around at the couple sitting in the back seat, "Aaron, sorry to hear about your grandmother."

Grandma Abba Martin had passed away earlier in the month, on the fourth of April. Only a couple of months after the Martin Christmas gathering; all the aunts, uncles and cousins returned to Stephenville to lay their beloved mother and grandmother to rest.

"I 'preciate it Sally," Aaron replied, "Her mind wuz getting so bad, she couldn't remember anythang. I remember one time last year; I went over to visit her an' I met Uncle Cliff coming out of her little house. When I went in an' asked 'er about 'im, she told me that she hadn't seen 'im in a long time."

"Weren't you grandsons her pallbearers?"

"Yes, we were. It wuz the last thing we could do for her."

"Aw, that's sweet," Missy added.

One forlorn cloud passed in front of the moon, hiding it's light, and the lonesome call of a dove in the distance began the unexpected ending to this night.

"Listen, he's sanging a love song to his mate," Sally whispered.

"Woo-OO-oo-oo-oo," the dove sang again.

Sally said, "That makes me think about a song." "Which one," Missy asked.

"'Always.'"

"Oh yeah, that's a good un," agreed Aaron.

"I love the tune." Sally began humming.

"Aaron an' me sung it over at his house the other day," Willie spoke up.

"They play it all the time on the radio — I heard 'em say that Irvin Berlin wrote it for his wife as a wedding gift," Sally said, "He must have really loved her. I like it better than 'I Lost My Heart in Monterey'."

"Yeah, it's the bee's knees; let's sang it," Aaron suggested, "Sally, you got a pretty voice, you start it."

Sally began singing:

> *Days may not be fair always,*
> *That's when I'll be there always.*
> *Not for just an hour,*
> *Not for just a day,*
> *Not for just a year,*
> *But always.*

Aaron joined in singing harmony,

> *I'll be loving you, oh always*
> *With a love, that's true always.*
> *When the things you've planned*
> *Need a helping hand,*
> *I will understand always.*
> *Always.*

Sally continued humming the melody; Aaron looked at Missy and saw tears in her eyes.

"What's wrong?"

"I want to go home," Missy began moving away from Aaron.

"Are you sure?"

"Yes."

"Well, why don't we jest ride around fer awhile?"

"No! I want to go home!"

"Okay, we'll go."

"Sally, please come an' sit back here," Missy insisted.

Sally and Aaron exchanged seating, and Willie got out to crank the Chrysler.

"It's got a 'lectric starter," Aaron told him.

Willie got back in, and Aaron pointed to the starter switch on the floorboard. "Step on that switch right there."

The Chrysler started, and Willie shifted into first gear, beginning the quiet ride back to Missy's house. She got out of the car without speaking.

"What wuz wrong with her?" Aaron asked.

"I don't know, maybe I'll find out later," Sally told him.

Willie drove the few blocks to Sally's house, and she got out of the car.

"Man, that wuz weird," Aaron said, "Everything seemed okay 'till we sung that song."

"Well, my advice to ya is to leave her alone; yore jest gonna keep gittin' yore heart broke.

THE FINAL CHAPTER

June 6, 1927 . . .

News that the State of Texas did not grant Snow a new trial and that sentencing would be carried out on Monday traveled fast through Erath County. A higher court had affirmed the lower court's decision in F. M. Snow's case. The crowded courtroom became silent as Judge Keith entered and took his seat at the bench.

"You may be seated," he told the standing observers, "bring in the defendant."

Sheriff Hassler brought Snow into the hot courtroom, a sharp contrast to the frigid cold days during the murder trial.

"Mister Snow, please remain standing. I have the obligation to pass sentence on you today, and it is an obligation that I don't take lightly, and be assured, sir, that I find no pleasure in doing so."

Snow nodded his head.

"The State of Texas has confirmed your conviction and you were not granted a new trial. Is there anything you wish to say before I pass sentence on you?"

"I don't see my lawyers, are they supposed to be here?"

"No, they're not here, but there is nothing your lawyers could do for you today."

"Well, I jest wanted it to be right an' all. Can I say sump'um?"

"Yes you may."

Snow turned to face the court observers, "I want everybody to hear, but I can't talk too loud. It ain't right fer y'all to put me to death like this but maybe I'll git off yet, an' then, maybe I won't; the Judge ain't said, but if I'm put to my death, I want to be buried by my old sweet mother. I ain't mad at none of you, an' if I'm killed, I hope to meet y'all in Heaven."

Judge Keith cleared his throat, "Francis Marion Snow, you have been found guilty by a duly sworn jury and under the laws of the State of Texas, the decree of this court is that you will be put to death on the fifteenth day of July, nineteen hundred and twenty-seven. A warrant will be issued to the warden of the state prison directing him to execute you by passing a current of electricity through your body sufficient to cause your death. Now, you will be turned over to the sheriff of Erath County who will transfer you to the warden at the state prison in Huntsville, Texas."

Judge Keith signed the execution orders, and Sheriff Hassler took Snow to his vehicle parked just outside the courthouse. Hassler sat with Snow in the back seat, while Deputy Webster drove the car; Deputy Pearcy setting beside Webster as a passenger rolled down the window of the hot car. The long trip to Huntsville was ahead of them.

"Well Snow, I guess this is that last ditch you were talking about," Hassler said.

"Shore looks like it," Snow smiled.

Hassler and his two deputies, after arriving at the Texas State Prison System in Huntsville, delivered Snow to the warden, Norman L. Speer. Speer took custody of the prisoner and issued a receipt to Hassler:

> "Received of Sheriff D. M. Hassler, one condemned man, F. M. Snow, from Erath County. Signed, N. L. Speer."

Hassler presented a Death Warrant to Speer, ordering the execution of Snow on July 15, 1927.

Subsequently, Texas State Governor Dan Moody issued Proclamation #20829 on July 11, 1927 giving F. M. Snow a twenty-eight day reprieve so that the Board of Pardons would have sufficient time to examine all the records of the case. Moody set Snow's execution date as August 12, 1927.

The Martins sat down to eat breakfast on this June day; the sky was clearing after a night-time rain shower. The birds were tweeting, greeting the new day.

One of the young roosters was trying to welcome the new morning with a pitiful sounding crow.

"That was a crow?" Millie laughed as she looked out to see a Rhode Island Red strutting around in the front yard; trying puff up like the full-grown rooster.

Always hungry, the chickens once wandered over to the Rivers' place and while there were stealing the dog's food, and adding to insult; they were drinking water from the dog's dish. Hootus snapped at one of the thieves, and the rooster squawked and jumped backwards, alarming the rest of the brood.

"Madison, I don't think you should be eating all that fat meat," Millie said as her husband cut and placed another piece of fat pork on his plate.

"Yeah, just look at my ole grandpa; just imagine how long he'd lived if he hadn't eaten all those eggs an' fat meat an' gravy an' sech as that. You know, Grandma said it would get him some day. An' it did; he only lived to be ninety-two years old."

"Oh, that's the same thing you say every time."

"I saw Herman Starnes the other day," Aaron commented reaching for another biscuit, "I kidded him about us thankin' it wuz his head in that cellar. He laughed an' told me he still had his head, but it weren't doing him that much good these days."

"Yesterday, when I was over at the store, I was telling Miss Jenkins about Virgil McElroy's conversion," Millie mentioned.

"It's a curious thang about ole Virgil McElroy," Madison began, "y'all recollect when I told you about witnessing to him?"

"Yes, I remember," Millie replied.

"Ole Virgil asked me why nothing seemed to bother me an' why I always seemed to be in sech a good mood. I told him I have peace that comes from God through the gift of salvation."

"Missy's daddy," Aaron thought to himself.

"He told me he used to go to church, a long time ago an' he'd heard about God an' Jesus 'an all that religious stuff, but after his wife fell an' was killed, he got real bitter an' quit going."

"Daddy, is that why he's so mean?" Aaron asked.

"I suppose so son; anyway, he told me he jest about quit believin' in God when that happened; that's what he told me anyway. I 'spect that's why he started drankin' an' robbin' an' being so ill-tempered. So he asked me if it wuz too late for him to accept the Lord an' find some peace. I told him, 'Virgil, it ain't ever too late.'"

Aaron asked, "What did you tell 'im then?"

"I did the best I could. I told him 'bout how I got saved one summer at a revival. He listened to me an' I laid out the plan of salvation by reciting all the Bible verses for getting saved that I could recollect, an' they weren't too many. But I had the jest of the thing like all people are sinners, an' God sent His Son, Jesus to die as payment for our sins."

Then Aaron remembered the revival that summer he met Missy; that summer that she was saved.

"Ole Virgil told me he wanted to be saved, so I prayed the sinner's prayer with him an' asked him to go to church with us the next Sunday. But, Brother Bays told me the next day that he wuz in church Wednesday night, an' he made a public profession of his faith right then. I thank that Heaven rejoiced that day."

"Halleluiah," Millie declared.

"Daddy, did you ever have any doubts if you were really saved or not?"

"Shore I did, I 'spect everybody wonders about it from time to time, 'cause it takes a powerful lot of believin' to believe in something that ya can't see. I remember that summer I was saved — the preacher said it was a free gift an' all I had to do was take it. I couldn't figure it out at first 'til he said that I should be sorryful for my sins an' believe by faith that Jesus Christ had died for my sins an' was raised up from the dead. He said faith was kinda like settin' down in a chair — you believe it's gonna hold ya up, so you don't worry 'bout how it holds ya up. So, yeah, I guess everybody wonders, but just read your Bible an' your faith will grow. It's so simple that even a child of eleven can understand it; I did. I guess if it cost us more, it'd be easier for us to believe."

"That brings back some memories of the good ole days before we were married," Millie smiled, "when the revival wuz goin' on; 'bout all that Momma did was the washin', ironin' an' cookin'. We always had the preacher an' singer to come to our house at least once for dinner. After they ate, the preacher an' singer usually took a short nap, then they all congregated on the front porch to visit an' most of the time, they had a Bible discussion."

Millie chuckled, "I 'member one time, my aunt an' uncle an' cousins came to visit durin' the revival. We thought maybe we wouldn't have to go to church that night, but about five o'clock, Momma said, 'let's get supper ready an' everybody get ready so we can go to church tonight.' My cousin Raymond said, 'I don't believe I'll go tonight.' Papa told him in no uncertain terms that 'as long as you're visitin' here; you'll go to church when we do.' Well, he went."

Aaron, now nineteen years old, had worked and saved to buy his first car, a 1925 Chevrolet Superior Roadster. Starting to John Tarleton College this fall would be a change and quite a challenge from the small school at Pony Creek, but the car would allow him to live at home and commute to college in Stephenville.

"Son, I need for you to open the store today, I'm goin' to be workin' in the fields," Madison told Aaron.

"Okay, Daddy."

Aaron finished his breakfast and drove to the store in his "new to him" Chevy. It was about mid-afternoon when Daniel McCarey came into the store.

"Hi Aaron," he said.

"Hey, how ya doin'?"

"Doin' good, say, is that yore car outside?"

"Yeah, I jest got it a couple days ago."

"That's a fine lookin' piece of a automobile."

"Thank you, you'll have to go ridin' in it sometime."

Ruth Rivers came into the store and got a bag of flour, a box of Lipton Tea and a box of salt.

"Aaron, will you put this on my account?" she asked.

"Yes ma'am, I shore will. What's ole Elvis doin'?"

"Oh, he's out helpin' his grandpa today."

"Tell 'im to come see me sometime."

"Okay, I sure will an' you come over."

"Don't y'all go huntin' anymore?" Daniel asked after Mrs. Rivers left the store.

"Nah, I ain't got the urge to go anymore after all that happened; say, what are ya doin' tonight?"

"I ain't got no plans."

"I'll come pick ya up about seven o'clock an' we'll try out my car."

"That sounds like a plan."

"Ring-Ring"—the telephone rang—"Ring-Ring."

"That's our ring," Aaron picked up the telephone receiver.

"Hello, Martin's General Store; Aaron Martin speaking."

"Hi Aaron, this is Katie," his cousin was calling.

"Hi."

"It's my cousin, Katie," Aaron whispered.

"Mother said I could ask you over for supper tonight."

"Uh, okay, bout what time?"

"She said about five-thirty or six."

"Okay, but Daniel McCarey is here, an' he asked me to go out to his place tonight. I'll eat with ya'll an' go to see him later if that's okay."

"Ask her to come along with ya," Daniel interrupted — Aaron nodded his head.

"Katie, you want to go with me to Daniel's?"

"Sure!"

Aaron later closed the store and went home to change clothes. He told his mother that he was going to Katie's house for supper. He arrived just as Katie finished setting the table. Katie's mother, Rachel, had prepared a pot roast with carrots, potatoes, onions and a big pot full of green beans, fresh from the garden.

"Ask Mother if I can go with you to see Daniel," Katie whispered to Aaron as they finished eating.

"Aunt Rachel, that shore wuz good!"

"Well, thank you Aaron."

"I wuz thankin' 'bout goin' to see Daniel McCarey. He wants to see my car — would you care if Katie went along with me?"

"Is that Nancy McCarey's boy?"

"Yes ma'am, it is."

"Okay, but y'all don't stay out too late."

Katie cleared the table and stacked the dishes on the kitchen cabinet. She went to her bedroom and changed into a yellow cotton dress, brushed her hair and then announced, "I'm ready."

Katie and Aaron got into the car and started the trip to the McCarey farm, southeast of Selden. Being a June day, the golden sphere in the west was still giving light as Aaron stopped his car in front of the McCarey house. Daniel walked out of a barn and waved to them as they drove up. Katie and Aaron got out and walked to meet him.

"This is Katie, my cousin," Aaron told Daniel.

"Hi," and not being disappointed, Daniel flashed a quick grin.

"Hi," Katie returned the smile.

Not wanting to stare, Daniel's sparkling blue eyes darted toward Katie then back to Aaron.

"She's too pretty to be a part of your family," Daniel said.

"Yeah, I know it, sometimes we get lucky — y'all ready to go ridin'."

"I am," Katie replied.

"We can all git up here in the front seat," Aaron instructed.

"Katie, is it okay if I set here by you?"

"Sure."

Aaron started his Chevy, and drove down the lane and turned onto a country road. Tall trees began appearing on the west side of the road, blocking out the sunlight, and knowing that they were approaching the sight, the Snow murder house; a kind of eeriness was about — it looked dark and light at the same time. Aaron drove the car on past the house and then turned around at the Stephenville cut-off and drove back the way they came. After passing the Snow farm once again, he turned at the split in the road and headed toward Duffau.

"Do y'all want ride some more?" Aaron asked as they reached Duffau.

Katie and Daniel were enjoying being chauffeured through the country-side, making small talk, laughing.

"Yeah! Let's circle around to Johnsville," exclaimed Daniel and Katie.

Aaron then drove to Johnsville, then back to the McCarey farm.

"It wuz good to meet ya," Daniel said to Katie as she and Aaron were leaving to go back home.

"I had a good time."

"Y'all have to come back sometime an' we can go horseback ridin' but I don't thank you could ride a horse in that purty yellow dress."

Katie grinned and waved as they were leaving.

"I had fun," she told Aaron.

"Yeah, it would be more fun if I had me a girl."
He was thinking about Missy.

"My friend, Laura Dauber, told me that she
thought you were handsome."

"Yeah, sure."

Aaron thought to himself, "I don't have any idea
who she is; I'll bet she's got freckles an' pigtails an'
wears glasses. How am I supposed to picture anyone
with the last name of Dauber?"

He would find out! June rolled into July, and
then the hot days of August began. On one of his
trips to Stephenville, Aaron went to the Farmer's
First National Bank to make a deposit for the store.
Standing in line in front of him, at Mrs. Little's
teller window, was a petite young lady with soft
brown hair — she turned and smiled and Aaron
saw her emerald green eyes, with dashes of chestnut sprinkling her irises. He thought she looked
more like a doll than a girl; she was so pretty — he
had never seen anyone so beautiful.

The girl finished her banking transaction and
then Mrs. Little said, "Thank you Miss Dauber, come
back again."

Aaron, after the lovely creature left, asked Mrs.
Little, "Who was that girl?"

"Laura Dauber."

"Oh, my stars!"

Sunday, August 7, 1927 . . .

"Since there's no church tonight, how would you like to go over to Daniel's?" Aaron asked Katie as the morning church service was over, "I saw him yesterday an' he wanted you to come with me again."

"Doesn't he have a girlfriend?"

"Well, he asked me to invite you to come along, so if he does have one, they must not be too serious."

"Do you think I should?"

"I don't see that it would hurt anything. Wouldn't you like to go?"

"Yes, I really like him."

"Well then, let's go to see 'em"

"Okay, what time?"

"I'll be at your house a little after seven; oh, by the way, do you thank that your friend, Laura, might want to go along? Is it too late to ask her? I kinda met her at the bank the other day."

"She has a beau now, but I'll ask her."

Aaron and his family returned home from church where Millie had already cooked a fine Sunday dinner earlier that morning. She had the table set and the food served up before Madison, Aaron and the girls could get their Sunday clothes changed. "Ya'll best git in here and git your vittles," she hollered.

After enjoying fried chicken, black-eyed peas, corn on the cob, yeast rolls and gravy; Aaron sat down in the living room and picked up the weekly newspaper, the *Stephenville Tribune*. He read the headline:

"Triple Slayer Faces Electric
Chair on August 12th"

"They's finally gonna execute that ole man Snow," Aaron said, "It seems like it's been a long time since all this started."

"Yep," Madison responded, "I hope he's made amends with his Maker."

"I'll never fergit that night when me an' Elvis wuz out there, jest having a good time. Elvis is like I am, he don't want to hunt no more."

"It wuz hard on everybody; Hassler ain't gonna run for sheriff again. I don't know if that's the reason for his decision or not."

"Daniel is kin to the Gristys; he said they don't talk about it. They have to go by that ole murder house whenever they have to go into town."

"I think Mister Sam is going to be the new district judge," Millie said speaking of Sam Russell, "he'll make a good one, but I think Judge Keith was a fine judge too an' he was fair."

"He'll do us a good job," Madison agreed.

A bit later, Aaron looked at the clock that was striking six o'clock.

"I'd better start getting ready to go," he thought.

Deputy Ross Pearcy, Justice of the Peace Watson and their friend, Leslie Hancock, had driven to the penitentiary in Huntsville earlier in the day on August the eleventh, hoping that F. M. Snow with impending death facing him might reveal facts about other murders.

"Sir, you are soon to meet your Maker, an' we just wanted ask you a few more questions," Pearcy began.

"Alright," Snow responded.

"There was a body found several years ago in San Saba that didn't have its head attached . . ."

Snow interrupted him, "I don't know a thang 'bout it."

"Okay, fine, then how about Palo Pinto County?"

"It won't do me a bit of good to say anymore."

"You could have a clear conscience."

"My conscience is clear — you got the wrong man."

Captain Hickman and Ranger Stewart also wanted to question Snow about the unsolved murders. Hoping for a confession, they visited Snow a short time before his scheduled execution. But, this too, failed to materialize; the fated man remained silent. His only comment was to one of the guards, as he was being strapped to the electric chair, "There has never been a better man to sit in this thang."

Captain B. L. Schram, the acting Warden, issued the order and Francis Marion Snow was executed on August 12, 1927 at 12:13 a.m. by "causing a current of electricity with the sufficient intensity to cause death to pass through the body of F. M. Snow."

Dr. E. L. Angie, the legal prison physician, pronounced him dead at 12:19 a.m., six minutes after the application of the electricity.

Neither friends nor relatives of the dead man claimed the body, so he was given a decent burial in the prison cemetery at Huntsville, Texas on August 13, 1927.

Thus ended one of the bloodiest and most hideous crimes that the country had ever seen at the time — one of the most grueling murder cases ever tried in Texas. It was finally put to rest.

A few days later, Aaron, alone in the house, was sitting at his kitchen table; the table at which he had sat every day for nearly all of his nineteen years. It was late afternoon; the bright sun of the day was no longer illuminating the dimmed room. Madison, his daddy, was working at the store; Millie, his mother, had gone to Stephenville to take his two sisters shopping for school supplies. It was quiet and almost lonely without his family.

Aaron's thoughts drifted back and forth, as he reflected on the happenings of the past couple of years. He thought about the murders, school, church, the parties, and most of all, his first love. His mind wandered back to the kitchen table where he was sitting. "It's my table," he thought.

But he knew that before long, the table would be thought of as his mother's and daddy's. He was becoming a man. He would soon be on his own and only visit this table on weekends and holidays. He wondered if he would ever marry and have children of his own. He thought that one day; he probably would. He wondered if he would ever find the love he felt with Missy. He knew the answer.

Then he thought of his friend Elvis — they had been best friends since their early boyhood days. He hadn't seen much of Elvis lately; Elvis hadn't attended any of the socials or just dropped by as he used to do. He wondered why?

Knock, knock, knock, "Hey Aaron, whatcha doing?"

"Elvis, I's jest thinking about you. Where have ya been?"

"Aaron, I'm real sorryful I ain't been around. You know with the murder an' trial an' everything an' all. I guess I jest didn't want to be reminded of it."

Oh that's all right, but I've missed ya. Tell me whatcha been doin' to occupy your time."

"Oh you know, been trying to stay hid and been doing a purty good job of it." Elvis kidded.

"No, I mean tell me what you's really been doing."

"Well you know the ole Jackson place next to us?"

"Yep, I shore do."

"Well, the Nicks family rented the place an' moved in there. They's got this here daughter, Sharon, an' she sure is somethin' pruty. I been spendin' a right smart of time with her. We take walks in the evenin' or jest sit around. You know, stuff like that. I ain't never felt like this about nobody before. 'Specially a girl. I think it's purty serious."

Then tears came to Elvis' eyes, "I wish it wuz all good news, but here's the worst part; ole Hootus died the first of last month."

"Oh no, Elvis. Tell me it ain't so."

"Yes it is," Elvis said with a trembling voice, "he come down wit a bad case of the rhum'tism. Couldn't hardly walk or git around. I fixed 'im a bed in the barn where he could lay in the shade an' be comfort as much as possible. That there rhum'tism shore wuz rough on 'im.

Aaron shook his head as Elvis continued.

"There toward the last, I'd brang 'im his meals an' water; but he wouldn't eat much. An' then one day, I walked out to the barn an' there he wuz. He wuz gone. Me an' Sharon buried 'im down by the creek under a big ole cottonwood tree. Best dog I ever had."

Elvis' tears turned to a smile.

"But, Mister Swanzy brung me another pup last week. Looks jest like ole Hootus did when he wuz a pup. Mister Swanzy said he wuz Hootus' great-grandchild. I named him Hoot Junior. An' he is a hoot; digging holes, tearing up Momma's garden, chasing everythin' that moves an' barking all night long. But I luv 'im."

"I'm glad ya got another dog. Maybe he'll be good at huntin'. I'm shore sorryful about ole Hootus, but tell me, whatcha gonna do now that you grad'eated? Gonna go to college?" Aaron asked.

"Naw, I can't see where college's got nothin' to offer me. I bought me a team of mules an' Mister Morrison said I could farm his lower field next year. Ain't much, about twenty-five acres. Spect I'll plant it in cotton an' see how that turns out. Grandpa told me he would help me out with some seed money to git started. Hope it all works out, 'cause I shore do like to plow."

"I 'spect it will 'cause ya know that farmin'," Aaron said.

"Well, I got's to go. Sharon said she's cookin' supper fer me; don't want to be late.

"No, ya shore don't!"

Elvis walked out the back door, stepped down on the first step — hesitated, then turned around and walked back through the door.

"Hey Aaron."

"Yeah, Elvis."

Aaron looks at Elvis, Elvis looks back at Aaron and finally speaks.

"What'd ya say we go huntin' an' set some traps tonight?"

EPILOGUE

Aaron, along with his cousin, Katie, and her friend, Laura, spent a lot of time at Daniel McCarey's farm in Selden during August of 1927. They rode horses down country roads under ribbons of moonlight, explored an old house, and enjoyed many picnics. Their summer romances faded when school days returned in the fall.

Two years later, the Wall Street Crash of 1929, Black Tuesday, happened. The depression that followed didn't make much of an impact on the good people of rural Erath County. They were poor folks before the depression, poor folks during the depression and poor folks after the depression was over. Their lifestyle of raising most of their food in gardens; and cattle, hogs and chickens in pens meant that they ate just as good during the depression as before the crash.

Missy and Aaron were together one last time, a little over fifteen years after the summer that brought them together. Missy, crying, asked him, "Why didn't you fight for me? Didn't you care enough?"

Ned and Ida Gristy, being too close to the story, rarely ever spoke of it. Ned Gristy died in 1946. Ida Gristy lived to be one hundred and one years old, going to her eternal rest in 1991. Both were buried in the Indian Creek Cemetery.

Mr. Samuel G. Swanzy lived to a ripe old age, and continued his habit of walking around the courthouse square in Stephenville and giving nickels to the small children he would meet. He was born in 1885 and died in 1966. He is buried in the Oak Dale Cemetery, north of Stephenville.

Uncle Will Savage was born in 1863 and lived on this earth 89 years. His motto, worth remembering, was, "if you can't say something good about someone; don't say anything." He rarely spoke his motto, but lived it every day. Aunt Florence Martin Savage lived an additional 13 years after the death her husband and died at the age of 92. They both were interred in Allard Cemetery just north of Rocky Point.

Herman Starnes and his wife had two daughters and a son. He ran a plumbing business in Stephenville for years and later owned The Old Place Antique Shop. He died on September 18, 1994 and is buried in the East End Cemetery in Stephenville.

Louis Savage, the author's great-granduncle, was actually killed by a lightning strike in 1912. His daughter is still living in Stephenville and turned one hundred and two years old in 2014; she still has a sharp mind.

Dee Hubbard (Doc) Hamilton spent his last years in a nursing home in Stephenville. He died in 1995 and was laid to rest in Indian Creek Cemetery with only a simple funeral home grave marker for his headstone.

Sheriff David 'Med' Hassler served as Erath County's sheriff for only one term. Public records provide few clues about Hassler's life after the years he served as sheriff. He and his wife, Mary, had three children. He passed away in 1957 and was buried in the West End Cemetery in Stephenville.

Deputy Sheriff Alfred Ross Pearcy later partnered with W. N. "Boone" Brown to form the Brown and Pearcy Motor Company in Stephenville. Pearcy died in 1972 and was buried in the West End Cemetery.

Sam Morris Russell served as district attorney until 1928, and then served as twenty-ninth district judge until 1940, at which time he was elected to the United States Congress and served until 1947. He resided in Stephenville until his death in 1971.

Texas Ranger Captain Thomas R Hickman, born in Cooke County Texas in 1886, continued to maintain law and order in North Texas investigating boundary disputes, murders and bank robberies, including the Santa Claus Bank Robbery in Cisco — the Christmas of 1927. He was chairman of the Texas Public Safety Committee at the time of his death on January 29, 1962.

Granddad Harold D. Keller and wife, Martha, sold their farm and moved to Stephenville in 1952. He went to live with the Lord in 1968 and Grandma Keller joined him a few months later. They were laid to rest, side by side, in the Valley Grove Cemetery south of Stephenville.

Missy lost her battle with this life at the age of fifty-three. She is interred in the Indian Creek Cemetery.

Cecil Ray, who loved baseball and rodeos never returned to Erath County. He passed away in Fort Worth at the age of sixty-five and was laid to rest in the Nancy Smith Cemetery in Somervell, County Texas.

Elvis Rivers told his story many times. and continued to farm in Erath County till a few years before his death. He died in 1986 and was buried in the Pony Creek Cemetery.

And Aaron Martin; he is a compilation of many different people of different times. The first part of this character was born in 1884 and died in 1944. He is buried in the West End Cemetery in Stephenville. A small part of him loved farming, trading farm equipment and flying airplanes. That part of the character died in 2002 and is buried just east of Lampkin, Texas. Another part of this character has a loving wife, two beautiful daughters, and a handsome son and owns a local business in Stephenville. Still, another part of the character of Aaron worked in government service for over forty years, is now retired and lives on a lake in Central Texas.

. . . maybe more another day, I think I hear Aaron calling me.

ABOUT THE AUTHOR

Carroll C. Martin was born and has resided his entire life in Erath County. He worked part-time in a convenience store during his high school and college years where he met many of the colorful characters included in his first novel, *Ashes Upon The Snow*. He worked in the banking profession and later retired from the Stephenville Police Department after twenty-five years of service.

Carroll said, of his law enforcement experience, "It came in mighty handy in describing the murder scenes, investigations, court room tactics and other legal proceedings that you find in my story."

Carroll and his wife, Melinda, live just east of Stephenville on a mini farm where they raise chickens, ducks, guineas, goats and donkeys. They have one son and two daughters and a passel of dogs and cats.

Carroll can be contacted on Facebook at *https://www.facebook.com/ccokemartin* and by email at *cmartin@martincomputers.com*. Visit his website at *www.carrollmartin.com*